Acknowledgments

I would like to dedicate this book to my family and friends whom I love greatly.
And a shout out to all the people I have ever met, you have no idea how you have influenced me.

Southside Dreams

B. K. Ray

URBAN BOOKS
www.urbanbooks.net

Urban Books
10 Brennan Place
Deer Park, NY 11729

ISBN-13: 978-1-60162-031-6
ISBN-10: 1-60162-031-4

First Mass Market Printing September 2007
Printed in the United States of America

10 9 8 7 6 5 4 3 2 1

Submit Wholesale Orders to:
Kensington Publishing Corp.
C/O Penguin Group (USA) Inc.
Attention: Order Processing
405 Murray Hill Parkway
East Rutherford, NJ 07073-2316
Phone: 1-800-526-0275
Fax: 1-800-227-9604

chapter one

If the world had stopped, Dorothy Evans would have gotten off. The world did not stop, the Jackson Park El train did. It was the Garfield stop; Dorothy's would be next at 63rd and King Drive, the street named for the slain civil rights leader, the street once known as South Park, and before that, Grand Boulevard. Before that it was prairie land. At least that's what the neighbors told her when she was a little girl.

When she was little, the neighbors were always telling her stories about their childhood. They talked about Greenville and Jackson, Mississippi; North Carolina, Arkansas, and the two or three other places they all had seemed to come from. She remembered her father, drunk and laughing about the old days on 39th or 31st, between the stockyards and Cottage Grove, where all the black people on the South Side of Chicago lived.

They spoke about the old days like it was some time of magic, about how they all pulled together because only one of them had a job, and the parties they used to have. She'd heard how they knew Duke Ellington or Louis Armstrong before they got rich and famous. They never talked about how shitty the times were. It must have been shitty then because it was shitty now. This shit had to have come from somewhere.

The El train pulled into the King Drive station. Sixty-third street, the street made infamous by the whores and pimps of the Sixties. It wasn't near as bad as the legend, but it was still bad, and a hell of a place to hang out and party. But it wasn't just 63rd. There were 55th and 47th Streets as well, all with clubs that had drinking and dancing. The music was better then, too. Not like that rap shit Dorothy's children listened to today.

Dorothy looked over the platform and saw a totally different 63rd Street, not the one she used to jam to, the one where she could hear Martha Reeves and the Vandellas or Smokey and the Miracles. This was not the street where she saw the Temptations and the Impressions. She actually met one of the Impressions once. He lived on 87th Street, just a few miles from where she was living now. Life got that close to her.

Sixty-third Street today was a hellhole. It was full of shit people living shit lives, and Dorothy knew she was just another one of them. Presently, there was the matter of negotiating the steps, the crowds and the bums to get to Walgreen's. She had to get her prescription for the evening. Sometimes it would last two evenings, but lately she was lucky to make it one. After maneuvering through the crowds, she went into the store and headed straight for the liquor section.

Dorothy looked at the row of bottles, wondering which one she would be with tonight. She compared the prices, from the ultimate cheapest to the sale-priced good ones. Tonight it would be one of the better ones. She wasn't feeling that bad, and this was definitely going to help make her feel better. She paid for her vodka and headed out to 63rd Street. She walked down King Drive to 61st then turned east toward Eberhart.

She could have walked down 63rd to Eberhart, but that would have meant walking down the 61st and 62nd blocks of Eberhart. Those were the kinds of blocks that had those drive-by shootings. Those were the blocks where women got raped and children disappeared. Drug dealers and all that kind of shit was over there. Dorothy would walk down her own block of Eberhart and that was it. Those blocks across 61st Street may as well have been on the other side of the world.

Sixty-first Street smelled of the ever-present scent of smoke from the barbecue shack there. It was powerful enough to draw Dorothy through the doors, with the intent of getting a few wing dinners for herself and her grandchildren. Her grown-ass children could fend for themselves.

Inside, Dorothy took her place in the line. In front of her was another one of those bum-ass niggas that seemed to be everywhere nowadays. They didn't wash, and they didn't seem to be bothered by the stench they created. Even worse, they didn't care who they bothered with their odor. Dorothy tried to breathe around him, and she tried not to look at him. He stepped up to the window and ordered a large order of necks and backs.

Dorothy looked up at the menu for the first

time in a long time, and saw two different order sizes of necks and backs. The world was coming to that—po'-ass niggas ordering backs and necks. She imagined that one day she would be standing in that line getting a bucket of necks and backs and thinking it was a good thing. Twenty years ago, there was no such thing as a wing dinner, so maybe a bucket of necks and backs wasn't far fetched, not far fetched in the least.

Ten minutes later, the wing dinners were ready. Dorothy gathered her bags and headed back up 61st Street. Across the street was that boy everybody knew was a drug dealer. He, his friends and his fancy-ass car sitting in a vacant lot. It was a damn shame to spend all that money on a car just to sit in a vacant lot with it. Well, he got his mama a big-ass car too, and she drove all over everywhere in it. Dorothy looked away as a bus passed by her.

She turned the corner at Eberhart, her block. It looked the same as it did yesterday, but it was so different from when she was a child. There were lawns when she was a child, houses were cleaner, and everybody didn't hang out on the front porch. Now, in front of each house there was a patch of dirt. No point in calling that a lawn. When she was little, she didn't play in the front because it was a lawn. Now there was no lawn, so she said nothing about her grandchildren playing in the dirt.

Next door to Dorothy's house was a family that always had somebody pregnant. When they moved in, they were three nice girls. Now they had ten or eleven children among them. They were always on the front porch, them and their little nigga boyfriends who were always moving in and out of the house. The mother died and the father lived in the basement or something when he wasn't at the tavern around the corner trying to get laid. It was a damn shame what was going on in that house, and it was a damn shame Dorothy had to live next door to it.

Dorothy's grandchildren were playing with some of the little hoodlum children from next door when they saw her. They ran to meet her, especially excited since she was carrying bags. She handed DeShawn the bag with the wing dinners in it. He and Laneka ran into the house. Danny's car was parked in front of the house. She really didn't want to see him or talk to him today. Where the hell did he get a car from anyway? Maybe she did want to see him and find out where that car came from. But not today. Today she just wanted to eat and have drink or two, just like yesterday.

Dorothy waved at the girls on the porch and went into her house. Regina had the phone stuck to the side of her head. Talking on the phone and hanging her ass out of some nigga's car seemed to be Regina's forte in life. It obviously wasn't bad enough that she hardly kept up with the three children she had, the oldest of whom was getting into more and more trouble, but she wouldn't pay shit on the bills until Dorothy threatened to have the phone cut off. Dorothy rolled her eyes at Regina and continued on to the kitchen. The kids had brought the food in and were all ready to fix plates. They were taking plates out of the dish drainer.

"Regina, why didn't you put the goddamn dishes up? Shit, you in the house all day. The least you could do is to clean up. You ain't paying no rent; you don't pay on the goddamn bills. Do something to earn your keep around here. Clean the damn house up."

Regina looked at her mother and hung the phone up. "Why you come in here hollering and screaming? I just finished washing them from lunch. It ain't like they ain't clean."

"Why you just finishing the lunch dishes? You should have done them hours ago. I'm tired of coming home to this shit every day."

"Don't be taking that shit out on me."

"Regina, long as you in my house, I'll take out on you what I want to. Do us both a favor and get out of the kitchen, then just stay out of my way 'til tomorrow sometime. It'll be the best for both of us. Just let me get my dinner and stay the fuck out of my way."

Regina walked by her mother, frowning. Soon after, Dorothy heard the front door slam. She reached into the cabinet and got a glass, put in some ice, poured some vodka, and took a sip. She added some water from the faucet and took another sip.

With three wings and a handful of almost cold fries, she went into the living room and sat in her chair. The television was about six feet in front of her. It was an old floor model, still watchable, though the colors were slightly off and a green ghost followed everything on the screen.

If she ever got the money, she was going to buy one of those big televisions, one with a remote that did everything. The remote she had barely worked, but it didn't really have to. The television was on all the time, and Dorothy really didn't care what she was watching. In a while, her eyes would be closed and the television would be a distant sound, like an old memory.

The show on was one of those five-character sitcoms that remedied the real world a half-hour at a time. Dorothy needed every remedy available. She was tired of everything that life was offering: the shitty job, the fucked up children, the tunnel with no light at the end.

There had been a time of great hope in her life, hope she would be living like the people on television, with a house worthy of living in, a car worthy of driving, and the only worry being how to get more. What she got instead was a wide variety of bullshit to contend with.

A sip of vodka was like Novocain for the pain. Shit, a big swig could make nothing better, but unlike so many other things, it didn't make anything worse. With her eyelids at half-mast, Dorothy surveyed the front room. The couch was old and sunk in the middle. It needed to walk on its last leg to the trash heap. In the winter, the draft coming through the front window felt like a fan. The gas bill got so high it took all year to pay off; just another way Dorothy managed to stay behind.

White people on television managed to stay on top of things. Dorothy managed to stay behind them, way behind them. She was behind on every bill there was, including the ones from the cheap-ass furniture store where she bought the couch. She was still paying on furniture that had fallen apart. That was fucked up. The shit was nowhere near as good as the money she spent on it, but it was the only place she could get credit.

Now that her credit was fucked up, she was actually better off dead. But dying was something she didn't know how to do. She'd thought about it many times, even more lately. Being dead meant no more bills or the dumb shit that went along with them. No motherfuckers calling her up on the job, threatening her with all kinds of silliness. No more of her children's bullshit. No more. Just let this thing called life be done. She took a hard gulp out of the glass.

The door opened and her eyes focused on Reginald as he walked into the house. He spoke to her, and she spoke back. He went into the kitchen and made a call on the telephone. Before long, it was over and he left the house. He was probably going to church. That seemed to be all he ever did. He had to be the holiest sonofabitch she knew.

She took another swig from the glass and got nothing but ice on her upper lip. She went into the kitchen and refilled the glass. This time she did not stop pouring at the halfway mark. Leaving the kitchen, she heard the door open and close again. Her eldest son, Danny, walked right by her and headed into the basement. At least this time he didn't have any of his hoodlum friends with him. Before she could settle in her chair, he was out of the basement and out of the house.

Dorothy got up and walked to the front door, not to look at her son, but just to see what was out there. There was always something going on in the front of her house. Regina could have her ass hanging out of somebody's car window, or Danny and his hoodlum friends might be sitting on the porch trying to fuck one of those little whores next door.

Regina was right where Dorothy thought she

would be, but Danny was nowhere in sight. There was a cooling breeze coming in the screen door. It was like one of those nights when she was a little girl. She watched lightning bugs and remembered the time she would have chased them, her father sitting on the porch with her mother next to him. Back then, there was every reason to smile.

There were still white people living in the neighborhood when her family first moved in. Jewish shopkeepers owned all the stores, but there was nothing wrong with that. She and the other little kids would come into the front only at night. All the parents would sit and visit each other. They lived as though they had just crossed the Jordan into the Promised Land, and the future was beautiful. They had a television, they had a radio, they had a car and Daddy had a good job. They had a refrigerator; they had a life better than some of the white people on television. There was no way to know it would never be that good again.

She looked at her grandchildren, and she knew they would think the same thing if they got to be her age. They wouldn't know they missed the whole damn boat and they didn't have a snowball's chance of getting on it. She could tell them to do well in school so they would have a chance, but that was a lie. She told her children that, and they even did well, but look at them. Danny, a "B" student, and that wasn't enough. Here he was, twenty-seven years old and still in the goddamned house. Shit happened. Over and over again, shit happens.

There was nothing wrong with Regina or Reginald. They were average students, maybe a little better than that, but it wouldn't have mattered if they were "A" students. Dorothy knew this. She knew it because Anthony was an "A" student. He was smart as hell, and all it ever got him was a jail sentence. His being smart didn't come to shit but heartbreak. Maybe he was too smart. If ever there was a motherfucker that was too smart for his own good, it was Anthony. He was so smart, he had already been to jail so many times, and he was the same age as Danny. He didn't go to jail for drugs or gangs or murder—nothing like that. It was always some off-the-wall, crazy shit he did, and that was just the shit he got caught for. There was no telling what he didn't get caught doing.

So what was there to tell her grandchildren? She could tell them this was as good as it was going to get. That it was a downhill ride from here. She could tell them to go ahead and get a crutch for life because they were going to need it. She decided to tell them nothing. Let them find out for their damn selves how fucked life was, and leave it to them to fuck it up some more.

Laneka and DeShawn played in the front yard in the dirt that used to be a lawn in what used to be a good neighborhood in a world that used to be worth living in. They didn't understand how fucked up things were. And there was no way for Dorothy to tell them how much worse things were going to get. They were certainly going to get worse.

Dorothy swallowed more of her drink and looked toward 61st Street. She could hear music coming from the car Regina had her ass hanging out of. "What kind of fucked up music are kids listening to today? What kind of shit is rap? What is it about?"

She could understand some of the lyrics and even identify what they were talking about, but most of that shit she couldn't understand what the hell they were saying. And what she could hear, every other word was "fuck" or "shit." There was no way anyone would have thought to say that shit on a record when she was growing up, and it certainly wasn't going to get on the radio. Half of that shit no one would ever say at all.

All the people out there looked like drug dealers or gang bangers. This was the kind of world her grandchildren had to grow up in. This is what their fond memories of childhood would contain. This is the world her children were leaving for her grandchildren. She had left her children a better world; at least she thought she had.

Dorothy left the door and returned to her chair. This was her throne in her shit kingdom. She looked at the mail sitting on top of the television. Without getting close enough to see it better, she knew a cut-off notice from the electric company was in the pile. The bill had come at the wrong time of the month. There was probably one from the phone company too. If it weren't there, it would be on the way.

She didn't have the money to pay both of them off. The phone could go, or the kids could pay it. After all, they used the phone more than she did. Hell, they used all the damn electricity too. They used everything, and they ate like they had never seen food before. There was no stopping this shit. Couldn't even slow it down to catch your breath. This is the world we live in. Fuck the world.

Dorothy took another swig that emptied the

glass, let her head roll back and looked at the ceiling. The ceiling was white; it had been white forever. The living room used to be her favorite room in the house. This was the room the television sat in back when all the neighbors came down to watch the *Jack Benny Show* or *Amos' n Andy*. Her father sat pretty much where she was sitting now, with a drink, but he was rarely drunk.

The ceiling was white when Daniel walked her home from high school, back when he had promised her the world. When she sat next to him on the couch, her mother would walk through to keep an eye on them. They would sneak kisses as soon as she left the room. They didn't watch television. They listened to WVON on the radio. They would practice doing the bop, or at least that is what they told her father they were doing. No, this is not what those promises were about, but this was the reality of it. Daniel was not there, and she was.

The ceiling in the living room was white when they took the dead body of her grandfather out of the room her grandchildren were sleeping in today. When her father died on the job, when her mother finally lost the battle to cancer, when the letter came in the mail . . . the ceiling had always been white.

The white ceiling was about the only thing that was the same. Once she had been in a family, now she felt alone. Even though her children were there, they didn't know her. They didn't know shit about her, not like she wanted them to. They didn't know what her life was like then or now. They didn't know what it was like to work a full-of-shit, go-nowhere job. They didn't know what it was like to live in fear of losing that job, or how loosely shit was held together. They had no idea how close they were to it all falling apart. They just knew that she came home from work, bitched and drank herself to sleep.

When she thought about it, she didn't know them either. They were not the children who used to smile and hug her when she came into the house. They were not the children who were eager to show her their homework and fill the old refrigerator door with their artwork. All of a sudden her children were gone, replaced by teenagers who didn't like each other and who liked her even less. Now, they had become people she didn't like. Reginald wasn't as bad as the rest of them, but he could start in on that church shit and ruin your nerves with it.

All her children used to go to church. Reginald was the only one all that church shit seemed to stick to. He went to church at least four times a week and all day Sunday. The preacher wasn't there as much as Reginald was. Dorothy went to church, but she wasn't sure why. Maybe it was what old black women did when they didn't know what else to do. Go to the mourning bench and cry your goddamn eyes out.

She knew she liked to hear Reginald sing. He had such a voice. He could have been a professional if he'd gotten the right breaks. But was content with his life the way it was. He was just singing for Jesus, singing and believing that the Lord was somehow was going to work it out for the best. She had heard so many people say that, but no one knew when or how. Was Jesus working it out now? Was this God's answer to her prayers? If it was, then Jesus must be a government worker, 'cause there wasn't shit getting done.

She looked over at the television. When was she going to look back and wonder how she got over? For now, she just wondered. As far as "over" was concerned, she had only seen people getting over on television. So, she went to church to hear Reginald sing, and while she was there, maybe she could find out why God didn't love her as much as He did those people on television.

There was no way sin could be the reason. She sat in her house and had a drink. She didn't bother anyone. It wasn't like she was one of those rich-ass white people that drank and killed people with their cars. She didn't even have a car. Sin didn't have anything to do with it. There were bigger sinners in the world, like the sinners she worked for. If it wasn't a sin to pay people shit, it should have been. But then God's concern wasn't with what you had and were stopping other people from getting. Who you was fucking, now God was big on that. Yeah, He wanted to know who you were fucking and whether or not you was going to have an abortion. Yeah, God didn't care if you paid your bills, but He gave a shit over your getting high or having a drink.

To hear the preachers tell it, that is what God concerned Himself with. They were hypocrites. They were screwing everybody, and God didn't say shit to them about it. God didn't care where you got your money from, as long as you gave Him His cut. He didn't even care if you had enough, as long as He got His cut. He never told you what He did with His cut, but then He was God, and you weren't.

Dorothy sat up in her chair. Someone on the television was laughing. They were always laughing on television. They even laughed when they read the news. How the hell could anyone laugh after they read all that shit about people killing each other? Did it ever get to them? Did they ever feel like just shouting into the camera, "You all is a bunch of dumbass motherfuckers"? Did the people that made you scared to leave your house ever feel anything when they read the news? Hell no. They weren't paid to feel; they were paid to scare you. Scare you with a straight face and then a smile.

Dorothy got up from the chair slowly. She steadied herself, walked into the kitchen, and poured herself another drink. The front door opened and shut. She heard Laneka and DeShawn run upstairs. Jaleel walked into the kitchen.

"Where you been that you coming in this late at night?"

"It ain't late. It ain't even nine o'clock."

"So, where you been?"

"Over to the playground."

"You know better than to be there when the streetlights come on. Ain't nothing up there in the dark but trouble."

"Yes, ma'am."

"Go on and get yourself something to eat, and you be careful. Have your ass in this house and off the street when them streetlights come on. You hear me?"

"Yes, ma'am."

Dorothy turned and walked out of the kitchen. She didn't even know why she went through that with him. Probably out of habit more than anything else. If his mother didn't care what he was doing, why should she? Jaleel was going to wind up like all them other niggas out on the street. He was going to wind up like Danny.

Dorothy knew Jaleel was going to wind up like Danny, but she didn't know how Danny wound up the way he was. There was no point in life where they tell you that the rules with your children change. Danny had been such a sweet little boy. One day a sweet little boy, and it seemed the next week he was a bad-ass teenager. He was out there, and there was no way she could get to him to bring him back. When he came back from the service, he was worse than when he went in. He didn't get killed while he was in the Army, but he seemed intent on getting killed after he got out, running with those no good hoodlums like he was.

Why couldn't he get a job? Reginald had one, so there must have been jobs out there. Shit, why couldn't she get a real job, instead of the bullshit she called making a living? She wasn't making a living; she was making a slow death.

She turned off the television and walked up the stairs. The children were watching the television in their room. She walked by it to her room and opened the door. There were still clothes on the floor, still clothes draped over the chair. They would be there tomorrow unless they walked away tonight. She closed the bedroom door behind her.

Inside the room, she undressed. Sitting in her underwear, she finished off the last from that bottle of vodka, hoping it would be enough to put her to sleep. Tomorrow was another day, not all that different from any other day, but another day just the same. Tomorrow she might win the lottery and this nightmare could end. Tomorrow she might even play the lottery. She knew she wouldn't win. She never won anything. Everything she had, she worked for.

She turned on the radio and lay down on the bed, pulling one sheet up to her neck. Again tonight there would be no dreams, just the cold blanket of black that came between her and relentless reality. She would slip through the cracks of consciousness to the music on the radio, remembering the times when she did dream.

chapter two

Anthony Evans stepped onto the Green Line train, the California Avenue stop, and found a seat. He looked toward the jail he'd just left. He couldn't see it, but he could still feel it—the screams, the clanking of the bars opening and closing. It seemed the last ninety days were nothing but those sounds. Anthony smiled because he was through with it. Now it was just a memory that he could look back on, instead of looking out from.

The train car filled with men who looked a lot like him. They were probably on their way to work, somewhere on the second shift, where they almost never got more than seven dollars an hour, and almost never thirty hours a week. Jobs that paid enough for one night out, and maybe you could go in on a bag before your dough was deadened.

Anthony had worked enough second shift jobs to know the drill: up at 10:00 and off to work by 12:00 or 12:30, depending on how many buses you had to catch. Slip on your headphones and hit the streets. All the normal people were already working their normal hours, including your girlfriend. You would get off at 9:00 or 10:00 and head home. You got to relax for four or five hours, then sleep and repeat. It was better than nothing, but nothing was all it ever was.

Anthony watched the abandoned buildings that filled the West Side become the big buildings downtown. He looked out of the window at the people in the streets downtown. All the white men with their ties on and their sleeves rolled up.

They looked like they were doing what they wanted to do, like they weren't suffering. Suffering was all Anthony ever did. He looked for black men. They were there, a few in suits, a lot more waiting to change buses to get to that second shift.

Anthony wondered for the ten thousandth time in his life, who was behind it all. He knew they were white men, but who were they? They could afford to bankroll politicians from aldermen to presidents, and they could afford to keep them in their pockets. How did they continuously manipulate the masses into doing the wrong thing so many times?

He didn't believe they were racist, not in the Ku Klux Klan sense of the word. They simply held their interests over those of everybody else. They did whatever they could to increase and maintain the power they inherited, the power their fathers and grandfathers had stolen. He knew they were not the Horatio Algers they liked other people to believe in. To hell with hard work; smart work was more effective. It didn't matter who they had to roll over to get where they were going, because they did it. And they did it without regret. They made their moves with no regard for the lives they may have ruined, as long as their lives got better because of it.

They lived in ivory towers surrounded by their loyal minions of board members and management. They had golden parachutes and golden tombs. They had so much money they had lost count. They could and did ruin the lives of thousands of people with the wave of a pen, and no one could do anything about it. They pulled off the ultimate smoke and mirror trick—they made the masses pay attention to something else while they did what they wanted to do.

They had successfully blurred the lines. There had been a time when the enemy was easy to spot. He was white. But now color and motive were no longer the same. There were black people who, while not as powerful, refused to use what power they had to benefit the masses. They just shut up and pocketed the dough. Now there was a large gray area where everything got jumbled into something that Anthony could not discern.

Anthony changed trains downtown. He didn't like riding the old El. That train went from the po'-ass West Side to the po'-ass South Side. His aunt rode that train, the Low-End Line. He hurried to the subway station before he did something that would land him back in jail. Something like grab one of those white men in a suit and throw his ass out in the middle of the street and commence to beating the shit out of him. Or he could snatch one of those white ladies' purses just to hear her scream her ass off.

While he waited on the train, a brother tried to

sell him a *Muhammad Speaks* newspaper. The Black Muslims, who were increasing their populations in the prisons, felt they were on the path to righteousness and freedom. They understood some of what Anthony argued, but they split on the ideas of leadership. They believed in Farrakhan or the Honorable Elijah Mohammed. Anthony didn't, nor could he be persuaded to. He would not follow someone whose house he could not visit, or someone that stood to make money off of him.

He thought it was funny how they could so easily see Christianity being used to opiate the masses, but they couldn't see how Islam accomplished the same ends using the same means. Anthony reasoned that religious zealots were closed-minded and empty-headed. Once again Anthony figured the men who wanted power were behind it all, but few people looked at it that way. Anthony was not an atheist. Although there was no doubt in his mind about the existence of God, it was the powers of men that he could not reconcile.

Anthony watched as the passengers on the train changed from black to mixed. He figured the White Sox must have been playing today. Anthony looked at a white man with his family. He tried not to confuse power and color; he knew better. But there it was staring him in the face—a white man with the power to have leisure time. These white people were sitting on the train on their way to a place so close to a slum they could spit on it. Inside the park, they would sit and cheer and drink beers that ran five dollars a cup, and across the street three niggas would be splitting a wine that cost a dollar a pint.

Anthony got up and went into the next train car. As he passed the white people, he watched them tighten up. He watched the fear blink in their eyes, and he smiled. This was all he had on them: everything they read in the paper and saw on the evening news, everything they knew about niggas but wouldn't discuss. They were polite, and simply referred to black people as "them."

They felt safe on the train because there were enough of them to be witnesses at the trial. Had something happened, they were most certainly going to see justice done, and done in a big way. "Each one kill ten," he whispered under his breath as they left the train.

After 35th, the train was all black, like it was supposed to be. Anthony looked out at the traffic on the highway until the train pulled into the 63rd Street station. There was no bus coming so Anthony decided to walk home. He walked over to 61st Street then headed east toward Eberhart. Anthony looked at all the things that had not changed on 61st Street: the liquor stores on every corner, the bums standing in front of them, the young girls and their babies, the old ladies clutching their purses as they walked up and down the street.

61st Street had continued its downhill slide while he was gone. There was a new beauty supply store on 61st and Calumet, one of those Korean stores. Anthony wondered how anyone could shop in those stores. The Koreans had those funky-ass attitudes toward black people. Black people treated them like they treated all the other economic pimps that passed through. Anthony looked through the window. Where did these people come from, and why did they come here? They made no pretense about their dislike for black people, so why didn't they take their asses to some people they did like, some people like the white people in the suburbs? They could make their money and kiss asses too.

Anthony spat on the window and continued up the street. Garbage spilled out of a garbage can and onto the curb at the corner of King Drive and 61st, already littered with broken glass from what looked like hundreds of broken bottles. He had not even made it to the house, but already he was tired of what he saw.

He wasn't bothered so much by what was there as by what it represented. It was the constant fucking decay, the ruined lives, and the fact that there was no force making it better. Some motherfucker that had never been on 61st Street was doing this. Actually, it was a bunch of motherfuckers, and they remained nameless and faceless to the people whose lives they were ruining.

He thought about kicking the garbage can over, but he realized there was no point to it. He crossed the street and saw the all too familiar sight of Sweets and his entourage in a vacant lot between Eberhart and Vernon. Sweets sat on the hood of his car while everybody around him stood up. Sweets saw Anthony too.

"Well, well, well, if it ain't ol' crazy-ass Tony Evans. What was you in jail for this time, trying to shoot the president or some shit like that?"

Some of Sweets' boys started laughing. Anthony looked at them. Some of them he knew, some he didn't. "Oh Sweets, how you gonna play me?"

Sweets got off the car and headed across the street toward Anthony.

"Yo, Family, I'm just fuckin' witcha. I mean, you always broadcasting that political shit like you gonna change the world or something."

Anthony walked up to meet him. They shook hands, twisting their fingers to signify the gang alliance of Family. Anthony wasn't an official gang member, if there were such a thing. He didn't run with them, he didn't operate with them, but they were a significant part of his environment. He knew enough Family to have the protection they offered in jail. He didn't disrespect them, and they didn't disrespect him.

"So, Sweets, what's been happening on this end?"

"I can't call it. Just trying to get my dough rolling in a proper manner."

"Yeah, I see you ain't hurting."

"Just trying to live my life is all. I know you ain't been to the spot yet, so I ain't gonna hold you up. All right, stay up now."

When Sweets turned around, Anthony looked at the crowd around Sweets' car, all pipeheads and wannabes. A hell of a group of people to call your friends. He turned and walked away.

Anthony turned the corner of Eberhart, and he could see Laneka and DeShawn playing in the dirt in front of the house. They saw him and ran to him. The people sitting on the porch next door saw him too. They applauded as the children dragged him to the house. He waved and spoke then went inside.

Regina was on the phone, like she had never moved. Anthony smiled at the scene. There was a familiar comfort in seeing her that way. Laneka let go of Anthony's hand and ran to her mother's side.

"Ma, Anthony home. Ma!"

Regina turned away from the stove and looked toward the dining room. She told whoever she was talking to that she would call them back later and hung the phone up. "So, they let your crazy ass out of jail, huh? It's about time. I was starting to think they dumped your ass in the nut ward where you belong."

"I'm glad to see you too."

"So, how was life in the pokey? You wasn't in there having sex, was you?"

"It was the same as always. And since when is it your business who I'm doing?"

"You know all them kind of boys be having the AIDS and shit."

"They ain't the only ones. Motherfuckers from around here gonna start dropping dead from that shit soon enough."

"Why you always got to be so serious about shit? That shit gonna put your ass in a early grave. You think about shit too much."

"That's the problem. Too many people ain't thinking about shit. That's why shit so fucked up. You ought to know, but then again, maybe not. Anyway, what's been going on around here?" Anthony said.

"Same shit. Ain't nothing changed."

"That's about what I thought. Oh well."

"So, what kind of shit you gonna get into now?"

Anthony smiled. "I'll think of something. Reggie in the house?"

"Nope. He at work."

Anthony turned around. "I'll get back."

Anthony heard Regina back on the phone before he could get to the stairs. The stairs creaked like they always had, in the same familiar places, and he saw the same cracks in the paint on the wall and the ceiling. Shit, it looked like the same toys were in the hall. He had no reason to expect things to be any different, yet each time he came home, he wanted it to be a better place than when he left.

He went into his room and lay across his bed. It felt good and familiar. Staring at the ceiling, he realized that nothing was going to change—at least not for the better, at least not until the man downtown with the money changed. The man downtown with the money didn't give a shit about 61st and Eberhart, and he wasn't going to change because of them.

The ceiling looked the same as it did when he first came into that room. He remembered it like it never happened at all, like it was something that he had made up. It was in April of 1968: Martin Luther King was killed on the fourth, his father was killed on the fifth; by the tenth, his father was buried and he was walking into this room.

His cousins, people he had never seen before, looked like they were aliens from another planet, and so did all the kids in kindergarten. He didn't feel scared; he felt more alone than anything. He was the kid whose father was shot by police, and he had never seen his mother. Forever the orphan.

The room had not changed in all those years. It

had proven to be as much of a prison as any jail he had ever been in. Actually, it was worse. You knew why you were in jail, and the bars were a lot easier to see. Your family could visit, but they didn't have to do time with you.

Still, it was his home, and it had its benefits. He did have a family now. Before, there was just his father. Now he had what amounted to brothers and a sister. His mother had died when he was born. He never knew what happened or why. Maybe his father was going to tell him one day, but his father had been killed before that day ever came.

Uncle Daniel came and got him and brought him here. He had been here ever since. Being brought here was not the worst thing that ever happened to him; being stuck here was. Other than the times in jail, this was his experience. He was still living with his aunt, and he knew he was going to stay. He heard about those noble souls who worked their way through school, but that wasn't going to happen for him. School was out. He'd been thrown out of high school and gotten a G.E.D., but that wasn't holding him back. It was his record. He'd already been to jail six times. Anthony knew the people he needed to help him, would not.

Then there was his son. The worst part of Anthony being doomed to this existence was that he really was in no position to help his son. He could get a job, but it wasn't the kind that would pay for private school or a college education. If it weren't for the state, there would be no health care. His son, the product of a fucked up relationship, was living with his fucked up mother in a fucked up house.

The door opened and Danny walked in. "Yo, cuz, what up tho!"

Anthony stood up. "Hey yo, man. What up witcha?"

They shook hands Family style, more out of habit than anything else.

"I got a couple of killers. Why don't you come smoke one with me?"

"They got any of that shit in them?"

"Yours don't."

"Sounds like a plan to me."

They went downstairs and out the back door. A few of Danny's friends were in the backyard, including his sidekick, Tiny. As soon as Tiny saw Anthony, he ran up to him and hugged him.

"Yo, Family, what up? You just getting out today? Ain't that some shit."

He turned to the other two men in the yard. "Y'all know who this motherfucker is? He the motherfucker that wrote that shit on the wall at city hall a few months ago. He the man."

As Tiny beamed, Anthony shook hands with the other two men. Actually, they were all proud of him. He had done something far removed from what they did. He struck straight at the man. They didn't know how, nor could they imagine a way to. Anthony thought of little else. It had become a bad habit that was going to do him in the way drugs ruin other people's lives.

A few joints were lit and passed. Anthony got one that didn't have any cocaine in it and held onto it. As they talked, Anthony found out that there was a change. A little white girl was now working in the liquor store where he had been working. This was the first time that Anthony even thought about his old job. Tomorrow he would go see if he could get it back.

When Danny asked him what was he going to do with the rest of the day, Anthony didn't hesitate to say he was going to see his son. Danny related that he heard the boy's mother was on the pipe. Anthony didn't care about her. It would be better if the bitch just up and died so he could take his son.

Danny rolled him a few joints because he knew that Anthony was going to walk to his son's house. It was on 103rd Street, which was quite a walk from 61st Street, but that was how Anthony liked to get around. Anthony knew Danny would have given him a ride, but he didn't want it. Danny gave Anthony three joints and a twenty-dollar bill.

"Got to look out for my cuz."

Danny was about the only one Anthony accepted things from, and even that was a rarity. They were the same age and almost joined at the hip until high school, where they started taking different paths. Danny left for the Army, and by the time he got back, they were too different to be as close as they once were. Despite all the changes they had been through, they would still look out for each other.

Anthony took the joints and the money and smiled. "Good looking out. I'm gonna pull up camp. Thanks for the get high, and a damn good get high it is."

"Yeah, you ain't gonna get no shit like that in jail. Did Family look out while you was in?" Tiny wanted to know.

"Yeah, but it ain't like I really needed it. I just

did ninety. It wasn't like I was doing a stretch in the state."

"Yeah, but people get deadened in the county too."

"Yeah, but I can take care of myself. After all, I'm a bad motherfucker in my own right."

Danny looked at him. "Yeah, you a bad motherfucker, but watch your ass over there around 103rd Street. They Friends out that way, and them some cutthroat motherfuckers."

"I'll get back." Anthony turned and walked out of the yard to the front of the house.

The five-mile walk would take about an hour and a half. Because it was so hot out, Anthony knew better than to rush. He walked straight down King Drive; that was the easiest way to go. At 71st Street, he stopped in a small grocery store. The Arabs in the store watched him cautiously as he walked to the cooler. He saw them looking and hated them for it. He knew why they did it, but he hated them for it anyway.

He looked one in the face. "What the fuck you looking at?"

The Arab averted his eyes. Anthony pressed. "You give everybody this treatment, or am I special? Somebody need to rob y'all ass blind, following motherfuckers around 'n shit. Fuck you motherfuckers."

The Arab was visibly nervous. Another one came out from the back as Anthony was putting the forty-ounce on the counter. The second Arab was older and surer of himself. "You don't talk to my people like that."

"Man, fuck you and every motherfucker that

looks like you. Y'all ain't shit but some fucking Jews in head rags, goddamn it."

"That's it. You leave my store. Leave or I'm going to call the police. I don't have to take this shit from you. I don't have to take this shit from you."

Fear had flamed up in the Arab, and Anthony was fanning it. Anthony noticed another one come from the back room. He knew that he would be the one with the gun.

"I'm going to pay for this beer and then I'm going to leave. Then and only then. Not unless you gonna give me the beer for free."

The third Arab stepped closer to the counter, then the door opened and two little kids came in and disappeared into the aisles. Anthony looked at the third Arab. "Motherfucker, you ain't slick. I know what the fuck you up to. Let me put it to you like this: if you shoot me, this store won't be here tomorrow, so just let me pay for my shit and I will be on my way."

The younger Arab, the first one to see Anthony, the one that hated the job of nigga watching, stepped up to the register. "One dollar and eighty-five cents please."

Anthony handed him the twenty and waited for the change. He wanted to spit on the other men in the store. When the young man handed Anthony the change and bagged the forty-ounce, the young one looked at Anthony and said, "My mellow."

Anthony smiled and took the bag. "Good looking out."

He turned and calmly walked out of the store.

He was glad that the niggerness of the area was inflicting itself on the shopkeeper's children. Given enough time, they would be drug addicts and whores of one sort or another, just like the people they took money from. Blackness was a power-filled thing, and no one understood the implications of that power.

Anthony walked over to the park across the street and sat down. Children were playing on the swings like they were living a normal life. Anthony could hear the boys on the basketball courts shouting "Open!"

They were stylin' and profilin' on the courts, surrounded by other boys and men who wanted to play, and the girls in shorts who served mostly as distraction. This was the epitome of summer. Across the park there was a little league baseball game, complete with a few parents in the bleachers. Anthony watched them, and for a moment he believed the American dream. He opened the beer and fired up a joint. The scent of reefer brought a freeloader from the basketball court, but Anthony didn't mind. He passed the joint and the beer. Sitting back and cooling out, he enjoyed the brief respite.

When the beer was finished, Anthony got up to leave. The man asked Anthony for a joint, but Anthony turned him down. The man thanked Anthony for what he had shared and Anthony left, continuing south down King Drive with an hour's walk ahead of him. He walked on, occasionally smiling because the reefer told him it was the thing to do. He watched the buses and cars, looking for a pretty woman to pass by.

Anthony liked King Drive. In a way, it represented the progressiveness of black people on the South Side. There were no white people on King Drive. There were people with money, but none of them was white. He looked at the houses across Nat King Cole Park. They had the big yards, front and back, the manicured lawns, and the nice cars parked in front. There were actually old ladies in sun hats working in their gardens.

Some of these people had been in this neighborhood a while, probably since the early Sixties, when there were still white people living on South Park Avenue. This was Chatham, super middle class black America. These people weren't necessarily just doctors and lawyers. There were some retired factory workers in the mix, as well as account executives of all sorts.

This would be a good place to call home even if it was getting a little rough around the edges. The gangbangers, drug dealers, and assorted petty criminals were there, but death was not an everyday thing. These people were still surprised by a rape and murder that happened a mile away. In Anthony's neighborhood, it was a surprise only if it happened next door.

There was even a university nearby—a primarily black, soon-to-be famous university. The reefer let Anthony dream of living over here. He knew it would never happen because he was not one of these people. He hated them for abandoning neighborhoods like his. He knew these were the type of black people who would readily shout, "There that nigga goes! Get him!"

He waited for the day to come when they would run out of niggas to point at, and then they would hear someone say that, pointing at them. It would be sweet. But for now, they locked their car doors when he walked by, the women clutched their purses a little tighter. For now, they were just dark-skinned white people.

He lit another joint. He wanted to be stupid to the point he didn't think of things like that. The reefer and the sunshine got the best of him, and he walked on smiling and stupid. Soon he was on Vanessa's block. He rang the bell, and soon enough she answered the door.

"What the fuck you want?" she said, hardly looking at him.

He pushed the door open and was hit by the odor of smoked rock cocaine.

"I want to see my son, and somehow I hope he ain't here."

Vanessa stepped aside and let Anthony come all the way into the house.

"He upstairs sleep. I wouldn't be getting high around him."

"You worse than I thought. Do your people let you get high in the house?"

"Damn. You can smell it?"

"Hell yeah. I'm standing here getting a contact off of the shit."

"I better open a window or something. I just smoked a little in the basement. Are you sure you can smell it?"

Anthony walked into the living room and sat down on the couch. Finally something had changed. This house was fucked up. The television was gone, the stereo was gone, the house looked like shit. Vanessa's younger brothers came out of the basement. The thought flashed in Anthony's mind, *the family that gets high together, dies together*.

Her brothers nodded their hellos to him. He understood their uneasiness. They were Friends, and they had been all their lives. They considered Anthony to be Family, so as long as there was no disrespect, it was okay.

Anthony looked at Vanessa. "What happened here?"

Vanessa looked around the room. "About a month ago, I think it was on the Fourth of July, somebody broke in and stole all our shit out the house. We was at a picnic. It was fucked up."

"Did they ever catch who did it?"

"You say that like they was gonna actually go out and look for them."

Anthony looked at Vanessa and smiled. That was something she would have said a long time ago. When they met, she was as cynical as he was. They were both young and angry then. She was thinking about joining the Nation of Islam until he talked her out of it.

They met on a bus. She was reading the Holy Koran on her way to school downtown. He was on his way to a second shift. They started talking, and the conversation was good. She didn't go to school; He didn't go to work. They wound up at a bar near her school where they sat and talked until the bar closed. They went home, and they talked some more on the phone.

Anthony thought he had found his princess. He was glad she was going to school. She tried to talk him into going, but he felt like he had to be at work. Vanessa got pregnant and Anthony went to jail. Vanessa had the baby, and Anthony went to jail. The baby got teeth and Anthony went to jail.

When Anthony wasn't in jail, they were together. If he wasn't being arrested, he was coming to her beaten and bleeding. This was not her dream. He found out when he was in jail waiting for a trial. A phone call and it was over with.

Anthony looked at her now. He thought about the time he would have killed someone for her, and this is how it turned out. There was Maxwell. He was going to be the true prince in the tradition of princes, not like the white ones in fairy tales, but the black ones in Africa that grew up to lead nations.

"I look fucked up, don't I?"

"You look like a geek. Is the shit that bad on you? You geeking for it? How does that shit feel?"

"Ain't no thing special about it. When you high, you happy. When you not high, you wish you were. Ain't nothing special about it at all."

Anthony leaned forward in the chair. "Vanessa, I thought that you would know better than to become involved in that shit."

"A lot of people felt that way about me and you. But hey, you hear people saying don't fuck with it, it will get you. You be thinking no, not me it won't. You fuck with it and you like it. You like it again and again. Next thing you know, you geeking. I thought it wasn't going to bother me. Sometimes I think I can beat it. Then something will knock the shit out of me and it's back on me."

Maxwell stood at the top of the stairs, listening to the voices below. He hesitated for a moment, listening to his father, then he slowly walked down the stairs. He walked slowly toward his mother, keeping an eye on Anthony the whole time.

Anthony watched his son walking across the room into his mother's arms. Anthony leaned into his face. "Hey, Max. How you doing? God, you look so beautiful, just waking up and all."

Vanessa leaned down and whispered into his ear, "Go on over there and say hi to your father."

"Yeah, come on over here and see your daddy."

He swept Maxwell off of his little legs and hugged him. "I missed you so much, boy. I missed you."

"I missed you too, Daddy. Why you been gone so long? Mommy said you wasn't coming over here no more."

Anthony looked at Vanessa. "Why you tell him some shit like that? I wrote to you and told you what to tell him. I ain't do nothing I am ashamed of."

He looked at Maxwell in his arms. "They put your daddy in jail, but I'm out now."

Vanessa mumbled loud enough for Anthony to hear, "At least for now."

Anthony put Maxwell down and took hold of his hand. "Fuck you, Vanessa."

"Don't be using words like that around my baby," she said.

"What kind of words? Words like 'his mother ain't shit' or 'his father ain't shit'? You been filling my son's head with all kind of dumb shit since I been gone. There ain't a lot I can do when I ain't around, but I'll be damned if I'm gonna let you talk that shit in my face."

"You just watch what you saying around him."

Anthony turned around. "Yeah, right."

He looked down at Maxwell, who was clearly on his side. "Let's go to the park and hang out. If that's okay with you, little boy."

Maxwell bounced and smiled. "Yeah!"

Anthony and Maxwell walked the two blocks to the park. There were other kids playing on the swings and the monkey bars. Anthony led Maxwell to the sandbox, where he was content to play. Anthony put him on the baby swings, keeping Maxwell all to himself. He told him it was because he was too little to play with the other children. That was true, but more important to him was that other children weren't good enough to play with his son.

Their parents were drug addicts and alcoholics, punks and bitches, the next middle class to sink to a new low. There was nothing they would not do, but they did nothing they would readily admit to. Vanessa was like that. She felt like she could beat the monkey she wouldn't admit was on her back. That was the way her parents brought her up to be. Her father was an un-admitted alcoholic.

Maxwell was going to have it hard, and he wouldn't know it. Or maybe he would be like Anthony and know that all of his life he was in the wrong place, in the wrong skin, in the wrong time. Watching him play on the slide, Anthony wanted Maxwell to have a better life than his. He could skip the dumb and unnecessary shit. He could have a chance at an education. He would, if there was anything that Anthony could do about it.

Maybe his record wouldn't matter. Maybe Anthony could go to school and make the life he'd dreamed of when he was young and didn't know the truth. Maybe he could be home from work by 6 o'clock every evening, help Maxwell with his homework, and put him to bed. Anthony could live like a "bougie," one of those people that he hated with a passion, one of those people that closed the door behind them.

It was a dream. Even if he didn't carry it with him, it would still be in his face, the way to live, the way to be. But it was impossible. Even if he did make it through school, what about after school? That is where all the trouble would be. He could go through school, making the best grades, and there would be nothing on the other side for him. Then what? That thing about being black, holding him back. He was never going to be less a black man than he was. He wasn't going to be an African American. He was always going to be a nigga, a black American, the product of racism in America. He would wear his niggerness, because he was proud to have survived it. Then some white man would tell him no, and Anthony would kill him.

He could get that degree and still go nowhere, be working in the mall, making money that was a joke. Working every day, still in the second shift, pissed off and pissing off. There were no promises, and everything was so much of a gamble. There had to be a way to make the odds better, if not for him, for his son.

He could buy all the way into the American dream and sell out to corporate America. But the more he thought about it, the more he knew he couldn't do it. He couldn't go to work every day and smile in the faces of better-paid white men.

He'd passed that point a long time ago. He also knew that as much as he detested that world, he would have to get his son into it. That was the one with the money, and money bought freedom, just like it did two hundred years ago. It was a paper chase and nothing else, bottom line.

After taking Maxwell back to his mother, Anthony smoked a joint and got on the Cottage Grove bus home. By mistake, he got off at 63rd Street and decided to walk the few blocks home. He started west down the street and turned at Eberhart. Even before he got to the corner, he could see the police lights flashing off barred store windows.

His walk slowed as his muscles tensed. As far as he was concerned, there was nothing about police to like. With the crackdown on drugs going on, the police were constantly taking license with the Constitution. Anthony figured the real name of the campaign should have been "Bust a Brother."

Anthony had already spent more than a few nights in jail for interfering with arrest procedures, and he had the scars to prove it. A somewhat askew triangle was in the middle of his chest, placed there by a police flashlight. A similar one was on the back of his head.

Run-ins with the police made Anthony feel as though he stood his ground when it counted. Before he made it to the evening news, his exploits had only gotten him local recognition as crazy. Messing with the police was something even the hardest gangbangers would not do, but to Anthony, it was something that had to be done. The police, more often than not, violated laws, as opposed to upholding them. Somebody had to put them in check.

When he turned the corner, he saw a single police officer holding a man against the hood of the police car. There was nothing unusual about that, so Anthony stopped to watch. He knew that they could get crazy after they had you in cuffs.

Aside from the police officer and the man, the block was empty. There was no one out on the porches or anything. There must have been shooting that drove everybody inside. Anthony walked closer, hanging in the shadows so he wouldn't attract the cop's attention unnecessarily.

Anthony could hear the officer speaking to the man, but he couldn't understand what he was saying. In the blinking lights on the squad car, Anthony could see the fear in the man's eyes. It was the same fear Anthony imagined slaves would have had when they were being taken back to the plantation.

With the man still down on the hood, the police officer grabbed the man's hair, raised his head up as far as he could pull it, then slammed his face into the hood. He did that twice. When the officer raised the man's head the second time, Anthony saw the purple blood on the hood. The strobe lights on the squad car turned the scene into sequential images.

Before he could actually think about it, before he could remember that he'd just gotten out of jail, before any consequences came to mind, Anthony had stepped into the light and yelled, "You punk motherfucker! You ain't shit but a pussy with a bullet!"

The police officer let the man's head fall back to the car. He looked around to see where Anthony was. The officer shouted in his most authoritative voice, "You, hold it right there."

"Fuck you, pussy!" Anthony shouted back. "If you want me, motherfucker, come with it."

The man had slid to the curb and the officer shouted again. This time desperation was making small cracks in his voice.

"I said hold it right there!"

"Fuck you!" Anthony shouted again before he disappeared into the shadows.

The sound of footsteps on the pavement was all that Anthony needed to hear. He moved silently to the darkness, into a gangway that would give him passage into the alley.

The small space between the two buildings was black dark, but somehow the flashing blue light seemed to be following him. The officer was running to catch him. He made one perfect silhouette at the street end of the gangway, in the flashing blue light, and then he was lost in the darkness behind Anthony.

The gangway smelled of urine and was full of wind-whipped trash and God knows what else. Some paper rustled under Anthony, betraying his position to the officer behind him. "I said stop or I'll shoot!" the officer shouted.

The cop was closer than Anthony first thought, but he wasn't worried. Anthony was at the alley end of the gangway. Ducking down, he turned the corner. The cop was halfway through the gangway. Anthony waited for the cop to stick his stupid face around the corner, assuming that Anthony had run down the alley. The cop came through the gangway without hesitation, stopping just long enough in the alley for Anthony to get a bead on him. Anthony jumped him, half blocking, half tackling him.

The officer bounced off the corner of the building, falling to the pavement in the alley. His gun slid across the alley. Somehow, the light in the alley enabled them to see each other's faces. In daylight, the cop would have been a black man; however, under the streetlight in the alley, he was a blue-faced demon.

Before the officer could realize what happened to him, Anthony had picked up his gun and jumped over him, running back up the gangway and onto Eberhart. In the front, the man who had been slumped on the hood was gone. Anthony ran across the street and through a yard. He could hear a dog barking as he ran down the alley.

When he reached 61st, he stuffed the gun into his pants, looked around, and calmly crossed the street. After he reached the house, he went into the back and smoked his last joint. He waited for his nerves to calm down before he went into the house. Dorothy was sitting in her chair, making the noises she made when she was passed out drunk. He walked by her, went upstairs, and put away his victory, a victory in the form of a fully loaded, standard police issue .38 revolver.

chapter three

Danny stepped out of the liquor store onto the broken sidewalk. His dark brown eyes adjusted to the dark street. His skin held a bluish tint under the beer sign that hung over the doorway. He held a forty-ounce bottle of cheap malt liquor in his right hand. With his left, he twisted the top of the paper bag over the top of the bottle.

He heard Otis calling out to him, but pretended he didn't. He didn't feel like being bothered by Otis, not now. He'd just shut down his spot, and Otis probably wanted to cop. Otis caught up to him as he turned the corner.

"Yo, man. Uh, Sweets is looking for you. Didn't you hear me calling to you?"

Danny looked at Otis with mild contempt. "Where he at?"

"Where he always be. In the lot by Vernon, chillin' out."

"All right."

"Yo, Family, you gonna let me hit that forty?"

"No."

"Oh, Family, how you gonna play me?"

"I'm gonna play you like I ain't gonna give you none. That's how I'm gonna play you."

"You ain't right."

"Fuck you."

Danny left Otis with his hands in the air and his mouth open. He headed down the block. Sixty-first was lit by sporadic signs screaming "beer and wine," "laundry and cleaners," "prescriptions filled." The signs fell on deaf eyes. Sixty-first Street was only for the people who lived there. At night, even people that did live around there avoided the area. Unless they were dealers, addicts or other assorted hustlers, 61st Street, dipped too low into the criminal underbelly for the almost normal citizens of the area to be involved with.

Danny uncapped the forty and took a deep swig. He could see Sweets and his ever-present crowd across the street. He'd known Sweets before the dough was rolling for him. Now that he had the money, Sweets was like a spider. Drugs and money were the webs, and he could keep the crowd until they died. Danny didn't really care for him. Sweets was still young, and he didn't believe his shit stank.

Sweets called out to Danny first. "Oh, Family, let me get witcha right quick."

Danny answered, "Hey, Family, what you know?"

Sweets crossed the street alone to approach Danny. They shook hands, twisting their fingers Family style.

"Hey yo, Danny, check this out. Man, I'm looking to spread the wealth. Look, why don't you make this move with me? I got connections, man.

My shit is rolling. Man, you know I got about three spots and I'm about to make a move on a house. Got to get my paper straight on this paper chase."

"You know, I got my own shit and it's proper, but good looking out, asking and shit."

"Look, man, I don't want Family out in the cold on this move. I mean, you can still make your money. Shit, you can probably double your income. See what I'm sayin'?"

Danny looked at him, trying to peep Sweets' move. "I'm straight. Thanks for asking."

"Hey, all right. I was just looking out for Family, that's all. But you sure you don't want to make this move? You might lose some money if you don't come on board."

Danny looked over Sweets' shoulder at all the people around his car. "Family, you look like you got all the help you will ever need."

"But hey, I can always use the help of a pro like you, my man. You ain't never caught a case on you, so you must know what you doing."

"I like my own game, but like I say, good looking out."

"Yo mellow, just let me know if you change your mind."

"I will."

Danny turned around and headed home. Sweets wanted Danny to work for him, but Danny wasn't stupid enough to buy that shit about him never catching a case. Sweets never caught a case either. Sweets paid off a flunky on the force for the low down. Danny was just lucky so far. The real reason Sweets wanted Danny was because Danny didn't get work from him. Danny was probably the only person in a five-block radius that didn't depend on Sweets for work.

It would be all right as long as Sweets didn't try no vicious shit. If he did, then Danny would be ready for him. Sweets had made his play, and now the shit was over. Danny wanted to leave it alone. He could just be conjuring up some bad drama for nothing.

Danny hesitated in front of his house. It looked just like all the other houses on the block. There was the patch of dirt in the front, the same bricks. The whole block looked like it had come out of a mold that had been stamped all over the South Side of Chicago.

He took another swig from the forty and went inside, where the only light was coming from the television. Old mail was sitting in front of the picture of his father. In the picture, browned with age, his father wore a military uniform. The photo could have been one of Danny five years ago.

His mother sat in her chair, a drink in one hand and a cigarette in the other. Danny hoped that she had drunk herself into silence and wouldn't be hollering and screaming. He didn't want to go any rounds with her tonight. She never knew how close she came to having him snap on her like she did on him.

His nephew, DeShawn, was sitting next to his mother on the floor, watching television. Laneka sat next to him. Danny looked at the television, then he looked at DeShawn. "Did your mother fix anything for dinner?"

"Yeah, she fixed some tuna fish."

"Is there any left?"

"Yeah."

Danny started to walk through the dining room. "Don't eat all that goddamn tuna!" his mother hollered at him.

"Fuck you," he mumbled under his breath.

He looked through the cabinet and found a clean bowl, filled it with the tuna fish, careful to leave some in the refrigerator. He took the bowl and the forty into the basement with him.

The basement offered respite from the heat upstairs and outside. Its coolness welcomed Danny, as did the musky, damp odor that old basements have. He exhaled some of the tension from the street, but he would not relax. He sat on his bed, eating the tuna fish and drinking beer in the darkness. There was a knock at the window. Without getting up, Danny yelled, "Who is it?"

"Me, Tiny."

Danny walked to open the window. "Yeah, man. What up?"

"Yo, Danny. What'cha into, man?"

"Just chilling out. Come on around to the side."

Tiny, like most men named Tiny, was anything but. He probably weighed 350 pounds, give or take a few. He moved quickly for his size and was at the side door in almost no time. Danny turned the light on when he went up the steps to open the door.

"Yo man, what up? How come you ain't out serving?"

"I don't feel like it. That's the good thing about being self-employed. When you don't wanna work, you don't have to. I just felt like coming in, plus my spot is starting to get too hot. What you doing?"

"Ol' girl was getting on my nerves, so I just pulled up camp."

Danny agreed. "As if shit ain't already hard enough on a nigga, people want to ride your ass 'cause they had a fucked up day."

Tiny sat on the bed. There was no place else to sit besides the floor. Tiny reached into his shirt pocket and pulled out a crumpled pack of Newports. He fumbled with the cigarettes for a moment, then freed one from the pack and lit it. After he lit the cigarette, he placed the lighter and pack on the bed. Danny motioned toward the pack, and Tiny nodded. Danny lit a cigarette.

"So, what you into?" Tiny inhaled.

"I don't know. I got some work, but I was thinking about hooking up on some more. But then the spot is so hot. Johnny Law all over the place, looking for a kill 'n shit, so I can chill for a moment. I got money, don't owe nobody shit, but when I do get out, I'm gonna need some help. I was thinking about taking stupid-ass Otis as a runner."

"You can trust Otis like that?"

"All the motherfucker got to do is run. Then he can have some money for hisself and quit bumming all the damn time."

"If you down for it, then I'm down for it."

"You want to hit this brew?"

"Yeah, pass it."

Danny passed Tiny the forty-ounce. "You got anything on you?"

"Yo, man, I always have something. Come on over by the window. We can smoke a couple of these thirty-seven fifties. I don't want the ol' girl smelling this shit. Man, she'll really start tripping. But hey, sometime I just don't give a fuck."

Danny and Tiny went over to the window. Danny handed Tiny a joint and took one himself.

Tiny lit his, took two hits and passed it. Danny took a deep drag. They could smell the burning cocaine.

"Yeah, this shit is hitting now."

Danny took another drag and passed it back. He held the smoke as long as he could before he blew it out the window, watching to make sure the smoke from the end actually went out the window and not back in the room. Tiny passed the joint and Danny took two more hits. They repeated the pattern until the joint Tiny was holding was almost burned out. Then Danny lit up the other one. After the second joint was gone, they sat back on the bed.

Tiny turned on the black and white television that sat on the dresser. "You know if there's a game on?"

"I'on't know, man. I don't be that deep into the shit. Now, I can keep up with basketball and football, but they play baseball too damn much."

Tiny lit a cigarette and passed the pack to Danny. "Man, you hear about James? He got deadened yesterday."

"Nope, I ain't heard nothing about it."

"Who you think did it?"

"I'on't know. James had his hands into so much shit, ain't no telling who wanted his ass. Shit just caught up to him."

Tiny leaned back against the wall. "You would have thought Family would have been looking out for him."

"Family can't be everywhere, and then again, ain't no telling. He might have crossed Family. Motherfuckers start that geeking and they'll steal from they church."

There had been a time in Danny's life when James was his hero. James was the one that hipped him to cooking. James funded him at one time. James had been rolling better than Sweets. He just wasn't high profile like Sweets liked to be. When James had his shit proper, there was no telling how much money he was rolling. He started hitting his product and hurting himself. Then one day, he was just another geek with a little respect. The last time Danny saw him, he had knocked on the basement window talking about the old days. Danny gave him a fifty bag and sent him on.

"Wasn't he a runner at one of Sweets' spots?" Danny asked.

"Yeah, I saw him over on about Fifty-seventh and Calumet a few weeks ago."

"That's fucked up. Back in the day his shit was righteous, then his shit fell and he was geeking on the streets."

Danny leaned back and looked up at the beams in the ceiling. James was just another nigga in long line of niggas dying in the game. This was the game. Dealing turned out to be a lot of people's life's work. Danny reminded himself that this was supposed to be a temporary situation, that one day he was going to move on to something more serious. He didn't know what he would move to, or when he would make that move. Maybe that was the way all the players thought. Danny took the forty-ounce and poured some of the malt liquor on the floor. "Here's to one more nigga that ain't going to jail."

Tiny took the bottle and poured a little on the floor. "Yeah, he was straight. To my boy, James."

Tiny took a deep swig and passed the bottle to Danny. He took a swig and set the bottle on the floor. "I talked to old Sweets today."

"Yeah, what was that nigga talking about?"

"He wanted me to come and work on one of his crews or some shit. He must be fucking with some serious drugs. He was trying to play me like I just got here. He gonna try to be all soft about it 'n shit, saying he was gonna look out for me."

"So, what did you tell him?"

"Get the fuck out of my face."

"Like that?"

"Naw, I wasn't going to be disrespectful 'n shit, but that is what it amounted to."

"How's he taking it? You know that motherfucker ain't used to having motherfuckers turn him down."

"He was straight, but if he wants someone to suck his dick, he got all them motherfuckers that's holding his jock to do that."

Tiny sat up and smiled. "You know what his problem is? He be watching too many gangster movies 'n shit. He feel like he gotta control everything and everybody got to be under him. I ain't mad at him. He just don't seem like a person to trust."

Danny stepped out a cigarette. "Yeah, man, he done sent about ten young boys to the state for his ass. Everybody know that he got to send some over to keep the heat off his ass. Tripped out thing is that all them youngsters know they gonna go, but they don't know when."

"You think he gonna start any shit?" Tiny asked.

"I can't see it happening, but then again I can't

call it. Man, I'll gun that motherfucker if I have to. I hope he ain't gonna get stupid on me 'n shit."

Tiny stood up. "Man, I'm gonna set out. Just let me know when you gonna go to work. I'll ride with you."

Danny got up to let him out. "Man, don't say shit to Otis if you see him. I want to catch that motherfucker when he ain't got the time to think about shit."

"Man, you letting that motherfucker ride, you better be the one thinking about it." Tiny walked up the steps to the side door.

Danny followed him. "He'll be all right. Get him some straightener and he'll be fine."

Tiny left. Danny went back into the basement. After sitting there, ignoring the baseball game on television, he went upstairs. He walked by his mother, who was sitting in her chair, watching the television with a blank stare on her face. "Where the hell you going?" she asked, her words slurring into one long, barely distinguishable sound.

Danny continued walking as though he did not hear her. It was obvious that she was drunk off her ass, and he didn't want to do rounds with her tonight.

"I said where the hell you think you going? Damn it!"

Danny knew everything that could happen from this point. He could go on out the door, then she would get up and scream at him through the door, or he could stay and she could scream at him in his face. It was a fucked up thing when your mother was drunk in public. The next-door neighbors would see her if she got up and went to the door. Either way, they would hear her.

He looked down at her sitting in the chair. "Ma, don't start no shit tonight. Just drink your shit and stay your ass in the chair," he said, heading toward the door.

"Damn you, motherfucker. You don't tell me what to do. You don't tell me a damn thing. You tell me where you got that goddamn car from. You tell me where your money come from. You tell me where all my money be going. You tell me that, if you want to be telling me shit. You tell me that, goddamn it."

"Ma, leave me the fuck alone. Just sit there and drink your shit, okay?"

She was struggling to get up out of the chair—or struggling with the idea of getting out of the chair. Danny could not tell which, and she could not get out of the chair. "You don't tell me what's okay, goddamn it! I fed your little heathen ass. I raised your heathen ass, and this is the respect that I get. Damn you! God damn you. I fed all your little hungry asses. I'm still feeding all your hungry asses. I'm still feeding you. You don't tell me shit!"

This would have been a good time for a joint. Why couldn't his mother be a reefer head? Smoke a joint. Fuck that—smoke a bag, and go her ass to bed. That drinking shit was a gamble. She could drink sometimes and don't bother nobody, then she could drink and curse out the mailman. She should get high. That could be like a treatment for alcoholics. They should get them high. They could get high and leave everybody else the hell alone.

"Ma, I'm gone. You bring your ass to that door and I'ma knock the shit out of you," he said, heading to the door.

"Oh, nigga, now you bad. You a big, bad-ass man now. You gonna knock the shit out of me. Motherfucker, I brought your ass into the world, I'll take your monkey ass right the fuck out of it! Where is my gun? Motherfucker, I'll blow a hole in your ass you could fly a plane through. You'll knock the shit out of me. Like hell you will!"

Dorothy was starting to stand up. "Motherfucker, I'll show your ass who's bad, goddamn it! Let me get my shit. I'll show you who's bad."

She stumbled back into her chair, and Danny headed on out the door. He could hear her cursing behind him, but she wouldn't get out that chair for a few more hours. She might not get out until the morning sometime. He ran down the porch and got into his car.

He drove a classic dope dealer's car, a 1985 Chevy Caprice. It could easily ride six niggas deep, no problem. The message in the back window said it all—"My Bitch." He had the booming system and a 16-channel police scanner. They had tried to take it from him, but he was never caught with anything. He rarely carried more than he could throw out the window without really missing it.

Danny got the car the way a lot of dope dealers got cars—he bought it off someone who needed to pay legal fees to stay a shorter time in jail. Shit was funny. They were seizing shit left and right, so the car was almost never in the owner's name. They kept changing the laws to make the lawyers rich. There wasn't a law out there you couldn't pay your way around. You were deadened if you got a public defender. So when you got busted, you tried to pay your debt to society up front so you didn't have to go to prison. Just another way that money changed hands in the paper chase.

A Saturday night would find somebody out somewhere. Maybe he would go to Max's spot. The music was always bumping there, and the bitches was easy. He could use the company. His stash was straight, and he had some money in his pocket. Yeah, Max's would be a good move.

He parked two blocks away from Max's. He knew there would be no parking close by, but the reason he didn't even look to park close was because the cops would be close. They were always close. They might have just been in the area to get the payoff, or they might have been looking for someone to bust. Either way, he didn't want to be involved with them. Besides, the farther you could run, the better the chance you got away.

He stopped at a liquor store on the corner to buy a pack of Newports, a half pint of vodka, and some chewing gum. He swigged the vodka before he got to the spot. It made his buzz complete. He was high off of everything, and in every way he wanted to be.

From the corner, he could hear the music and he could see a small crowd of hard legs in front of the spot. The door opened and bass thundered down the street, then it almost disappeared when the door closed. Danny watched the boys in front. They were played-up dope boys. They had the earrings, the gold chains, the hair-cuts and braids, the clothes and the money. They were flexing in front of the club. Danny just hoped that they weren't into starting shit right now.

"Yo, Family, what up?" one of them asked, looking Danny up and down as he approached the door.

It was a look Danny knew too well. He was being sized up. The dope boy looked at Danny and wanted him to cower or at least not stand up to him. It was some ancient call of the wild shit. Danny knew this ritual all too well. You go out, get all drunk or highed up, and then you and your homeys get into a fight. Then you have that collective memory of that time you kicked somebody's ass at the club. Do it often enough and you get a reputation for your violence. Do it one time too many, and instead of having memories, you become one.

Danny nodded in the dope boy's direction and continued toward the door. The boy was flagging Family colors. Everybody knew that Max's was a Family spot, but Danny thought his attitude was getting out of line. Danny had been a member of Satan's Family as long as he could remember. He had attained his respect; he was an elder son. In the Family, an elder son only had to look up to Family Men. They could operate how they wanted, as long as they didn't disrespect a Family Man. There was no way this young punk could be an elder, and who was this motherfucker anyway?

"Yo, motherfucker, I just look like this. Don't be trying no stupid shit. I'm an elder, motherfucker. You give me my respect."

"Oh, my fault, Family. I didn't mean no disrespect. My fault."

"I just don't play that shit. I ain't the one."

"Everything's chill, Family."

"Bet."

Danny walked up to the door, looking back. When he opened the door, the music hit him full on. The bass was pounding and somewhere under it was a song. The bar was crowded, at least from what Danny could see before the doorman blocked his view.

"Five dollars."

Danny watched him say it instead of hearing it. He reached into his pocket and pulled out a wad of bills, found a five and gave it to the doorman. The doorman moved and Danny walked into the bar. He watched a waitress wind her way through the crowd with a tray full of drinks. The air was stale with cigarette smoke and alcohol. The air conditioning was on, but it was still hot. The heat, for all its intensity, seemed to have little or no effect on the revelry.

On the dance floor, bodies rhythmically smashed into each other. It was just a sexual ritual, a payoff in the paper chase. The women at the bar ranged from innocent to nasty in their dress and manner. The men simply reflected what they thought was cool. It was fun to watch, but it was more fun to participate. Danny ordered a beer from the bar.

With beer in hand, Danny surveyed the bar. Sweets and his crowd were in the corner. Danny nodded to him; Sweets nodded back. Danny looked at the women at the bar. There was no one there that he immediately recognized, but that was neither good nor bad. He looked at the men hanging around the bar, waving their hands, trying to get some point across or just trying to score some points.

He saw a table with three girls and no men sitting at it. He went up to the table and asked the prettiest one to dance. She shook her head, so he looked at the other girls sitting at the table and walked back to the bar. Again he looked for someone he knew. It was going to make the difference tonight. He wouldn't have to explain himself to someone he knew, and tonight, he didn't feel like explaining.

He saw a girl at the other end of the bar, someone he did know, a girl called Melissa. She reminded him of a girl named Candy, who was all that before she let that rock bet bad on her, fucking around with that powder. Now Candy was just another fiend with a number.

He slipped through the crowd until he got to the other end of the bar. "Hey, Melissa, what's up with you?"

"Danny? Where you been? Who you up here with?"

"I'm up here with you. You looking fine enough to take a big bite out of. What you been up to?"

"Nothing. What you doing?"

"I'm telling you I came up here looking for you."

"Yeah, that's why you ain't called in two weeks."

"Bullshit. I called you twice last week alone. Your answering machine must be broke."

"That's funny. I got everybody else's messages."

"Ain't your number 767-8105?" Danny knew it was the wrong number.

"No, it ain't. It's 767-8150. Who you been calling?"

"Well, whoever it is got some nasty messages on they machine."

He looked at the red dress she was almost wearing. "So, you up here with anybody I might have to kill?"

"I'm up here with some friends of mine."

Danny set his beer on the bar and took her hand. "C'mon and dance with me."

She got up and he let her lead the way to the

dance floor. He smiled one wicked smile as he watched her walking in front of him. She was a collection of curves. Her behind looked perfectly round, on top of some perfectly round thighs, above some beautifully rounded calves. Her walk was hypnotic, hips swinging evenly on both sides, chocolate-covered legs in high heel shoes that fell exactly in front of each other.

Melissa reached a spot on the floor that was as close to empty as they could find, and she turned around to face him. A slow song was coming on. She eyed him up and down. She was sizing him up and he knew it. He just hoped that he measured up. The music was filling in as they moved closer to each other. She put her arms around his neck, and he reciprocated, placing his arms around her waist.

At first they danced at a distance, touching only where necessary. They each watched couples dancing around them. Some were dancing just like they were, like strangers. There were others whose intimacy was apparent, or at least they had intimate intentions.

Danny decided to make a move and he pulled her closer to him. At first there was a little hesitation, then she gave way. He could feel her now. To dance this close was totally different. He could feel the fabric of her dress on his shirt. He moved his hand to the small of her back, and the other hand he brought to the nape of her neck. He leaned down and whispered in her ear, "I hope this ain't all there is."

"What you mean by that?"

"I mean that I hope we can get closer than this."

Melissa smiled. "We'll see."

He let his hand slide down her back some more, until it was resting on her behind. She looked up at him. "You better watch it."

"I want to do more than watch it. Can't you tell?"

"Why should I give you the good treatment?"

"Because I can do you better, and you know that."

The song ended. Before anyone could let go good, there was another slow song. Some of the couples separated. Danny held tighter to Melissa, and she held on to him, getting lost in another slow dance. They never let up, never missed a beat. Her face rested on his chest. If it had been another place and time, it would have meant the same thing.

Like a bird in a groove, Danny thought. That was something that Uncle Dave would always say when shit was going right. Danny never really knew what it meant, but he liked the way it sounded. They were lost in a groove, someplace where they could close their eyes and let the music play them like someone playing a violin or a saxophone. They took half steps side to side, pushing closer to each other. It was times like this that Danny wondered what a real relationship was like, what having a wife would be like. Coming home from work every day to a loving touch.

The song ended much too soon for both of them. They stood there for a moment, reluctant to let go. The bass of a much faster song beat through the air. Danny let his arms drop, not wanting to let her go at all. "So, how you gonna act?"

Melissa looked back at him. "What are you gonna do?"

"Why don't you come take a walk with me?"

"Okay."

They went straight out the door. There was a new set of dope boys standing around. All of them followed Melissa with their eyes. One of them said, "I can do you better!"

Melissa took Danny's hand and they walked by the crowd. Danny took her to the car. They kissed twice before they got there. "You awful bold," she said, getting into the car.

"You got to be in this world or you ain't gettin' shit."

"You know I like you," she said, smiling.

"I hope so. I hope you don't go kissing all the men that will be fools for you, 'cause if you did, you be too busy."

They kissed again—a long, passionate kiss that allowed Danny to fill his hands with her. "I better be getting back. My girlfriends are probably wondering where I am."

"Before I let you go, those numbers was 8150, right?"

"Yeah, and you better call tomorrow too."

"I'ma call later tonight."

"Well, if I don't hear from you by tomorrow, I'll forget you existed."

"Bet."

They got out of the car and walked back. There was another set of dope boys in the front. Danny kissed her goodbye in the front of the club, and the dope boys whistled. One followed her into the club. Danny turned around and walked back to the car.

He drove by his spot and saw someone sitting

on the steps where he sold his rock. That was not right. He parked in front of his house, got his gun from under the seat and walked back up the block. The man on the porch watched Danny walking toward him.

"Yo, man, what you looking for?"

"I'm looking for you, home team!"

"I got fat dimes and fatter quarters."

"Straight," Danny said as he got close enough to see the man's face.

The man went to get his stash out of the bushes. Danny pulled out the gun, holding it behind his leg. When the man turned around, Danny was pointing the gun in his face.

"Motherfucker, what you doing working here? This is my spot. Why the fuck you working here? This is the kind of shit that will get a nigga deadened. I don't know who you are, but I'll fucking take you out in a minute."

"Oh, Family, Sweets said I could come work this if it wasn't nobody here. It wasn't nobody here, so I worked it."

"Man, this spot don't belong to Sweets and he know it. I should just take your ass out for being here. But since you Family, I'll just say it was a misunderstanding. Get your shit and go on. Don't be back this way."

The man took his stash down the street. Danny stayed looking around to see if there was someone else around. The spot was empty. He walked back to his car and drove the car to his house, wondering if he should have killed that man and let Sweets know what was up. Maybe he should have shot him, just to send a message.

chapter four

The alarm on Reginald's watch went off, but he really didn't need it because he would never oversleep on a Sunday. He stopped the alarm out of habit, then sat up and looked out of the window. This had to be the pit of dreariness, to wake up and look out at Eberhart. If he had stayed over at Dennis' apartment like he'd wanted to, he would have awakened to a view overlooking Lake Michigan on South Shore Drive.

Eberhart was no lake, but it was a place that should be under the lake. He sat up and stretched, got out of the bed and stretched again. He was surprised to see Anthony in the bed on the other side of the room they'd shared almost as long as Reginald could remember. So, Anthony was home from jail, at least temporarily.

Reginald left the room so he wouldn't wake Anthony. As long as Anthony was asleep, they wouldn't argue. Reginald took a shower. On the way back to his room, he stopped in the kids' room and woke DeShawn and Laneka. He also needed to wake his mother and find out if she was going to make it to Sunday school today. If she wasn't going to Sunday school, he hoped that she wasn't going to church at all. If she were, he'd have to leave class early to come back and get her to make it to the service on time.

He went into his room and dressed. He looked at himself in the full-length mirror on the closet door, changed his mind then changed his clothes. He settled on a mint green linen suit, a purple shirt, and a green paisley tie. He decided that he looked good enough in it.

After he got dressed, he knocked on his mother's door. "Ma, you gonna go to Sunday school?"

"How much time I got?"

Reginald looked at his watch. "About forty-five minutes."

He was lying. She had an hour easy, but he knew if he told her an hour, she would take longer than that, and he didn't want to be late. She had little if any regard for other people's time.

The kids were downstairs eating a breakfast of cold cereal and Reginald joined them. "Are you all ready for Sunday school today?"

DeShawn looked at him. "As long as none of them fat ladies be trying to kiss me. I don't like them old fat ladies."

"DeShawn, those ladies are just being nice to you, and you be nice back to them. At least when you make faces, don't let them see it. Okay?"

"Okay."

"Laneka, what about you?"

"Yeah, I guess I'm ready. What you got to do to be ready? You got to give me some money to put in the offering thing."

"I'll give you some money, and I want you to put all of it in the offering. You hear me?" Laneka nodded. "You too, DeShawn." Reginald said so that Laneka did not feel as though she were being picked on solely.

DeShawn nodded. Reginald knew that the money he gave them wasn't going to make it to the offering. It was a tradition. When his grandmother gave him money, he didn't put all of it in church either, and the rest he would buy candy with. He didn't mind, because they didn't have enough candy in their lives.

He could hear his mother upstairs moving around, so he assumed that she was actually gonna go and not fake him out. After eating breakfast, he sat in the living room and re-read his Sunday school lesson. It was about David and Jonathan. This was nothing that he hadn't heard before. Actually, there was little in church that he hadn't heard at one time or another.

Maybe it was time for him to take it further. Maybe he should announce his call to the ministry, but he wasn't sure if that was what it was. It could be that he just wanted it so bad, that he wanted to be a church leader, a pastor someday. He would pray on it more. If God wanted him to preach, then he would, but in the meantime, he would be content to continue his music ministry.

His mother finally came down the stairs. She was dressed, and she looked so pretty. Reginald was proud of how his mother looked. All that drinking she did, she should look a lot worse. She was wearing that yellow dress he had just gotten her. It was on sale, and with his discount it didn't cost that much. As dark as she was, she would have never chosen a bright yellow dress for herself. She had grown up believing that dark-skinned women shouldn't wear bright clothes. He had a time convincing her to even try it on. Seeing herself in it was all the convincing she needed.

"I told you, you would like that dress, and I knew that you would look good in it."

"Thank you."

"Are you ready to go?"

"Did the kids eat? I don't want them sitting up in that church all morning on an empty stomach."

"Yeah, they had some cereal. They'll be all right."

"Well, let's go then."

The four of them walked out to Reginald's car. It wasn't as good-looking as Danny's car, but it was functional. The children got in the back and were immediately quiet. They knew that they wouldn't get any money until they got to church, and the better they acted, the more they would get. Reginald had told them that months ago, and it got them to behave perfectly for the ride.

Dorothy checked herself in the rearview mirror before letting Reginald take off. Reginald repositioned the mirror and drove off. He turned the radio to a church broadcast, not so much to hear preaching, but to hear the choir.

"Turn that thing down. Shit, it sounds like you in the pulpit. The children gonna lose they hearing."

Reginald turned the radio down. The ride would be over in a few minutes, especially since there was almost no traffic at 9:15 on a Sunday morning. He pulled into the church parking lot. Out of habit he looked at the sign in front of the church: *Gethsemane Baptist Church, Rev. Odell Warden, Pastor*.

The children got out on Reginald's side of the car and waited for their grandmother. "C'mon, Ma. I gotta put the alarm on and I can't do it with you in the car."

"Reginald, ain't nobody gonna steal this piece of shit car out of a church parking lot. Just park it next to the pastor's Mercedes. Won't nobody even see it."

"Ma, these people around here will steal your dirty underwear while you peeing. You just can't be too careful."

Dorothy got out the car. Reginald turned the alarm on and gave the children three dollars apiece. Then he walked ahead into the church, leaving his mother, still walking, in the parking lot.

Reginald got in the church and went straight into the basement. It was immediately cool. He greeted some other church members with a genuine "Good morning."

They spoke back, lacking the same sincerity. Reginald looked at them as they walked by him and thought, *The hearts of men are full of evil intent, even since their youth.*

Some of Reginald's classmates were already in the classroom waiting. They all spoke to each other, sat down, and re-read the lesson. The bell rang, but the teacher hadn't arrived. Reginald stood and stretched out his hands to the people on either side of him.

"We don't have to wait for him to get here to pray. Roxanne, why don't you lead us in prayer?"

Roxanne stood, her dress slightly smaller than it should have been. Not that she was fat or anything, just that her clothes were always deacon-catching tight. She stretched out her hands for her neighbors to take hold. She closed her eyes and lowered her head.

"Lord, first of all we'd like to say thank you. Thank you, Lord, for waking us up this morning and clothing us in our right minds. Thank you, Father, because You didn't have to do it. You didn't have to bless us with this morning, Lord, but You did. Thank you for giving us a saving grace this morning, Lord, and thank you for filling us with Your Holy Spirit, Lord. We need You, Lord, because we can't make it on our own, Lord. We're like blind men, Lord. We don't know the way. We thank You for showing us the way, Lord. We thank You for sending us Your son, that all who believeth on Him might be saved and have life everlasting. We ask that You bless the teacher this morning. Fill him with Your spirit. We ask that You fill us this morning, Lord. We ask that you fill us with Your Holy Spirit, that we might go forth and proclaim the gospel that will save men's souls. These and all other blessings we ask in Jesus' name. Amen."

The rest of the class said "Amen" and sat down. They returned to reading their lessons while they waited for their teacher. Within a few minutes, Edward came in, followed immediately by Mark, a new tenor in the church choir. Edward was the minister of music. Even though he made no noise when he entered the room, his entrance was in no way subtle.

He wore his blue minister of music robe. He looked almost angelic, with his hair combed into large, neat waves on his head, and his beard neat and trimmed. He looked like he could have passed for a black version of the white Jesus that had hung on the wall in his grandmother's room. He placed his bag on the floor next to his chair. He reached into the bag for his Bible and his teacher's copy of the Sunday school book. Mark took his seat next to Edward and quietly opened his lesson book. He hardly looked at anyone in the class. Reginald noticed the hickeys on Mark's neck. He smiled at Edward, who smiled back and opened his Bible, giving his attention to the class.

"David and Jonathan's friendship begins in the eighteenth chapter of first Samuel. My Bible reads that the soul of Jonathan was knit with the soul of David, and Jonathan loved him as his own soul. This is the kind of love that God would have us to have for one another. Because our souls are knit in the body of Christ, we should love each other as we do our own souls. Can anyone add to that?'

Reginald was trying to be sincere and pay attention to the class, but his eyes kept straying to a class across the hall. Tremont, a quiet, brown-skinned young man sat in the class, alternately reading his Sunday school book and his Bible. He hardly looked away from the pair of books in his lap, when all of a sudden he answered a question and sprang to life. Reginald watched as Tremont began speaking nervously then gained confidence as he continued to speak. Tremont was very assertive in his argument, and the whole class agreed with whatever he had said. When he finished, he sat down, beaming.

Tremont must have felt Reginald watching him. He looked at Reginald then sheepishly looked away. Reginald continued his extreme examination of the young man until he was sure that

Tremont wouldn't look back at him. Reginald then returned his attention to Edward, the class and the lesson on David and Jonathan.

Edward was still talking about the relationship between Jonathan and David to the whole class, but directed his attention to Mark. Mark sat quietly his chair, holding his head down the entire time, but Edward was beaming at him. Did Edward have to be so obvious? Why didn't he just send everybody else out of the room, and they could just have their little lesson right there on the floor? Reginald rolled his eyes at Edward and prayed that the class would come to a quick end. After forty minutes of Edward's semi-sermon and the class giving the same answers to every question, the bell rang. Edward ended his personal sermon for Mark, collected a small offering, and prayed the class free.

Roxanne took the money and the attendance chart then went to the Sunday school office, where they properly recorded the ten dollars collected from the ten people in the class. Reginald went out to the parking lot with Edward, followed by Mark. He watched Laneka and DeShawn going off to the liquor store to get their Sunday offering of candy for the service. "Don't spend all that money down there, and you better have put some money in Sunday school," he shouted after them.

Edward lit a cigarette and walked toward the front of the church. Reginald walked with him, with Mark taking his place as a concubine behind Edward. Reginald knew what Mark was going through, and of all the people he could be going through it with, Edward was probably the worst. Edward was loud and always attracting attention to himself. Mark looked like a dog that had been caught stealing out of the kitchen garbage. But all that would pass. For now, though, Reginald felt pity for him.

"So, Reggie, what's been going on with you?" Edward asked.

"Same stuff, different days."

"I heard that Michael was sick."

"Michael who?"

"You know, he used to go over to Ephesians, him and Darryl."

"Okay, now I know who you talking about. Does he have it?"

"Yeah, I think so."

"Man, it seem like everybody is just dropping like flies. I'm tired of going to funerals."

Edward flicked his cigarette into the street. "He's out at County. Why don't we go and see him? As a matter of fact, I'm going to run over there after service. Why don't you come with me?"

"Yeah, I will, but I got to take my mother and my niece and nephew home first. Why don't I drop them off and then meet you at your house?"

"Okay."

Reginald heard Tremont's name mentioned from behind him. He turned around and Tremont was now standing about ten feet away from him. Reginald stepped toward him. "Tremont, how are old are you now?"

"I'm fifteen," he answered, barely lifting his head.

"You sure are a big fifteen. So, are you going to join the choir this year?"

"Well, I was thinking about it."

"Well, you know we always need some more

men in the choir. If you want to, why don't you come to rehearsal this Thursday? If you need a ride, I'll give you one."

"I'll bet you would," Edward said under his breath.

"Sure," Tremont said to Reginald. Tremont took off in the direction of the liquor store. Reginald turned back to Edward. "So, why were you late for church this morning?"

Edward gave Mark a knowing smile. "There were some things I had to take care of before I came to praise the Lord."

Mark blushed and Reginald frowned. "I'm sure there was."

Edward started walking back toward the church. "We better get inside before you all get fined."

"You all go on. I'll be there in a minute."

Edward turned and continued to the church, Mark following quietly behind him. Reginald looked toward the store to see if Tremont was on his way back yet. There were children coming down the street, but Tremont was not among them. Reginald thought about going to the store, but there was nothing he wanted from there besides Tremont. He decided that he'd do best by going into the church.

He walked to the basement in the church. The room dividers were all down, and someone had begun singing the devotional. There were still a few deacons downstairs, gawking at the women in the choir when they should have been upstairs participating in the call to worship.

The choir members held hands and joined in the singing, and the deacons left. Edward was leading the singing, with Mark standing next to him.

Reginald sang halfheartedly. As the song ended, someone began a prayer. Other members of the choir added praise to the prayer. Reginald didn't add anything today. Usually he would, but today he just didn't feel up to it.

After the prayer, Edward announced, "Show time, folks."

The choir members spent the last few minutes straightening up and making sure all the robes were zipped up before going to the service upstairs. The choir members arrived in time to join in the last of the call and response between the deacons and the congregation. When the choir had taken its place around the congregation, on cue, the congregation stood. One of the ministers approached the pulpit and started a prayer.

"Heavenly Father, we come here today to say thank you. Thank you, Lord, for waking us up this morning and clothing us in our right minds. Thank you, Father, because You didn't have to do it. You didn't have to bless us with this morning, Lord, but you did. Thank you for giving us a saving grace this morning, Lord, and thank you for filling us with Your Holy Spirit, Lord. We need You, Lord, because we can't make it on our own, Lord. We're like blind men, Lord. We don't know the way. We thank You for showing us the way, Lord. We thank You for sending us Your Son, that all who believeth in him might be saved from damnation and enjoy everlasting life. We ask that You bless the speaker this morning. Fill him with Your spirit. We know that You are a doctor for those in need of healing. You are freedom for those imprisoned. You are food for the hungry. But Father, there are those out in the world that don't know You, Lord, that don't know You are a waymaker when there is no way. We ask that You fill us this morning, Lord. We ask that You fill us with Your Holy Spirit, that we might go forth and proclaim the gospel that will save men's souls. These and all other blessings we ask in Jesus' name. Amen."

The congregation sat down, then Edward struck a chord on the piano. Reginald joined the last few choir members in line around the congregation. He didn't like devotion when his grandmother brought him to church, and he was glad he could avoid it now.

The choir started a synchronized sway in time to the music Edward was playing. As soon as he was sure everyone was in step, he gave the signal, the music picked up, and the choir began the march. The altos and tenors marched on one side of the church, and the sopranos, bass, and baritone marched on the other. When the last member of the choir reached the choir stand behind the pulpit, the choir began singing.

The congregation clapped and sang along. Almost unnoticed in the joy, the pastor Odell Warden made his entrance. The song ended and the congregation stood up for the congregational selection. After that, the first collection was taken. While the plates were going around, Reginald looked for his mother. She was sitting with DeShawn and Laneka in the middle of the church. He wondered if she had already drunk from the half pint of vodka she always carried in her purse.

She was never going to be saved, not like he was. She was going to drink herself into an early grave, and there really was nothing that he could do about it. He knew he could pray all he wanted to, but if she didn't want to change, she wasn't going to change. He wondered why she even came to church at all. Maybe one day when she was sitting there, something would reach her and make her see the need for God in her life.

He could see Laneka and DeShawn fidgeting, probably passing candy back and forth to each other. He wished there was some way he could keep them involved in the church, so that what happened to their mother wouldn't happen to them. He survived like he did because of God and nothing else. He hadn't become a gang-banger or a drug dealer; he wasn't a drug addict and he didn't have children all over the city. So he had sex with men. He wasn't hurting anyone, and he wasn't hurting himself.

Then he saw Tremont sitting three rows in front of his mother. Tremont sat next to his grand-mother. Should he try to get next to him? Tremont reminded Reginald of himself at that age. He was into the Bible too. Reginald wondered if there were any other similarities between them, and he wanted to find out.

The collection was taken and the choir sang another song. Reginald sang lead, but he just wasn't into it. The audience clapped and sang along, but it definitely wasn't his best performance. After that, the choir sang the Lord's Prayer, then the tithes were collected. After a long prayer, the choir sang again. The pastor began his sermon. The sermon was about the same thing it always was—the weary and the downtrodden. By the end, the pastor had taken the congregation through his ranting and raving, and had brought them to tears.

Some women fainted, some were filled with the spirit and some openly wept. Reginald watched his mother crying. She held her composure, but there were definitely tears streaming down her face.

This was the only place he ever witnessed his mother cry. She never cried at home. If she did, no one ever knew about it. He guessed that since so many other people had given in to their emotions, she felt it was all right if she did. Reginald enjoyed the fact that his mother was touched at all. Someday, maybe she would be touched enough to change her life.

Reginald watched Tremont when he was not watching his mother. Tremont was as interested in the sermon as was anyone in the church. He wondered what Tremont was thinking about, and hoped the boy was thinking about him. He knew that was far-fetched, at least for now. He made a mental note to speak to him after church about joining the choir.

The pastor finally closed the sermon and gave the invitation to join the church, but there were no takers this Sunday. After another song and announcements, the pastor gave the benediction. Reginald went to the bathroom with Edward while he removed his robe. Edward insisted on wearing the robe, even though the rest of the choir agreed it was too hot to be in a robe for three hours.

While they were in the parking lot talking to other members, Reginald saw Tremont and his grandmother heading for the bus stop. He walked over and offered them a ride. Edward reminded Reginald that they had a commitment for the afternoon. Reginald said that he could still make it because Tremont didn't live that far from him.

First Reginald took his family home. He watched his mother to make sure she got in the house okay. Before he drove off, he could hear Regina screaming at her children. After they were some distance from the house, Reginald asked Tremont over his shoulder, "So Tremont, what do you think about joining the choir?"

"I don't know. I don't think I can sing all that well."

"Well, why don't you just come to rehearsal? You won't have to sing a solo on Sunday or nothing like that. Mrs. Ford, wouldn't you like to see your grandson in the choir?"

"Of course I would."

"See. I'll call you on Thursday. Your number is in the church directory, isn't it?"

"Yeah."

"Then I'll call to make sure you coming."

"All right."

"Okay, see you then."

He drove for a short while and dropped them off in front of their house. He drove to Edward's house like he said he would, where Edward and Mark were waiting for him. They went to Cook County Hospital, and went directly to where they kept the AIDS patients. Michael, the friend they were looking for, had been discharged and was at home, a 20-minute drive from the hospital. They decided to visit him there.

Reginald dreaded seeing Michael. It had been a long time since he had last seen him, and he knew what to expect. More than a few of his close friends had died of AIDS. It wasn't just that they died from AIDS, it was that the disease would eat them up first. When people first started dying, he reacted like everyone else, avoiding them. Then a close friend, an ex-lover, came down with it, and watching him die changed the way Reginald felt about AIDS patients. He broke down and he touched the man, and then he touched anyone he knew who had it. He touched them because there was so little else he could do, and Reginald's friend had told him, right before he died, how much the touch meant to him.

Despite seeing so many die, he still couldn't get used to it. The worst way was to see people die by themselves after their families had disowned them; to see them in the hospital alone, unvisited for weeks at a time. Reginald often wondered how his family would treat him if he had it. So far, he only had to guess, but the minute he sneezed or coughed or experienced the smallest touch of diarrhea, the fear would grab him. At first he didn't want to be tested. Too many people he had been intimate with years ago were dying from AIDS now. Knowing turned out to be better than not knowing when he tested HIV negative. There had been a lot of praying around that test.

They rode in silence. Reginald and Edward made it their mission to visit AIDS patients two Sundays a month. If they weren't going to see someone in particular, then they would go to an AIDS hospice just to lend a hand.

These rides were always quiet. Perhaps Edward reflected as Reginald did, each of them thanking God the entire ride that it was not him who was afflicted. He hoped that HIV or AIDS was not a reflection of how God felt about homosexuality. It was not a curse from God, but it was definitely a curse. It wasn't that God didn't love you if you had AIDS; it was that almost nobody else did. As they pulled up, it occurred to Reginald that Mark might never have been on such a visit.

"Have you ever seen someone with AIDS?" he asked Mark.

Mark shook his head.

Edward turned toward Reginald. "He'll be all right. He'd have to see it sooner or later. Besides, he can go with us whenever we go."

"Okay, if you think he'll be okay."

Mark looked scared as they approached the door. Reginald agreed he was bound to see it one day, and there was no time like the present. Edward knocked on the door. It took a while for Michael to answer it.

"Hey, Mike, how you doing?" Edward asked.

"I'm okay. I just got out of the hospital yesterday."

Edward shook his hand then gave him a hug. Reginald followed suit. Mark was visibly scared, but he shook Michael's hand in spite of it. Michael walked slowly through the house. He sat in his living room on the couch, where next to him was a television tray holding about thirteen different bottles of medicine. "So, what's new?"

"Well, we think the pastor has a new boyfriend. He's the new church secretary, and I'll bet he's taking dictation off Odell's lap."

"You know your pastor is a whore," Mike said, smiling. After having visited so many men with AIDS, Reginald and Edward knew they appreciated some normalcy, and nothing was more normal in the church community than gossip.

They sat and visited with Michael. His mother looked in on him once. It was good that his mother was there for him, and they knew she needed a break too. They talked for about two hours. Edward and Reginald both sang, and Michael, through his tears, joined in. They were all crying by the time the song ended. Michael thanked them for coming by, and they hugged him again. Before they left, Reginald promised he'd bring Michael some reefer that he could get from his brother.

After they left, they went to dinner at Edward's house. They always felt pretty good after these visits. Mark lay down and took a nap. Reginald and Edward listened to a church broadcast on the radio and decided that later, they would attend the Jordan River broadcast that night.

The Jordan River Baptist Church was packed to the rafters. The pulpit was filled with assorted dignitaries. There were assorted ministers and pastors, a few aldermen, and the esteemed pastor of the Jordan River Baptist Church, Bishop John H. Perry.

The announcer took the stage, to the left and a little lower than the pulpit. The choir sang "Swing Low" as a back-up for the announcer. She began in her nasal tone, "Good evening, and may God bless you. Welcome to the weekly broadcast of the Jordan River Baptist Church. We are coming to you from our sanctuary located at 5640 South on Cottage Grove Avenue in Chicago, Illinois. We are under the divine leadership of the Bishop John H. Perry. In the name of our Lord and Savior, Jesus Christ, we'd like to thank you for joining us in this service of worship to our Lord. Whether you are sick and shut in, in prison, or just listening in the comfort of your home, we'd like for you to know our prayer lines are open.

You can reach a prayer partner at 312-424-2204 or 312-424-3707. Send your letters of comment, your prayer request, or your tithes and offerings to Jordan River, 5640 South Cottage Grove, Chicago Illinois, 60647. We begin our service with a selection from our young adult evangelical choir."

The announcer left the microphone and the choir behind her began to sing. After the song, the announcer took the stage again. "Now we will hear a prayer from our own associate pastor and assistant overseer, the Reverend Jackson L. Jenkins."

The Reverend Jenkins approached the microphone behind the pulpit and began his prayer. "Heavenly Father, we come here this evening to say thank you. Thank you, Lord, for waking us up this morning and clothing us in our right minds. Thank you, Father, for being with us in our home, and for being in our cars with us. We thank You, Father, for keeping an eye on us in these dangerous times. Thank you, Father, because You didn't have to do it. You didn't have to bless us with today, Lord, but You did. Thank you for giving us a saving grace this evening, Lord, and thank you for filling us with Your Holy Spirit, Lord. We need You, Lord, because we can't make it on our own, Lord. We're like blind men, Lord, we don't know the way. We thank You for showing us the way, Lord. We thank You for sending us Your Son, that all who believeth in him might be saved. We ask that You bless the speaker this evening. Fill him with Your spirit. We know that You are a doctor for those in need of healing. You are freedom for those imprisoned. You are food for the hungry. But Father, there are those out in the world that don't know You, Lord, that don't know You are a way-maker when there is no way. We ask that You fill us this evening, Lord. We ask that You fill us with Your Holy Spirit, that we might go forth and proclaim the gospel that will save men's souls. We ask that You touch those out there listening to us, Father. Touch those in the hospital beds, touch those in the prisons, touch those in the halfway house, those in the streets, those who find themselves without a home. We ask that You let them know that You not only can make a way, Lord, but that You are the way. These and all other blessings we ask in Jesus' name. Amen."

As soon as the prayer ended, the choir offered another selection. This time the song was a fast one and accomplished what it was supposed to; by the end of the song, people were running in the aisles, filled with the spirit. Reginald, Edward and Mark joined in with the choir. After that selection, the announcer read the list of names for the sick and shut in, then she read off another list of those in prison who listened. The "Warriors of Prayer" were still on the prayer lines for those in need.

Then the offering was taken. The minister called out for those whose offering was over one hundred dollars to be the first to give. Then he went down in denominations of ten until he was accepting offerings under twenty dollars. After the collection was blessed by a three-minute prayer, it was taken away by a horde of deacons. Reginald wondered just how much money they had collected that night. He also wondered if all the people in the over-one-hundred-dollar bunch actually gave over one hundred dollars. After all, what were they going to do if they asked for fifty and all you came up there with was ten? Would they send you back and tell you to wait your turn, or would they take the ten and shut up?

Edward told him he need not think of such things, it didn't matter. They were here for the show. The visiting choir was about to sing. To sing as a visiting choir at the River was quite a trick to pull off. First you had to get someone from their music department to attend your church. Of course, they had to be recognized. If the choir got a favorable review, then your choir would get an invitation for weeks or even months away. Edward was on the waiting list to get someone to come out to hear the choir.

The whole thing worked out well for everyone involved. The visiting church choir would bring a large contingency of visitors, the visitors would give money, so the River would benefit. The visitors would benefit from the exposure that being on the most popular church program in the city would bring. If your choir sounded good, people would like it, and people knew if they liked your choir, they would come to your church and give money.

The visiting choir sang well. They had the people in the aisles in the spirit. The audience wouldn't let the choir stop singing. Actually, it was a combination of the audience and the organist. The choir would end the song, the audience would continue clapping on the same beat, and the organist would start playing again. The choir would start singing, and the people would continue clapping to urge them on. Reginald stood up and clapped and sang with the rest of the audience.

The church finally calmed down, and the announcer stood and introduced the pastor. He thanked the choir for giving their all, and proceeded with his sermon. The sermon reached its peak with the choir singing against the preacher preaching, and the congregation urging them both on. The announcer took the stage again while the preacher was still preaching and thanked the radio audience for listening. She invited them to listen again, and the broadcast ended. The service ended ten minutes after the broadcast did.

The church emptied into the parking lot and the basement. Reginald, Mark, and Edward went into the parking lot. Reginald went to his car, got in and started it up, though he didn't drive off because he wasn't sure where he wanted to go. He could go home and listen to all the hollering and screaming that was undoubtedly taking place, or he could spend the night with Dennis.

He wouldn't have to have sex if he didn't want to. He could just stay with Dennis. More often, Dennis had been bringing up the idea of Reginald moving in. There was no reason he shouldn't. He decided that he would stay with Dennis tonight. He would stay as a friend, a potential roommate. He didn't want a lover, not Dennis anyway. Dennis would have to understand.

chapter five

Dorothy looked east up 61st Street. She didn't see a bus, so she headed west toward King Drive. She knew she had a better chance of getting a seat at the El stop on Cottage Grove, but she felt safer at the King Drive stop. She walked, looking nowhere but where she was going. In her right hand she held her bus pass; her left hand was in her purse holding a .25 automatic.

It was just after 8 o'clock, and the liquor stores were open and already attracting their unemployed customers who stood in front to bum money for a drink. Dorothy ignored them, and if one walked toward her, she would send him away with just a look. She reached the El station and climbed the steps. The ticket agent possessed the same disposition as everyone who worked for the public, with the public, didn't receive tips and hated their job. Dorothy felt the same way at work but couldn't act like that because she relied heavily on her over-taxed tips. But for now, she was a customer, ignored like the rest of the teeming masses passing through transit gates.

Dorothy lit a cigarette while waiting for the train. She looked around at the station. It had been reconstructed less than a year ago, but there were already gang symbols on the walls and it stank with the ever-present smell of urine. Well, at least it wasn't rusted and the paint wasn't peeling, like before they fixed it up.

There were two guards with dogs on the platform. Dorothy didn't understand how they chose what they would guard and when they would guard it. The El guards—for that matter the whole city—gave the nights over to the gangbangers and hoodlums of all sorts. What they failed to realize was that by giving away the night, all that crime was spilling into the day. In the morning, the guards were there, and the crooks were watching to see when they would leave so they could have the station. At least they were there in the morning.

Inside the train, the heat carried the odor of urine. What was it that made so many people piss in public places? The train pulled out of the station, heading downtown. A beer can rolled out from under one of the seats and made its way down the center of the train car. As soon as it was in her reach, she kicked it away. She looked out of the windows at the back porches of the apartments the El passed by. Broken glass sparkled around cars that should have been abandoned if they weren't, and all sorts of other garbage littered what could have been the back yards of these buildings.

Occasionally, she would see children playing or men as nasty as the alleys they were in, standing around, passing a soon-to-be broken bottle between them. This was the world full of nothing; nothing places filled with nothing people on their way to their respective nowhere. Maybe it was seeing the same monotonous shit every day that filled her with disgust. The same shit in one long-ass row, a row that stretched behind her as far back as she cared to remember and was all the tomorrow she could depend on.

A bag lady got on the train at the 31st Street station. She stank. Dorothy wondered if there was someplace that homeless people could go and bathe. It was bad enough that you had to look at them. Why did you have to smell them too? There were enough things in Chicago that assaulted the senses; homeless people could shower or something. It ought to be mandatory, especially in the summer after a rain. The police ought to just go out and round them up, take them to jail, and make them bathe. She smiled to herself, thinking how silly the idea was. There weren't enough police to do the job that they were paid to do, but maybe the mayor could start a task force.

Dorothy watched the woman coming down the middle of the train car. For a moment, she felt a pang of fear that the lady might sit next to her. Dorothy was somewhat relieved when she sat across from her.

The lady set two shopping bags between her legs and settled in for the trip. She cast her eyes downward and never looked up. Dorothy tried to ignore her, but her eyes kept returning to the homeless woman. The lady had on too many clothes and not enough shoes. The torn purple hi-top gym shoes hardly covered her feet at all. Dorothy wondered if the lady had been riding the trains all night. Now that the train traveled from one ghetto to another just passing through downtown, this would be the train to ride. No white people, no one to protect, no police.

The train pulled into Madison Street Station. Dorothy left the pissy car and the bag lady behind. The air outside was as fresh as air gets in downtown Chicago. The crowds had achieved their motion, moving through the streets like crazed ants. Some were rushing, some were dragging their feet going to wherever they felt they had to be. Dorothy made her way to the counter at Woolworth's.

In the back room that got the workers away from the customers, there had recently been talks of layoffs, cutbacks, and pay reductions. Actually, there was always talk of such things. They hung over the heads of workers like that pie in *The Three Stooges* short. The constant threat of the loss of income had kept most of the workers in compliance with the whims of management, though others had jumped ship with a hearty "Fuck this shit!" going off to great uncertainty.

Dorothy spoke to the other workers in the back room when she entered. Her friend Gerry was almost ready to go out on the floor, but Dorothy convinced her to stay until she was also ready. They talked about what they had seen on television, what was going on in their respective households, and who was sick in the hospital. Being sick was a frightening thing when there was no health insurance. Actually, there was health insurance—

insurance that took money out of your check, insurance that had a five hundred dollar deductible, five hundred dollars that you never had, money out of your check that you couldn't spare. Why bother? If it got bad enough, you could always go to County and let those Republican taxpayers in the suburbs pay the bill. The irony was that people in management made more money and their health insurance cost less out of a bigger check. They could afford to finish off the deductible, while Dorothy couldn't even afford to look at a deductible. Crossing the chasm from being part of the labor force to being part of the management farce was unheard of and impossible.

"Shit, as long as I been working here, I ought to be running this place," Dorothy said.

"Yeah, you hear them women on television talking about a glass ceiling. Well, we in the concrete basement. Shit, we don't even see the motherfuckers that are ruining our lives. If it weren't for all the shit we got from them, we wouldn't know they existed," Gerry said, rolling her eyes at the thought of white women with six figure incomes complaining about shit.

"Yeah, ain't that some shit. We down here taking money for these motherfuckers, fucking with these crazy-ass customers, and all them niggas upstairs want to do is to see how much money they can fuck us out of. Let there be an opening in management, and what do they do? They bring in some white boy from another planet that can't even open a cash register, and they put the motherfucker in charge of us and we been here for ten years."

Gerry stepped behind Dorothy to tie her apron. "You know I used to think it was that college shit, but that ain't it. How can they expect somebody to get a degree on the wages they pay? Besides, experience got to count for something."

"The only experience we got is letting them fuck us like they do. Then they want to put some shit in our work record about our fucking attitude, like this kind of shit is supposed to make us happy."

They walked out together, putting on their business faces, smiles that might get them tips instead of the scorn they felt. They looked into the same faces they had seen so many times before, like the faces of little old white people who refused to or couldn't afford to move to the suburbs, the faces of little old black people who were on the last legs of their lives, people with nowhere to go and no one to listen to them moan, people who had to be around people and who were willing to spend for the attention. There were the young men out there who rode the buses with their wives and mothers and now waited with a cup of coffee until they made their way to the second shift somewhere. It was the miracle of common victims that brought them all so temporarily together, crossing all the known lines of division so easily.

In the first chair, as usual, was Tommy. He was always the first person she served when she worked the early shift. He had already eaten and was drinking from his third cup of coffee. Retirement and a wife who didn't want him in the house brought him here at first. That was years ago. The last few years it was nothing more than habit. When Tommy first started coming, he was old and worn. Now he was older and worn out.

Dorothy refilled his cup and passed him some cream and sugar. "So, how you doing today?"

"Oh, I'm all right. I went to see my wife today. She getting along okay. I suspect they gon' let her come home soon enough. After I leave here, I'ma go over to the hospital to see her."

Tommy sipped coffee, opened his newspaper and read. That was how the day would almost always start. From this point until she took her lunch, Dorothy stayed on her feet. She had to know when to rush, when to take her time, when to snatch money from someone's hand and when to stop and talk. She navigated her way through the day like the professional she was. No one could tell how much she hated her job.

The first five hours were a blur of faces and snatches of conversations that seemed to run into each other. As long as things ran smoothly, there would be minimal interference from the white boys upstairs. Even if they didn't come down, they made their presence felt with the video camera over the cash register, the electronically printed tickets, and the computerized cash registers. At the end of the day, they knew just how much money you were supposed to have, they knew how many times you opened the register and when you opened it. They knew everything that was ordered and everything that was served.

All this technology was to make their already easy job easier, so they could spend more time cracking the whip. After all, labor was considered a controllable expense. Labor didn't pay bills according to the beliefs of management, because labor was a bill, a big bill. Labor didn't bring in customers, not like those little signs in the window or the new attractive menus did. They could spend money on stupid shit, but they couldn't pay the people who worked for them. They were the new breed of slave owners, and if there were any God, any justice in the universe, they would go to the same place in Hell where slave owners were kept.

Lunchtime for the workers came after the lunch crowd had come and gone. Dorothy and Gerry went to a nearby bar called The Upstairs. Dorothy ordered a vodka martini and Gerry had a rum and cola. They ate sandwiches they had stolen from the lunch counter. They talked about the shit in their lives, their shit children, their shit jobs, and the shit they had to put up with in general. They weren't seeking answers, and they were not trying to better define their problems, just let off some steam. It was do that or curse somebody out.

They got back to the lunch counter feeling a little better than when they'd left. They smiled more and chewed Doublemint gum, even though management frowned on gum chewing. With the smiles, the tips got better and the day quickly wound towards 6 o'clock.

After work, Dorothy decided to stop at The Upstairs to get one for the road. One went too fast, so she ordered a second. She wondered if the bartender thought she was alcoholic. Fuck him if he did, and fuck him if he didn't. People can think whatever they want to think. If they weren't paying her bills, fuck 'em.

A lone man sat at the other end of the bar.

Dorothy knew he was looking at her. She gave him no encouragement. The drama men brought with them was hardly worth the effort now. All he could do was sleep with her, and there was no promise that it would be good, so there was no point in gambling on it.

He got up and walked toward her end. Dorothy ordered another drink and paid for all of her drinks.

"Hi. How you doing?"

"I'm just fine, thank you."

"Mind if I join you?"

"Well, I'm about to leave, and I really ain't in the mood for company, so I guess I would mind."

"No harm in asking."

The man turned around and walked away. One of these days, she was going to talk to someone and they weren't going to walk away. The dream of ever really having a man she could depend on was fading, but every once in a while it reared up and she felt the loneliness eating away at her.

She looked out of the window to the women standing at the bus stop on State Street. She wondered if they were going home to husbands and boyfriends. She wondered what it was like to go home to someone.

She finished her drink and looked at her watch. It was getting near 7 o'clock. There was no way she was going to catch the Low-End Line this late. She would just walk over to Michigan and catch the King Drive bus. She gathered her few things and left.

She stood on the corner, the bus pass in one hand and her gun in the other. She was downtown, but she wasn't safe. She was never safe. The bus came and she boarded. The bus was mostly empty, so she sat at the front, where she could see the driver and he could see her.

As the ride went on, the bus got a little more crowded. At 31st Street, a tall, lanky boy got on. He walked through the bus, eyeing everyone on his way to the back. Dorothy surmised he was on crack or some shit like that. Dorothy kept an eye on him, figuring he was up to no good. He sat in the middle seat at the back of the bus. He looked at everyone on the bus, and he saw Dorothy looking at him.

When the bus stopped at 59th, Dorothy got up to be ready for the next stop. She looked to the back and he was still sitting there. For an instant, she thought to wait until 61st Street, but the thought was gone before she could ponder it. He looked back at her then she looked away. When the bus reached 60th, Dorothy stepped off. Before the bus pulled off, the boy got off at the back door.

She looked across the street and stuck her hand in her purse to get a hold of her gun. When she felt it properly in her hand, she shook it to make sure it wouldn't get caught on anything on its way out of her purse. The streetlights were coming on, but it wasn't dark yet.

She crossed King Drive and continued walking home. When she got to the first alley, she gave a half look around to see if the boy was following her. He was behind her, about a half block. The rest of the street was empty except for a few lightning bugs coming out of the grass.

Dorothy wondered if he was following her, and if he was, should she speed up or slow down and allow him to pass? "Fuck it. This motherfucker is going to have to catch me," she whispered to herself.

She was walking as fast as she could, and at the street, she gave the half look again. This time, he was closer to her. She saw he was wearing gym shoes, so she couldn't hear him coming up on her. Down the block, there were a few people on porches. She decided to keep going. Eberhart was the next street.

Dorothy shook the gun one more time, just to be safe. Once she crossed Vernon, she kept a lookout for him. Before she reached the alley, she could see him break into a run. She shook the gun loose and pulled it out of her purse. With the gun out, she turned to face him. He was almost up on her when he saw the gun. He stopped dead in his tracks, almost falling forward.

"Oh, lady. Oh, I wasn't going to do nothing. I was just going to run by you. I didn't mean no harm."

Dorothy looked into his lying eyes. "I don't think we have to worry about what you were going to do to me. You better worry about what I'm going to do to you."

"But lady, I was on my way to my friend's house. I don't want no drama."

"Shut the fuck up and lay your ass on the ground." The young man dropped to his knees with his hands still in the air. "All the way to the ground, goddamn it. Do it and live to tell the story."

He lay down and looked up at Dorothy. She was pointing the gun to his head. She started walking around him. He watched her. "Put your head down. I don't want to look at your ugly-ass face."

She walked around to stand in back of him, knowing that he was trying to figure out what she was doing. She didn't even know what she was going to do. She did know she wanted to hurt him and hurt him bad. He lifted his head up to see what she was doing. She put a bullet in the chamber of the automatic then walked around to stand in back of him. He lifted his head again to see what she was doing

"Put your fucking head down."

The boy lay back down on the ground. When Dorothy was sure he wasn't looking, she kicked him as hard as she could between his legs. He immediately balled up in pain. She jumped back to get out of his reach and kicked him again, this time in the back of the head. He tried to grab her leg, but she jumped out of his way. She looked for another place to kick him. She kicked him in the back. He rolled over to try to grab her, but again she jumped out of his reach.

It had become a dance—spot, kick, jump. All the times she kicked him, she didn't get what she wanted. She wanted to hear something break on him; she wanted to give him a constant reminder not to fuck with people he didn't know. Out of the corner of her eye, she could see someone running toward her. Whoever it was kept shouting out her name. With a quick look, she saw it was Tiny. Judging by his speed, she wouldn't have too many kicks left.

She spotted an opening on the balled up boy, aimed at his head, but missed and kicked him in the knee. She heard and felt a bone in his knee break. She jumped back, ready to kick him again, but Tiny was already there. Tiny picked her up and turned around, placing himself between her and the boy on the ground.

"That sonofabitch tried to rob me, so I commenced to kicking his ass. So, if you move out of my way, I can finish fucking him up."

There were finally other people coming down the street. Tiny looked at the boy, still balled up on the ground.

"Man, I ain't do nothing to that bitch."

"Oh, Family, show some respect,." Tiny said to him.

"Man, look. I wasn't going to do nothing to her. Call the police. I think she broke my leg."

"I should have put a hole in your ass. I still can, goddamn it. Try to fucking stick me up."

Tiny told one of the boys in the gathering crowd to go and get Danny. As it turned out, no one knew the boy on the ground. The boy didn't know the address to the house where his friend lived, but he knew which house it was. Tiny pointed out to him that if his friend didn't show up, bad drama surely would.

Danny arrived and Tiny gave him a quick summary of the situation. Dorothy was still shouting at the boy on the ground. The boy was making no attempt to get up because he wanted to be able to protect himself in case the crowd showed its violent disapproval of what he tried to do.

"Yo, mellow, I don't know what you was going to do, but it ain't going on!" Danny shouted then kicked him dead in his face. With that, the crowd collapsed on the boy.

They kicked, hit, and stomped on him. The crowd dispersed at the sound of a police siren approaching. The boy was left on the ground, his clothes torn, some ribs and other bones broken. He lay bleeding, waiting on an ambulance.

Dorothy left with the rest of the crowd. Danny and Tiny were ahead of her. She made no effort to catch up to them. The people she walked with asked her how she was. She felt fine. When she reached the house, she lit a cigarette and sat on the porch. She could hear the siren from the ambulance taking the boy away. Tiny and Danny were sitting on the steps too. They were all silent until the ambulance was gone. After the wail from the ambulance died out, Tiny spoke.

"Damn, Mrs. Evans, you was kicking the stuffing out of him."

"He ought to be glad I didn't shoot his ass first. I didn't want to try to explain all that shit to the police and have them take my gun. I just wanted to break something on that motherfucker so if he ever tried some shit like that again, he would have something to remind him not to be fucking with people he don't know."

Danny stood up, looked at his mother then went into the house. Anthony came up on the steps. He looked at his aunt. Her clothes were disheveled and her hair was a mess. He smiled at her. "Well, well, well, if it ain't good ol' Aunty Big Bad, wrecking the lives of evil doers in the hood."

She smiled back, basking in the glow of her victory. "Damn right. I don't play that shit. Motherfuckers got to know not to be fucking with me."

Danny came out of the house. "Hey, Tony. What's up?"

"You tell me."

"I can't call it." Danny looked at Tiny. "Yo, man, let's go and make this move."

Danny walked past his mother on the porch then he and Tiny took off for 61st Street. Anthony went into the house. Dorothy looked toward the place where she left the boy in the street, shook her head at the whole incident then went into the house.

Inside, she went right up to her room and got a bottle of vodka out of the closet. She sat on the bed and poured some into the glass that was always on her nightstand. She did not notice how much she was shaking until she lit another cigarette. Taking a healthy swig of vodka, she sank on the bed, lay back and blew smoke to the ceiling.

She sat up and looked at herself in the mirror, realizing she looked like shit. She stood up, went to the closet and started to take off her clothes. As her pants were falling to the floor, she noticed a quarter-sized spot of blood near the bottom of her pant leg. She thought about the boy, how he looked the last time she saw him, laid out and bleeding from his mouth and his nose. He was somebody's child. She thought about when she went to get Danny from the hospital after he broken his arm getting into a fight, or the time that Reginald got hit by a car when he was eight. Twice she had to take Regina to the hospital after one boyfriend or another had beat the shit out of her. Her face looked like she'd been in a car accident with a brick wall. Anthony would never go to the hospital, but he came home bloodied and bruised too many times to count. Someday she would be doing the same for Jaleel, DeShawn, and Laneka.

She stood in the doorway of the closet, looking at the bloodstain on her pant leg. All of the violence that had just passed, still fresh in her mind, seemed so useless. She walked over to the bed and sat down, still holding the pant leg, and she started to cry. She let go of the pants, lay down, and buried her face in a pillow.

Today, because of her, somebody would be going to see their child in the hospital. Nurses who didn't seem to understand the difference you could make just by touching your child would hold them back. Doctors going in and out of the room where your child was laying, treating you as though there was something you didn't understand about the child you carried, the child you'd taken care of all of his life. Doctors treating you as though you would interfere with the healing of your own child. Policemen standing around trying not to be in the way, but always being in the way. They stood between you and your hurting, bleeding child. Today was someone else's turn to go through that. Today someone else was going to get their broken, bleeding child from the doctors, hospitals and police with their variety of papers that need to be filled out, initialed and signed. Today was someone else's turn, and for the sake of that boy, hopefully there was someone else.

There was knocking at the door. At first Dorothy didn't even hear it. When the knocking became more insistent, she responded. She took a deep breath and defensively asked, "Who is it?"

"It's Reginald. Can I come in?"

"Gimme a minute."

She sat up and reached for a tissue then wiped

her face and took a long sip of vodka. She took another look at the bloodstain and threw the pants in the closet then put on her robe. She sat back down on the bed and took another sip of vodka.

"Come in."

Reginald opened the door and looked at his mother.

"Ma, are you all right?"

"I'm okay. You just getting in from work?"

"Yeah. I heard you got into a fight or something. What happened?"

"Some young guy tried to snatch my purse or some shit. Then after that, things got out of control. I really don't want to talk about it now."

"Are you feeling okay? I mean regardless of what happened, I want to know do you feel okay now," Reginald asked, the Christian care registering in his voice.

Dorothy took a sip out of the glass then set it on the nightstand. "I've felt better before and I'm sure I'll feel better again."

Reginald crossed the floor and sat on the bed next to his mother. He looked at her face. There were no bruises or scratches on her face. She saw him looking and looked away, took the glass off the nightstand and held it with both hands in her lap.

"Look, I'm as all right as I need to be right now. I don't need you to come and baby-sit me. If I did, I'd let you know. Right now I just want to take a shower, cool off, and be alone. If I feel otherwise, you'll be the first person I call. Okay?" She patted him on the arm.

"I just wanted to make sure you are all right." There was that caring look on his face.

"I'll be fine," she said.

Reginald left. Dorothy looked at the clock on her dresser. It was 8:30. She took another long sip from the glass and set it on the nightstand, then left her room to take a shower. She looked in on her grandchildren. All three were watching the black and white television that she watched in the morning. "You all make sure you get that television back in the kitchen. I don't want to have to come looking for it. I don't think I'll be in a good mood if I do. Do I make myself clear?"

Jaleel looked away from the television for a moment. "I'll make sure to take it down there tonight."

She looked at him and wondered how long it would be before she was going to get him from the hospital or the police station, or even worse. To think about it, it was strange that he was in the house this early. Usually he would be out until at least 10 o'clock. "Where is your mother?" she asked into the room.

Not that Dorothy cared one way or the other where she was. Regina didn't go to very many places. She was either downstairs on the phone or hanging her ass out of some boy's car window in front of the house. She was anywhere except with her children.

"She downstairs somewhere."

This time, Jaleel did not look away. Laneka and DeShawn never even glanced away from the television, like they were in some hypnotic trance. It was frightening to watch them look at television like that. She wished there were something else they could be doing—reading a book, out chasing lightning bugs or something—anything that got them away from sitting slack-jawed in front of the idiot box like that. Fuck it. They were not her children. Even if she was the one that made sure they didn't go around hungry and bare-assed.

She went into the bathroom and turned on the shower. The water trickled out of the faucet. The water pressure was fucked up, the tiles were falling off the wall, and the linoleum on the floor was worn through. After ten minutes of manipulating the faucets, she found the balance of temperature and pressure.

The shower was over quickly. Dorothy didn't feel like standing up that long. She left the shower feeling cleaner and wanting another drink. She sat with the drink and the radio on, going through the ritual that ended her day. While listening to dusties on the radio, she rolled her hair and smoked cigarettes, taking short sips until the glass was empty. She refilled it once.

The radio did what it always did; it brought back memories with old songs, mixing emotions with lyrics, showing time and distance. That was the danger of dusty radio. Occasionally there would be a song that would trigger a strong memory, like one of those songs from the Delphonics or Martha Reeves and the Vandellas from the mid-sixties, back when she had so much hope and the world was still a new and fresh place.

She was married, pregnant, and not quite out of high school, but it was okay. They were going to do just fine. Danny was born and Daniel, Sr., got a letter saying he had to go. He came back and left, then Reginald and Regina were born. Daniel came back once more to bring Anthony home. He left again, and then the letter came, and nothing had been right since.

She should have married again, but nothing seemed right. She never got to say goodbye to Daniel, and she never really got to move on. When the time finally did come, time was all but gone. Sure, there were men that professed their love for her. They would have taken care of the kids, but Dorothy just couldn't do it. She couldn't let go of the pieces of a dream that got blown into small bits.

The last roller was in place and she lay back on the bed. This time, the radio seemed to hold her still. She could listen to the dusties all night long, dreaming of dreams she once had. Looking at the ceiling, she realized that she hadn't eaten since lunch. She went to the door and called Jaleel to her room. "Go downstairs and fix me a plate."

Her words were starting to run into each other. Maybe she ought to stop drinking, at least until she got something into her stomach. Jaleel appeared with a plate of red beans and rice. She quickly finished off the plate of food, and soon she finished the last drink.

Still listening to the radio, she looked out of her bedroom window to the street below. She could see her daughter hanging her ass out of a car that had pulled up in front of the house. There was music coming from the porch next door, and some kind of racket from up the street. People let their hoodlum children play in the street all hours of the night.

Everything was the same as it was the night before. Everything fell right back into the groove where life belonged, or where it stayed because it didn't know how to get out of it. Once again, she thought about the boy in the hospital, his mother standing in the hall as they tried to put her son back together.

Why would that boy try some shit like that? What the hell was wrong with him? Was he on drugs or something? He could have gotten himself killed trying to snatch a purse. What about Danny? She remembered how cold he was, kicking that boy in the face. He never said a word to her, never asked how she was doing or anything. She wondered if there was something wrong with Danny. Fuck him. He was on his own now. She had done what she was supposed to do, she kept clothes on his ass and made sure he had something to eat.

She looked at her daughter. At least now she was standing up talking to some boy. The kids were safe in the house, but that was no reason for her to go running up to cars like a five-dollar whore. If these men were so interested in her, why didn't they stop long enough to get out and talk to her like a lady? Shit, they didn't have to because she would go running up there before they had a chance to get out the car.

Who the fuck did Reginald think he was? It was not his job to take care of her. He needed to be looking out for his own damn self. He was always going up to that church. It was all right to go occasionally, but he lived in the damn place. There was certainly something wrong with that. It was like he was in a cult or something. Any day now he was going to sell off all of his worldly goods and give the proceeds to the church.

Shit, all them motherfuckers is grown. There was nothing she could say to them now. They were as grown as they wanted to be. She couldn't tell them shit. She was through with them all. She was just waiting for the day when they would all move the hell out of her house. She was tired of their shit, tired of the shit at work, tired of all the damn stupid-ass fools out there sticking people up and winding up getting the shit kicked out of them. She was tired of all the shit that she was forced to call life.

She left the window and went to lie down on her bed. It was not enough. She poured herself another drink and took a swig straight out of the bottle. She lay back down and let the vodka and dusties sing her to sleep.

chapter six

Mice and roaches stole about the kitchen floor in brilliant silence. They ran on hormone paths etched by repetition, across floors and the ceiling, behind baseboards and cabinets. They trespassed washed dishes and garbage alike. They ran along the baseboard, behind the refrigerator, and atop the stove in their nervous search for sustenance.

The light clicked on and everything scattered for cover. Danny entered the kitchen and walked straight for the refrigerator, trying to crunch roaches all the way. "Fucking bugs." He cussed them out loud.

His eyes were red and his stomach was empty. He'd just finished a joint and it was time to feed his munchies. Opening the refrigerator, he wondered aloud, "What kind of vittles do we have tonight?"

He pulled out and examined various aluminum foiled bowls. He fiddled with bowls of old greens, peas, rice, some meat from a week ago, all of which were returned to their resting place. A Tupperware bowl turned out to be the prize of the hunt. "Shit yeah, boy," Danny whispered.

Danny took the chili out and poured it into a pot on the stove. While it was heating, he foraged for something more immediate. He snatched the box of generic fruit ring cereal and a bowl from the doorless cabinets. He got milk out of the refrigerator and emptied the contents of the box into the bowl. There wasn't enough milk to fill the bowl, so he ate handfuls of the cereal until he achieved balance.

He ate the cereal while standing over the cooking chili, occasionally tasting the chili to see if it was hot enough to eat. When wisps of steam rose from the pot, he grabbed another bowl out of the cabinet and filled it to the rim. He placed the pot in the refrigerator and took both bowls to the basement.

With the lights out, the dance of the vermin resumed. It continued uninterrupted until the dawn pushed most of them back between the walls. Dorothy came downstairs in her robe, a lit Salem dangling from the corner of her mouth. She was pulling the rollers from her hair, putting them in her pocket as she crossed the floor. She counted the rollers as she pulled them from her hair. After a good night's sleep, she could have eight out of her hair before she reached the kitchen doorway. This morning she had six. The nights were getting longer and she was getting less sleep.

She stood for a moment in the doorway of her once modern kitchen. Paths had been worn into and through the linoleum. As soon as the idea and the opportunity occurred at the same time, she was going to have that goddamn hole by the sink fixed. The basement was becoming more visible through it all the time. The fucking chairs had to be replaced—the whole dinette set, for that matter. The refrigerator was acting up again, and only two eyes on the stove worked anymore. Too much shit. Fuck it. Let it all fall down.

She thought about the boy yesterday, her compassion replaced by cynicism. "Damn lucky I didn't shoot and kill his dumb ass." She kicked the incident out of her mind and began her morning ritual. Reginald would be coming down any minute, if he spent the night here last night. It was his life. He could stay where he wanted to, but he was still going to help her with the goddamn bills. The last man had passed out of her life some time ago, so there was no man to help. Reginald and Regina would have to pay the phone and the light bill, and that was that.

She filled the tea kettle with water. The creaking floor had long ago become the score to her morning coffee-making ritual. She sat in the only chair that still had a back on it. She claimed the chair as hers as long as she was in the house. The effort was not to save the chair from the same fate that had befallen the other three. It was only to delay the inevitable.

She moved the ashtray from the counter to what was left of the table. The table was little more than four metal legs with a gray-flecked white Formica top. Around all of the edges were burns from cigarettes lacking ashtrays. The cigarette-burned table and the worn floor had no specific history; they simply happened. Around the kitchen, the rest of the damage did mark points in history. The scenes of battles, accidents, and crimes fell helter-skelter around the room.

She opened the freezer door and pulled out a big bag of chicken wings, setting them in the chipped and stained porcelain sink. If she could just find someplace to start replacing all this shit, then maybe it would not be as bad as it was, but it was too much of a gamble. She could get a new stove, then the refrigerator would give out, or she could get a sink, and the table would fall apart. It was just easier and less worry to replace the shit that was beyond use while jerry-rigging the rest.

Long forgotten fights between whomever sped up an already rapid decay, and what was not the result of a fight was the effect of malevolent neglect. She remembered when she threw an iron at Danny for coming in the house too late when he was sixteen, and bouncing Regina off the cabinets. She remembered fighting her own mother, and the fights between her parents.

She listened as Reginald made his way around upstairs. She listened as his footsteps led to the bathroom, then she could hear the water making its way through the pipes upstairs. She reached into her robe pocket and pulled out a comb. The teapot began to whistle, so she walked to the refrigerator, got out a can of evaporated milk and made a cup of coffee.

Almost as soon as she went upstairs, Reginald came down. He turned on the nine-inch black and white television that was on the counter, and jerked the wire-hanger antenna around until he hit the sweet spot, getting the picture down to itself and its primary double. Reginald fixed himself a cup of coffee and sat down at the table.

Soon Dorothy returned with her cup of coffee and sat in her chair at the table. "Reginald, you are going to have to pay the phone bill this month. I can't make it this trip."

He took a sip from his cup. "I'll pay what I can on it, and the rest will have to wait for next month. You ought to be trying to get some money from Regina. She the one on the phone all the time."

"You just do what I told you to do, and I'll take care of Regina."

"You want me to give you a ride this morning?" he asked, sensing the need to change the subject.

"What time you leaving?" she asked, relieved that he did not pursue the inequity of Regina using the phone more than anyone and paying the least on it or any other bill in the house.

"In about a half-hour."

"Yeah, I'll be ready to go by then."

All right. Reginald took his coffee upstairs with him. Dorothy settled in at the table, watching some white children somewhere in suburban America shout, "Good morning, America!"

DeShawn crept into the kitchen. "Good morning, Grandma," he said, rubbing his eyes.

"Good morning, DeeDee. How you this morning?"

"I'm all right."

DeShawn was in his underwear, his hair matted to his head, and his face was dry and dirty. He walked across the kitchen floor, sat in one of the backless chairs and began watching television.

"You want some breakfast?"

"Yes."

"Well, let me see if there is some cereal and some milk."

Dorothy took the box off the top of the refrigerator. There was nothing in it. She looked in the garbage can that was next to the sink and saw the empty milk container in it. "Goddamn it. Go down in that basement and tell Danny to get his ass up here now."

DeShawn went into the basement. Dorothy sat at the table and lit another cigarette. Soon DeShawn was back in his chair in the kitchen. A minute later, Danny came upstairs.

"What?" he asked. Indifference was confined to the edges of his voice, enough so that she would know, but not so much that she would care.

"Did you eat all the goddamn milk and cereal last night?" she asked, more interested in his answer than the tone of his voice

"It wasn't hardly nothing in there," he answered. He knew exactly where the conversation was going, because they had been through this so many times before that he could mouth the next words with her.

"Then why did you leave this empty-ass box on top of the refrigerator? If you eat the shit up, then throw the goddamn box out. I swear, you niggas kill me with this trifling shit. Go to the store and get some more cereal and get a gallon of milk too."

She reached into her pocket and pulled out a roll of bills. She counted out six ones then thought about the six rollers that morning and wondered if she should play the lottery. She started to hand Danny the money but stopped. "You got money to run the street all goddamn night, then you got enough money to buy some cereal and a gallon of milk."

Danny went back into the basement. DeShawn stared blankly at the television. Dorothy took a pull off her cigarette and a swig of coffee. Laneka came down and sat at the table too. The side door opened and closed as Danny left for the store.

The three of them watched television in silence until Reginald came downstairs and Dorothy left with him. The two children continued to wait at the table, and were joined by their older brother. Danny came back in, gave them the milk and cereal, then went back into the basement. Regina came down in her nightgown and frowned at her children. "When y'all done, there better not be one bowl left on that table either."

She looked at the chicken wings in the sink. "Goddamn, we ought to be able to fly eating so many fucking chicken wings."

The children ate in silence, dumbstruck by the television on the counter. Regina walked over to the telephone and dialed a number. "Hello, is Mrs. Shields in? Well, when she gets in, can you tell her Regina called? Thank you. Bye."

She held the switch hook down then let it up and dialed another number.

"Hello. Is Kenneth in?" There was a pause. She wasn't sure of what she would say, but it didn't matter anyway. She needed money, and he was a place to get it. Checks were not due for another two backbreaking weeks. She wanted to get a job and leave welfare and dumb-ass niggas alone, but for now, getting these motherfuckers to take care of their children was job enough. They were always trying to duck out of shit, talking about other shit they had to do. Well, they got to do this. Fuck all that other shit.

"Hello, Kenny . . . Yes, I am calling about some money . . . Bullshit. You got money. Why you always trying that bullshit? I was hoping that this time we could skip the dumb shit and just do what we both know you gonna do . . . This ain't about whether you will or will not. That ain't the question. The question is how much and when . . . He's your child, and he needs clothes and shoes for school, unless you think he should go barefoot and bare-assed."

While Kenneth pled his case, Regina looked at her children, twisting the phone cord in her fingers. "DeShawn is six years old. You would think that you would be used to the idea of him going to school . . . No, I ain't got to use the money myself . . . Then you go ahead and take him shopping, but I want to see the receipts from what you buy him . . . Because you be buying all that cheap, off-brand discount shit . . . Better yet, you can take me and him . . . Bring the bitch. That bitch don't stop no show . . . 'Cause she is a bitch . . . Fuck all that. This ain't about who you sleeping with. This is about getting DeShawn clothes and shoes for school."

Regina paced the floor, looking in cabinets, opening the refrigerator and looking at her children sitting at the table. Jaleel got up, put his bowl in the sink, and left the room. Then her other children put their bowls in the sink, but they sat back at the table.

"Hell naw, I ain't gonna let you have custody . . . Ain't a goddamn thing wrong with this environment . . . Like I'ma let that stupid-ass hooker take care of my child . . . Because she is all that . . . She the one that start putting all that shit in your head in the first place. You ain't said a damn thing about custody before he was five, now you talking stupid shit . . . What's the matter? Can't that bitch have her own babies? . . . If you want to be the father so damn much, then why the fuck do I have to call you and tell you that he has to have clothes? Why the fuck we got to do this dance whenever I need some money? If you want to be a daddy, goddamn it, you can start right the fuck there . . . I don't care. Adopt one of them niggas off T.V. You ain't getting my son. I don't care if you gave birth to him . . . You take him shopping. I'm going along because I want to, and don't do no stupid shit. I'm telling him what you said. Don't let him down again . . . Bye."

Regina hung up the phone and left the kitchen. Laneka looked at DeShawn. "She was talking to your daddy. You gonna go live with him?"

"No."

"Why not?"

" 'Cause I don't want to. I'ma stay here with Grandma. Plus, I ain't got to live with him no way."

"What if he gonna get you all the toys you want?"

"I might."

"Well, my Grandmother gonna get me all the toys I want."

"Grandma ain't gonna get you no toys."

"Not Grandma, my other Grandmother, my father's mother. She gonna do it 'cause my father is dead."

"No she not."

"Then your father ain't gonna get you no toys either," Laneka almost shouted.

"I don't want no toys from him," DeShawn said, frowning at his sister.

"Then he ain't gonna get you no new gym shoes either."

DeShawn reached up to the television and turned the channel. "My Grandma gonna get me some new shoes. I don't need my father to get me nothing, and Grandma ain't gonna get you nothing, nothing at all."

"Shut up. She is too. I can get what I want to get." Laneka was annoyed.

"Grandma ain't gonna get you nothing, and Ma ain't gonna get you nothing, and ain't nobody gonna get you nothing."

Laneka got up and went upstairs, leaving DeShawn alone at the table. He could hear her telling on him. He hadn't done anything, but he knew he would get yelled at anyway. He sat there, watching television, waiting for his mother to call him. Soon enough, she did. DeShawn left the kitchen with the television on.

For about twenty minutes, the television entertained the walls and the few roaches that were forced to forage in the light of day. Anthony came into the kitchen and fixed a bowl of cereal. He watched the white people and the wannabe white people make fools of themselves on a talk show. The people on those shows never got it together, but that was the point. America the dysfunctional.

Danny came up, and they both stepped outside to smoke a joint. They came into the house, red-eyed and smiling, and sat down at the table.

"So, Danny boy, what the hell is up with you?"

Danny shook his head. "Not a damn thing."

"Now that's a damn shame. A man like yourself ought to be up to something, even if it is no good."

Danny spoke, smiling at the memory. "I went to Max's the other night and saw Melissa. Man, that bitch was looking finer than a motherfucker. Man, she got ass mo' lotty-dotty. I've been trying to hook up with her."

"So you think she trying to give you the slip or some shit like that?"

"Naw, I don't think it's like that. But I tell you what—I'm gonna stick to it, though. So, what's up with you?"

"Same drama. Looking for a way to get my money right." Anthony looked out the window toward the alley.

"You know I could hook you up. It ain't no thang to me," Danny said.

"Naw, man. I got to get my shit at least semi-legit. You know they'd like to get my ass on something like that. Besides, I ain't got the patience to deal with all them geeks, man. I'd have to knock them motherfuckers out as soon as they start that begging shit. Man, them pipeheads might try you out. I just can't get with it."

Danny ran his fingertips over the roll of money in his pocket. "Well, if you need some dough, you let me know. I'll look out for ya. Hey, I do what I gotta do. I need to get me a lackey. One of them motherfuckers I can toss a bone to every now and again, and he'll do everything I tell his ass to. Man, I be up in some of these motherfuckers' spots and shit, and Family will tell the motherfucker "get brew", and the motherfucker will do it, too, just like a little bitch. And the motherfuckers be so loyal, they'll suck dick if Family ask them to do it."

"Speaking of such, what is Reggie's gump ass up to?"

"He's still in the church. Man, now that's some tripped-out shit, all them fags in the church. Then they wonder why ain't no real men in the church. Ain't no room in the motherfucker." As soon as Danny spoke, he regretted that he had brought up church at all.

"The reason why ain't no men in the church is because all them pastors want to do is to pimp bitches, and when a man is a bitch, it just works out easier for them. See, they always talking that shit about 'submit'. Fuck that. Fuck them." Anthony scowled at the thought of them.

"Man I don't want to hear that. You bringing my high down. Now I'm gonna have to smoke another joint to feel better. Come on."

"Bet. Let me finish these vittles first," Anthony said, happy to be released from his impending tirade.

Anthony started to eat. Danny sat back in his mother's chair. "Yo, man, you ought to go back and see that Greek motherfucker and see if he'll give you your old job back. He got some white bitch in there now. I think she his granddaughter."

"Yeah, I think I will go see old Mr. Popolous and see what's up with him."

"Come on, man. Let's go and smoke this joint," Danny said.

Anthony finished off his cereal and joined Danny outside. The television went back to entertaining the roaches that were out foraging. Regina came downstairs and put Anthony's bowl in the sink with the other dishes. She ran the water to wash the breakfast dishes. She picked up the phone, dialed a number, waited, then put in her code and hung up the phone. She turned to the sink and started washing the dishes. The phone rang and she snatched it off of the hook. "Hello?"

She turned off the water and sat down in her mother's chair, speaking softly, smiling into the phone. "I was starting to miss you. I know better than to wait around for you to call, and it took you too long to call me back. I'm wondering why."

She twisted the phone cord in her fingers. Catching a glimpse of her toenails, she wondered if she should polish them. She stood up and looked out the back window at her brother and cousin smoking reefer by the fence. "Well, I guess that's a good enough excuse—I mean reason . . . Well, my sixth grade teacher used to have a sign on his wall that said 'excuses are tools to build monuments to nothing.' So, that wasn't an excuse . . . Yeah, I'll try to get with you this weekend . . . I have children and I just can't dump them anywhere . . . Yeah, I do live with my mother, but they ain't my mother's children . . . Yeah, if it's late enough . . . We'll see . . . All right. I'll talk to you then."

Regina hung up the phone and returned to washing the dishes. After she finished, she went back upstairs. The television continued entertaining ghosts in the kitchen. Anthony passed through on his way upstairs. Jaleel dribbled a basketball to the refrigerator door and looked in, hanging on the door and finding nothing. Jaleel dribbled out the back door. Danny came in, fixed a large bowl of cereal and disappeared into the basement. Laneka and DeShawn danced through the kitchen and out the back door. A few minutes later, they came back in to get some cold water.

Anthony passed through on his way out as the children were running out the back door. Regina came in and began to make lunch for her children. The television was ignored but still on. The phone rang again; again Regina snatched it off of the hook. "Hello?"

"Yes, Mrs. Shields, I did call you this morning. It's almost time for school to start, and Jaleel will be needing some new shoes and clothes and stuff. I was wondering if you were going to take him shopping this year . . . Well, ma'am, I'd like to take him, but I just don't have the money this year. I've got two other children that are going to school too, and I would appreciate all the help I can get . . . I don't know. It's really hard to tell if I'm doing the right thing staying home to raise my children . . . Since my youngest is going to be in school all day this year, I'm going to try and get a job that will still let me be home when they get here . . . I mean look what happened to Johnny. Do you ever wonder if he would have turned out differently if you would have been home with him instead of working all the time? . . . Mrs. Shields, you know like I do, raising children is a full-time job . . . I do what I can, and sometimes asking for help is all I can do . . . Hopefully one day it will be different, but that's one day, not today . . . The bottom line is are you going to help? If you aren't, then why are you putting me through all this? And if you are going to help, why are you putting me through all this? . . . I don't like having to ask for help. I don't like being on welfare. I don't like being a single mother, but it's something that I have to do . . . Of course I love my children. Do you think I would go through this if I didn't? When I said I don't like being a single mother, it's true, I don't. I'd rather be married to a man that would love and take care of me and my children. But since that ain't happened yet, I got to do what I got to do . . . Rather than that, since he hardly get to see you anyway, why don't I let him spend the weekend with you? . . . In about two weeks, because all the stuff he needs will be on sale then . . . Okay . . . Thank you, Mrs. Shields."

Regina hung up the phone. "That bitch," she breathed out.

Danny ran up the stairs and without even looking at Regina, he picked up the phone. He looked at his beeper and dialed a number. "Yeah, man. What up? . . . You gonna be at the same spot, right? . . . This shit is straight, ain't it? I don't want to be getting no bullshit . . . I'll get with you in a minute . . . Bet."

Danny hung up the phone and stared at the basement door. "Where are you going?" Regina asked him.

"None of your business," he said, ignoring her.

"When Mama find out what you doing, she gonna kick you out of the house."

"I ain't doing shit to worry about. So, since I ain't worrying, you ain't got nothing to worry about either."

"Everybody ain't stupid as you think they are," Regina said, rolling her eyes.

"Watch yourself. Don't start no shit, won't be

none," Danny said and left the kitchen for the basement. Then the side door slammed as he left.

DeShawn came in the back door. His mother watched him. "Boy, don't be running in and out of the house all day. Where your sister? What she doing?"

"She in the front. She ain't doing nothing," DeShawn said, walking carefully around his mother.

"Go out there and tell her to come in here so I can comb her hair. And you all stay off of that curb."

DeShawn got a cup out of the cabinet and turned on the water, letting it run to get cold. Regina looked at him. "What are you doing?"

"I'm fix'na get me some water."

"Get the water after you get your sister."

DeShawn put the cup down and headed for the door.

"Boy, turn that water off. Shit, we ain't got no water to be wasting," Regina shouted at him.

DeShawn turned off the water and headed out the back door. He came back in with his sister.

"Laneka, go upstairs and get the comb and brush and the hair grease."

Laneka ran off upstairs. DeShawn turned on the water again. Regina shot him a look, so he quickly filled his cup and turned off the faucet. After drinking the water, he went back outside. Laneka came back with a comb, brush, a big jar of blue hair grease, and a bag of barrettes.

Regina put the television on the counter and sat in her mother's chair, Laneka sat between her legs. Regina loosened all the braids in her daughter's hair, then she took a spray bottle of water and wet Laneka's hair. Laneka sat and tried to watch television between having her head twisted to accommodate her mother's comb and brush. Twelve braids and one soap opera later, Regina was finished.

"Go and get DeShawn and tell him to come here so I can comb his nappy-ass head."

Laneka ran outside and soon DeShawn came in. He took his seat between his mother's legs. She immediately sprayed his hair and started to comb. DeShawn tried but could not resist crying.

"As soon as I can, I'm taking you to the barber and cut all your goddamn hair off. I'm sick of going through this shit just to comb your head."

When she was finished, DeShawn got up and went back outside. Regina got up and opened a can of store brand cooked spaghetti and meatballs. When the food was hot, she went to the front door and called her children in the house. Jaleel was nowhere to be found. Laneka and DeShawn came in and sat at the table and ate. Regina loomed over them while watching the soap opera. Occasionally, Regina would shout at the characters in the soap. The back door opened and Chandra walked in with a one-year-old riding her hip and a four-year-old trailing close behind.

"Hey, Chandra, what's up?" Regina said.

Chandra came in and sat in one of the backless chairs. She set the baby on her thigh before giving her the bottle she was crying for. Her son sat on the floor not too far from his mother.

"Ain't a damn thing happened worth mentioning. I been sitting in that goddamn welfare office all day, waiting to see the dumb-ass caseworker. These motherfuckers want to get everybody off welfare, just kick your ass off, and then they don't give a shit about what you do. But see, when you start knocking white motherfuckers in the head and taking they money, they gonna act all surprised."

"You went over to the one on Sixty-fourth and Maryland?" Regina asked.

"Yeah, and they ain't got no air conditioning, and you can't hear the television. You have to wait four hours to go talk for twenty minutes. I wonder what the hell them people be doing back there."

Regina dumped the bag of wings into the sink, and began rinsing them. After they were rinsed, she would lock them and pile them on a plate. "Most of the time they ain't doing a damn thing. But if I had to look at poor-ass, stanky niggas all day, I'd want to put that shit off as long as I could too."

Chandra laughed. "Yeah, they do be some funky asses up in there."

Laneka and DeShawn finished eating, so Regina sent them in the front to watch cartoons. Chandra's son joined them. Chandra sat the baby down on the floor. "Oh, girl, guess what."

"What?" Regina said, barely taking her attention off the wings.

"Latrice boyfriend getting out of jail next week, and she didn't even tell him she pregnant."

"Who the father?"

Chandra rolled her eyes. "Don't know. I heard it was your brother."

"Ain't no way Danny been with that heifer and not get some kind of disease."

"But shit, it could have been anybody. Hey, your nigga goin' to jail ain't gonna stop the show."

"That reminds me. I got to take Jaleel to see his father some time before the next two weeks. His mother is getting out of line, and he gonna have to snap that bitch back in line."

There was a pause as they both watched the television. "Check it out. Tracy and DeeDee getting married. Ain't that some shit," Regina said.

"Tracy who?"

"Tracy that used to go with your brother."

Chandra looked perplexed. "My brother ain't went with no girl named Tracy."

"You know, the girl that had James' baby." Chandra still didn't know. "Remember she used to get high with us when we was in school?"

Chandra smirked. "Oh yeah, now that's a clue. Like there was someone in school that didn't get high with us."

"She used to live over on Champaign, then she moved out to Altgeld Gardens, then after she had her second baby, she got sick and had to live with her mother again. Her baby died, then she got pregnant again."

"You talking about TeeTee?"

"Yeah, TeeTee and DeeDee. I guess they gonna name they children C.C., ReeRee and Mimi."

Chandra laughed. They returned their attention to the soap opera. During a commercial, Chandra broke the relative silence. "Is it true that James is dead?"

"Yeah. Somebody shot him in the head over in the playground. Boy, the way these niggas killing each other is ridiculous. I guess they waiting for the day when it ain't no niggas left to shoot," Regina said matter-of-factly.

Chandra shifted in the backless chair. "Didn't he have like six or seven kids?"

"I think so. It might have been more. That nigga was pissing babies. But back in the day when he had his money right, they was just giving it up to him. I don't think he ever really took care of any of them. The welfare people probably shot his ass. They got tired of taking care of his babies when he was laying on his ass."

Chandra picked her baby up off of the floor to see if the plastic diaper was full. It wasn't.

The back door opened and Anthony came into the kitchen. "Hey, Chandra."

"Hey, Anthony. How was jail this trip?"

Anthony smiled. "Like you don't know. Oh yeah, I forgot you was passed out the last time you went."

Chandra smiled. "Ha ha ha. You so funny you ought to have your own T.V. show—the crazy-ass nigga show."

Anthony continued to smile. "I got my job back. My money will soon be straight, so I can take care of my baby."

Chandra watched him going to the refrigerator. "Where you working?"

"At the liquor store where I been working."

Laneka ran into the room crying. She stopped in the doorway so her mother would take notice of her.

"Girl, what is wrong with you?"

"De . . . Shawn . . . hit . . . me!" she said, heaving through her tears.

"DeShawn, get your scrawny black ass in here right now!" Regina shouted toward the front room. He came and stood next to his sister in the doorway. "Get your ass over here." His mother was clipping her words in anger.

He walked over to her, trying to stand out of her reach. The kitchen seemed to hold its collective breath as Regina turned away from the wings in the sink and faced her son. She bent down to him. "What did I tell you about hitting your sister?"

Dorothy appeared in the kitchen doorway just in time to see Regina slap DeShawn twice, once on either side of his face. The second slap knocked him into the stove.

"Regina, don't be knocking him into the furniture like that. If you gonna hit him, hit him. Don't use him to break the furniture with."

Regina looked back at her mother. "He ought to be glad I didn't throw his ass down the basement steps. I'm tired of him and his sister fighting all the time."

"Like you didn't get into fights with your brother when you were little," Dorothy said.

"Like you didn't knock the shit out of me when I did." Regina snapped back.

"Like I still won't knock the shit out of you." Dorothy turned and went upstairs.

Regina glared at her children. "You all get your asses back in that front room and I don't want to hear shit out of you."

Both of the children left the room, shoulders shaking, tears running down their faces.

"Well, it's nice to know some traditions never die," Anthony said, and he went upstairs.

"Fuck you," Regina said as he walked through the door.

Regina and Chandra resumed their conversation as the oil was heating up to fry the wings. Danny came in with Tiny on his heels. Tiny spoke to Regina and Chandra, and they spoke back. Danny asked if there were any calls for him. Regina told him no.

"Say, Danny, did you know that Latrice is pregnant?" Chandra asked.

"A better question would have been, do I care if Latrice is pregnant? The answer is no," Danny answered.

"They say you the father."

"Like I would touch that skeezer. Don't be listening to that gossip."

"Well, her boyfriend getting out of jail soon."

"Once again, Chandra, do I care? Once again the answer is no."

Danny and Tiny left the house. Regina continued cooking dinner, talking with Chandra. After the wings were cooked, Regina made some off-brand macaroni and cheese, and a small pot of string beans. With dinner cooked, she called her children back into the kitchen and fixed plates for them and Chandra's son. Chandra didn't want anything to eat; at least she said she didn't. Regina fixed herself a plate and they went to the front porch.

Reginald came into the kitchen, fixed himself a plate and took it upstairs. Dorothy fixed a plate and took it into the front room. Danny came in and took three chicken wings into the basement with him. Jaleel came in and fixed a plate. He sat at the table and ate while rolling the basketball around with his foot. Anthony took three wings out of the back door with him. DeShawn finished, scraped the bones into the garbage, and put his plate in the sink. Chandra's son followed suit. Jaleel finished and left his plate on the table. Laneka sat there. She had finished her two chicken wings quickly, and the macaroni and cheese was gone. It was the string beans that were giving her trouble.

While she sat there, poking each string bean with her fork, she dreamed of the day when her husband would take her away from where she was. They would live in a big house, a house that was new, not an old house like this one. And she would never make her kids eat things that they didn't like. She would have a dog and a cat. It would be a Lassie dog and one of those long-haired cats like on television.

She would have a nice car when her husband came and took her away. She would work down-town in an office building, and she would be rich. She would be so rich that she would have a maid. The maid would clean up everything, and Laneka wouldn't have to. Laneka's children would have all the toys they wanted, and they would have color televisions in their rooms, and they most certainly would have separate rooms.

Her little girl's hair would be easy to comb, and it wouldn't hurt. If it did hurt, then they would go to the beauty shop and get their hair done. Laneka wouldn't holler and scream at her children. They would hug instead of fighting.

She looked at the paint peeling on the ceiling. Her home would be beautiful, just like the ones on television. Her couch would be new, and she would have a big-screen television. Her husband would come home every night, and he would kiss her at the door and call her honey. They would eat the fabulous food that the maid would cook, and they would sit on the couch and watch television together. The Lassie dog would be lying on the floor in front of the fireplace, and the cat would be looking out of the window.

Her children would call her Mom, and she would have a big beautiful car, so they could go on rides in the country when they wanted to. They would live on a nice street in a nice neighborhood. She would have nice friends to gossip with on the phone, and they would go shopping together. They would go to the mall and go to any store they wanted to, because they had all the money they needed.

Laneka choked down the last string bean. She slowly walked to the garbage and scraped off her plate. Then she put it in the sink. She took one last look around the kitchen and slowly walked out.

After about an hour, Dorothy came in. She scraped the bones into the garbage then put the plate in the sink. She took her glass, which was half-filled with vodka, and ran some water in it. Dorothy lit a cigarette off of the stove and took two swallows from her glass. She turned off the television and the ceiling light. Regina came in, scraped her plate and put it in the sink. Reginald came in soon after she left. He scraped his plate and put it in the sink.

The kitchen was dark and quiet until Danny came back in with Tiny. They cleaned out the rest of the chicken wings, then sat in the kitchen drinking cheap malt liquor out of forty-ounce bottles. "So, man, are you straight?" Tiny asked.

"Got some more work today. Will be back serving tomorrow," Danny answered.

"You sure about Otis?"

Danny smiled. "He's gonna be my lackey. He'll be straight."

Tiny took a swig of the malt liquor. "It's your call. You the man."

Danny took out some rolling papers and started to roll some joints. Before he rolled them, he added ready rock cocaine to them. "My man, let's go and smoke these thirty-seven fifties. You'll feel better. I'm sure of it."

Tiny followed Danny out of the back door. Jaleel came in and hung on the refrigerator door before proceeding upstairs. Anthony came in, looked in the refrigerator and went back out. Regina came in and beeped someone on the phone. When it didn't ring in ten minutes, she turned the light off and left the kitchen.

Jaleel came through the kitchen again. This time he looked out of the back door before he left. The roaches and mice were creeping once again. Behind the stove, a cricket chirped because that was all he knew to do.

chapter seven

By 8 o'clock in the morning, 61st Street was starting to get its rhythm. Buses ran one behind the other, jamming up on the corners. Traffic flowed, jerking from Cottage Grove to St. Lawrence and then on to King Drive. Old people and women walked up and down 61st Street, feeling a degree of safety that no other hour offered. The loud radios were gone, and the alcoholic bums were just coming out of their stupors. The drug users, both dealers and addicts, had retreated to the shadows. Sixty-first Street for that hour was Anywhere, America; Hometown U.S.A.; anywhere but 61st Street.

Anthony watched the people getting on the bus. They were up to their necks in the grind, racing to be on time for their particular abuse. Contrary to whatever campaign the Chicago Transit Authority was running, people only caught the bus because they had to. They might catch the El for convenience, but people mostly caught the bus because they didn't get paid enough for a car.

Catching the bus, you will not have a car, you will not have decent health care and you will not have enough food to eat. The only things you will have are a hard time and the knowledge that nobody gives a fuck.

The Arabs and Koreans began sneaking into their various shops. The metal shutters were rolling up and the bars were coming off the windows. The doors were being unlocked to sell some more suffering to the community—some more beer, some more wine, some more liquor, cigarettes, candy, and chips. Some more made in Taiwan-China-Mexico-Uruguay-Philippines pieces of shit that you could only wear or play with once before they tore, turned green, or broke and put somebody's eye out.

Anthony spat on the sidewalk, at nothing in particular and at everything. He shook his head at the suckers on the bus and continued on his six-block walk to his particular abuse. His shit of a job, where the only benefit was that it was something to bitch about.

The blocks ahead offered shade from the relentless sun. Children, still crusty around the mouth, were already taking their places on the dirt patch lawns in front of the houses. There was no wind, and the air smelled unwashed and stale.

Anthony ignored his surroundings by traveling in a marijuana haze. To him, it was a comfort that his mind was fogged and he was unable to hold any train of thought for too long. He stood in front of the liquor store for a minute as if to let the wind blow the reefer smoke off him, except there still was no wind.

He knocked on the window, and soon enough,

Mr. Popolous was peering his round, hairless white head through the bulletproof glass to make sure it was Anthony and not some other heathen scum. The store seemed darker than Anthony remembered, and even more of a hellhole than before he left. Mr. Popolous unlocked the door for Anthony to come in. They spoke as though there had been no absence between them.

Anthony went to the back, where he knew the new stock would be waiting. Anthony never understood why Mr. Popolous pretended to have a grocery store by having these things delivered. It was probably a marketing move—start off having kids come in to buy milk, bread, and chips, then as soon as they were old enough, they would get their drink, cigarettes and rolling papers there as well. But there were a lot of items on the shelves that predated Anthony's employment.

The back door was wide open, but the burglar bars were locked. Anthony could see Mr. Popolous' two-year-old El Dorado sitting in the back. The car was bright and shiny, not only because of the brilliant sunlight, but because of the decrepit background it stood against.

Across the alley was a shell of what was once someone's home. The decaying heap now only held the lives of vermin and weeds tall enough to grow through where the windows would have been. In what would have been a back yard, some men stood around in a loose circle, trying to figure up enough change for a half pint of cheap wine.

The back room had not changed. There were fresh cases of bread near the door, and the usual cases of beer and wine that had to be refreshed daily, or at least it seemed that way. Anthony dove right in. It was work that his body remembered. It was work that was effortless and painless, and it dulled his mind even more. He moved all the cases of bread toward the front door, so that when Mr. Popolous buzzed the door, he could shove all of them through with his foot.

The door was buzzed, and Anthony pushed the cases of bread into the actual store. The three aisles that made the store were about twelve feet long. The fourth aisle was the cooler that held the beer, pop and wine. The counter with the bulletproof Plexiglas partition formed the real wall. This was the wall that kept the customers, their sticky fingers, and their guns at a safe distance.

Mr. Popolous sat on a tall stool in the corner so he could look through the Plexiglas and watch the door. As soon as the door opened, he would slide to his feet and wait on whoever came in. They mostly wanted cigarettes or a pint or a half pint of something; or they could get the forty-ounce bottles of malt liquor that went by super macho names, now simply called ghetto water.

Mr. Popolous would joke with the customers as he waited on them. After being such an integral part of the neighborhood for so many years, he actually became part of the community; but every night he would leave, and they would stay.

As Anthony crammed the last loaf of bread on the shelf, he looked in the bubble mirror at the end of the aisle. In the next aisle over, he could see a little boy, about eight or nine years old, stealing some potato chips. The boy looked up and down the aisle to see if he was being seen, then stuffed a bag of chips under his shirt.

Anthony made no attempt to stop him. Mr. Popolous had asked him repeatedly to do everything that he could to "stop the little heathens" from stealing in the store. Anthony felt that since they were stealing from thieves, he felt no moral reason to stop them. If he saw someone stealing, he would ignore him or her and go into any other part of the store that offered him cover.

Anthony was going to get his fifty dollars a day, under the table, whether they stole or not. Unfortunately for the little boy, Anthony wasn't the only person who saw him stealing. Had it been a dope addict or wino, the little boy would have gotten away with it clean, but it was a little old lady who went to church for a hobby, who witnessed his stealing. She immediately told Mr. Popolous.

Moving as quickly as he could, Mr. Popolous came out from behind the safety of his glass. When Anthony heard the door click, he sensed what was happening. He headed to the back room. Mr. Popolous grabbed the little boy before he could get out of the store. "What is under your shirt, young man?" he demanded.

The little boy tried to make a run for the door, but the old lady stepped in his way.

"Why are you trying to run?"

Mr. Popolous grabbed the boy by his shirt. The boy wriggled loose and tried for the door again. This time he made it only to find out it was locked. Mr. Popolous grabbed him again and dragged the boy behind the Plexiglas with him. The little boy was starting to cry.

"This is no time to cry. You are going to go to jail." Mr. Popolous sneered at the little boy.

Anthony watched through the cracked back

door. He wanted to go out and set the boy free. He knew if he went out there, Mr. Popolous would fire him. This had gone past the stage of right and wrong. This was the place of principle, where the lies truly lay.

Mr. Popolous thought nothing of selling the liquor that tore apart so many families, cigarettes that were proven to kill the users, and food that was not healthy in the least. For that, there were no principles involved, unless it was the profit principle. But let somebody try to steal a bag of chips, principles fell from the heavens.

Anthony was trying to keep his own principles in check. He wanted to go and save the boy. He wanted to beat the shit out of Mr. Popolous, beat him until him and his fucking principles lay bleeding on the floor. As much as Anthony hated to admit, what held him back was the same thing that Mr. Popolous held dear—profit. Anthony knew his chances of legitimate employment were all but nonexistent, with his criminal record a dead weight against any attempt at the American dream. Meanwhile, this man who was quite simply a drug dealer making a decent living off the rampant destruction of people's lives, wanted to bring a little boy to justice.

Anthony had more to think about than morals and principles. There was his son. It wasn't a matter of being a good role model. As a good role model, he should go and body slam the old man, yet it was a matter of money that held him in the back room. Maxwell's mother was going to do everything she could to insure that Anthony's access to his son was as limited as possible. He couldn't just go to jail, and he had to keep the dough rolling in. This was as close to a legitimate job as he was going to get. That scared little boy in Mr. Popolous' grip just wasn't enough to jeopardize his income over. Anthony smiled when he thought about it. He was becoming middle class.

The police were soon there, taking the little boy away. They would probably take him outside and let him go somewhere. This crime was hardly worth all the effort and paperwork involved. Even though Mr. Popolous wanted to press charges—at least he said he did—he knew the little boy was going home. But at least he put a good scare into him.

However, if the little boy got his hands on a gun, which he was going to do sooner or later, it would be Mr. Popolous who would be full of regret. When the police had taken the boy away and Mr. Popolous felt better, Anthony got a beer out of the cooler and sat in the back on top of some boxes. He had the rest of the day to do whatever. There was no reason to rush. Anything that did not get done today could wait until tomorrow. He was going to get paid the same no matter what was accomplished.

There it was again, money looming over his head. When it got to the bottom line, money was all that counted. If you had it, no matter how you came by it, it was the shit. It commanded respect like nothing else; it was the difference between living and dying slow. It wasn't just what it did for you, but how you could make it do more for you. You could get it dirty as hell today, and it would come clean later. Buy your way out of the ghetto, you and all your bad habits. Even better, it made the ghetto a lot easier to live in.

Anthony sat there, sipping the beer, thinking about money and how to get it, when the door opened. It opened with more force than Mr. Popolous ever used. He looked at the young, blonde lady standing in the doorway. She was dressed in black from her head to her combat boots. Anthony guessed she was about twenty-two years old.

She stormed across the room like one of Hitler's youth and stood over him, pointing at the beer in his hand. "You ain't supposed to be drinking no beer, and I know you didn't pay for that."

Anthony looked up at her. "First of all, who the fuck are you, and what is your motherfucking problem?"

The white girl glared at him. "Don't worry about who I am. Worry about having a job tomorrow."

Anthony took another sip out of the beer then looked at her again. "Fuck you," he started. "Fuck you and fuck everybody who looks like you. Coming in here talking like you the shit. My mother is dead. Don't nobody talk to me like that. You best carry your little light ass out of here before I snap all over you."

She looked down on him, her lips parted, but she said nothing. Anthony smiled at her confusion. "If you ain't gonna make a move then carry your ass."

Anthony figured that the girl went up front to tell her granddaddy that he had been disrespectful, and that consequently he should be taken out in the alley and be beaten and shot, or hung. She came on like super feminist, but she wasn't ready for no nigga, not up close. Feminists had boxed up the world like they wanted as far as white men were concerned, but niggas were something that the rules didn't apply to.

Maybe the little white bitch was doing what little white bitches do by helping Daddy look out for the dough. It didn't matter whether the money was immoral or illegitimate; it was the family money, and it was her job to make sure it wasn't going to any two-bit niggas. But let a white motherfucker in a suit come through, he could have them giving up all the money. Sell them some stocks and bonds and skip town on their asses with all of their money. The law would be lost trying to look for him.

A white man in a suit could run a scam on a million of them at once, and if he got caught, he might serve a year in Club Fed. But let a nigga hit one of them in the head for fifteen cents, and they would be ready to hang his ass from a tree with a quickness. Only way a nigga could get away with shit is to pull the scam on other niggas and maybe two stupid white people.

Anthony knew it wasn't simply a matter of color, but color was an intricate part of the equation. The equation of oppression could not effectively exist without color or ethnic differences. But the most important part of the equation was money. It could override everything else, and whatever your color was, you still had to buy your freedom, keeping in mind it cost a lot more than it did 150 years ago. The question was still the pursuit of money, and the li'l white bitch was anal about not losing hers.

Anthony knew every week they took about $30,000 out the back door in a paper bag. It was money from this store and another store that they owned. He wondered if the old man was willing to die for $30,000, or would just let it go and call it a loss. Thirty grand was a lot of dough. It may not have been enough to die for, but it was certainly enough to kill for.

Thirty G's, the price of one week's suffering, could really help Anthony out. Actually, it wouldn't help him at all, but it could help his son. It could pay for a college education, or it could at least get him in a private school.

Anthony knew his life was all but over with. He wasn't going anywhere and he wasn't going to do anything. His son, on the other hand, still had a chance, but the only things in the way were money and his mother. Maxwell's mother had the chance once, but she got caught up in the "right now" syndrome and blew it. With that kind of a role model, Maxwell was going nowhere, right behind his mother. That "right now" thing was killing most people. Forget the future, forget anything that might in some small way benefit the future. Vanessa joined the legions of people that believed only in the "now" of life—no plan, no planning. Get laid, get high, 'cause tomorrow we might die, and if we don't, we will have another day to get laid or get high.

Anthony didn't want his son to be like that, and he wondered how he would be an example for him, the way his father was an example for him. His father died in the struggle against oppression. It was a noble death. Police gunned him down after Martin Luther King was assassinated. They killed King, and they would kill any other nigga that might get ideas. He had left Anthony the torch to carry, and Anthony would do the same for his son, but unlike his father, he was going to have a plan for his son. There was no plan for Anthony. His father was killed and that was the end of that. Anthony knew he was going to die, so he had insurance policies for his son.

He had to get a plan for his son so he wouldn't wind up going downhill like so many other people in his mother's house where he was supposed to be growing up. He knew if his son came with money attached, unlike Anthony, there would be people that would be glad to take care of him and see that he came up well. Thirty grand would definitely kick start a plan, but what was Anthony going to do after he got the money, besides go to prison? He couldn't go to prison; that was out. Jail had been enough. Besides, if he died, prison wouldn't be in the calculation. The problem came back to a plan. This is why so many revolutions failed; there was a great plan for a revolution, and no one knew what to do next.

Anthony finished the beer and decided that he needed to think of a plan. In the meanwhile, he had to get back to work. He opened another beer and set it in the floor in the corner, in case the little Nazi came back with Daddy. While he moved boxes from one side of the room to the other, he wondered whom he could choose to best take care of Maxwell.

Reginald was the first person to come to mind. He was working, and he wasn't into no silliness. With Reginald, sexual abuse would be out. But he was all into that church shit, and it didn't seem that he would ever peep the scam that was being perpetrated on him. Reginald would stay with that shit until he died. Anthony was sure he didn't want his son to come up in church. If he wanted to find God, he would have to make it an intellectual pursuit, not that singing, crying, go nowhere shit people called religion. Reginald was a religious ritualist, like all the people he went to church with.

Regina was too fucked up with her own children. Even if she had all the dough she needed, she would probably lay up and let some knucklehead nigga get it all. She could be so misled by the thought of love, that she would let that happen. Besides, with her children, Maxwell would wind up like some mistreated stepchild or some shit.

Aunt Dorothy was too old. Besides, he had already been enough of a burden on her. It would be nice if she could retire. As fucked up as her children were, raising children was obviously something that she was not all that good at. But then again, maybe she learned from her mistakes. With her drinking habit the way it was, probably not. Besides, she was losing it. Every time she got drunk, all she talked about was that she was finished raising children. Actually, she wasn't and she knew it. She was raising Regina's children now.

Danny was the last person to choose—a drug dealing, gang-banging man called Daddy. That didn't seem right, but if you look past the television labels, there was a lot more to Danny, and Anthony knew it. Danny would never have gotten caught up in the bullshit he did if he had gotten out when the getting was good. But where there needed to be bridges, there were breaks, and that was the way the cards fell. It wasn't like Danny was a genius, but he wasn't stupid either. He had never been arrested, and he was still alive. For a drug dealer, that was quite an accomplishment.

If Danny put his marketing talents to use in a legitimate setting, he would be on his way to living the lite version of the American dream. Maybe no big house in the 'burbs, but he would definitely be doing better than he was now. When Danny was selling nickel bags of reefer, he was the one that put ten papers in each bag. Now that he was selling rock, he had put together the thirty-seven fifty set up. It was about two joints and a dime of cocaine for fifteen dollars.

Still and all, even with his marketing savvy, there was no way that Danny could do it in his present situation. One little slip-up and he would be off to prison or dead in the playground. He would have to be willing to make a change in his life. If he could get a degree and turn his mack up in the real world, then he would be straight and proper. The one thing that would really make a difference would be if Danny were willing to make a change.

It wouldn't be so much a change as it would be getting back on track. Anthony thought about when they were little, how they would lie in the bed and tell each other what they would be when they grew up. Anthony wanted to be a lawyer, like Perry Mason on television. Danny wanted to be a businessman like Darrin on *Bewitched*. Anthony smiled because in their own way, they were close to that.

With six convictions on bullshit, Anthony needed Perry Mason. Danny was a businessman. Somewhere, they got off track, way off track. Trying to remember where the deviation from the dream occurred was futile. It could have been a trip to the principal's office in the third grade, or trying to get laid in the eighth grade. There was just no telling. A pair of gym shoes in the window, a fight; it was nothing in particular and it was everything. Anthony had long ago passed the point of no return, but hopefully Danny still had a good way to go.

Anthony thought about what kind of future his son had. He couldn't be sure that it would be better without Anthony or with him. He would like to see Maxwell grow up, make faces at his choice of friends, see the grades he got from school, graduate from college, all that good shit. But if there were nothing done, that wouldn't be the future at all. He would go to school, join a gang at ten, get on drugs, go to jail and/or die.

It would be nice if Maxwell's future could be his future too, but that wasn't going to happen. Going to school was out. How was he supposed to eat in the meantime? Maybe his life could be like one of those people they put on television all the time to show you that you could make it in spite of the odds against you. He could go to school and sleep in the locker, steal food out of the cafeteria kinda shit, and some kindly professor would put him up and give him old clothes to wear.

He would get his degree; then some kindly benefactor would see his struggle and give him the break he needed. Then he would learn to shit roses. He had a police record and notoriety. He had a very short temper, and it would be only a matter of time before he would fuck some white boy up for looking at him the wrong way. Then he'd be out of a job, with a bad reputation. That wasn't his world, and he was locked out of it anyway. He had to give his son a better chance than that. He was going to do it or die trying.

The way to do it was to go out blazing. Maybe he could kill a few police officers. That would definitely get him shot. At the worst, it would just get him a severe ass kicking. He could kill a white girl. Kill a white girl *and* a police officer—a white police officer. Fuck, he could kill a white woman police officer. His ass would get deadened for sure behind some shit like that. If he didn't get killed, he could always plead insanity.

Anthony imagined himself standing before a judge explaining his plea. "Your Honor, I was insane. I was undeniably, irrefutably insane. Knowing what I know, knowing about Emmett Till, knowing about the Scottsboro boys, knowing about the monster from the Black Lagoon, I know that white men will kill for their women. How could I possibly have been in my right mind when I committed this act? Now, I know that if I wanted to kill someone and get away with it, I could kill another nigga, long as he wasn't too young, or I could have killed a Mexican or Puerto Rican man. Even if I were to throw myself on the mercy of the court, I would still get the chair, the rope, or the needle for killing a white woman. I know I would get deadened. Now, a person that wants to die is crazy, probably a manic depressive or some shit like that. So, your Honor, I submit that I was insane when I killed that white girl—crazy as a road lizard, a few bricks shy of a load, elevator doesn't go to the top, a real live Looney Tune."

The door to the back room opened and Mr. Popolous came through. He wanted Anthony to go in the front and take care of customers while he and the Nazi bitch went to lunch. Anthony took the seat by the cash register. He took money from the endless parade of addicts that came into the store. There were alcoholics, nicotine fiends and snack food junkies. It was no wonder that black people lived to the ripe old age of fifty.

These people were fattening up the white man every day, day after day. At the end of week, they would have left their share of his money, damn fools. All those so-called leaders trying to get people to spend their money in black-owned stores. Too bad all the black stores weren't liquor stores, or even better, if they had some whiskey made by black people. Instead, it was a bunch of white motherfuckers, or they were Korean or Arabs. Every time a black man opened a store, he was out of business two weeks later. What the hell was up with that? Ain't nobody had an answer for that shit. And when niggas did succeed, they weren't doing shit to help another nigga along unless he could give them some money for it up front. But this time, it was a little different. They were giving money to a black man. They didn't know it, but neither did the white man they thought they were giving it to. Anthony sat on the stool, smiling, taking the money like it was his.

* * *

Danny sat on the front steps of a vacant building about a block down the street from his house. Tiny sat two steps below him, and Otis paced back and forth in front of the house. They watched the cars going up and down the street, looking for anyone interested, and anyone too interested.

Danny watched an old raggedy car pass in front of the house then pull around the corner. He knew who was in the car, and he stood up, expecting the person to walk back around the corner. Surely enough, an unkempt man came around the corner. "Yo, Dan-nay, why don't you come on 'round the corner and see what I got for you?"

"Big Al, what kind of bullshit you selling today?"

"Oh, Family, you know me. I got the goods, baby. Come on and take a look. And you know it ain't even got to be a sale thing. We can make a move like in the old days and trade."

Danny walked over to him. "Motherfucker, you know you talk mo' shit than a li'l bit, and you need to have your ass kicked."

They shook hands, giving gang recognition. Big Al answered, "You know my name, my claim to fame. So come now, and let's kick this game."

Danny and Al walked around the corner to where Al parked his car. He opened the trunk and revealed three televisions. Danny pointed to the smallest of the three sets. "Is that one color?"

"Yeah, and peep this. I even got a remote for it."

Al rifled through the trunk until he fished out a remote control and handed it to Danny. Danny looked at the remote then at Al. "Yeah, but do the shit work? You could have dug this shit out of the trash somewhere."

"Oh, Danny, you wound me, my man. Of course it works. Check this out. I got this shit for five dollars. These motherfuckers broke into the Radio Shack over on Cottage Grove and stole this thing, and they didn't even know what it did."

As Al spoke, he plugged the television in, then took the remote from Danny. "Bam! In living color, goddamn."

The television came on. The picture was nice and clear, especially compared to the one that sat in the kitchen. Danny took the remote from Al and turned the channels.

"So, how much you want?"

"Fitty."

"Get the fuck out of here."

"Come on, bro. Outta the box you would have to give up a deuce ball easy. I'm giving this to you for a quarter of what it cost. Man, come on now. Work with me on this."

"Man, how can you talk that straight outta the box shit? This motherfucker look like you got it out of a garage. It ain't like I really need a television. I'm doing your ass a favor being here at all. You know I don't even like to buy hot shit."

"So, what you talking about?"

"I'll give you three bags for this shit."

"Man, come on. You standing on my money."

"Three bags, man," Danny reiterated.

"Fuck it. All right, bet."

"Help me get this shit to my house."

"Oh, you know I got to charge for delivery." Big Al smiled his toothy grin.

"Nigga, please."

"Nothing ventured, nothing gained."

Al set the three televisions up in the trunk. Danny

went around the corner and walked up to the steps, where Tiny was still sitting. "Yo, Family, I'm gonna make this move with Al. I'll be back in a short. Hold down the spot and keep an eye on Otis' goofy ass."

Danny walked back to where Al was parked and got in the car. Once at the house, he went in the side door and put the television in the basement. He paid Al with three fat dime rocks, and Al dropped him off back at his spot.

Danny returned to his place on the steps. He watched the traffic to see if there was anyone slowing down. There was. He ran out to the car.

"Yo, man, you got any nicks?" the man in the car asked.

Danny looked around. "Nothing but dimes, no change."

The man handed Danny a twenty-dollar bill, and Danny reached into his pocket and produced two dime rocks. He handed them to the man and the car took off. Danny turned and headed toward the curb, watching as a young mother and two children came down the block toward him.

He turned to Tiny. "I know this bitch ain't expecting to get served with no kids on her."

Tiny stood up. "If she geeking, she geeking. Kids don't mean shit."

"I ain't serving no bitch with no kids on her."

The girl was close enough to Danny for him to recognize the pleading look in her eyes. She walked up to him. "You got any dimes?"

"Bitch, what the fuck is wrong with you? You don't bring no kids to a spot. You ain't getting shit here. You better take that shit somewhere else. I won't serve around no kids."

"Please. I just couldn't find nobody to watch

them, and I wanted to get some. Come on now. I promise I'll never do it again. Just help me out this once. Please."

"Hell naw. I ain't serving. Carry your ass off somewhere."

"Please?" she said with her eyes wide, hoping he would change his mind.

"What part of 'hell no' is confusing you, goddamn it? I said no. Now get the fuck on away from here!"

The girl turned around and meekly walked away. Danny turned toward Tiny. "Can you believe that shit? I mean that's the kind of shit that be on the news."

"Man, you should have let her have it. I mean it ain't like she left them alone in the crib or nothing. She was just trying to get a li'l get high, and she didn't want to leave her kids alone. Now, that's the kind of shit that winds up on the news."

Danny looked at the ground. "You right, and when you right, you right." He turned to the girl, who was making her way slowly down the street. "Hey, baby. Yo, girlfriend." She heard him and turned around. "Come on and get one."

She turned around and came back. She set down the baby she was carrying, reached into her bra, and pulled out a ten-dollar bill. Danny had the rock in his hand, and traded it for the ten in hers. "Look, baby, a drug spot just ain't no place to have no kids. I mean anything can happen. Somebody might want to do a drive-by on me, or the man might come through. Shit, anything can happen, and you don't want your babies around for that."

She thanked him and headed off in the other

direction. Tiny and Danny both returned to their place on the steps. Otis continued to pace in front of the building. They sold a few more bags to a few people in cars. Other than that, they sat and waited for the next customer to come up.

Danny watched a man from the opposite corner, coming down the street with the look of a geek all over him. His clothes were tattered and his hair wasn't combed. He looked thin—the kind of thin a long relationship with drugs would get you, the kind of thin white girls were killing themselves to get to. The man was killing himself, but he was having fun doing it. The man approached Danny, waving so that Danny could see the ten-dollar bill in his hand. Danny got a dime rock out of his stash and got ready for the trade. He took the money with one hand and handed the rock with the other. It looked like they were doing a ritual greeting of some sort. The man turned around and headed back in the direction he came from. Danny looked at the money as he was putting it in his wad. It was the tips of his fingers that told him first, then he looked at the back of the bill. It was bad money.

The man was across the street and moving away faster. "Hey, motherfucker! Hey!" Danny shouted. The man continued walking, pretending not to hear his shouts.

Danny took a running jump off of the curb and shouted again. This time, there was no mistaking it. The man heard Danny and started to run, but Danny was already too close to him. He reached out and grabbed the man by what was left of the T-shirt he was wearing. "Yo, man, give me my shit."

"What's up, Family?" The man turned around, struggling to sound ignorant of what was happening.

Danny let go of the shirt. He could hear Tiny coming up behind him. "Motherfucker, don't try to play me. Give me my shit or I'ma start beating the shit out of you."

"Man, I gave you the money for it. I paid for it. I paid for it, man. I gave you the money."

Danny swung on him, hitting the man in the side of the head. "Give me my shit, motherfucker. I ain't gonna ask again." The man reached into his pocket and gave Danny the dime rock back. "You better had, motherfucker." Danny turned around and started to walk back to the steps.

"Can I have my money back?" the man asked.

"Hell no. You gambled and you lost. You better leave while you still got the chance, trying to treat me like I just fell off a truck 'n shit."

The man turned around and walked away. Danny handed the ten to Tiny as they walked back across the street. "Man, look at this shit. These geeking-ass motherfuckers will try to give you toilet paper if they thought they could get away with it. And the punk wanted his money back. He better get the fuck out my face before I deaden his ass."

"Man, how the fuck you know it was counterfeit?" Tiny asked him.

"Man, when you feel money all the time, you can tell by the touch. Feel that one and feel some real money. You can feel the difference."

Otis stopped walking long enough for them to settle in then he walked over to the steps and sat down. "How much longer we gonna be out here?"

Danny looked at him as though Otis were an alien from another planet. "What, motherfucker? Do you have something to do, somewhere to go? When it's time to go, you'll know. See, that's why niggas ain't got real jobs. They always worrying about getting off. They ain't happy 'til a motherfucker let them off permanently, then they want to bitch about that. Otis, just keep your damn eyes open. It ain't like there's heavy lifting involved here."

"Well, can I take a break for a minute, I mean to sit down or something?"

"Yeah, but if the man come through, then your ass better be flying."

Otis sat on the steps. Danny looked for another customer coming down the street. That was all he had to do, look for prospects and problems. He could see his nephew, Jaleel, walking down the street dribbling a basketball. He was walking to the playground. Jaleel never bought a basketball, because he never had the money to buy one. But even when you couldn't buy one, you would still wind up with one somewhere in your life. You could steal it, find it, or get it on circumstance, but you would own a basketball.

The dope game was like that. You could go looking for it or it could just fall in your lap. Sometimes it could be just circumstance and opportunity meeting. The only thing you needed to get into it was a little money and a lot of hunger. Danny figured that if you were black and you lived in the city, you knew a drug dealer. The more of them that you knew, the more likely it was that you would become one, especially if you didn't turn into a geek first.

You could make all the moves by yourself, but it was better for you if you were on a crew. A crew had more people looking out, and there was always the idea that you might somehow be able to confuse the law if you needed to. As a player in the dope game, you had to believe that you were smarter than the law was, but Danny never counted on that. He knew he was smart, he just hoped that the law was lazier than he was. For the most part it was, but Danny knew, unlike so many of his contemporaries, that it was just a matter of time before he would be prosecuted to the fullest extent of the law. He started with the idea of getting a few things then getting out, but upkeep was another matter of cost that he hadn't figured on. One day he was going to get out of it, get a real job and leave this bullshit behind. He only hoped he got out before his day came, either the day when they took him away or the day when they carried him away.

Danny watched a girl coming down the street. It was Angela, a girl he used to kick it with. He dreaded having to talk to her. He wanted to send Tiny down to deal with her, but she had already spotted him too. Danny stood up and walked down to the sidewalk. He stood there, his arms crossed over his chest. She smiled; he didn't.

She was definitely geeking. There had been a time when he thought she was fine, but that was some time ago. Now she had those flat titties under her tube top, and she had the geek thinness on her. She was fucked up. He wasn't happy to see her.

She walked toward him, still smiling. Thirty

pounds ago, that smile might have had some effect on him, but now she looked like a black skeleton with glowing teeth. "Hi, Danny. How you doing?"

"I'm straight."

"Do you remember me?"

"Yeah, Angela, I remember you."

"So, what you doing?"

"I'm doing what I do."

"Damn, you ain't got to be like that."

Danny didn't move. His face stayed the same; his eyes looked behind her, through her. She stepped up closer to him. "How you gonna treat me?" she asked, looking up to him.

"What do you want?"

"Can you let me have a dime?"

"Nope."

"Come on now. I'll turn you on to some of this," she said, pointing at her crotch.

"I'll give you a dime for ten dollars."

"Come on now. I got six dollars. Give me a little help."

"Look, I ain't the Red Cross. I ain't into helping, especially if I'm helping people stand on my money. I can't do that."

"Please, Danny. I just need a little help."

"I ain't the one."

"Yes, you are. You the one. You the one that got me started on this shit. If it weren't for you, I would have never touched this shit."

"Hey, peep this. All the time we was kicking it, did you ever see me touch a pipe? Did you see me hitting the antenna? Hell naw. You ain't never seen me straight up smoke a rock. I'll smoke it in some weed, but you way past that. You somewhere I'll never be. If anything, I might have let you get high with me, but I never turned you on to the pipe."

"Yeah, but it was you that got me started period. I would not be doing it at all if it weren't for you getting me high."

"Either way, it ain't my problem now. I don't smoke the pipe, and I ain't giving you nothing."

"Danny, please. Just this once."

"Angela, you trying to make your habit my habit, and that ain't gonna happen. I can't do nothing for you."

"I'll bring you the money back. I just want some to have for now. I'll bring you the money."

"I'll tell you what. Instead of bringing me the money back, why don't you wait 'til you have the money, then get high?"

"Danny, please," she begged.

He turned around and walked back to the steps.

"You sonofabitch! I'm gonna trick on your ass. Don't look out for me. I'll drop a dime all over your ass," she shouted behind him.

Danny turned back around, walked over to her, and stood close to her, looking down into her face. He pointed in her face, his index finger touching the tip of her nose. "You even think about it, I'll fuck you up with a quickness, and if I go to jail, I'll kill your ass first thing when I get out. Don't be making empty threats."

He pushed her in the face. "Now get the fuck away from me." Danny turned around. She got up off the ground and walked the other way.

"You think she gonna trick?" Tiny asked.

"No."

"Man, why she even come like that? Boy, when people be geeking, they get way out of line," Tiny continued.

Danny took his place on the steps. "Man, just drop it."

Otis took his place at the curb. He started his pace in the usual way, then he took off running. The squad car at the other end of the block sped up. Danny and Tiny ran into the building and out the back. The crossed the alley, hopped a fence and ran through another yard, then walked as nonchalantly as they possibly could down Vernon. They reached the corner of 61st Street and headed east, walked to the alley between Eberhart and Rhodes, then went into Danny's backyard. They waited a minute for Otis. When he did not show, they went into the basement through the side door.

About fifteen minutes later, Otis knocked on the side window. They let him into the basement. "So, did they catch you?" Danny asked.

"Nope. I ran through a few yards and the alley then they let me go. I waited a while to make sure, then I came here."

"Straight," Danny said.

They went into the yard and smoked a few thirty-seven fifties then decided to walked down to the liquor store and get a few forties. Danny told them he was going to make a move, and they could come if they wanted to. They all got in the car and drove out to the suburbs.

They listened to the police scanner while they rode. The scanner said the same thing over and over: "Black male with a gun" or "Black male shot."

They pulled up on a block that was typically suburban. Danny stopped and told them to wait in the car. He ran inside one of the houses then returned just as quickly as he had left. He got in the car and they headed back to the city. Danny put his stash in the house, rolled a few thirty-seven fifties, and they decided to go get something else to drink. They made the walk down to 61st Street and stopped in the liquor store, got a pint of brandy and headed back to Danny's backyard. Once there, they smoked thirty-seven fifties and passed the drink between them.

They finished getting high and decided to go for a walk until the spot was properly cooled down. They were walking west down 61st Street when Sweets called Danny from across the street. He was talking the same game as before. Initially, Sweets was hesitant to talk around Tiny and Otis, but Danny assured him that they would find out anyway.

Tiny expected Danny to do that. After all, they had been friends for a long time. Otis was surprised to hear it. He was not highly regarded by anyone in the neighborhood. Most people thought of him as little more than an alcoholic bum. He was usually not privy to first hand information.

Sweets looked at all of them, then his eyes settled on Danny. "You know, Family, you'd be much safer in a house, and you wouldn't have to worry about little altercations like the one the other night. I'm sorry that happened. He must have misunderstood where I told him to go."

Danny told him that they would think about it; they would have to talk it over. Sweets was quick to throw in some more of the benefits, the primary one being that he wouldn't have to worry about copping or cooking again. Everything would be supplied for him, ready to sell.

When Sweets finished his sell, they retreated a few feet away. Danny was looking at the personal profit they all stood to gain. Tiny told him that he would be under Sweets' thumb if he took the deal. Then Otis brought up the house on 55th Street.

All he had to do was mention it, and they all knew what he was talking about. A year ago there had been a house on 55th that was doing the best business in the area. They had four crews running 24 hours a day, seven days a week. Then one morning the crew coming in found the crew they were to relieve all dead. There had been blood all over the house, and five bodies in it. No one ever knew exactly what happened. The favored rumor was that the police came, killed everybody, and took the profits. There was one that DeeBees did it. DeeBees were the rival gang, also known as Friends or the Devil's Best Friends.

Some people thought it was an inside job; that some other Family had done it. Some just said they was robbed, period, no gangs involved. Maybe it was a customer that felt he was short-changed, or somebody lost a girlfriend. Whatever it was, no house had that kind of money running through it since.

They decided as a group that the loss of control and the danger involved were not worth it. They returned to Sweets with an answer.

Danny looked at him. "Well, Family, it ain't gonna happen. Thanks for looking out, though."

Sweets wasn't ready to be turned down. "Look, Family, I can't make you take it, but I suggest that you think about it some more."

They all understood the threat implied in what he'd said. Danny stood up to him. "What the fuck is that supposed to mean?"

"Just what I said," Sweets replied, lacking any emotion.

"Oh, Family, you ain't got to come to me like that. Be straight with me."

Sweets started to say something but looked over Danny's shoulder and said nothing. He smiled and faced the ground. Tiny looked behind Danny and saw someone running toward them from across the street.

Tiny tapped Danny. "Yo, man, you know this motherfucker running up on us?"

Danny turned around to see someone he immediately recognized as the man that was on his corner the other night.

"What the fuck?"

Sweets, still wearing the same smile, said, "Yo, Family, meet my homey, Maniac."

Maniac stopped running three feet in front of Danny. "Yo, motherfucker, you pulled a gun on me the other day. What the fuck is up with that?"

Danny turned and looked at Sweets. "This how you gonna play me?"

"I ain't got shit to do with this."

Danny, still ignoring the man in his face said, "I thought you was gonna look out on this."

"It ain't my call."

The crowd gathered in anticipation of blood. Tiny moved toward Maniac, slightly in back of him. Otis, not sure what he should do, moved into the crowd. Maniac stepped closer to Danny.

"Where your gun at now, motherfucker?"

Danny had participated in the song and dance rituals that preceded a fight since his first fight in the second grade. He was supposed to give some type of verbal response. He could explain his way out of it, or he could heighten the challenge. As much as Danny knew the ritual, he didn't feel like going through it. He swung on Maniac, knocking him to the ground.

The crowd opened up enough so Maniac could hit the ground before he hit anyone else. While he had expected the prefight rituals would last a little longer, now he saw the concrete rushing toward his face. Before he bounced off the ground, Danny was on top of him. Danny flipped him over to his stomach then grabbed the right side of Maniac's collar with his left hand. Tightening his grip on the collar, Danny dug the knuckle of his thumb into the base of Maniac's throat.

He wrapped his right arm around Maniac's head then leaned over and whispered into Maniac's ear, "You ready to die, you punk-ass motherfucker? You ever look like you gonna fuck with me again and I'll deaden your ass with a quickness, and I won't need a pistol. I'll kill you and hold you close so I can hear you die."

Maniac wanted desperately to get some air, but he couldn't find the strength to throw Danny off of him. He heard every word that Danny said, but it sounded like he was dreaming. He passed out. When Maniac went limp, Danny held him just a little longer before letting him fall to the ground. Danny stood and shouted at Sweets. "You a punk! You acting like a fucking DeeBee. You ain't shit. Your word ain't shit. Fuck you."

"Don't ever call me a DeeBee again. Don't be disrespectful."

"Fuck you."

Danny turned around and walked away. Tiny and Otis followed. Sweets smiled to his crowd and had some of his boys help Maniac up. The crowd went off in different directions.

Danny was pissed. "Man, you see that shit? That motherfucker wanted me to run a house for him, and then gonna try to do me like that. Fuck him. If I want a house, I'll have my own goddamn house. Running with that motherfucker, I'm liable to wind up like James did."

Tiny saw what was happening. "Yo, man, don't let this shit get out of proportion and shit. I mean don't be thinking on that revenge tip 'n shit. Ain't no sense in letting it get out of hand."

"Hey, I know this. If he try to pull some shit like that again, I'm going over to 57th and see Big Daddy and get his ass deadened. I can't believe he was gonna let one of his boys jump me in the middle of the goddamn street. I should have smoked his ass, but there was too many people there."

They got another half pint, went in the backyard and smoked another thirty-seven fifty. Then they went in the basement and watched the new television. The news was on. More dead niggas was the top story. They watched in silence, knowing that one day they could be in the "more dead niggas" segment of the news.

Danny spoke about what they were all thinking. "You know there will be some bad drama behind all this shit."

Both Otis and Tiny shook their heads.

"Look, I'll sell this shit I got today in a low key way. Other than that, I'll be off the street for a while 'til this shit blows over. Are you all straight?"

Tiny and Otis both nodded. They sat and watched the news some more. There was another story about the governor manipulating education money, giving the school children in Chicago a good "fuck you." Not that it made a difference in their lives, because they were long out of school. It did feel like another blow for being black though, like another lock on a door they weren't going through.

"Yo, man, why don't y'all pull up? I'm gonna chill. Hey, if you need anything, come through and I'll look out."

Tiny and Otis got up and shook hands with Danny, then left out of the side door. Danny went into the basement and unplugged the television. He brought the television and remote upstairs to the kitchen, leaving them on the counter. He went back into the basement, checked his money and his stash, then laid down and went to sleep.

chapter eight

The work day over, the mass exodus from downtown began. The sunlight bounced off the glass and steel structures, almost eliminating shadows. Reginald walked out of the doors in the alley between Wabash and State Street, heading for the El station on Randolph and State. The El came, crowded as usual; a crowd of fallen hairstyles, stale perfume, and body sweat. Just eight hours ago, everyone was clean and smelling fresh. Most every building downtown had air conditioning, so people must have saved their sweating for the ride home. The crowded El and the jarring of bodies back and forth was the music and the dance for the end of the work day.

Reginald didn't mind. This was better than being at work. This is what the workday was all about; this was the gem in the crown—getting off and going home. Besides, he parked near the 22nd Street station, so he wouldn't have too far to ride; being crushed for a few minutes was more than worth the trip home.

As the train jerked its way down the alley between Wabash and State Street, Reginald thought about going to his mother's house after work. That is what the place had become—his mother's house. It was hard to think of it as his home. He had spent the last couple of days at Dennis' apartment. It was only a matter of receiving his mail there and moving two more loads of clothes. As for now, he was without a place to actually call home. He was in between homes. He wasn't all the way out of his mother's house, and he wasn't all the way in Dennis' house yet either. If he were Catholic, he'd be in Purgatory.

Reginald didn't like living in the house on Eberhart. They were only his family as a matter of biology, and even that wasn't certain. They were nothing like he was. They didn't concern themselves with the things that concerned him. They only had their name in common, and that wasn't enough.

Not being with them was good for him. He didn't have to explain himself to them—not that he wanted to. As far as he was concerned, the less explained the better. If there ever came a time when he did explain himself, he would rather there be some distance between them. He could tell them on the phone and be done with it, or even better, he could never tell them.

When the El stopped at 22nd Street, Reginald stepped through the doors and took a deep breath. He stood on the platform, looked out over Chinatown, and wondered if he should stop and get something to eat on the way to wherever he was going. Walking down the steps, he decided against Chinese food. Maybe he would get some chicken.

The car was too hot to sit in, so he turned on the engine, turned on the air conditioning, and waited outside. He sat on the hood of his car, looking at the Chicago skyline. It sat big, broad and not too distant, like the life he wanted that was still out of reach. He wondered if he would ever get to live that life or if it was only for people who lived their lives on television. Although he did like the industry he worked in, he did not have the job he wanted. Although he was in the choir, it was not quite the ministry that he wanted. Everything he wanted seemed to be around some corner or maybe at the next exit. It felt as though everything he wanted was just on the other side of some big thing he had no control over. He would simply have to trust that God would lead him to the fullness of his life.

He got in the car. The radio was tuned to a gospel station. Reginald sang along as he crawled through the southbound traffic down King Drive. Out of habit, he turned east on 61st Street. Since he'd made the turn, he might as well see his mother. Maybe they would have something to eat. Dennis certainly wouldn't have anything to eat at his apartment, at least not anything cooked. While he was at his mother's house, he could take some more clothes with him as long as Anthony wasn't in the house. If he were, then Reginald would keep on his way.

He knew Anthony would be confrontational, and Reginald didn't feel like it tonight. It was always the same thing with Anthony, always complaining. If it wasn't the almighty white man he was ranting and raving about, it was the church, or something else legal that so many other people seemed to enjoy. He never ranted and raved about drugs or gang banging. He must have been in full agreement with those things, considering what he did and the people he did them with.

Since Anthony had gotten out of jail, Reginald had seen him once and said nothing to him. If they did talk, Reginald would try to keep it to "Hi" and "Bye." He knew it was only a matter of time before he got into a shouting match with Anthony, especially if Anthony was high or drunk or something. If anyone in the family already knew that Reginald was gay, it was Anthony. It seemed like Anthony knew everything, except how to stay out of jail. So what if Anthony did know? He could go into his tirade about how homosexuality decimated the black gene pool. Anthony was forever on his black kick—black this and black that. If it wasn't black, it was the white man. There was never anything about God. God overcame color.

Reginald was so lost in his mental arguments against Anthony that he drove right past Eberhart. When he reached the stoplight on the corner of 61st and St. Lawrence, he made a conscious effort to think of something nicer, like the fact that choir rehearsal was tonight, and he was going to pick up Tremont. Now that was definitely something more positive, picking up Tremont. Just the idea of Tremont made Reginald smile. He wondered if it was Tremont or the lust for Tremont that made him smile. Since Reginald hardly knew him, it must have been the desire that made him smile. This was a wonder of love, the fact that someone could speed up the beat of your heart just by the thought of him.

Maybe his attraction was because Reginald

knew Tremont never had sex with a man, and that made Tremont a virgin. In a way, this didn't matter, but then there was the idea of introducing someone to this idea of sexuality. Of course, there was no way he could absolutely be sure that Tremont was virgin, but in his daydreams, he was. In his daydreams, Tremont was not only willing, but also grateful, very grateful.

One of the things that Reginald knew about hormones was that they reacted to each other, so surely Tremont must have felt something for him. Reginald drove along, wondering what Tremont would be like. He wondered what course their relationship would take, if it would even get off the ground.

Singing along with the songs on the radio, Reginald wondered what Tremont was really like. Even more to the point, what would Reginald be like around him. Reginald had never been with a virgin before. He wanted to do it right.

Reginald pulled into the apartment building parking lot. He shook off his thoughts long enough to park and lock the car. Once inside the apartment, he checked the answering machine, but all the messages were for Dennis. He called home to check for messages. Regina told him that some guy called but wouldn't leave a message. Reginald hoped that the mystery caller was Tremont, although it didn't matter because he was going to call Tremont anyway to make sure he was still coming to choir rehearsal. While looking up the number Tremont had given him, he wondered if he should apply constant pressure or wait until Tremont gave some certain signal to put the move on him. Since Reginald had never been with anyone that he supposed was a virgin, he didn't know what to do.

He lay back on his bed because he wanted to enjoy the fantasies of how this could go, comparing his first time to his fantasy of Tremont's first. Reginald was 14 years old, and on a convention trip with Reverend Warden. On their first night there, Reverend Warden got some wine and they drank it. Reverend Warden took a shower, and after he came out of the bathroom, he suggested that Reginald take one. When Reginald came out of the shower, Reverend Warden lay naked on the bed.

Reginald remembered the uneasy feeling he had in his stomach. It was like he knew what was going to happen, and he knew it was wrong; like a train coming at him, and he was stuck on the track. The pastor called him from across the room. Reginald's head was swimming, partially from the alcohol, partially from fear, but mostly because he knew what was going to happen. Reverend Warden reached into Reginald's robe and began stroking him. Reginald, as if he were hypnotized, let him. Then the reverend pulled him closer.

The pastor of the church performed oral sex on Reginald. The sensations added to the dreaminess of the whole thing. It was the first time anyone had done anything like that to him. Not much later, it was the first time that Reginald had done anything like that to someone else. On that trip, he had oral sex with the pastor two or three times a day, every day he was there. They had anal sex twice, once on either end. Before the one-week trip ended, Reginald was looking forward to those sexual encounters. He actually didn't want to come home.

The relationship with the pastor continued after they returned. It was during that time that Reginald began to take more notice of the men in the church. He joined the choir soon after and found he was far from alone. He just seemed to be among the kind of people that he felt the most comfortable with. It seemed like he grew up in a very short time, especially from that trip with the pastor. That was all so very long ago, back before AIDS, condoms, and commitment mattered for sex.

When it came to the reality of his relationship with Tremont, Reginald knew it was all just fantasy, and as much as he could fantasize about it, it could easily come to nothing at all. It was hard enough to be sure that someone whom you were certain was gay was attracted to you. This was out there. Still, no matter how far out there it was, Reginald was going out there to get it. Lately he had become the caretaker in his relationships. He was doing the pursuing, the wooing and the romancing. He couldn't remember who the first person he actively pursued was, nor could he remember how he did it.

He was certain he had become an aggressor in his relationships, but this was still some other thing and had to be treated as such. When he was younger, though not by much, he had been the boy. Back then, it was easy to believe that those men genuinely cared for him, and the things they gave him were out of admiration. But now that he was on the other side of those same tracks, he knew things to be different.

There was more than one boy he had helped because of what the boys were doing for him. It was not that they were actually boys; it was the simply the way Reginald related to them. He imagined his relationship with Tremont would be different from all those previous. He and Tremont would first establish a friendship. It would be the kind of friendship he always wanted with a lover, sort of like the one he had with the pastor back in the beginning.

After he became involved with the pastor, there was no need the pastor left unmet, and now if the pastor needed anything, he knew he could count on Reginald for it. Reginald wanted to have a similar relationship with Tremont. Reginald preferred to think the difference the reverend made was more spiritual than anything else. He avoided imagining that things could have happened differently than the way they did. It was water under the bridge and could not be undone, so he made an effort not to stress over it. If it weren't the pastor, it would have been someone else. He tried not to waste his time thinking about who he could have been or ever being different from who he was. Before his trip with the pastor, Reginald was a lot more like Danny and Anthony; he liked girls. He liked to console himself with the thought that he still did like women.

Somewhere in him, he still dreamed of having a wife and children. He could see his wife sitting in the pews, their children sitting quietly next to her, listening to him deliver the word of God. It was just a matter of finding the right woman. For now, he would be happy with his male friends. Being gay was only temporary. Before he went on that trip with the pastor, there was a girl in the choir that he liked. He just didn't know how to approach her. There were other girls too, and he'd had sex with the girl next door, but after the trip, there was a whole new dynamic he was dealing with.

Girls had competition for his attention. The major difference was that he did nothing as far as men went. He didn't have to chase them, they chased him. He didn't have to woo, he didn't have to romance, not with men. All he had to do was be there. After a while, girls seemed to more or less disappear, and all his friends were men in the church—not just his church, but churches all over the city. Even those churches that professed to have no homosexuals in them.

Reginald found the number and gave Tremont a call. He was pleased when Tremont answered the phone. It turned out that he was still interested in going to rehearsal. He wasn't as excited about it as Reginald would have liked, but that was okay. It would change. Just to help precipitate the change, Reginald reminded him that the Lord's praises were serious business, not to be taken lightly. Reginald hoped that he had tinted it to Tremont's liking.

After eating a microwave dinner, he sat in the front room listening to gospel music on the stereo. He turned the air conditioner on full blast until the room became too cold, then he turned it off again. Within minutes, the room was hot again, so he turned it back on full blast, since it would not come on by itself.

When the time came to leave, he did so quickly. He pulled up to Tremont's house, and saw Tremont waiting on the front porch. Reginald took that as a good sign.

"So, how was your week?" Reginald asked as soon as Tremont was settled in his seat.

"It was okay. I mean didn't nothing happen."

"You ready to go back to school yet?"

"Yeah, I guess so."

"What are you going to be when you grow up?"

"I don't know. I kinda want to be a preacher."

"Why a preacher?"

"I don't know. I just kind of feel that it's what I want to do. I mean I study the Bible a lot 'n stuff. I just think that it's what God wants me to do," Tremont said sheepishly.

"Well, I know how that feels. I still think that is what God wants me to do too, but for now I'm into my musical ministry. What do you think of joining the choir?" Reginald asked, hoping he was not too enthusiastic.

"Well, I just want to see how it goes, you know, to find out if I'm comfortable with all that."

"There are a lot of preachers that began in the choir. As a matter of fact, Pastor Warden started in the choir in his church. You've heard him break into song during the sermons on Sunday, so you know he can sing."

"I didn't know he used to be in a choir."

"He's not the only one. Like I said, a lot of preachers used to be in the choir." Reginald parked the car and they went in the church.

The beginning of rehearsal was a lot like the beginning of church, requiring a certain amount of socializing to occur first. There was gossip that had to be spread, people who had to be talked about and talked to, fingers to be pointed and hands to be waved. Like everyone else, Reginald participated. Tremont stood near him, but he didn't say much more than "hello" to people.

The choir took their seats in the stand. Tremont sat next to Reginald in the tenor section, even though he had no idea what voice he was. Sitting in the choir stand, choir members continued to gossip, waiting for Edward. He finally walked in, followed closely by Mark, who promptly took his seat. Edward walked over to the piano. He put his bag down then clapped his hands.

"Okay, people, let's settle down."

The hum of activity died down. Edward waited for total silence before he began. It didn't take long; the choir knew what was expected and responded accordingly. Anyone who refused to cooperate quickly became an ex-choir member.

"First, I'd like to welcome a new member to our flock. Young Mr. Tremont Givens is joining our ranks this evening."

The choir responded with a hearty, "Amen."

Edward continued, "Maybe Tremont would like to say something about why he joined."

The choir members clapped to show approval of the idea. Tremont was taken by surprise, but stood up and began speaking. "First of all, I'd like to thank the Lord for giving me the opportunity to do this, and I would like to thank the members of the choir for accepting me. I hope I can bring some glory to the Lord and to Gethsemane Garden Church."

Tremont sat down and the choir clapped again. Reginald was beaming for Tremont. He was genuinely proud of what he'd said and the fact that Tremont didn't lose his composure when he spoke. Reginald leaned over and congratulated him. Edward settled the choir down and asked Reginald to lead the choir in an opening prayer. He stood and extended his hands for the people sitting on either side of him. He gave Tremont's hand an extra squeeze as he took it in his.

With the rest of the choir holding hands, Reginald asked if there were any prayer requests. Someone wanted a prayer for a friend; someone else wanted a job; someone else wanted to have a prayer said for his mother, who was ill. Another person asked that her husband be prayed for. With no more requests being shouted out, Reginald bowed his head and began his prayer.

"Heavenly Father, we come just to say thank you. We thank you, Father, for giving us this opportunity to thank You. We come here, Father, to become better at giving You praise, to be better at singing Your praises, to be better at being Christians, so that someone will see Your light in us and give You the glory. We ask that our singing of Your praises touch the hearts of saints and sinners alike, so that all men might realize they are nothing without You.

"We ask that You help us to put aside our differences, so that through unity we accomplish the things that we cannot as individuals. We ask that You bless us by giving us the discipline that will change our efforts into our accomplishments. Father, we ask that You extend Your healing hand, Father. We don't have to know the names and addresses because You already do. We know You can heal, Lord, and we ask that You touch this woman and make her whole. Father, someone asks that You touch a friend. Father, we don't have to know the extent of their relationship, because You do, Father.

"We ask that You might open a heart, or bring about a healing, or do whatever You see fit. After all, Lord, it is Your will that be done, and as much as we may profess to know the will of God, ultimately, God, everything is up to You to judge, and only You know what is truly right. Father, someone else is looking for employment. We know that if we ask You for bread, that You will not give us stones. We ask that You remove the obstacles, Lord, and that You reassure this person that their search is not in vain, that if they persevere, there will be rewards.

"Lord, somebody wants their family healed—their family, Lord, the most sacred of Your institutions, Lord. We ask that You give this family peace and patience, Lord, so that they may work out their problems under Your loving gaze, so that they might have Your peace in their house, and that Your love will light up their home. And finally, Lord, we would like to thank You for adding to our numbers so that we might add to Yours. In Jesus' name we pray. Amen."

Reginald squeezed both of the hands he was holding, again giving Tremont's hand an extra squeeze. After everyone sat down, the secretary read the announcements. It seemed the choir had received the necessary eminence to garner an invitation to sing at the Jordan River broadcast. The choir rejoiced in the news.

The actual rehearsal took almost three hours. They rehearsed in sections and as a whole, learned new songs and perfected familiar ones. Besides, there was always talking or something going on. They liked to think of it as camaraderie.

Church members actually came and sat in on

the rehearsals because they found them entertaining. After rehearsal ended, Edward asked Reginald to meet him at a restaurant they frequented. Reginald watched Mark as they spoke. He was his usual silent self. Reginald was starting to think there was something wrong with Mark because he was so dependent on Edward. He wondered how Mark acted when Edward wasn't around.

Reginald asked Tremont if he cared to join them. He said he would have to call and ask his grandmother, so Reginald pointed him to the phone. Tremont came back smiling, with the permission he needed. Reginald was glad to see him smiling. Maybe there was some way to get him out of his shell. Reginald was definitely going to give it a try.

Edward told Reginald that they would have to meet at the restaurant because there was something he had to take care of. Edward took off with Mark, and Reginald and Tremont got in Reginald's car. In the car, Reginald turned on the radio but kept the volume low so they could talk.

Tremont noticed the station. "Do you always listen to gospel music?"

"Pretty much."

"Why? Don't you like other kinds of music?"

Reginald paused to think of his answer. "Well, it's not that I don't like other kinds of music, because I do. It's just that I prefer to listen to gospel. I've got a lot of friends that make gospel records, and I plan to do the same someday, and I want to show my support for them. Besides, other music, especially that stuff they call urban contemporary, is just about sex. It's not that I'm against sex; it's just that there is more to life than getting laid.

Besides, I like to think of my life as God-centered, and gospel music keeps me thinking about God."

"So, you really dedicated your life to Christ, huh?"

"Well yeah, but that doesn't mean I'm like a priest or something. I mean I still do other stuff, and I have things that I struggle with."

"Like what?"

Reginald would have loved to tell him everything right then and there, in honesty and truth. "I don't know, just stuff. I'm sure you have stuff you struggle with too. And it's probably stuff you don't readily want to talk about. After all, Paul said don't cause your brother to stumble."

They pulled into the restaurant parking lot and went in. Reginald told the waitress that they were waiting on Edward and Mark, and to send them to their table when they came in. They settled into a booth near the back. Reginald watched Tremont while he was reading his menu, beaming like he was during Sunday school.

"Do you mind if I order some wine?" Reginald asked.

"Do you think Christians should drink alcohol?"

If this was a test, it was too easy. Reginald smiled. "I don't see it as a sin, if that is what you mean, but I don't think Christians should be drunkards either. While drinking isn't a sin, I think being drunk too often is."

"It's okay if you order it. I was just wondering what you thought about it."

Reginald laughed. "Do things like that bother you? Moral questions, I mean."

Tremont smiled. "Well, I do want to go into the

ministry, and it seems that every time you get one question answered, two more come up."

Reginald looked away. "Yeah, life is a series of tests and questions. Don't ever feel like you got all the answers. I think it makes God laugh at you."

"How is that?" Tremont asked.

Reginald smiled. "Well, in order to keep you humble, God will often put something in your way to show you just how powerful you are not. He usually does it just when you think you got all the answers."

The conversation hung in the air for a moment when Reginald looked at the traffic outside the window. The waitress came by and Reginald ordered a bottle of wine and four glasses. She set the bottle on the table and left the glasses.

"Would you like some?" Reginald asked Tremont.

Tremont was caught off guard. "Well, uh, yeah. If you don't mind."

Reginald poured just a little in the glass and set it in front of Tremont. "If the waitress comes by, that's not yours. Okay?"

"Okay."

Tremont quickly took a sip and placed his glass on the table. Reginald poured himself half a glass and took a drink, then set the glass back on the table. Reginald started looking out of the window again.

"Reginald, why aren't you a preacher?"

Reginald turned his attention to Tremont. "Why you asking me that?"

"Well, the way you was praying tonight, it's just that . . . Well, it was so different from when you usually hear people praying, so I figure you ought to be a preacher. That sounded like the stuff that preachers say."

"Well, to be honest with you, I do think about it. Lately, I been thinking about it more and more. I really don't know what I'm waiting on. I guess I just need that little push. I guess God is just dealing with me."

"I think you would be a good preacher."

"Thank you. That means a lot to me coming from you."

Edward and Mark were coming toward the table. They sat opposite each other, just like Reginald and Tremont had. Edward sat next to Tremont, and Mark next to Reginald. Reginald poured wine for both of them. Soon they ordered their food. Reginald reminded Tremont that he was treating, so he could order anything that he wanted. Tremont modestly ordered a hamburger plate.

While they ate, Reginald and Edward did all the talking. They talked about other people in gospel music, whether it was someone in a choir in another church or someone they knew who made a record. Tremont listened intently and Mark sat in his usual silence. Reginald poured everybody some more wine, winking at Tremont when he poured a little in his glass. Tremont smiled and quickly drank it. After the plates were taken, they finished the wine and paid the bill. Reginald and Edward talked a little more, then got ready to leave. They got in their respective cars and drove off. Reginald watched Tremont watching the other car pull out of the empty lot.

"What do you think is wrong with Mark?" Tremont asked Reginald.

Reginald was caught off guard. He wasn't ready for this line of questioning. "What do you mean?" he asked as though he didn't know immediately what Tremont was talking about.

"I mean he don't be talking at all."

"I guess he just don't like to talk."

"Why he follow Edward around like a little puppy?"

"I don't know. I guess they're friends. There's nothing wrong with that, is there?"

Tremont thought for a minute. "I don't know. It just seems kind of weird is all."

They rode the rest of the way to Tremont's house in silence. As they were pulling up to his house, Reginald asked him what he was thinking. Tremont looked at him across the car.

"I was wondering how you got to know all that stuff about the Bible."

"I know what I know the same way you will. Studying the Word as often as you can. Don't think nobody is just going to tell you stuff, because you will be waiting a long time for that. God could just fill your head up with it—well, actually He does fill your head up. You just have to give your head to Him. You keep on studying, and one day you'll know more than I do."

"I don't know. It just seems so hard, and like you say, ain't nobody gonna tell you anything. Then there's all that stuff you want to do that you ain't supposed to be doing. Man, it just seem like it's too much."

Reginald reached in his glove compartment and got out a pen and a piece of paper. He wrote down the number to his mother's house and to

Dennis' apartment. "If you have questions, you can reach me at one of those two numbers, or leave a message and I'll call you."

Tremont took the paper. He sat looking down at it. Reginald wanted to take him in his arms, kiss him, and make him believe that life wasn't as hard as it seemed. Instead, he put both of his hands on the steering wheel.

"Well, being a Christian doesn't mean that you won't ever sin again. What it does for you is to give you forgiveness when you repent. Even then, it doesn't mean that you will have an easy victory next time. The one thing you can try to do is to not let yourself be consumed by sin. Everybody falls. It's the good Christian that will get back up and do his best to continue to do right. A good Christian realizes that everybody falls and you learn to forgive others." Reginald stretched out his hand and placed it on Tremont's shoulder. "You stay in there. You'll be just fine."

Tremont nodded. "Yeah, I guess I will. Talking to you is definitely better than talking to my grandmother. She just be like, 'Do this' and 'Do that,' and that just don't be getting it."

Reginald let him go. "Well, like I said, you have a problem, I want to be the first to know about it."

"Bet." Tremont got out of the car. Reginald waited until he was sure Tremont was in the house before he drove off. He wondered what Tremont really thought of him, and he wondered if he would ever call. Reginald would be there for him if he did.

Reginald knew better than to be condescending. It was hard to be fifteen, even in church. The clock in the car read 1:00. He didn't feel like turning in right away, so he decided to go to a club, maybe have a drink or something, or even someone. He drove around trying to decide where to go. There were a few clubs he thought about that were on the South Side. He thought about going north but changed his mind. He wanted to go someplace where they didn't play all that loud music; just a bar or something where other men were. He settled on a club called The Tropic, a place he used to frequent some time ago.

The idea of The Tropic brought back memories. Not too long after things cooled off between him and Reverend Warden, he started noticing other men in the church, especially in the choir. When he started running the streets, telling his mother he was going to some church function, he often wound up at The Tropic afterward. He never got carded there, and he would order Screwdrivers. When the men he was running with were sure that he and the reverend were no longer an item, they moved in like vultures.

Actually, there were a few of them that didn't wait quite that long. The more he ran with that crowd, the more gay men he met. A lot of them belonged to choirs in other churches. He'd had a lot of fun, but that was all so long ago. More than a few of them had died of AIDS by now, and there were still some that were living with it. AIDS changed a lot of things; mostly, it killed his friends. He wondered if he had it. He was going to be tested again someday soon. Until then, it was protected sex and prayer.

From outside The Tropic, Reginald could hear the music coming through the door. It was loud, but not loud enough to keep him out. Just like back in the day, in the front were a bunch of whores, not necessarily the kind that sold sex for money. They made their living off of relationships. Not that there was anything wrong with it, Reginald was doing that once. It was now something he would rather not be bothered with.

Inside, he was immediately reminded of the way things used to be in there. Sex. Cheap sex, free sex, just sex. The men out front were remnants of that time. There was nothing wrong with them doing what they did; it was just that the time for that had passed. Maybe it was just the way of youth. Reginald knew it wasn't for him, so he wondered why he was there at all.

A good drink was an available excuse, and Reginald decided to use it. He went to the bar and ordered a Screwdriver. The bartender was new, so it was a lot more orange juice than Reginald cared for. He turned around and walked to an empty table, something that was rare in the old days. *The old days,* Reginald thought. He wasn't old enough to use a phrase like the old days.

He felt like one of those old, lecherous men he used to point at and make fun of. He decided he would finish his drink and leave. He sat down and took a sip. Someone came up and sat at the table with him. It was someone Reginald did not recognize. The man sat in the chair.

"Don't you know Edward?" he asked.

"Yeah," Reginald said, thinking it might be one of Edward's friends.

"You know he has it," the man said.

"No, I didn't know."

"Yeah, well he got it all right."

"So, what are you, his doctor?" Reginald asked, perturbed.

"No, I heard."

Reginald cut him off. "You ain't heard nothin'. Why you want to go around lying like that? Ain't life hard enough already? Why you got to go causing confusion?"

"I was just—"

Reginald cut him off again. "About to leave."

One of the most vicious rumors that could be spread involved AIDS. It was a quick way to lose friends. Reginald knew that Edward didn't have AIDS, but he would think about it when he saw him. He hoped that it wouldn't affect their relationship that much. Why did that man say that? People going around starting bad drama. Reginald finished his drink and left. The Tropic had a lot of history, but that was all it had. It couldn't provide him with the kind of relationship he wanted—something that he could be proud of, something without all the lies and petty jealousies that invaded so many of his earlier relationships. He wanted someone he wouldn't grow tired of looking at. He hoped that Tremont would be that someone.

On the drive home, he thought about what he'd told Tremont. Reginald didn't want to be Tremont's hero. Reverend Warden had been Reginald's hero, but that was a long time ago. Now it was harder for Reginald to define his relationship with the pastor. Sometimes he would sit in the choir stand listening to the pastor preaching, and he would believe the pastor was everything he appeared to be. He would be the same man Reginald looked up to as a child; the same man everybody else in the church, save a few, would see. He was the man leading them all to Heaven, the man that brought the gospel to them. He was the man that taught Bible study, explained salvation, the man that they were sure had walked the Roman Road. He was the next best thing to Jesus.

Then there were other times when Reginald looked in the pulpit and saw nothing more than an old, fat-assed sissy in there. A two-faced hypocrite telling people how to live their lives when he lived a lie. It was never pointed out to him, but Reginald noticed that the pastor almost never preached against homosexuality. When he did say anything about it, it always ended with "love the sinner and not the sin."

There was one thing the pastor would say that would cause Reginald to cringe if he was listening. He would stand in that pulpit and scream out, "I'm not what I ought to be, but I'm not what I used to be."

Often when he heard that, Reginald would think, *You ought to be honest, and you used to be younger*.

People said that in church all the time. It was just one of those things church people said. There was no way to qualify it. They didn't tell you the difference between then, whenever then was, and now. What did you do when you knew he was lying? Dennis would often tell him that it shouldn't matter to the people in the pews if the pastor was gay. Being gay wasn't the bad thing here, it was lying; it was having people look up to you while you were lying down to them.

There was nothing Reginald could or would do

about the pastor. He knew of instances where the pastor of a church was outed by an ex-lover, and the church would side with the pastor. They would claim the forgiveness of God and the frailty of man. Reginald didn't want Tremont to think those same things about him years down the line, he was sure of that. He was not sure what to do about it.

He knew in the seat of his mind, where no lies can be told, that if he knew the pastor was gay, he would not have gone on that trip with him. He also knew that he would not be going to that church now if he weren't gay and knowing what he knew. He wondered if Tremont was a bigger person than he was, if Tremont would accept him in spite of his homosexuality. He hoped against hope that Tremont would love the idea, that he would have found himself a new home.

Being gay wasn't bad; no, it wasn't bad at all. People only felt that way because it helped them to feel better than someone else. Sure, the Bible said it was an abomination, but it also said the point of the law was only to show the imperfection of man. Reginald could live with being gay, but could other people let him live being gay? It was something that bothered him, and he was sure it bothered other gay men in the church trying to find the proper balance between God and Nature.

It would be nice to say that you would never do it again and that you had, in you, the strength to walk away from it, but it would only make God laugh. It was easier just to try and find a place where you could live and be happy.

These things were never far from him, although

he tried not to give them too much thought. They were still constantly with him, sometimes more pronounced than others. He chose to think about Tremont, all the way home, until he was sleep and could think no more.

chapter nine

Dorothy looked out her bedroom window. It was raining. It had been raining for some time, raining as though it had no intention of stopping. Big, fat raindrops splashed in puddles on the street. Leaves that the rain had torn from the trees were floating in the gutters, on their way to clogging up the sewers with other accumulated garbage.

Dorothy was considering all the adjustments she would have to make today. She would have to leave a little earlier, and she was working the breakfast shift, so Reginald wouldn't give her a ride. He probably wasn't in the house anyway. She stood up, put on her robe, and began pulling the rollers from her hair, starting the trek downstairs into the day.

Maybe she had a little too much to drink last night, or maybe it was the weather, but she felt heavy today. Life felt heavy. She went through all the normal pre-work motions: she took food out of the freezer, she put on the water for coffee and she smoked a cigarette. Already she was tired, and she wanted to go to bed and stay there.

There was a smell coming out of the basement. It smelled like something funny had burnt up. It smelled like reefer, but it smelled different, sweeter. She had smelled this before, at the Cottage Grove El station. There was a girl on the platform smoking a joint that smelled like this. She knew whatever it was, Danny was the one that did it. No one else in the family would straight out fuck up like this, not in the house.

Danny was really starting to think that his shit didn't stink. He was always pushing her limits. He had done it in school, and he did it when he ran off and joined the Army. He never said a word to her about it, just upped one day and was gone. The bad part about it was that he knew joining the Army was the last thing she ever wanted any of her children to do.

The thought came and went that it might be somebody else in the house, but that was ridiculous. Not Regina, not Anthony, definitely not Reginald, and hopefully not Jaleel. It could have been one of Danny's friends, but they wouldn't have been doing it if he wasn't. There was no point in running questions about it in her mind, since she knew it was Danny. She knew it in the seat of her mind where there were no lies.

That truth lay heavy in the back of her skull like a lead tumor. It was the same truth that told her that Reginald wasn't receiving any calls from women, and all the men that called sounded like they were one step from becoming women. It told her that Reginald's being in church all the time wasn't a good thing now and it never was.

It was the same truth that told her Regina paid more attention to boys in the street than she did her own children. The truth that told her Anthony was so far out of control, she no longer recognized him, and that scared her. It was the same truth that told her in a small still voice that she drank too much and too often. It was the same truth that told her things weren't going to get any better, no matter how hard she wished.

The rain did not let up on the way to the train. The umbrella she was carrying, meant more for pleasant showers, blew open and collapsed three times on the walk to the station. And of course, the buses were nowhere in sight. At least for the first time in a long time the station didn't stink of piss. The El, on the other hand, stank. Period.

The homeless people had taken the train for shelter, and the smell sat in the air, a constant reminder that there were no windows that opened on the train. The train and the people on it were the least of her problems, and they could wait their turn. She remembered the smell from the kitchen. She knew it was burnt cocaine. Danny was the only one of her children that would have done some shit like that. He was not only smoking it, he was probably selling it.

He had to be doing something illegal. He didn't have a job, but he had a car and those expensive gym shoes. He'd gotten that color television from somewhere. So, there was no question that he was selling it, but what was Dorothy supposed to do? Scream and holler at him? That was the normal reaction to his stunts, and so far that did not accomplish a damned thing. She could shout until she changed colors: Danny was going to do what Danny wanted to do.

Dorothy looked out of the train window and saw a billboard that made her laugh. The sign gave an 800 number to call and turn in drug dealers. Of course, you could remain anonymous. If everybody did that, the phone would be ringing off the goddamned hook. Every black body in America knows a drug dealer. It's impossible not to.

Dorothy thought about the ones she knew. There was the infamous Hughey Brooks; everybody knew him, and they knew what he did. Even the police knew, and they did nothing. Then there were all those small-time dealers that hung out in taverns, trying hard to impress whoever and each other. She watched the billboard being soaked by the rain. For all the good it did, it should be 1-800-FUCK-YOU. Danny could do whatever he wanted and there was no way to stop him, but she would never turn him over to the police. Danny had to know the consequences of getting caught. Dorothy knew too. They could seize the house if they found cocaine in it. Then the house would be their problem, whoever they were.

Dorothy got off at her regular stop. The umbrella was totally useless, so she left it on the train. The rain wasn't as heavy as when she got on the train. She hoped her rain scarf would be enough to get to work with. She made her way through the crowds. It wasn't 7 o'clock in the morning and already there were crowds downtown. She walked with her head down, trying to keep the rain off her face, but it hardly helped at all.

She wondered how Regina would fare in life. It was not looking good so far. She was twenty-seven, with three children and nowhere near a man in her life. That was her problem; she wanted a man to save her, and that wasn't going to happen. Dorothy knew that road well. Even if by her wildest imagination Reggie had AIDS and Danny wound up dead in a ditch, Regina was going to outlive them all. She was taking the long way through hell. She picked out miseries like they were shoes to wear to the ball—pretty but painful.

Regina was the child of misery and suffering. Pregnant when she was fifteen, and nothing had been right since. Dorothy never asked Regina about her sexual initiation, because she didn't want to know about it. She could hope that the first time was the time Regina got pregnant, but that was just wishful thinking and as far as Dorothy wanted to carry it. When Dorothy suggested that Regina have an abortion, it was as though she'd asked Regina to shoot herself in the face.

Regina mistook teenage problems for not being loved, and a baby was going to love her forever. Where did kids get that bullshit? Regina seemed to forget that she was a baby once and that there was a distinct possibility that the relationship she had with her mother she would probably share with a child one day. No one ever thought that far into the damned future. Dorothy knew she didn't. As far as she was concerned, her future was whatever the fuck would happen in the next ten minutes. Why should Regina listen to her mother anyway? Her mother was living the life of misery; what the hell did she know about how to live?

When it came down to it, Dorothy didn't know a damn thing, not anymore. The only thing that Dorothy could show Regina was how not to live her life. "Don't devote your life to one man. When he is gone, then what? You get a letter and a medal with another man's picture on it." Dorothy's life wasn't shit but a warning, telling others what not to do.

Regina learned to keep men in her life, to keep the drama high. After all, high drama is a sign of living. Regina, who was still very pretty, kept the boys coming as Dorothy looked on from the sidelines in disapproval. After what seemed like an endless line of boys, there was another child born. Dorothy watched as Laneka's daddy did everything he could to disappear, quickly running his route straight to the grave.

Jaleel's father pulled a good disappearing act. He got Regina pregnant then he went to jail for twenty-five years. That relieved him of all of the responsibility of being a father. He was the furthest one, still in orbit around Regina. Dorothy had to give it to her for keeping that man in check, even though he was in prison.

Regina could lead the way for the next generation of suffering in the world. Regina had all them babies' daddies and with no daddy of her own. She just kept the men coming so she could keep them going. It had to be like a hobby to her. That was the only way Dorothy could see her playing with all these men like she did, keeping all those daddies and would-be daddies orbiting her like moons in her gravitational whims.

Anthony was a daddy in orbit, but that was because he wanted to be. Actually, he wanted his son to orbit him, to be the very center of his universe. Dorothy remembered him bringing his baby boy over to the house when he came from the hospital. He was definitely the pride of Anthony's life. Anthony was going to be Maxwell's hero. Not that he would do it the way Dorothy hoped. She hoped he would go to school and get a job that allowed him to take care of his family, to be that somebody that others could look up to. But that was asking too goddamned much. Instead, Anthony wanted some other shit altogether. He wanted to be a mythical figure like his father was to him. His father was a hero, not a punk getting shot in the back looting a jewelry store. He definitely was not a junkie, not to Anthony.

Who was Dorothy to tell him the truth? She thought that she should, but it was a lie that had grown beyond her control in her silence. His father was just another junkie nigga, shot in the riots after King was killed. Her little white lie had grown into a noble myth, and his junkie father had become a hero of epic proportion, getting slain for the cause of truth, justice, and the rights of the oppressed black man worldwide.

Anthony was going to be a hero to his son, like Anthony's father was a hero to him. In another day and time, Anthony might have been a hero, but not today. Today he was a damn fool pulling dumb-ass stunts. Unlike his father, Anthony was not just going to die; he was going to explode. And he was going to do it like Daniel did it, with nothing left to bury. On that day, he would be a hero and join his heroic parents, wherever they were, and be dead, talking about going down for a righteous cause. Anthony would be surprised when he got to wherever he was going to find out that his parents weren't in the gallery of heroes, just two stupid-ass junkies who were better off dead.

Maybe it was time that Anthony found out the truth about both of his parents. Not that it would make any great difference to him now. Dorothy could not think of why she had not already told him. Both of his parents were dead; now Dorothy was his parents. He was as much her child as Danny was, and she had failed both of them, all of them. In the seat of her mind, where no lies could be told, she took the blame for putting them on their roads. Even deeper, she knew that she didn't put them on their roads. She put herself on a road that they just followed.

The rain stopped just before the workday ended. She looked out of the front window before she went into the locker room. She didn't want to go home. There was no home; there never was. It was a lie she told herself to lighten the load. It did not work. Her bed was there, and that was all the reason she needed. The bed was a good place to be. All she had to do was to get her coat and her purse and be on her way.

As soon as she opened the door to the locker room, she could hear someone crying in the corner. For a moment, she thought to offer comfort, but as her eyes traveled the room, she could see the white envelopes sticking out of the lockers in what seemed like random order. The knot that was tying itself in her stomach told her that she would be the one needing comfort soon.

There was a letter in her locker. She could hear other people mumbling in the room. It sounded like she was hearing it through the wall. She pulled the envelope out of the locker vents and removed the letter it held. She skipped the heading and the words jumped at her. "Dear Dorothy Evans, We regret to inform you . . ."

She folded the letter back up. She didn't need this, not now. Besides, it didn't matter what followed. There was no good news that started with those words. Those words, "We regret to inform you," bounced around in her head. They ran circles in the neuron-synapse firing sequences. She felt faint as the words stretched into memories. *We regret to inform you that the man to whom you pledged your love, the father of your children and defender of his country, has in that act of defense been blown to very small pieces, pieces too small to send home. So, here's the consolation prize—a beautiful purple heart with some ancient white man's picture on it. We thank you for your support, and offer our sincere condolences. Here's a few thousand dollars. Go and get yourself a car.*

Dorothy sat on the bench provided for employees in the locker room. Within moments, she was standing again. There was no point in staying around. She wanted a drink—a big, long drink. She got her purse out of the locker and got the miniature out, drinking it where she stood. She remembered the bottle that was sitting on the shelf in her closet, a new one that she put there yesterday.

There was a bottle on the shelf in her closet, at her house. In the house where her oldest son would deal drugs to boys who would try to stick her up and get the shit kicked out of them. In the house her daughter would run out of, up to cars like a three-dollar whore, with all of her daddies in orbit. In the house where her son, who had a friend in Jesus, Mark, Matthew, Luke, Bob and God only knows how many other little sissies, resided in his holy-ass closet. In the house where her crazy-ass nephew would stay while he was out of jail, until he got caught doing some other stupid shit. In the house filled with heartaches and heartbreaks. The same house they carried her dead father and her dying mother out of, the same house she brought her babies home to, the same house Daniel brought his orphaned nephew to. The same house that she never saw her husband in again, dead or alive.

The worst thought was the one screaming that there was nowhere else to go, and there never was. Now she could get on welfare. Maybe her drug-dealing son would take pity on her and buy her a fur coat and a big car. She could take her son that had AIDS to the hospital with her new Medicaid card. She could be like Regina, keep the men coming and going, and don't give a shit what her children think.

The letter burned in her hand, then in her purse. She could not stop thinking about the letter, about Danny or Reginald or Regina or Anthony. Her grandchildren would occasionally pop up on the perverse merry-go-round of despair that she operated in her mind, along with Daniel, Sr., Mama, Daddy, bottles of vodka and cut-off notices. Her mind in a haze, she cleaned out her locker. Fuck this place. She threw the empty miniature bottle against the wall.

Ride the stinking-ass El train to 63rd and King

Drive. The bum motherfuckers had gotten off of the train, but they left their funky-ass smell behind. Take the train to the hell called home, through all the little hells that lit the way. If there had been any pity this morning, it was more than gone. Fuck the poor-ass motherfuckers in their shit homes. Fuck the motherfuckers on the train that still had jobs to go to tomorrow, the people that could make small dents in the hills of bills that came through their mail slots every day. And a special fuck, a big nasty fuck filled with some deadly painful shit for the assholes in management.

She furiously bumped into people getting off the train. In the station, she could smell the burnt cocaine again, or was she imagining it? No. There were three people over there passing a joint nervously between them. She stopped and looked at them. They looked like three different-sized black skeletons with clothes on.

Is that what Danny did to people? Did he make them look like that? Did he sell them that shit that sucked the life out of them? And if she smelled it in the house, was he sucking the life out of himself? It was not enough that he sold misery to others; he also indulged himself, so it was just a matter of time before he became a little brown skeleton.

The girl in the group looked around the platform. Her eyes met with Dorothy's. There was not a hint of pain or regret in them. They made Dorothy want to go for her gun, if the look meant anything at all. Fucking people deserved the shit they got, because after all, they ordered it.

Outside of the platform, the sun was shining

bright and hot, like it had never rained at all. The sidewalks were filled with pedestrians, if "pedestrians" was a nice word for bums, addicts, and alcoholics. Fuck them sonofabitches too.

Across the street, Dorothy could see that boy, the one that had the big car and the crowd that followed him wherever he went. He was sitting on the hood of one of his big cars, ignoring the people around him. He called one of his loyal minions to him and pulled a wad of money out of his pocket. It was as big a wad as she had ever seen John Frazer pull out. He peeled off a couple of bills and handed them to the man least twice his age. The man acted as though the boy had done him the greatest of favors to send him to the store.

How was she supposed to tell Danny that this was not the life he should be living? She could tell him that he should live like her—work your ass off and wind up with a letter that regretted to inform you. Yeah, give up the life of big cars, furs coats and paid bills; go out in the world and collect your fucking letters that regretted to inform you. That was what life was all about. Whoever dies with the most regrets to inform goes to Heaven, no questions asked. To go to Hell meant that you went to Heaven and got a letter that regretted to inform you.

She could point out how Reginald was working, and that he had a car. It wasn't a big car, but it did the job. Be a big fucking sissy like Reggie was, then you could fuck your way into the world, or at least you could get fucked to the top of the ladder. Or maybe he should be like Regina and be on welfare 'til the day he died. Yeah, go on welfare and get people to orbit you somehow, like Regina and her orbiting daddies. Orbiting daddies were better than dead ones; he could ask his crazy-ass cousin Anthony. He could tell him just as well, if not better than Dorothy did, how to live your life hating the people that you worked for. How to fill up on hate and other people's shit until you exploded in their faces, the way your daddy did.

Dorothy realized that she was standing on the corner staring at the boy across the street, and now he was staring back. He probably thought that she was one of those old ladies he filled with disgust, the old ladies he scared by being somebody they read about in the paper or saw on the T.V. news every day during the ten hours that the local newscasts were on.

Before she could continue, he was getting off the car and heading toward her. Dorothy shook the gun loose in her purse. Remembering that she had her raincoat, she pulled the gun out and hid it under the coat, which was slung over her arm. She should have left, and she knew it, but instead she remained rooted to the same spot. As he crossed the street, he motioned for the crowd to remain behind him. They obeyed. There was no way that Danny would ever want to live like that.

"Hey there, Miss. Ain't you Danny's mother?"

"Yes, I am."

"Could you tell him something for me? Would you do that, ma'am?"

"What do you want me to tell him?"

"Just tell him that Sweets is looking for him, and that we can still make that move. He'll know what I'm talking about." Sweets smiled.

Dorothy stood there. She wanted to shoot him,

to unload the whole clip on him. She hated him for having the things he did and getting them in the shameless way he got them. It made a joke of her whole life. She went to work every goddamned day she could, and didn't have shit to show for it. She struggled inside the whims of her customers, her managers and motherfuckers she had neither seen nor met. Here it is they tossed her to the fucking side like it wasn't shit, and this nigga sitting up here dealing fucking drugs making more money than she would know what to do with. He pulled out wads that could choke a horse, and she did not have enough change to choke a cat. But she did have a goddamned letter that regretted to inform. Where was this motherfucker's letter that regretted to inform? It was people like him that made other people want to deal drugs and snatch people's purses after they got off the bus. There he was, right there in her face, acting like she didn't know, or even worse that he didn't care whether she knew. "Yeah, I'll tell him. You said your name is Sweets, right?"

"Yeah, Sweets."

He didn't move.

"Is there something else I can do for you? 'Cause your standing there is making me nervous," she said, her finger caressing the trigger on the gun under her coat.

"Oh, I don't mean no harm," Sweets said, backing away, smiling.

"Yeah, the last boy that said that is in the hospital."

"Yeah, I heard about that."

He turned around and went back across the

street. Dorothy wasn't going to tell Danny shit. Fuck that drug dealing motherfucker. He just did that to mess with her mind, but he didn't know that other than killing her children in front of her, there was no messing with her mind. Her mind was as messed with as it was going to get.

Dorothy finally reached Eberhart. There were her grandchildren playing in the dirt in front of the house. Danny, Tiny, and Otis were sitting on the front steps. Next door, the young girls and their constantly growing brood sat on their front porch. Actually, the children were spilling off the porch, past the dirt patch lawns, into the street. It wasn't bad enough for her that she had to watch her own drama; she had to watch theirs too.

Dorothy put the gun back in her purse. She still didn't know how to confront Danny about the shit in the house. As bad as she was feeling, she decided not to bring it up at all. She walked up to the porch. Everyone spoke except Danny. She said her hellos and started to go in the house, but turned around.

"Danny, you got any money?"

"Yeah."

"Well, could you run around the corner and get me a wing dinner? One of those big ones, with about six or seven wings. Get the kids some tips and fries, will you?"

"Is that all?"

"Well, you could bring me a six pack of beer, and if you see a newspaper, bring it home. I've got to look for a new job."

"Why, what happened?"

"I got laid off today."

Tiny broke in. "Sorry to hear that, Mrs. Evans. It's going on like that all over. My mom got laid off a few weeks ago. She collecting unemployment now."

"Well, I can wait until tomorrow to make that trip. Right now I just want to take a load off and deal with today's bullshit."

She went into the house in time to watch Danny and his friends walking down the street. She wondered if it was just that simple. Just ask him to do it and it was done. She was going to see how far he would go.

Regina had the phone stuck to her ear, the only other position she knew besides hanging her ass out of a car window. Dorothy rolled her eyes and went upstairs. She went into her room and pulled the vodka off the shelf. She took a healthy swig and poured some into the glass that had a permanent home on the nightstand. There was no point in rinsing it out, because anything that could survive vodka was worth swallowing. For the first time that day, Dorothy smiled.

She took off her uniform and hung it up for what may have been the last time. She had been laid off before and went back when things got different. She put on her robe and lay across her bed.

DeShawn brought her food up to her room. It was just as well, because she didn't feel like leaving her room today. She didn't feel like watching the white people or the black people in T.V. Land winning their way through the world today. She turned on the dusty radio station and listened and remembered.

She opened the dinner and ate one of the wings

and a few fries. Dinner could wait. Besides she had a taste for the rib tips. She called to DeShawn to bring her some up. He did. Actually, he brought five of them to her. She picked over the rib tips and took a healthy gulp of vodka.

The day came rushing back at her. She'd lost her fucking job. Her low-wage, no-benefit-having, shit-catching piece of a job. She reached into her purse and took out the letter that regretted to inform. She unfolded it and read it all the way through this time. She was laid off because they were downsizing, whatever the hell that meant. If they wanted to cut some waste, they could have removed management. A deep breath and another big sip. This was worse than she wanted to admit.

Getting another job was not that big of a deal, not that the one she lost was all that much of a deal either. It was just that she would have to go looking for another job. She could get a job as a waitress anywhere, and it was going to be another go nowhere job. She had already been nowhere; she spent most of her life being nowhere, and now she would have to go there again, this time on a different bus.

She had not planned for this. She had not planned for any of this. How the hell could anyone have planned for shit like this? Dorothy didn't have a plan, not when Daniel Sr. went into the Army or when he never came back. There was no time to plan anything. Dorothy had a plan now. She planned to get drunk, wake up tomorrow with a hangover, and get drunk again.

Her arms were hurting, her feet were hurting and her back was hurting. She was hurting all over in different flavors. A pain flared in her arm then got lost in the forest of pain. Another stiff drink would numb all that pain shit. Dorothy ate the rib tips then ate another chicken wing. The radio was playing some old blues, some of that crying-ass music. It fit her mood. Dorothy wanted to cry.

The drug dealer was moving around in the kitchen downstairs, and the closet saint was either in church or with one of his friends. He was hardly ever in the house anymore, so good goddamn riddance to him. She should have asked him if he was gay. She should have pinned his happy, soul-saved ass down and asked him. Not that it mattered one way or the other, but it seemed like something she ought to know. He was her child and she should know. The idea of it felt like some kind of betrayal. How the hell could he be gay? Where did that shit come from? What the hell was he doing with his life? What the hell was she doing with her life? No matter what happened to her children, she still had to live her life. What was she going to do?

Her head was swimming in dusties and a second strong drink. The rib tips settled into her stomach like lead weights. Another drink and she might be sick. Hell, she may as well. She was already sick. She was sick of the bullshit that she was forced to call her life. She lay back on the bed and looked at the ceiling.

The good ol' cracks in the ceiling. They had been there since she had, maybe longer. They had been growing, but you never saw them grow. There were more of them now. Either that or she was seeing double. She felt lightheaded more than drunk. She sat back up. To hell with the cracks.

She sat up, looking straight into the mirror. She stared at the woman with no job whose family was shot to hell. The woman stared back. Things would change. Damn right, they would. They were going to get worse, a hell of a lot worse. They always do, and she was living fucking proof.

Tomorrow was another day. It was time to call this one a night, even though the sun was nowhere near setting. She took off her robe and laid it on the floor next to the bed. It could find its way to the closet some other time. She sat in her underwear and poured another drink, took a healthy sip and set the glass on the nightstand then lay back down.

The sheets were cool. The cracks were still in the ceiling. The globe was still over the lightbulb, just like when she was a little girl sleeping in her parents' bed on a scary night. She could hear the children watching television in the next room. Her oldest grandson probably wasn't in the house at all. She could hear her daughter in the front of the house, laughing, probably hanging her ass out of somebody's car window—probably that boy, Sweets. Fuck all of them.

Fuck the drug dealer, the fag, the whore, and the fucking maniac. She did what she was supposed to do. She fed all of them, all of the hungry mouths in the house. She fed the ones she bore and the ones she didn't. Feed the little motherfuckers. Like a crazy bird, feeding all the little motherfuckers.

Dorothy watched the globe on the ceiling until her eyes shut. The light was never on. She could see the globe from the light coming in the window, so she watched the light until her eyes shut. Then she listened to the music until she blacked out.

There were no dreams in her sleep. She stopped having dreams a long time ago. She lay there, her stomach gurgling alcohol and grease, spewing cholesterol into her arteries. The worries spinning in her mind were never far enough from her for her to feel any comfort. The old gospel song lied. God had given her more than she could bear. Somewhere between the last stars and the first light, her heart gave one last heave, ruptured, and collapsed. She never felt the tingling in her extremities working toward the center of her body as the flow of blood stopped. One soundless pop, and the world stopped for Dorothy Evans.

chapter ten

DeShawn stood on the back porch watching the garbage truck at the end of the alley. He ran down the back steps and through the yard to the back fence to see if the truck was moving, or if the men in it were taking one of their breaks, sitting and drinking at the end of the alley. When the truck jerked to the next house, he ran back inside.

He walked through the kitchen and dining room to the foot of the stairs in the living room. He stopped where the carpet had worn through. His brown house shoes were the same color as the wood he was standing on. He swung on the banister and shouted up the stairs. "Mama, they coming down the alley!"

Regina yelled back down, "What?"

DeShawn ran up five of the thirteen steps. "The garbage truck is coming," he yelled again.

"Bring me one of those plastic bags out of the kitchen, and hurry up."

DeShawn ran into the kitchen and searched under the kitchen sink for the plastic bags. Before he could remove one of the yard-size plastic bags from the roll, his mother was calling for him to hurry up again. He ran through the house, his torn house shoes pounding on the brown carpet and the bare spots his feet touched, until he was standing at the door to his mother's room. Regina was sitting on her bed, gathering the trash in her room to go out. She was temporarily overwhelmed by what she saw. There were clothes everywhere, and try as she might, she couldn't find the waste-paper basket that was supposed to be in her room.

"Jaleel," she called and waited.

Jaleel came and stood in the doorway. Regina spoke to him without looking at him. "I know you in there getting all that garbage ready to go out, aren't you?"

"It's already ready, Ma."

"Well, go and get the garbage out of Reginald's room, and I better not see one piece of paper in your room when I get in there. You hear me?"

Jaleel didn't answer. Instead he turned around and walked away.

"Nigga, you better answer me when I'm talking to you. I don't know who the fuck you think you are, but you better answer me."

"Dag, Ma, I was just going to do what you said do."

Regina snatched the plastic bag from DeShawn and handed it to Jaleel. "Don't give me no shit." Jaleel took the bag and left the room. DeShawn stood there planted to the floor.

"What are you still doing here? You seen my garbage can?"

DeShawn shook his head and turned to leave the room. Before he could get out of the door, Regina was shouting at him again. "Go look in my closet for the garbage can."

He walked across the room, careful to stay out of her reach, and looked in the closet. He returned to her with the wastepaper basket.

"What the hell was it doing in there?" she asked. DeShawn handed it to her and shrugged his shoulders. "I know, you don't know." Regina shouted, "Don't nobody in this house know shit. Shit just happens. Garbage cans just grow little legs and go hide in the closet, and don't nobody know a damn thing about it."

Regina looked down at her son. He was still in the same clothes that he had been wearing yesterday, his face was still crusty, and he had that shit in his eyes. For a moment, she wanted to laugh at him, his nappy hair and his little ashy ass. Then, plain as day, she could see his father's face on him, then it was gone. "Get your ass out of here and go wash up."

DeShawn ran into the bathroom. Regina gathered what trash she could into the wastepaper basket until it was stuffed. She went into the hall where Jaleel was standing with the plastic bag in his hand. She dumped the contents of the wastepaper basket into the bag.

"Did you get the garbage out of Mama's room?"

"No, you said get it out of Reginald's room, so that's what I did."

"Goddammit Jaleel, why don't you use some

common sense sometimes? The garbage men are gonna be here in a minute. Fuck it. I'll get it myself. Shit, I don't believe you sometime."

Jaleel handed the plastic bag to his mother and turned around and went to his room. Regina set the wastepaper basket on the floor. She knocked on the door to her mother's room. There was no answer. The door was opened slightly, so she called out to her mother. Still there was no answer. Regina pushed the door and watched it swing open. She hesitated, waiting for a response. There wasn't any. From where she was standing in the doorway, she could see her mother's feet. They were slightly off the bed, dangling in mid-air.

Regina walked slowly into the room. Her mother lay on the bed, still in her bra and panties. At first, Regina thought nothing of it. She'd seen her mother passed out more times than she liked to remember. The radio on the dresser was still on, playing the dusties like it always did. As she looked at the radio, Regina realized just how well she could hear it. There was none of the heavy, labored breathing that her mother would have after she passed out drunk. There was none of the gurgling, snorting, or other assorted noises that her mother would make. There was only the perfectly tuned radio.

Regina walked over to the bed and looked down at her mother. There was no rising or falling of her chest. Regina touched her arm. It was cold, and did not respond the way an arm of the living would. The fear of realization was causing the fine hairs on the back of Regina's neck to stand up. She gingerly touched her mother's neck. With nothing to feel, she quickly pulled her hand from the corpse.

"Jaleel. Come here," she called. This time, there was no anger in her voice. Jaleel came to the door, but he didn't come in the room.

"What?"

"Do me a favor and go in the basement and tell Danny to come here. Tell him that it's important. Forget that, tell him that it is an emergency, and hurry up."

Jaleel could hear the trembling in his mother's voice, a trembling that he'd never heard before. He knew to run. Regina looked around the room. She realized that she was still holding the garbage bag.

"DeShawn, come here."

DeShawn came to the door holding a wet washcloth. Regina was standing between him and her mother's body on the bed. She gave the trash bag to him. "Here, go get this out to the garbage. Put on a shirt and pants and get this out before the garbage men get here."

DeShawn turned around and went to his room to change clothes. Laneka was sitting on the floor watching the television. She hardly noticed DeShawn in the room with her.

Danny lay across his bed in his underwear. DeShawn's running across the floor and Regina's hollering woke him. He lay there thinking about firing up a thirty-seven fifty. If he did, he'd have to go into the back behind the garage, since his mother was going to be home all day. There was no point in catching drama from her, especially when it could be avoided. The joint could wait until later.

He listened as Jaleel ran across the floor in the living room, and through the house. He was surprised when the footsteps did not go out the back door, but instead continued across the kitchen floor to the basement steps. Danny wondered why Jaleel would be coming down into the basement. He sat up as Jaleel reached the bottom steps.

"Danny, my mother wants you to come upstairs. I think something is wrong with Grandma."

Danny looked at him. He was breathing hard from running through the house. "What you mean something wrong?"

"I don't know. Mama went into Grandma's room to get the garbage out, then she told me to come down here and get you. She said to tell you that it's a emergency."

Danny got out of the bed, put on his pants, and took off up the steps. Jaleel waited for him to pass, then took off after him. They both ran through the house and up the next flight of stairs. When they reached the top floor, Regina was standing in their mother's doorway, crying. Danny looked twice to make sure she was actually crying. It had been a long time since he had seen her cry, and even then it was because somebody hit her.

He came to the doorway. "What's the matter?"

"Mama's dead."

"What?"

"Mama's dead. She ain't got no pulse or nothing. She feels cold as hell, and she ain't breathing. Mama's dead."

Danny walked into his mother's room. Jaleel tried to walk in behind him, but Regina stepped in his way. From the doorway, Danny looked at his mother's body on the bed. He had never seen a dead body that didn't have a hole in it. There was no way she could be dead without a hole. The only time he'd seen a dead body without a hole was his grandmother, and she was in the casket.

He walked across the room and touched the same arm that Regina had touched earlier. It was cold and there was no life in it. He felt for a pulse on her neck; there was none. For the first time since he had come into the room, he heard the radio playing.

Regina sent Jaleel to his room, but she never moved. She didn't know what to do. She wanted to sit down, but the only chair in the room was on the other side of the bed. She looked at the body. It made Regina shiver to remember how it felt to touch her mother's arm. She watched Danny, and then he looked at her. As their eyes met, they both realized how completely helpless they were.

"I think we should call the police," she said, but didn't feel connected to the words. It seemed like someone else had spoken, but it was her voice. The word "police" snapped Danny back to reality. He had to get his shit out of the house. The police might want to search for some reason. Danny definitely didn't want to get caught with that shit in the house, not today.

"Yeah, I'll go and call them, but I got to do something first." He walked through the door. "Yeah, I'll call 'em in a minute."

Regina decided to go into the children's room. She stepped out of her mother's room and closed the door. She went into the kid's room. Laneka was watching television. Jaleel was sitting on his bed. She looked at him, and he looked at her. He knew. There was no way he didn't.

Laneka never looked away from the television. She could feel the tension in the room, but she wouldn't look away from the television.

"Laney, turn off that television. I have something to talk to you about."

DeShawn came bounding up the stairs and into the room. He looked at his mother and saw she was crying.

She looked down at him. "DeShawn, go sit on the bed." He started heading toward the bed. "No, better yet, come here. Laney, you come here too."

DeShawn stood where he was. Laneka got up and slowly crossed the room. DeShawn waited until his sister was closer to his mother than he was before he took a step toward her.

Regina reached down and held them by their shoulders, squatting until she was eye level with them. "Grandma has passed on."

Regina watched their unblinking eyes, seeing that they didn't understand. She looked at Jaleel. His face was buried in a pillow. She could tell from the way his body was shaking that he was crying. She returned her attention to the children in front of her. Her mind raced for the right words. The only ones she knew they would understand were the words she didn't want to use.

She took a deep breath, closed her eyes, and opened them. She could see the fear building in their eyes. Jaleel's crying was loud enough for everyone in the room to hear him. She tried to blink back some tears, but the effort was futile. They were streaming down her face.

She tried to focus on the children in front of her. She could feel Laneka's little body begin to shake. Regina took another deep breath. She'd formed the words in her mind, then let them come out of her mouth. "Grandma's dead."

She was going to pull them to her, but before she could, DeShawn jerked away. She looked at his little brown face for one blinking moment and it was gone.

"No, she ain't!" he screamed and ran away.

Regina stood up with Laneka clinging to her. She looked across the room to Jaleel, who was sitting up on the bed. She motioned for him to come and get Laneka. Jaleel seemed to take forever to get across the room, but soon enough, he was holding his little sister and she was holding him.

Regina turned and went into the hall. The door to her mother's room was open. She could hear DeShawn in her mother's room, screaming. Regina ran down the hall and hesitated at the door. DeShawn had her mother's hand and had almost pulled her body out of the bed. His face was full of tears, and in his raspy, worn-out voice, he was still screaming. "Grandma, get up!"

Regina ran to her son and grabbed him. When she pulled on him, he gave the corpse one last pull and it fell on the floor. The weight of the corpse made him let go. He screamed at his mother to let him go, but Regina held him as tight as she could. Her mother's arm hit Regina on her leg. She tried to ignore it, but she could feel where it hit and almost nothing else. Everything was in slow motion, between her son's screams she could hear the radio playing "More Love" by Smokey Robinson and the Miracles.

Regina took a deep breath and ran out of the room. She kicked the door shut behind her. DeShawn was still screaming, but not as loud as before. She took him into her room. She sat DeShawn down on her bed and held his arms. She looked at his face. His eyes were beginning to swell from his crying, and his nose was running. Through all the mess on his face, she could see the hatred in his eyes.

Why would he hate her? She didn't know what to say to him.

"You killed Grandma!" he screamed at her.

"What?" she asked, astounded.

"You killed Grandma."

"Don't say that, DeShawn. Nobody killed Grandma. She died, but nobody killed her."

"Don't nobody just die. You killed her."

He wasn't screaming anymore; he spoke softly. The tears were streaming down his face. Regina could feel the anger in her start to rise. How could he say some shit like that to her? It was her mother that died. Dorothy had been her mother a hell of a lot longer than she had been his grandmother. "Look, DeShawn, my mother is dead and nobody killed her. I don't ever want to hear you say something like that again."

She looked in his eyes for some kind of response. There was the cold, accusing stare and nothing else. She pulled him to her. He stiffened up, but she just held him tighter. Then suddenly he collapsed and became her child again, the same little baby that she brought into the world one cold-ass night in February almost six years ago.

She remembered her mother taking her to the hospital, standing in that blue gown in the delivery room next to her. Every time she had a baby, it was her mother who went to the hospital with her. She even went the last time, when Regina had an abortion. Regina remembered how neither of them spoke a word, but through the silence she could hear her mother talking about Regina hanging her ass out of a car window like a cheap whore. Regina had heard her say that so many times.

The abortion was without trauma, at least the kind you always hear about on television. It was a single operation with a little pain involved. It was a hell of a lot easier than bringing another child up in this world. Six hours later, they shared Mrs. Fields cookies on the bus ride home.

It was a hard thought to deal with. Her mother was dead and would never be there for Regina again. She would not be there to nurse the wounds when Regina came home beat up by a jealous man or woman. She would no longer be shouting about dinner being cooked and no one but her eating. After all the times Regina had wished her mother dead, she was not actually ready for it to happen.

With DeShawn still crying in her arms, she thought about Reginald. He would have to be told. Reginald could make the funeral arrangements because he was probably good at stuff like that. But before any of that could happen, Danny was going to have to get that body out of the house. What the hell was Danny doing anyway?

Regina took DeShawn into the room to be with his sister and brother. They were sitting on the bed. Jaleel was holding Laneka in one arm, and she was somewhere between the television and the reality around it. Jaleel was staring blankly at the television too. DeShawn came in and sat on the floor near them. Regina sat on the bed next to them. There was nothing else to do until the body was out of the house.

Danny was in the basement, holding a shoe box with about twenty-five plastic-wrapped dime rocks in it. He usually kept the box in the rafters in his room, but for now he wanted them out of the house. Twenty-five was a new low for Danny. He usually had between fifty and a hundred. He hadn't cooked any out of the last ounce he bought. He just hadn't had the time. He was going to cook it yesterday, but it was almost time for his mother to come home. It wasn't the smell; it was that he didn't want all the drama she would be serving behind it. Like the time she caught him with a half pound of weed in the basement right before he joined the Army. It was her finding it that made him decide to join.

He looked at the packs in the box. It didn't matter now. He could cook in the house all he wanted to. His mother wouldn't be serving any more drama. He could actually start serving out of the house full time if he wanted to. He sold a few bags to friends out of the house, but it wasn't a full-time thing.

He realized he would never sell out of the house full time. It was way too dangerous. It could never be a real spot as long as people were living there. But it could be a part-time thing, a little more than he was doing now.

He remembered he was going to call the police, and he'd come in the basement to clean it out. He could take his shit and put it in the garage, close enough to keep an eye on and far enough away to disclaim. He started up the stairs, and there was a knock on the side door. He looked at his watch. It was almost 10 o'clock. This was too early for anyone to be visiting, but it wasn't too early to be geeking. Danny eyed the door suspiciously. The knock came again.

"Who is it?" he yelled at the door.

"Yo, Danny, you serving?"

"No."

"Come on, Family, look out."

"What you looking for?"

"Just a dime."

Danny continued up the stairs, holding the box in one hand. He opened the door just enough to see through the crack. The door did not stop where Danny had intended it to. Instead, it kept coming. Danny tried to look in the doorway to see what was going on. He pushed back against the door. A foot came through the opening. The thought occurred and was gone for him to go in the basement and get his gun. It was too far away.

He braced himself against the wall. There must have been two people pushing from the other side. He wondered if someone from next door could see what was going on. There was no way for Regina and the kids to hear it. If these people got through the door, there was no telling what they would do. They could be some pipeheads looking to get high, or someone out for revenge. It could be DBs, but that wasn't likely. This was too far in a Family territory for DBs to think they could get away with this.

The foot had become a leg, then an arm. The

hand had a gun in it. Danny quickly disarmed the hand, but the gun fell down the stairs. There was still pushing at the door. Danny looked at the gun sitting on the floor at the foot of the stairs. He still wouldn't have time. Now there was most of a man through the door. Danny swung on him, hitting him three or four times before he was all the way through the door. The man was swinging on Danny. Danny ducked once and the door slammed open.

Danny pushed the man down the basement steps. Out of the corner of his eye, he could see the butt end of a shotgun about to slam into his face. He tried to step out of the way, or at least out of the direct path of the gun butt. The first blow hit him on the shoulder. The boy that Danny had pushed down the stairs was back on the landing, now with the gun in his hand. Danny hesitated as the man pointed the gun at him. This time out of the corner of his eye he could see the butt of the shotgun coming again. He did not move. His eyes shifted to a third man standing slightly behind the man with the shotgun. The butt of the shotgun slammed into his face.

Danny had a buzz in his head as he returned to consciousness. He was lying on the floor at the bottom of the stairs. It took him a moment to get his bearings. As he mentally collected himself, he let his hand roam over his chest to see if he was shot. There was no liquid anywhere.

He breathed a sigh of relief then felt his face. There was a sizable lump under his right eye. There was also a scrape on his face, but it wasn't bleeding. In the relative darkness, he could see someone had ransacked his room. The shoebox that held his stash was empty on the floor, his mattress was off of his bed, and the drawers in the dresser had been emptied. His clothes were no longer hanging up.

He slowly got up and walked across the floor. He straightened the mattress and lay across the bed. He could leave the rest for later. Someone was calling him. It sounded like it was so far away it was from next door. It was his sister, standing at the top of the stairs.

"You gonna call the police about Mama?"

"What?"

Regina turned on the light. "Are you still going to call the police about Mama?" She was coming down the stairs.

"What about Mama?"

"She's dead."

"What?"

Now she was at the bottom of the steps.

"What the hell happened here?"

"Ain't nothing happened."

"What happened to your face? What the hell you been down here doing?"

"Bump all that. What about Mama?"

"Mama died and you were supposed to be calling the police about it. Forget it. I'll do it myself. I done already called Anthony and Reginald. I thought you called the police an hour ago."

"An hour ago."

"Yeah, you was supposed to do something and call the police."

Danny sat up. His head hurt real bad. "Yeah, I remember now. Why don't you go on ahead and call them? I just need to lie down for a little while, then I'll take care of all of this shit."

Regina started walking up the steps. She looked at the open door at the landing and turned around. "You better leave that shit alone before you get deadened. We can't afford to lose anyone else in this family. Mama dead, Grandma dead, and our father been dead so long I don't even remember what he looked like."

"Chill out with that shit. Mama ain't even cold yet and you starting to sound like her already," he said.

"I got children in this house. If you want to get yourself killed, then find someplace else to do it." Regina turned around and went up the steps. She closed the side door, and went into the kitchen to call the police. She explained that she had a dead body in the house. The dispatcher was going to send an ambulance. Regina waited in front of the house for the ambulance. It came and she showed them where the body was. The children watched silently as the EMTs took their grandmother's body out of the house.

Anthony was coming down the block as the ambulance pulled away. He ran up the front stairs into the house, where Regina was standing in the doorway.

"Well, there she went," Regina said sullenly.

"I'm really sorry. She was like my mother too."

"Yeah. She was your mother too."

"In a bottom line kind of way, she was. Where Danny?"

"His stupid ass is in the basement."

"I'll talk to you later. How are the kids?"

"They'll be okay," she said as Anthony walked by.

Heading to the basement, Anthony hesitated at the bottom step when he saw the room. "What the fuck happened down here?" he asked.

Danny rolled over and looked at him. "I got bum rushed."

"When did this happen?"

"Earlier today. You know Ma died."

"Yeah, they just took her body away."

"Did they say what it was that killed her?"

"They didn't say anything to me. I was coming up the block when they was pulling off."

Danny sat up in the bed. "That straightener probably killed her. She was drunk off her ass last night."

Anthony sat on the bed. "Why you wanna talk about her like that? You don't know what it was."

"You know she got fired yesterday. She probably got fired for being drunk on the job."

"Danny, why you trippin'? You going through some of that psychotic shit they be talking about on them talk shows?"

"Man, I'm telling you, all that drink killed her."

Anthony looked at Danny in contempt. "Man, life killed her. Dying is something you get from living. So, what you gonna do about this shit that happened to you? You gonna go out and start some dumb shit that won't end until you dead?"

Danny got out of the bed and looked around the mess in his room for some cigarettes. He found some and lit one. "Yeah, man, that's what I'm gonna do. I'm gonna deaden somebody."

"Man, why don't you take the fact that you still alive as a sign to get out of this bullshit?"

"'Cause that ain't what it is. It's a sign that some motherfuckers slipped up and let me live, took my shit, and now they got to pay. Man, these motherfuckers come up in my house and took my shit, and I'm supposed to let that roll? I don't think so."

"Damn, Danny, I didn't know you was buying that bullshit wholesale."

"What bullshit?"

"All that gang bullshit about who the baddest man is. Man, that's bullshit they sell you so you don't mind dying."

"What the fuck else am I supposed to do? This is how I make my money, and this is a paper chase. Besides, this ain't nothing to do with gangs. I think I know who set this shit in motion. It was Sweets' ass, and he standing on my money. I ain't gee'n for that. It's a get back kind of world, so I'm going after what is mine. This is what I do. This is how I live my life; this is my world."

"Man, sell that bullshit to someone that don't know. You ain't got no real record, you ain't never been busted, so instead of looking for the opportunity to get out, you gonna go further into the dumb shit. Yeah, you could deaden his ass, then you go to jail, and your life from there is super fucked. Man, I'm telling you, look around. You better redirect yourself. All you got to do is get papers and you'd be straight. All you got to do is find another way to make money."

"Doing what?"

"You think about it. If I could get you into

school and you could get into some legitimate dough, would you do it, or would you stick with this dumb shit?"

"Fuck all that bullshit. You can't get me into school. You ain't got two nickels to rub together. How the fuck you gonna take care of me?"

"That ain't what I'm talking about. The question is, are you game for it? Think about it, because I'm about to get into some thick shit, and I'm gonna have the dough. You think about it."

Anthony got up and went to the stairs. Danny stepped on the cigarette he was smoking. He lay back down on his bed. Anthony looked back at Danny lying on the bed.

"You ought to go and see a doctor. You look fucked up."

"I don't need no doctor. I probably got a concussion. I don't need no doctor for that, I just need to get a nap. I'll be straight."

Anthony started up the stairs. "It's your life. Just think about what I was saying."

Danny closed his eyes. "Fuck that shit," he whispered.

Anthony went through the house and to the second floor. He stopped and looked in the kids' room. "How y'all doing in there?"

"Anthony, how did Grandma die?" DeShawn asked.

"I don't know. I really don't know."

"Did Ma kill her?"

Anthony stood in the door, not knowing what to say about that. He wanted to say yes, to tell DeShawn that they all helped to kill his Grandmother, that living like they did was enough to kill anybody and that he was surprised that any of them was still alive. The truth is a bitch.

"No, your mother did not kill her. She died, but no one killed her. If anybody killed her, it was the people at the store where she worked. Yeah, they did it."

"How did they kill her?" DeShawn asked. All three of the children were looking at him, waiting for his answer.

"They worked her 'til she died. They do that sometimes. They used to do it to slaves all the time."

Anthony backed out of the room, closed the door behind him, and went to his room. He sat on his bed, thinking about what he'd told the children. That is what happened. They worked her to death. There was no chance of health care that was cost effective. Whatever killed her, she was probably sick from it for a while, and she could still be alive if she could have had the chance to see a doctor.

Yeah, they worked her like a slave and then they fired her. Who the fuck was these people that they could make these decisions about people's lives, especially people that they don't know? These were the people that worked in an office somewhere, and they killed people they had never seen. They hid behind the idea of corporate togetherness, but they weren't together with black people. All the people that were fired were black, with a few token whites thrown in to stop any discrimination suits, like a rat in a trap that would chew its own leg off to get away. They needed to be shown what they were doing to people. Better yet, they needed to enjoy the pain that they were inflicting so freely on others.

The door opened and Reginald came in the room. "Why you tell them kids that the people at Mama's job killed her? That's not true and you know it."

"They killed her and I know it. You don't want to admit it because that would mean that they killing you too."

"Why couldn't it just have been her time to go? Why it got to be all that other stuff?" Reginald asked. "I just think it was her time to go, and no one killed her. Stop tripping. At least stop filling the children's heads up with that shit."

Reginald closed the door and left the room. Anthony started to follow him, but changed his mind. Reginald walked into his mother's room and sat on her bed. His mother had been through enough. God did her a favor to take her so soon. If only she would have turned her life around; if only she would have learned to trust God and not let so many things get to her; if only she would have been serious about her relationship with God.

Not a week ago, he was sitting right in this very same spot, wanting to pray with her or for her or something, and now there was nothing left to pray for. The end is always nearer than we like to believe. Reginald didn't want to die alone like his mother did. Even worse than dying alone was the fact that so few people would miss her. She never got to share with the world who she was. She never got to find out who she was.

Reginald had no doubts about who he was. He

was a child of God. He wanted to be sure that people would miss him because he had helped them. Sitting on his mother's bed, he decided it was time to enter into the ministry of the God he served.

With that behind him, he knew there was no reason to stay in the house any longer. After his mother was buried, he would leave. It would be the best way for him to get on with his life. He walked to the door, looked back on the bed, and wondered why he wasn't crying. He should be mourning. He figured it had not hit him yet. He hadn't really accepted the fact that she was not going to be there anymore. Maybe she was never there—at least she was never where he was.

Downstairs, the neighbors and the few friends that she did have were starting to drop by with their sympathies. Regina sat in what was once their mother's chair. She was crying. Reginald watched her from the top of the stairs. That was the way it always was. The one that raised the most hell with his mother when she was alive was the one that would do all the hollering and screaming when she died.

As soon as he hit the bottom step, he was being hugged. Soon enough, his mother's cousins would be there going through her bedroom, looking for things that they could steal. Reginald walked over to the chair where Regina sat. She looked up at him, so pitiful, like a wet, homeless kitten. Reginald reached down and hugged her. He found himself holding her like she was the last remnant of his mother. She was. Dorothy was dead.

Reginald was almost sitting in the chair with her. He was crying now. Dorothy was dead. He hadn't really needed her, but what was Regina going to do?

"You'll be fine," he told her.

"Where's Danny?" he asked when he stood up.

"He's 'sleep in the basement. He got beat up or something earlier today."

"What happened?"

"I don't know, but whatever it was happened in the basement."

Reginald went into the kitchen. Regina sat in the chair, still crying, occasionally looking out the front window. She wondered what her children were doing. She knew they were upstairs, probably looking at television. They were going to need new clothes for the funeral, another thing that she would have to find a way to take care of.

She didn't want to think that far ahead, but the questions were there. What was she going to do? Her mother had an insurance policy, but whatever that was would have to be split three or four ways, and it wouldn't last long. She would have to find a job. Her children would all be in school full time this year, so she would have more time available to work. Someone came in the front door, and she put questions of the future out of her mind. The present was enough of a problem to deal with.

Uncle Dave and Aunt Rose came in the house with a few of her mother's cousins. They were vultures. They came over and hugged her, then went into the kitchen and talked with Reginald. She knew they were going upstairs next. She hadn't even gone through her mother's things yet. She took a tissue and wiped her face. She was going to have to go upstairs before they did.

She got up and went up the stairs, checking in the children's room. Laneka and Jaleel were watching television. The bathroom door was closed. DeShawn was probably in there. She knocked on the door to Reginald and Anthony's room.

"Come in."

She walked in the room, Anthony was sitting on the bed looking out the window. "How you taking it?" Anthony asked.

"I'll get better. How you doing?"

"Me? I'm used to dead parents. I'll be fine."

"Aunt Rose is downstairs, and she got two of her daughters with her."

"You better get in there before they do."

"Yeah, I know. Well, I was just wondering how you was doing. I suppose that Reginald can't hold them off much longer."

"You want me to come in there with you?"

"Would you?"

"Yeah, I ain't doing nothing else."

Anthony joined Regina and they went down the hall. They both hesitated at Dorothy's door. Finally, Anthony opened it and they went in the room. DeShawn was sitting on his grandmother's bed.

"Mama, Anthony said that the people at Grandma's job killed her. He said they do it all the time, especially to slaves."

Regina looked at Anthony. He shrugged. "I didn't want him thinking you did it."

Regina went and sat on the bed next to DeShawn. She put her arms around him. He easily leaned in to her.

"Mama, was Grandma a slave?"

"No, DeShawn, she wasn't a slave."

"Then why did they kill her?"

"They didn't know no better. It was a mistake they made."

"Like when they shoot a little kid on a drive-by?"

She pulled him close to her, squeezing him a little. "Yeah, it was just like that."

chapter eleven

Reginald lay in the bed watching the sun rise over the lake. Yesterday seemed like a bad dream acted out in slow motion, from the time his sister had called him at work, until he was asleep in bed. Maybe it would be different when he saw her body. He remembered sitting on her bed, making up his mind to go into the ministry. He would tell the pastor today.

Hopefully today would be easier to go through than yesterday. He wondered if he should go to services at all, but he knew there was nothing to wonder about. That was what he did. Other people went out, got drunk, and partied. He did that too, but he lived to go to church on Sunday morning. It would help relax him. Besides, there would be the support of the people that he knew in the choir and the congregation.

He thought about what Anthony told De-Shawn. According to Anthony, white men did all of the killing there was to do. One way or another, white men had their hand in every death that occurred in America. Maybe there was some truth in what Anthony said, maybe it was her job, but even that was a choice she made. Reginald comforted himself with the idea that God took her before life got worse for her. Anthony could never accept that it was simply her time to go, something that had been formed before she was. Predestination was something that Anthony knew nothing about, unless it had something to do with the white man. Reginald tried to blink Anthony's conspiracy theory out of his mind, because it had to be her time. If it wasn't, how could she be dead?

After all that, the vultures descended. Actually, they couldn't get in the room because Anthony wouldn't let them. They were not related to Anthony and he knew it. He had no reason to be nice to them. He told Aunt Rose that Regina and DeShawn were having a talk inside the room and they were not to be disturbed. He actually shooed them away from the room, back downstairs into the living room.

Most of the people that came by were drinking. Reginald was amazed at how people liked to share the miseries of life, and even more, how they got miserable sharing them. They did the same thing they always did; they got drunk and started fighting over something.

It was the fight, or at least the almost fight that made Reginald decide to stay over at Dennis' apartment. Reginald knew he would have to break the habit of calling it Dennis' apartment. This would be his home soon enough. His mother was dead, and there was no reason to stay on at Eberhart any longer.

Reginald was lying on his back, looking at the ceiling in his room. He turned on his side and looked at the clock. If he didn't hurry, he would be late for services, having already missed Sunday school. He got up washed and dressed. The thought occurred to him to call his mother and see if she wanted to go to church. He corrected himself, thinking that maybe he should ask Regina if she wanted to take the children to church. He called and asked her, but she wasn't interested. He decided not to press it further.

He checked himself in the mirror, changed his tie and left the apartment, arriving at the church not long after Sunday school let out. There were people milling about in the front of the church and in the parking lot. He knew that there would be the customary onrush of sympathy-givers. He had been one more than once, and he would be again.

As soon as he parked in the lot, they saw him. When he got out of the car, they approached. He was going to let them offer their sympathies, and he was going to be graceful doing it. He stood in the parking lot for ten minutes, taking hugs and feelings from well wishers and people offering various assistance to him to help him get through this period of mourning.

Except for the announcement of his mother's death, church was pretty much a repeat of last Sunday's service. During the service, he got looks of pity from everyone in the congregation. When he sang, the whole congregation was in tears. It made him feel a little better to sing. It was only one song, but Reginald made the most out of it.

When the service was over, Reginald told the pastor there was something he wanted to talk about in the privacy of his office. Reginald went to the church office and talked with the secretary about having his mother's funeral at the church. After all the arrangements were made, he went to the pastor's office.

Reginald knocked on the door and entered when the pastor called for him to come in. He sat across the big oak desk from the pastor.

"Reginald, I'm really sorry about your mother, if there's anything that I can do, you let me know."

"Thank you, Reverend Warden. If I need anything then I will let you know. I came here to talk about something altogether different." Reginald took a deep breath.

"Yesterday after my mother had passed, I made a decision to do something I've been thinking about for a long time. I've decided to accept my call into the ministry."

"Reginald, you're going through some powerful changes right now. Are you sure about this? I mean this is a big step that you are taking."

Reginald shifted in his chair. "I would have liked my mother to have seen me do this, but she can't, and I really don't know why I've waited this long. I just want to find out what I have to do."

The pastor stood up. "Well, I don't think you will have a problem. I do want you to do some studying to prepare yourself. You will be presented to a panel of pastors that belong to our convention, and they will make the determination. Then you give your installation sermon. Are you sure about this?"

"Yes, Pastor, I'm sure as I have ever been about anything in my life," Reginald said.

The pastor reached across the desk and shook Reginald's hand. Then he came around the desk, hugged him, and kissed Reginald on the cheek. "I really feel good about this. I think you will make a fine preacher."

There was a knock on the door and they let each other go. The pastor called for the person to enter, and his new personal secretary came in, obviously displeased at Reginald's presence. Reginald excused himself and left the office. He went into the parking lot, where he was surprised to see that Tremont and his grandmother were waiting for him by the car. Edward and Mark were there also. Tremont expressed his sympathy, and so did his grandmother. Reginald asked them if they wanted a ride home, and they accepted.

Edward asked Reginald if he was going to be at Dennis' that afternoon. Reginald said he might make it there, depending on how things were at his mother's house. Edward and Mark left. Reginald got in the car and took Tremont and his grandmother home. There was no conversation in the car, just the church service on the radio.

He dropped them off and decided to go on to his mother's house. There would probably be a bunch of relatives and friends there. When he turned the corner, he knew that his guess was right. There were too many cars, and people were spilling out of the front door and all over the porch.

Reginald walked up to the house, took a deep

breath and went in. He was greeted with hugs and the sympathy of all the people standing around. Danny was nowhere in sight, but then Reginald didn't expect him to be. As Reginald walked through the house, he noticed that everybody was drinking. He started to go in the basement to look for Danny, but he was intercepted by one of his mother's old, drunk friends.

As soon as he got away from the woman's reeking breath, he wondered if people had that same impression of his mother. He knew he'd had that impression about her, because there had been more than one occasion when he'd run into his mother after she had started drinking and she wore out both his patience and his manners.

There were times that she was drunk, she would go from rambling to ranting and raving. She would start talking about how no one ever took care of her, and how she had to take care of everybody. She fed everybody—she fed her children, she fed other people's children, she fed everybody there was to feed, and she was tired of it. Whenever she got off in that direction, it was best to leave the room.

On those nights, and there were lots of them, she drank until she passed out. If she didn't pass out in the chair downstairs, she would come upstairs to drink some more. If she was upstairs and got into one of those moods, she could curse out everybody all night long, even though the closest person to her was either down the hall or downstairs, or maybe not in the house at all.

Sometimes she was content to have a few beers. She would be all right then, but if a bottle of vodka appeared, trouble was sure to follow. The liquor had definitely become a problem in her life, especially after her mother died. But she never let it stop her from getting to work, and it was at its worst when she didn't have to work the next day. She worked as much as she was allowed to, between and around layoffs.

To commemorate her death, everybody stood around drinking. They would probably be this way until she was buried. Reginald went upstairs to check on the children. They were not in their room. He looked in Regina's room, and there was no one in there. Then he went to his mother's room.

Regina and Aunt Rose were in there going through Dorothy's things. At least this time, Aunt Rose didn't have her two junior vultures with her.

"Where the kids at?" he asked.

Regina looked up. "They staying with Jaleel's grandmother. I thought it would be good for them to get away from the house until Ma was buried."

"Hi, baby," Aunt Rose said, tottering toward him.

She was drunk, and Regina was drinking too. "Hi, Aunt Rose," he said, leaning over to hug her.

When he straightened up, he looked back at Regina. "Where's Danny and Anthony?"

Regina continued to go through the drawers. "They in the basement or the backyard. They somewhere around here."

Reginald turned around. "Where you going?" Regina asked him.

"I'll be back a little later. I just got to get out of the house for a while."

James whispered back, loud enough for Reginald to hear.

"Oh, James, don't bother me. I'm glad to see all of you. I wasn't expecting it, but I am glad to see you," Reginald said.

Edward came up to Reginald. "I called everybody. I thought you could use a little cheering up. I thought you might be back here, so I invited them."

Reginald hugged Edward. "You were right."

As soon as he let Edward go, there was another to hug him, then another. They all expressed their sympathies. By the time the last one hugged Reginald, everybody in the room was crying, and someone had started singing. The others joined in, and the song went for about twenty minutes before they let it stop.

When the song ended, Reginald grabbed the bottle of wine, held it up, and said, "You all want some wine?"

They nodded and said "Yes."

He smiled. "Well then, y'all better go and get you some, 'cause this is mine."

The mood lightened up, someone left to go and get some chicken and other things for dinner. They were also going to pick up some more wine and some beer. Reginald was taken care of like a royal figure. Someone brought him a plate with his dinner; someone else kept his wineglass full.

His friends found a seat wherever they could in the small living room—on a chair, the couch, or on the lap of another guest. The conversation naturally turned to church gossip.

"Have you seen that boy your pastor been laying hands on of late?" James asked. Everyone from Gethsemane immediately knew he was talking about Marcus, the pastor's newest personal secretary.

Edward immediately jumped to the pastor's defense. "If Warden ain't sleeping with you, you don't know who he sleeping with. Why you got to be starting rumors and spreading malicious gossip?"

"Oh, Edward, hush," James started. "You know your beloved pastor done slept with every sissy in his church, and a lot of sissies that ain't. They don't call him the queen of Chicago for nothing. Every time the man preaches, he be digging for someone, slipping those little messages that certain people really understand."

Someone in the room agreed with him. "He know he be digging. All that shit he talks about returning in kind, he know he digging. He probably dug up that boy he got now."

Edward again defended the pastor. "He didn't have to dig him. That boy be all over the pastor. I guess he think the pastor gonna do something for him."

James continued. "He know he better watch himself, or he gonna wind up just like that preacher on the west side, or one of them priests that be playing with them young boys or something."

Reginald frowned. "Yeah, one of these days that is going to back up on him. I could see if he was just going to settle down with one friend, but he going through them like water."

"I'm telling you that Marcus has been all over the pastor since he joined the church." Edward said.

"Marcus is a little pain in the ass. Today when I went to see the pastor to announce my plans to enter the ministry, Marcus all but busted the door down to find out what we were doing in the pastor's office."

James clapped his hands. "Another man of God. Tell me, Reggie, when you got the call to the ministry, was it on AT&T, MCI, or Sprint? Just tell me, is God on the Friends and Family plan?"

"Be quiet, James. You just mad because won't nobody call you at all," Reginald said.

Everyone was glad that Reginald decided to become a minister, especially Edward. They talked for about two more hours before some of them had to get back to their various churches. The members of Gethsemane had to get ready to go and sing at the broadcast tonight. They all hugged Reginald again with promises that they would be stopping by his home all this week.

After they left, Dennis said he would clean up the mess, and Reginald decided it was time to return to his mother's house. Reginald turned up the church broadcast on the drive over there. He was glad that he'd had something to drink, but he was far from being drunk. Hopefully, it would make the people in the house easier to get along with.

The sun was about to set and the streetlights were popping on as he pulled up on his block. The neighbors were sitting on their front porch, much like they always did as soon as it got hot enough. Their kids were spilling off the porch, through the front yard and onto the street. The front door to the house was wide open. He looked around at the people in the house. There were some people he had not seen earlier, so he had to go through the whole hugging and handshaking thing again.

Reginald made his way through the house and into the kitchen. Danny and Anthony were sitting at the table with a plate of food and a can of beer in front of each of them.

"So, do you all want to know the funeral arrangements?"

Anthony took a sip of beer. "What is there about them to know?"

Reginald sat in what was remaining of the other chair. "Well, the funeral and the wake will be at the church on Wednesday, and the burial will be Thursday morning. I hope that you all don't have any thing to do on Wednesday evening around 7 o'clock."

Danny looked at Reginald. "Don't go there, Reginald. Don't start no shit."

"Anyway, it's going to be at the church. It won't cost us no money that way, and that is the church that Mama used to go to."

Reginald watched Anthony because he knew Anthony was going to say something. Anthony didn't disappoint him. He stopped chewing and took a swig of beer. "You know, that is a good thing. Probably the only thing the church is good for, burying dead people."

"Anthony, do us all a favor and don't start that jumping on the church stuff tonight," Reginald said.

Anthony rolled his eyes at Reginald. "Man, fuck the church. Fuck the church and every motherfucker in the church. You ought to be having the funeral there for free. Hell, they ought to be paying for everything, as much money as Aunt Dorothy, you, and Grandma put into that church. They ought to be giving you some money back."

Danny looked at Reginald and let loose one of those heinous, drug-filled giggles that bothered Reginald ever since he was teenager. It was a giggle that let Reginald know he was on the wrong end of a joke, and that he was a definite minority at the table. Things like this had been happening for a long time, often at the same table.

Anthony and Danny had been teasing him and lying on him ever since they were little boys. They never went at him one-on-one, but they would always gang up on him. When they would let him tag along on their adventures, he often wound up in more trouble than they did. He couldn't run as fast, so he was the one that was always getting caught. Then they would lie and say they weren't there.

Once, when he was six, they told Reginald that they were all going to play hooky from school. He did, they didn't. When there was no way he could explain the absence on his report card, his mother gave him a whipping with an extension cord. His grandmother tried to defend him, but his mother told him that he shouldn't have listened to Anthony and Danny.

They would go to what they called the clubhouse, which was a garage two blocks over, where they would hide the things they'd stolen or found. That garage was where Reginald had his sexual initiation. Anthony and Danny had convinced two of the girls from next door to come there. They brought Reginald, only to offer him sloppy seconds after they finished with each of the girls.

Reginald wound up having to wait three days until he convinced a girl to go there on his own. In the meantime, they constantly teased him, and until the girl admitted that the act actually occurred, they would call him a punk, saying that he was scared of girls.

The whole sex thing happened when Reginald was ten and Danny and Anthony were thirteen. After that, Anthony started getting into more trouble at school, then with the police. Danny began running with older boys in the neighborhood and getting high. That was when Reginald decided he wanted to be a preacher, and he started paying attention to what happened in church.

His grandmother was always encouraging him by telling him that he would become a great man of the Word. She would defend him from them and his mother whenever she thought it was necessary. Then she died. His mother neither encouraged nor discouraged his getting into the Bible. It was then that the pastor of the church took Reginald under his wing.

"Fuck the church." The words rang in his mind after Anthony said it.

"Fuck you, Anthony. You always talking that crazy shit, as if what you thought made a damn bit of difference in the world. The church has accomplished more than you ever will, you and your off-the-wall ass."

Anthony filled his fork with macaroni and cheese. He chewed and swallowed it, then looked at Reginald with one of those looks that Reginald had come to hate. His face was drawn up tight and serious. Anthony was about to launch into his usual attack on the church. It would be all the things that Reginald had heard him say a thousand time before: they don't give anything back to the community, they live off of old ladies, they deny people real relationships with each other and the God they say they served. Reginald chose to go to church. Why couldn't Anthony just accept?

"Reginald," Anthony began, "why you so quick to defend the church after what they did to you?"

Reginald was caught off guard. It took him some time to respond. "The church ain't done nothing to me. Nothing to hurt me anyway."

Anthony took his plate to the trashcan next to the sink. After he scraped the remnants into the garbage, he turned to Reginald. "Just answer me one question and I'll leave the shit alone."

Reginald held his ground. "What?"

Anthony crossed the floor, stopped in front of Reginald, and picked up his glass of beer off of the table. He leaned down in Reginald's face, but he spoke loud enough for Danny to hear. "Who fucked you first, the pastor or the minister of music?"

Reginald was stunned into silence. Danny was laughing out loud. Anthony held his smiling face close to Reginald's so he could watch the reaction on his face.

At first Reginald wanted to tell him to mind his own business, but that was too weak of a statement. The implications appeared to be that he could finally free himself from them with a declaration of some sort. The phrase "I'm gay and I'm proud" came to mind, but somehow it didn't fit the situation.

Danny was standing up laughing now. Reginald watched him. He had been sitting in mother's chair. Reginald wanted to tell, but there was no one to tell. There was no one to come to his defense here, especially if he didn't do it himself.

Anthony straightened up. "Why you sitting there with your mouth open? Oh, maybe you don't remember. Or could it have been both of them pulling a train on you 'n shit?"

Reginald got his bearings. "Why you fucking with me? What have I done to you that you have to come to me like this?"

Anthony bent back down into his face. "Somebody needs to do something with you. Be a man, Reggie. Be a fucking man."

Reginald scooted his chair back until he was out from under Anthony. "What the fuck is up with you? I am a man. I'm more of a man than you are. I am not limited by sex. I ain't got to tell nobody what I do behind closed doors. When did you announce to the world that you were straight, or that you don't have good sense?"

Reginald could feel his heart pounding. He stood up and looked down on Anthony. For the first time in a long time, he could see that he was taller than Anthony. He knew the way he stood up, the words he spoke could easily be taken as a threat. Deep in his heart, he meant it as a threat, a last act before fight or flight, and he was in no mood to run.

"I am the way I am because that is the way I

want to be. Or do I need permission to live my life the way I want to from you or the white man?"

Danny stepped back. "Doom, doom, goddamnit!"

Reginald turned to Danny. "Why don't you stop acting like a child? I mean we're all supposed to be adults here, or are you automatically ruled out because you don't do nothing but act like a child?"

Danny closed in on Reginald. "Oh, man, how you gonna act, coming at me like that? Talking that dumb shit."

Reginald straightened his back. "I'm talking about the way you live your whole life. You still messing around in gangs; with people that will hit you in the face with a brick or a stick, or whatever they hit you with. At least Anthony got a job."

Danny stopped in his tracks.

"Yo, motherfucker, I get my money. I got my dough rolling and in a proper manner. I make more money in a day than you make in a week selling dishes. My paper is straight, goddammit. You don't know what the fuck you talking about."

Reginald was caught up in the moment, full of himself. "Where you get your money? Drug addicts? You get money from people that are suffering, and the bad thing is you sell them the shit to make them suffer some more. But take it a little further. Where do they get their money from? They knock some old lady over the head to get five dollars to come and see you. The people that knocked you on the head took your money and went to get something to get high with. It's a vicious cycle that you got rolling, and you a big part of it."

Anthony sat back down. "Gee, Reggie, I don't

know. Sounds just like a church to me. Either way it's some old lady coming up off the dough."

Reginald returned his attack to Anthony. "Like you doing something to help people, writing nonsense on the wall. That ain't did nobody no good. It just got your dumb ass thrown in jail for three months. You talk all that mess about the black man this and the black man that. What kind of black man are you? You ain't accomplished a damn thing."

Anthony stayed in his seat. "Motherfucker, you act like the church has accomplished a damn thing, or someone in the church has done something. They ain't done shit. It's still a bunch of poor ass-niggas out there trying to make ends meet. That is unless they one of them fat-ass preachers that go about pimping everybody they get they hands on. They done sucked a whole nation of people into believing that life ain't shit but a pain, so you don't have to do shit but suffer while you here. They got people believing that they can't be responsible for their own life. They got to come and get them some Jesus. Jesus this, Jesus that, ask Jesus, call Jesus, get to know Jesus. Then they sell some Jesus to your dumb ass in a one-week supply, so you can come back next week and get a shitload of Jesus to go home and fuck up your family with. I don't know how you can sit there and talk about what Danny does. You just up there helping the pimp deal dime bags of Jesus dope 'n shit."

"See, Anthony, it would take somebody like you to say some stupid shit like that, comparing the Lord to a drug. If I had to be addicted to something, I'd rather be addicted to Jesus. That is what you need. You need to get the Lord in your life so you can get your act together and stay out of jail."

Anthony got up and pointed his finger at Reginald. "See, motherfucker, that is where you wrong. I know God. I know all about God, but it ain't the God you serve. It is a whole different thing. Where you say submit, my God says challenge. Where you say follow, my God says go, and where you say turn the other cheek, my God says kick his motherfucking ass. My God ain't no punk like your God is. If we was still waiting for motherfuckers in the church to do something, we'd still be picking fucking cotton in Mississippi. The only reason the church ever made a move is to get money. All that civil rights bullshit was just because the motherfuckers in the church wasn't getting paid like they knew they could. When they got paid, they shut the fuck up. If they was serious about all this civil rights shit, why is the black community as fucked up as it is now, and only getting worse?"

Danny saw his chance and jumped in. "And it ain't like them church pimps ain't bringing their money to me, because they are. I see it all. I see preachers and prostitutes, both of them on a Sunday afternoon. I see old-ass broads, I see young bitches, and I see gay motherfuckers too. I see friends of yours come through. So don't be trying to sell me that Jesus shit, 'cause it don't work. It don't work like rock work."

Reginald returned his attention to Danny. "Yeah, you know how that rock shit works, too, don't you? 'Cause it be working on you. I bet you ain't went one day in two weeks without getting high.

Have you? And how many friends would you have if you weren't dealing? Probably none."

Danny leaned back in his chair. "How many friends would your monkey ass have if you weren't sleeping with them? See, Reginald, your ass ain't in no position to be talking about nobody as fucked up as you are. You be talking all that Christian shit. I don't know the Bible that well, but I do know it say you ain't supposed to be having sex with other men 'n shit. But that ain't the most fucked up part of it. What's fucked up is that you tried to hide the shit. Trying to play us like we Boo-Boo the Fool. How fucking stupid do you think we are?"

Reginald rolled his eyes "You don't really want to know the answer to that, do you?"

Anthony took his seat. "See, there you go with that shit again, thinking you better than someone else. Motherfucker, you want to be all siditty 'n shit, but bottom line, you ain't better than nobody else. Bottom line, Reginald, you ain't shit, like we ain't shit. You just a different flavor of shit, so fuck you and your church-going, monkey ass. Fuck you."

Reginald was not ready to relent. "See, it's not like that at all. You all might think that I think like that, but I don't. Y'all might think I'm better than you are, but all I am is different than you are. I know how to stick with things no matter how rough it gets. Why didn't you finish high school, Anthony? I'm doing my thing and you ain't. You ain't doing nothing but stupid shit. You ain't never done nothing but stupid shit. Fuck you and your white-man-holding-you-back, fucking-with-the-police, stupid, going-nowhere ass. Fuck you."

Danny went to the refrigerator and got another beer. He returned to his chair and sat down, "Man, Reginald, you fucked up in the head. You really need to take a look at yourself. I know what I do is illegal, but that whole church thing is a scam and you know it. Every Sunday they up there taking in tall money, but they don't be setting it out to the people they get it from. They bring it to me or they throw it somewhere else in a bad habit. Lately it's all been going to lawyers. Every time you turn around there's some shit on the news about some priest or preacher fucking around with some young boys 'n shit. As soon as some shit like that happens, the whole goddamn church be ready to stand behind him and say what a man of God he is, and how he is such a big help to the community. The trip part of it is that some of the people in the church know he be doing it, and they still be on his side. You motherfuckers in the church talk all that bullshit about righteousness, but you won't stand for what is really right."

Anthony chimed in. "And to make matters worse, every Sunday the preacher pimp be up there in the pulpit, screaming at the top of his fucking lungs about how you shouldn't get high, and you shouldn't be fucking so-and-so, and all that other shit you shouldn't be doing. But they ain't got shit to say about the real problems in life. They ain't got nothing to say about minimum wage, or how fucked up it is for somebody to do what Woolworth's did to Aunt Dorothy. You never hear them talking shit about that. Is that how you gonna be, Reggie? Are you gonna be a punk-ass preacher pimp like the rest of them, instead of real and true to what you say you believe? Yeah, you gonna be just another gump-ass preacher pimp. Good fucking luck to you."

Reginald sat back down at the table. "Oh, I guess you gonna be some kind of hero, Anthony. You ain't going nowhere. You ain't got the attitude to be anything. All you ever want to do is fight—fight this and fight that. All that fighting you done ain't accomplished a damn thing. Dr. King wasn't about all that violence, and he was able to accomplish things."

Anthony shot back, "Accomplished what? The passage of a civil rights bill that ultimately didn't mean a damn thing. Take a fucking look around, Reginald. Look at this shit we living in. This is what Dr. King accomplished. Or are you gonna give me all that shit about what he was gonna do, but he got killed? If the shit hadn't been such a secret then anybody could have done it, but the fine church leaders always got to keep secrets because they think y'all ain't nothing but a bunch of dumb-ass suckers to follow them around in the first place. King ain't changed a damn thing, not on this block, not in this city. He ain't done shit, and I'm tired of hearing about him. You'd think the man was Jesus Christ."

Danny jumped in, "And you know he right, Reginald. King might have helped some people, but a lot of other people are a lot worse off. And all that dumb-ass church shit got a lot to do with it."

Anthony pointed at Reginald. "The most fucked up thing about the church is that they won't admit they fucked up. They just keep on running for Jesus, but they running in the wrong direction. They reason for being that way is that they have always been that way. Fuck the church and get the fuck out of my face talking about them."

Regina walked in to the kitchen just as Anthony finished speaking. Before Reginald could answer Anthony's accusations, Regina jumped in. "Why the hell y'all in here getting loud 'n shit? Mama just died, can't y'all pretend to get along until she buried? I mean we got people coming over to the house to show they respect and you all in here hollering at each other."

Danny looked at Reginald. "Well, you better put Reginald ass in check. Motherfucker come in here and started going off 'n shit. I was about to snap all over his ass and get him back in line."

Anthony chimed in. "Yeah, we was sitting in here all chill 'n shit and this motherfucker come in here talking that bullshit."

Reginald stood and looked down at them. They were sitting much like they were when he came in the room. "See, there y'all go acting like children. What is Regina gonna do? Is she going to put me on punishment, or is she gonna take me upstairs and beat my ass?"

"She ain't gonna have to take you upstairs. I'll beat your faggot ass right here and now," Anthony said, standing up.

Regina stepped in between him and Reginald. "Anthony, sit your ass down. If there'll be any ass kicked up in here, I'll be the one doing the kicking." She pushed Anthony back into his seat, but Reginald was closing the distance between him and Anthony this time.

"Let him go. If he wants to kick my ass then let

him go for it. I ain't scared of his ass." Reginald was reaching at Anthony over Regina's shoulder. "Come with it, motherfucker. It'll be a fight. I'm tired of him talking shit."

Danny stood up. Regina shot him a glance that put him back in his seat. She looked just like his mother, and the words coming out of her mouth sounded just like his mother. "Reginald, find your ass a chair and sit down. I wasn't bullshitting. There ain't gonna be no fighting in here tonight unless I'm doing it." She pushed Reginald back. He thought about hitting her.

"Regina, don't ever push me again. I am not your child. You put your hands on me again, we'll be fighting."

Regina looked up at him. "We ain't got to wait that long. We can go at it right goddamn now. I don't know what the fuck has been going on in here, but you better put that shit in check. I ain't the one."

Anthony stood back up. "Yeah, motherfucker, fighting with Regina is your best bet. I'll fuck you up."

Reginald headed toward the back door. "Come on, let's take this shit outside. I'm sick of your ass. Come on, let's go."

He went out the back door. Anthony followed, until Regina stepped in his way.

"Anthony, don't start no shit. He just upset cause Mama died. I know he tripping, but give him a break. You know you can beat him."

Anthony looked down at her. "You know that, and I know that, but I think I'm going to have to show him."

Regina turned to Danny. "Don't let them fight."

It was his mother's voice and her face again. This time Danny just sat there. "If they want to fight, that's their thing. I ain't got nothing to do with it."

In the backyard, Reginald waited for Anthony. He stood there wondering if the grace of God would get him through this in one piece. What was he doing? Anthony had been fighting all his life. Reginald never had to fight. Thanks to the reputations of both Anthony and Danny preceding him in school, no one ever challenged him to a fight.

Anthony slammed the back door shut. "What you talking about now, you punk motherfucker? How you gonna act?"

Anthony jumped over the back rail to the ground in front of Reginald. Regina came bursting through the back door as soon as Anthony hit the ground. She ran down the steps and stood between them, facing Anthony. "Don't start this shit, Anthony. Y'all ain't gonna do this."

Anthony reached over her and shoved Reginald. Reginald stood his ground and shoved him back. Regina didn't wait for any more licks to pass. She swung full on Anthony. He was caught by surprise. Before he realized it, he had hit her back, and she was lying on the ground. Reginald jumped over her and slugged Anthony. The hit knocked Anthony backward, and he fell against the porch railing. Reginald pressed his advantage. He swung on him again. This time it was a full swing, like in one of those cowboy movies. Unlike a movie, it didn't connect.

Anthony blocked the punch and caught Reginald in the mouth with a jab. Reginald took a step back and threw a jab. He hit Anthony in the chest, which only slowed Anthony down. Anthony caught Reginald under the eye with another jab. Reginald pulled back his fist like he was cocking for a punch. Anthony moved his arm to block. Reginald kicked him in the groin.

"You little bitch!" Anthony cried out as he doubled over in pain.

Reginald felt himself being pulled backward. Regina had gotten up and was yanking him out of the way so she could get to Anthony. When she saw him rolling on the ground in pain, she let out a chuckle. "That's what your ass gets."

Danny was standing on the porch looking down at Anthony. Reginald was standing behind Regina, who was still laughing at Anthony. Anthony began to get off the ground. He looked up to Danny. "Man, why don't you hand me my brew?"

Danny smiled down at Anthony. "What, ain't you gonna finish kicking Reginald's ass?"

Regina interrupted. "He better worry about me kicking his ass. He knocked me down."

Reginald felt like he was left out of a joke. He watched as Anthony walked back up the stairs to the porch.

Anthony looked at him. "Man, I ain't gonna fuck with you, but it's about time you stood up for yourself and that bullshit you believe in. You know how you felt, like you was tired of the bullshit that I was giving you, like you could have kicked my ass, even though you know you can't. That's how I feel all the time, about everything.

Now, if you could take that and bottle it, you'd be straight. Or you'd be gay, or whatever the hell you are."

Reginald was still looking confused. "So, you was just fucking with me, seeing how far you could push me?"

"I guess you could look at it that way. It's like this— the shit I believe, I believe, no matter what anyone else thinks about it. Danny's ready to die for what he is doing. It ain't about what you believe; it's about what you are willing to do for it."

Regina watched Danny coming out of the door with the beer. "Well, he better believe that shit somewhere else, so if he gets his ass killed, it will just be his ass."

Danny looked down at her as he handed the beer to Anthony. "What the fuck are you talking about?"

"I'm talking about you," she shouted back

"What about me?" Danny asked, holding the porch railing.

"You dealing that shit."

"What about it?"

"Don't be doing it in the house, 'cause I ain't gonna have my babies on the news. One of my children get shot while somebody trying to shoot your ass, you better put that shit in check."

"No. You better put that shit in check."

Reginald started walking toward the porch, "Danny, you shouldn't be bringing that shit in the house."

"Motherfucker, you don't even be in the house, so you ain't got shit to say about it."

"Don't be gone all day. We got a bunch of people coming over."

Reginald went down the steps and out the front door without having to hug anyone. He got in his car and drove off. He decided that he was going to the apartment. He stopped and got a bottle of white zinfandel, regretting that he didn't get anything to eat while he was at the house. Maybe Dennis would have cooked something. If nothing else, there were a hundred places to get something to eat all over the neighborhood, no matter which one he was in.

To his delight, there was a wind coming off the lake that should have kept the apartment nice and cool. He was going to go in, get something to eat, sit down and watch a baseball game. After that he could go deal with the drunks that were populating his mother's house.

He opened the door to the apartment. Instead of the peace and quiet he expected, he heard voices coming from the front room. The first voice he could immediately distinguish was that of a friend named James. His voice was deep and very feminine.

Reginald walked the hall to the front room. "Look, it's Queen Reggie," he heard James say as he entered.

There were about fifteen men sitting around in the front room. They were all friends of his. Some of them sang in the choir with Reginald, some sang in other choirs across the city. He could hear someone asking James to be quiet, telling him that Reginald's mother died yesterday.

"I'm sorry. I didn't know about his mother,"

Regina cut back in. "You be doing that shit in the house, I'm gonna drop a dime on your ass."

"You do and you won't live to tell."

Reginald stopped at the foot of the stairs. "What are you gonna do, you gonna shoot her? Or you gonna have Tiny kick her ass?"

Danny looked at him. "Shut your faggot ass up. If either you or her start interfering in my shit, I'll fuck both of your asses up."

Anthony spoke in the lull that followed. "Danny, man, think about it. There are kids up in the house. That shit that happened to you yesterday, they could have came up in the house and killed everybody. You ought to give some serious thought to giving that shit up while that is still your choice."

"Oh, Tony, now you gonna turn on me too? But hey, y'all can talk that bullshit now, but wait 'til the paper gets low, then see what you be saying. Wait 'til they ready to cut the electricity off, or you get a cutoff for the phone or the gas bill. Then what you gonna do? You gonna get the money from church, Reginald? Do you think your little bullshit-ass Mother's Day check can cover all that, Regina? Or maybe Anthony with his little bullshit job can do it."

Anthony took a swig of beer. "It ain't got to be like that. I told you I was gonna look out for you. Don't sweat the load."

"Man, Tony, fuck your plan. Fuck you, Regina, and fuck Reggie too. Fuck all y'all. Y'all and them drunk motherfuckers in the front room."

Regina took a step closer to the porch. "Danny, don't pull this shit now. Mama is dead. We ain't got nobody but each other now. It ain't like we had a whole lot before, but we got a lot less now. You say fuck us, but where you gonna go from here? Y'all better put an end to this dumb shit right now. It's time for this family to pull together, not fall apart."

Regina turned to Reginald. "What are you going to do?"

"What do you mean?"

"Are you going to move out?"

"Yeah."

"Shit, Reggie, now that Ma died, you know we ain't got enough money to do shit with. Why you gonna go now?"

"Mama left that insurance money, but I'll still help out with the bills, what I can. But I just don't want to live here anymore."

Danny started back in the house. "Yeah, he wanna live with his boyfriend."

Reginald walked up to the porch. "I just don't want to live here," he said apologetically.

Anthony, Reginald, then Regina followed Danny into the house. Danny took his seat at the table. Anthony sat back down. Reginald walked through the kitchen.

Regina stopped him as he got to the door. "You ain't leaving tonight, are you? Can't you stay as long as these people are here?"

"Yeah, I'll stay. I just want to go listen to a broadcast on the radio."

He continued through the house and upstairs. He went into his mother's room and sat on her bed; he turned on the radio on her dresser, and changed the station so he could listen to the Jordan River broadcast. It hadn't started yet, so Reginald looked to make himself comfortable. He lay back across the bed and thought about Tremont. He sat up, found the phone, and dialed the number.

Tremont answered the phone. Reginald took that as a good sign.

"So, how was your day?" Reginald asked him.

Tremont related the events of the day to him. He came home from church, his grandmother cooked dinner, and he watched television. He wanted to go to the broadcast, but there was no way for him to get there and back. Tremont was sorry to hear that Reginald's mother passed. There was a lull in the conversation. Reginald turned over on his stomach.

"Tremont, do you think I'm a holier than thou kind of person?"

"No. Why you ask something like that?"

"I don't know. I wonder if I come off that way."

They said their goodbyes and Reginald hung up the phone. The Jordan River broadcast began. He lay back, listening to the announcer. He looked around the room and noticed many things were already missing. He should have never let Aunt Rose near this room, but it was too late now.

The broadcast was the same as it always was, until the guest choir got up to sing. Edward announced that the song was dedicated to the memory of Dorothy Evans. There was a moment of silence, then the choir began singing "Beams of Heaven." Before the song was half done, Reginald was in tears. He'd lost his mother, and nothing in the world was the way he thought it was. He hadn't fooled anyone. He didn't get away with a damn thing. People knew. Anthony knew, Danny knew, Regina knew. He never told his mother, but she had to know too. There was no going back now. He was an announced homosexual man.

How was he going to be now? What was he going to do? And his mother was still dead, and she was never coming back. There was no one to run to, so he did what any Christian does in a hurting time—he prayed. God help him.

chapter twelve

Retribution. Anthony liked the sound of the word. It pushed the mission toward biblical proportions. Not the Bible according to Reggie and his faggot friends, but the bible as Anthony liked to believe. That shit they were reading out of the Bible in church, all that shit about "love thy neighbor," that was shit the white man perpetrated on people to keep them in line. There would be the day, or so Anthony believed, that God would deal out retribution like cards on a blackjack table. All the white players, and the black, Oriental, and otherwise that got caught up in greed and some cosmic power struggle would get twenty-two on the first play.

Talking to Reginald would always get Anthony to thinking about God. For the first time in a long time, Anthony had no doubts about his purpose in life. He had found his divine mission. Reginald might be a faggot preacher someday, but this was Anthony's calling. This is what God had prepared Anthony to do. This was just like Samson and the Philistines, like David and Goliath. It was up to Anthony to die a noble, blessed death in the footsteps of his father, but unlike his father, Anthony wasn't going alone. He was going to play it out like Samson and take some with him.

Anthony wondered if that was all bullshit. He wondered if God let it get like this for Anthony to straighten it out. And in the big scheme of things, would anything change? His cousins all thought he was bullshitting, or about to do one of those crazy things that got him put in jail. He wasn't talking out of the side of his neck this time. This time it was for real.

He couldn't tell them exactly what he was going to do. All they needed to know was that he was going to do something. Now, if he could just figure out what he was going to do so he would know. Maybe that was the beauty of this mission. It wasn't the accomplishment that became the end, it was the purpose. The purpose was to propel the future generations of his family out of the slum, both mental and the physical. This could be done.

Before Aunt Dorothy died, Anthony's purpose was simply to make a future for his son. Now, there was his whole family. Why didn't he see that before? He could take care of Maxwell, but how would he give Max a secure foundation to build upon? It was more than just money. There was the ability to make intelligent decisions, and the odds were low that he would be able to if there was no place to make a secure foundation.

Now there was retribution—justice, old world style. They, whoever they were, had killed Aunt Dorothy just as sure as if they had shot her in the head. Her death didn't make the news, not even a write-up in the newspaper, nothing. They would not even acknowledge that she died, or that they had anything to do with her death. They just sat, silently nodding their approval that another black person was dead. Let one of their own die, and they were ready to preempt soap operas for three days running.

Anthony shook his head. There was nothing he could do for his mother and father. They died too long ago and too far away, but Aunt Dorothy was another matter altogether. She was freshly dead, and the people directly responsible were all certainly still breathing. If they didn't know what they did, it was about even. Just like when they made up three different laws for hitting one cop in the face one time. In the course of defending himself, a nigga could break fifteen laws he didn't even know existed.

This mission was his gift from God, and Anthony was going to push it to the limit and play it for what it was worth. Now that the purpose was laid, there was only the matter of what to do. Anthony was certain that everything would come in time to pull it off, whatever time that was. He was tired of looking at the ceiling, so he pulled himself out of bed.

Today was another workday, another day of pulling dough for the white drug dealers in the neighborhood. But the mission added a new tilt to a familiar scene. He was not going to take money for the white man, but perpetrate and peep the white man's moves. The money, Anthony decided, was his for the taking. That tainted money that had been collected over the misery of so many black families on Chicago's South Side. This was neither irony nor poetic justice. This was the white man's justice, robber baron justice, the kind that made America great.

Anthony started his walk to work with a joint like he always did. He smoked, wondering what Mr. Popolous' life was worth. He could take the money without killing him, and that was the way it would be, if possible. The old man wasn't going to stand in his way either. As for the people in Woolworth's, they would meet their ends. Dying was a hazard of working downtown.

The workday went the same as it always did—stack this, shelve that, watch the young motherfuckers steal. Anthony watched Mr. Popolous take money from the masses. Mr. Popolous smiled and talked, just like he always did.

Anthony knew he didn't give a shit about the people he was getting money from. More than once he would tell Anthony what he really thought of some of the people who came to the store. This was done in the camaraderie of us versus them, but what Mr. Popolous seemed to forget was that Anthony was one of them, not one of us.

Maybe he did deserve to die for what he was doing. Maybe Mr. Popolous would prove to be an example for the Arabs and the Koreans to ignore. Or maybe it would just reiterate to them that black people were not to be trusted, only to take money from. Maybe all those people that had business in the neighborhood but didn't live in it would take their businesses back to their own neighborhoods.

Anthony knew that would not happen, but it was a nice daydream.

Mr. Popolous had given Anthony a job, or something quite close to one. The pay was under the table, so there were no benefits, not even for unemployment. Still, it was better than no job—not by much, but better just the same.

Mr. Popolous had given him a break and maybe Anthony would do the same for him. Since he only had to work half the day, Anthony decided to go and see his son. Vanessa hadn't totally denied him, so while the chance was still there to see his son peacefully, Anthony was going to do it. No serious drama the last couple of times he went over there, but he could feel the tension building. Soon enough she would snap on him, and the shit would start.

He took the bus to her house. When he got off the King Drive bus at 95th and St. Lawrence, he looked over at Chicago State University. He wondered what it was like inside the halls of academia. Were those people in there really trying to learn anything, or were they just trying to bullshit their way through to the big money?

There were some college students waiting at the bus stop with him. They were about all that fraternity bullshit. Watching them, Anthony decided there was nothing about them to like. They weren't lifting the masses, they were separating from them.

If they were lucky or had some key to the inside track, they would go and get good jobs, shop in the suburban malls, and buy a house away from the hood. Then they would constantly talk about the people that they left in the slums. It was the ritual of the black middle class, and Anthony hated them for it. They represented the lack of a middle ground. You couldn't stay and build, so you left. There was no way for you to raise your children in the slum, so why bother to stay? Anthony understood it, but he hated it just the same.

What most of them didn't realize is that everything they were running from they were taking with them wherever they went. Bring your old friends over to your new house. They bring their bad habits, your children bring their bad habits, and you bring your bad habits. Of course, they weren't bad habits while you had them, just when the neighbor's kid got hold of them and used them on someone's daughter. The next thing you know, there is a drug house across the street from your new house.

The whole scenario made for a bunch of strange circumstances for black people. Like walking up a down escalator, or like being that Greek dude who had to push that rock up a hill every day for eternity. Shit never got better, just slightly different. You could only run and wait for the bottom dwellers in the old neighborhood to kill themselves off, then you could move back and renovate.

Anthony thought of an old slogan he wrote on a wall somewhere in his life: *Urban blight = White flight, Urban renewal = Nigga removal.*

Anthony got on the 104 Cottage Grove bus with the same disdain he always had for people. This bus was the same as all the other buses on the south and west sides of the city. Women would get on first and stand in the front of the bus. The young men would get on last and fight their way to the back of the bus. Anthony thought about sitting next to one of the women on the front of the bus, just to feel the fear coming off of her, but he headed for the back instead. He sat in the very back, where the windows were scratched up with gang symbols and the nicknames of young lovers in hearts, which in another time would have been on a tree or a park bench. This was the thug section of the bus, only for the hard-assed of the working or nonworking classes.

The bus lurched off and Anthony settled in for the ride. When the bus reached 95th and Cottage Grove, a young Black Muslim got on with an arm full of newspapers. The man squeezed his way through the bus to the front of the thug section, which began at the rear door. He stopped and began his sell.

"My brothers," he began. "How many of y'all working for the white man? Better yet, how many of y'all working at all? See, that is why we as a people need to get and create our own. We need our own products, our own markets. We need our own economy. Black people in America spend enough money every year to rank eighth in the gross national product of all the nations of the world. Yet our children are hungry, our communities are overrun with drugs and all other manner of decay, and the evil that the government perpetrates on us seems to know no end, and these people are the ones that say they represent us. They don't represent us. They can't represent us. They don't even know who we are."

All the time he was talking, he was shoving the paper in the faces of those sitting in the back of the bus. Anthony knew it was only a matter of time before the paper would be shoved in his face. He watched the man walking toward him, still talking about the woes of being a black man in the United States. The man stopped in front of Anthony.

"My brother, just for a dollar, some serious knowledge."

Anthony looked up at him. "Get that bullshit out of my face."

"My brother, you ain't got to come to me like that. There might be something in here that will set you free, get your mind out of that trap."

Anthony pushed the paper out of his face. "Man, your mind is in a trap. That's why you out here getting pimped for them papers and Farrakahn is set up in a spot in Hyde Park. I don't know why y'all out here trying to push that shit on people. Everybody that wants one already got one. Why ain't you writing for the paper, or why ain't the motherfuckers that is writing for the paper out here trying to sell it? See, you all talk all that bullshit, but bottom line is you all can't even stop the A-rabs from selling liquor to your brothers. If you want to do something, get on them punks. After all, they your Muslim brothers. So, get out of my face with that bullshit."

The bus stopped and the man took his arm full of newspapers to the back door of the bus. He looked at Anthony and shook his head. Anthony yelled at him as he got off the bus, "Fuck you."

Anthony watched the man through the back window as the bus pulled off. He thought that since he was in walking distance of where he was headed, he should get off and start a fight with the man, but he remembered that he was going to see his son, and he focused on that goal. Besides, there was the whole mission, and there was no point in jeopardizing it this early in the game.

Anthony got off the bus at 103rd Street then walked to Vanessa's house. He could see her brothers sitting on the porch. They spoke as he walked up the steps. They were another problem of the middle class. Here they were in a position to leave the ghetto, and they wanted to be cool more than anything. In their neighborhood, cool was to be a DeeBee. They were card carrying, gun toting, drug using members of the Devil's Best Friends, or simply Friends, as they referred to each other.

Anthony spoke back to them and walked through the open front door into the house. Vanessa was sitting on the couch and she was not alone. The man didn't flinch when Anthony walked into the room. Vanessa straightened up out of what was an embrace with the man.

Anthony ignored the man totally. "I came here to see Max. Is he around somewhere?"

Vanessa apologetically excused herself from her friend and asked Anthony to follow her into the kitchen. He followed her with his usual air of indifference. The man on the couch followed them out of the room with his eyes.

In the kitchen, Vanessa sat on one side of the table and motioned for Anthony to sit on the other. Anthony took the chair she pointed at and turned it around before he sat down. He folded his arms on top of the back of the chair.

"So, what the fuck is all this about? I just

wanted to see my son. You can save this drama for someone you want to impress. I ain't the one."

"Anthony, who the fuck you think you are coming over here like this? Every day you do this shit. I done told you a thousand times to call before you come barging into my house. I mean give me some respect."

Anthony looked at Vanessa like she was speaking Chinese. "Vanessa, I came here to see my son, not to talk to you about stupid shit. Why don't you just go and get him? Or you can tell me where he is and I'll get him myself. You and that boy in there can go back to doing whatever you were doing. I ain't got nothing to do with that."

Vanessa leaned forward, putting her elbows on the table. "Don't be disrespectful. He ain't no boy. Look, I don't come barging over your house anytime I want to, so why you got to be that way with me? I mean you just came up in the house. You don't know what could be going on."

"Vanessa, I don't give a fuck what is going on. Why you serving me all this drama 'n shit? Just because you got some nigga in the living room with his dick hard and his head full of dreams, don't start tripping. It ain't about that. If you want to impress him, you better try with someone else, some other time. It ain't going on here now."

Vanessa shifted her weight in the chair. "I'm just tired of you doing this shit, dropping over every goddamn day just because you fucking feel like it. We ain't like that no more."

Anthony stood up and walked around the table. He stopped about a foot away from Vanessa. She got up and went to the other side of the table, stopping at the chair he'd just left.

"Motherfucker, don't be walking up on me. You don't want to go there."

Anthony walked around the table again. "Why you tripping on me? I just want to see my son. Now you bringing all this stupid shit. I'm telling you now, I ain't for this. Put that dumb shit in check and let me see my son."

Vanessa backed up until she was out of his reach. "Anthony, get the fuck out of my house."

Anthony sat back down. This time Vanessa screamed at him. "Get the fuck out of my house!"

Anthony stood up. "Bitch, you better quit hollering at me. I'on't know what the fuck is wrong with you, but I am not your child. Come to think of it, you better not be talking to my child like that."

Vanessa took a bold step forward. "Motherfucker, who you think you talking to? I'll talk to my child the way I want to. Fuck you, motherfucker. You can't say shit to me. And I'll talk to you any way I want to. What the fuck are you gonna do? You gonna beat me up or some dumb shit like that?"

"I'm telling you, don't holler at me."

"Fuck you, Anthony."

Anthony stood up and grabbed her collar, pulling her close to him. "I told you don't be hollering at me. I don't give a fuck about you. I'll fuck you up with quickness. Just tell me where my son is."

He pushed her into the sink behind her. She reached in the sink and pulled out a butcher knife. Anthony stepped up to her and knocked the knife out of her hand. He pushed her again.

"I'll wreck your goddamn life, you keep fucking with me. Silly shit like that will wind up with a bitch in hell, a nigga in jail. I don't even know why you pushing me 'n shit. I just want to see my son. I'm going to give you some time to get your shit together. I'm going to see my son."

Vanessa cowered by the sink while Anthony turned to walk out of the kitchen. The man that had been sitting on the couch was now standing in the doorway. Anthony looked him up and down. "What your pussy ass want?"

"My friend, don't be coming to me like that. Shit won't get better."

"I'll come to you like I fucking like to. What the fuck you gonna do?"

"My friend, you better put that shit in check."

Vanessa was standing behind Anthony. She talked over his shoulder. "Just let him out of the house."

The man stepped out of Anthony's way while reaching under his shirt. Anthony pushed him against the wall, and the gun fell to the floor. Anthony immediately reached down and picked it up. He walked through the living room and out of the house.

The man shouted out the door behind him. "Man, you gonna need it."

Anthony turned around and walked back up the stairs. "Am I gonna need it for you? You bad enough to try some shit? I can take care of you now, and you can still make the ten o'clock news, punk ass DeeBee."

The man retreated back into the house. Anthony walked off the porch. He looked down the street to where some children were playing at the end of the block. One of them looked like Maxwell, so Anthony headed in that direction.

The little boy at the end of the block turned out to be Maxwell, so Anthony took him to the park. He took one look back at the house to see Vanessa and the man standing on the porch watching him. When they were out of sight, Anthony hugged his son. He hugged him knowing there would not be too many more hugs.

The thought of leaving Max with his mother was burning in Anthony's mind. Vanessa and her gang-banging, drug-using and dealing friends were not going to be able to offer Max the kind of life he would need to take advantage of the opportunities that Anthony was going to get for him. Danny didn't promise to be all that better, but Anthony was betting on him. A little more convincing would be necessary, but Danny was going to come through.

They arrived at the park and Anthony put his son in the baby swing and pushed him. They played on the seesaw and in the plastic castle. With his son in the sandbox, Anthony returned to his dilemma. If Danny finally relented and said he would do it but then didn't, that would really be messed up. There was no way he would trust Vanessa. The money would be spent on drugs, and the only thing Max would come away with is some more poverty.

Danny was the only choice. The matter of convincing him was simply to put the plan in terms that Danny related to. Anthony knew he could tell Danny that the neighborhood was full of Friends, that Vanessa was a DeeBee. Danny would see the need to get Max away then. But how could he explain to Danny that he would have to go to school, get a better job, act in a dignified manner? That was the hard sell part.

He watched his son in the sandbox. It was all for him. All the rest of the bullshit could be dealt with. Bottom line, his son had to be taken care of. This was the only chance that any of them had to make it. If Maxwell didn't get out of the cycle, there was no telling how many generations would be stuck in the slum behind him. Maybe none. Maybe Max was going out early and he wouldn't have any children. Or even worse, he could go out and have children with fucked up mothers. All bets were on the mission. All bets.

Looking back, Anthony knew he should have been more selective about who he was fucking. That was hindsight. Anthony knew he fucked up then. Now it was going to take a plan to get his son out of the dumb shit. Vanessa was getting deeper into the drug scene, which is why she was laying up with a gangbanger. Any other knotheads she had could sink on the ship with her, but Max wasn't going down that easy.

Max left the sandbox and headed for the slide. Anthony watched him. He also looked for any situations that could be sneaking up on him, or any kind of situation that could end up in gunfire. This was no place for children to play, but it was all that there was. Beirut.

This neighborhood was better than his, but it wasn't better enough. The big difference between here and 61st Street was money and nothing else. This neighborhood just had further downhill to go than his did. Vanessa couldn't see how this place was the same as his, with the drugs, the gangs, the decay. Even with the money these people had, this was still no place for a child to grow up, only a place to grow old and die.

This was no nurturing environment. These people didn't know shit about raising children. The proof was all around them, parents that had no balance to their lives. They were in the world to get theirs, and whatever was left their children could fight over. Vanessa's father worked for the government almost all of his adult life, but neither of his sons could get a job. Making matters worse, their father would not help them to get gainful employment. Their father observed that he'd accomplished all he had without help, so they could too. Except it wasn't happening.

Somewhere down the line they had gotten off track and decided to do things for themselves and not for their children. Anthony didn't want his son to come up under those circumstances. He wanted Max to have every possible chance he could furnish, to get out of the slum. That is why Danny had to go to college and get educated about children. Danny had to agree to do this. He had to see what was at stake here. It was time they give up this dumb shit and get a real life.

Anthony knew that even if Danny went along and got out of his present situation, some of it was going to follow him wherever he went. It would have been better if Anthony could give all those things to his son, then he wouldn't have to trust anybody to do a damn thing. But Anthony knew he had denied himself access to the places where he could safely raise his son. He wasn't going to get credit, a decent job, or anything that he knew he could use to insure his son's future. Watching Max on the slide, Anthony knew he was doing the right thing for his son. He was going to give his son a future. It was just going to cost him his life.

It was time to go. Anthony wanted to leave before it got too dramatic to stay. He took Max's hand and headed back to Vanessa's house over Maxwell's protests. The boy never wanted to go back home, and Anthony didn't want him to go, but he had to stay clear of the law, so he knew it would be best to take him back to his mother.

Vanessa was standing on the porch, still looking for Anthony to come back. She knew he would bring Max back. Why was she serving all that drama? When he was halfway down the block, he hugged and kissed his son again. After he watched Max run to the porch, Anthony turned around and walked to the bus stop. The whole time he waited for the bus, he expected a group of Friends to come up on him, but it never happened.

The bus ride home was uneventful. Anthony was going over the mission in his head. There were still some loose ends that had to be tied. There was the large matter of getting Danny's commitment. That was the hammer. If nothing else, he could tell Danny what he wanted him to do, and just hope he had the sense to do it. Maybe there was some way he could tie the money up so that Danny could only use it for what Anthony wanted him to.

Anthony stopped at his insurance agent's office. He put stipulations on the benefits. It was amazing the way the money game was played. You could do whatever you wanted to, all the computers 'n shit. With money, all you had to do was make wishes, and it was happening. Poor people didn't have computers. The world was still way off for them, their children, and their children's children, especially since their children were having children. Poverty had to be the fastest breeder in the world. The only people in the world that couldn't have children were rich people, so maybe money couldn't buy everything.

So now the set-up, as far as the insurance went, dictated that Danny would get money as long as he stayed in school and maintained a 2.8 G.P.A. Anthony walked to the house from the agent's office. Danny was sitting on the porch, and Tiny was not too far behind him. Anthony could hear people in the house. All of this funeral shit—Anthony could not even remember his mother or father's funeral. He had never seen their graves. He didn't remember either of them having a funeral.

Funerals didn't have a purpose, especially for the dead people. The dead were dead. The living ought to have the good sense to leave them alone. Why did people have to look at them while they were dead? Was it to be sure that the dead were dead? Anthony had never seen his parents dead, but he was sure that they were dead. To hell with the dead.

Anthony walked up to Danny. "Yo, man, you been thinking on what I was talking about the other day?"

Danny looked down the street. "I can't say I

have. I don't really know what you were talking about. Besides, I got other shit I got to think about, like getting my dough rolling again. I can't stand the idea of being broke. It ain't my favorite flavor."

Anthony sat down on the steps next to him. "See, that's is what I was talking about 'n shit. You ain't got to be in the dope game no more, and you can still get your dough straight. Straight and legit."

"This ain't about the dope game. This is about motherfuckers out gunning for me. How the hell is straight and legit gonna deal with that?"

Tiny broke in. "Yeah, man, motherfuckers gunning for you got to be dealt with. Ain't no way around shit like that. Take a motherfucker out, and not to dinner."

Anthony looked at Tiny then back at Danny. "Who you think is out to gun you?"

"I'm placing my bets on Sweets' ass."

"Why you think he want you?"

"The motherfucker been watching too many gangsta movies and listening to too many rap songs. Shit done got to his head, and he thinks he can rule the world. But it ain't like that."

Anthony looked down the street. "If I take Sweets out, will you look out for me?"

Danny laughed. "Look out for you how?"

Anthony looked Danny in the eyes. "I want you to be a father to my son. I want you to go to school next semester and make the move to be what you said you wanted to be a long time ago."

Danny chuckled. "What the hell is that?"

Anthony looked down at the steps. "I don't

know. Whatever you wanted to be a long time ago—a doctor, a lawyer, accountant, businessman, any goddamn thing. Just whatever it is, be it the hell away from here. The bottom line is to be there for my son. That is what this is all about. His mother is all out of line, over there hanging out with Friends 'n shit. I don't want my son growing up in that shit. Besides, she geeking, and it's just a matter of time before she forgets about him."

Danny looked at him. "Where the hell you gonna be? You gonna be in jail for a long time this trip? Tony, man, you done snapped. First of all, how you think I'm gonna get Max away from his mother? And I don't know shit about raising no children. Besides, I got problems of my own to deal with."

"Don't worry about where I'm gonna be. If I take care of all that other shit, will you do what I want you to do?"

"How you gonna do all that?"

"Don't worry about it. Just will you do it?"

Danny stood up. "Man, I'll tell you what. If you do all the shit you say you gonna do, then yeah, I'll look out.

Anthony spoke again. "You got to look out for my son like he was your son and you wanted the world for him, no matter what happens to me."

"You got my word. If you go through all this shit, I'll take care of your son like he was mine."

Tony stood up and they shook hands. "Say goodbye to this dumb shit. You'll be out of here in a month at the latest."

Anthony turned to Tiny. "Man, you make sure this motherfucker stay on his word."

Tiny looked up at him. "Yeah, man, I will. What you gonna do now, Tony? You gonna do some more shit that will get you on the news?"

Anthony smiled. "Well, you just gonna have to stay tuned."

Anthony turned around and went into the house. He spoke to the people who were sitting around in the living room, drinking. He saw Regina sitting in the dining room, drink in hand and already drunk. Maybe her mother's death hit her harder than it hit the rest of them, or maybe she was a lush in the making.

He headed upstairs to his room. Reginald wouldn't be there, especially after last night. He walked into his room and lay across his bed, looking at the ceiling. He hadn't been out of jail for two whole weeks yet and all this shit happened. It wasn't just Aunt Dorothy's dying, but all the shit with Vanessa too.

She was definitely tripping. This was not the dream he had for a family. He wanted it to be a beautiful woman who supported him and his ideas, two wonderful children, and they would be happy the rest of their lives. When he met Vanessa, he thought she would make his dream come true.

They were going to do so much to change the world. They would start an organization that was not based on racial equality, but on the equality of humanity. They were going to welcome young people with big ideas and help them form those ideas into reality. The mission they had in mind was to encourage the different creativities that people had, because they knew that people were not alike, and to them that was a good thing.

His eyes traced over the cracks in the ceiling. He should have known she was not as different as he thought she was. Her interest came to be about money. When he met her, he thought she was about more than that. Anthony knew money did have its place, but it shouldn't be the centerpiece of their relationship.

Money was a fucked up place to be measured. He was never going to have enough because there were too many people with more. After a while, she reeked of the middle class paper chase, and by that time she was pregnant. She got on welfare so she could get the proper medical care. If it wasn't for that, Max might have been born in an alley somewhere.

After Max was born, things got worse instead of better. Vanessa was even more consumed with thoughts of money. Anthony tried to do what he could, but it was never enough. Then he went to jail again, and by the time he got out, she was seeing someone else. Vanessa had more than made it clear that she had given up on Anthony. She repeatedly reminded him that he had failed her. At first he believed her, but then realized that ultimately the only person he failed was Max. He failed Max because he chose Vanessa to be his mother. He was going to correct that any day now.

They were never going to be a family. They were just going to become statistics. When she had given up on him, he gave up on her, but he wasn't going to give up on his son. Even more important, he was going to make sure that his son wouldn't need her because Anthony knew the day was coming when she would give up on Max too. She would utter those words that Anthony knew were a curse. She would tell Max that he was just like his father.

The only thing left was for Anthony to insure that if Max were just like his father, it would be a good thing. If Max was like him, then he would do anything for his child, his family. Max would know what his father was like, so Max would want to be just like him.

chapter thirteen

Enough thirty-seven fifties and you didn't fall asleep. You could lie in bed, look at the ceiling, look at the wall, look at the floor, and you would just light up another one. It was how Danny would spend the time, daytime and nighttime, avoiding dreams where people would hit him with shotguns then shoot him. A dulled mind didn't retrace the steps over and over to see if there were somewhere you made a mistake, or if you did the right thing. A dulled mind wouldn't play it out further, where you would wake up and see the rest of your family lying in pools of blood on every floor of your house.

Since his mother died, Danny did the one thing he knew better than to do. He allowed himself to binge on getting high. He had no intent on controlling it, not for a while anyway. Thinking about it, he hoped that he had not gone too far. But then where the hell was too far? This is where addicts came from. It was shit like this that would create a geek on you. Maybe it was because his mother died, or all the shit that had happened to him, or maybe it was time to take some time off and get fucked up. It didn't matter because that was all that he wanted to do—get drink, get weed, get rock, get high.

The basement looked the same. It was the same shitty beams on the same shitty ceiling, but somehow the basement, the backyard, and the front porch were different.

Danny was getting restless. Maybe he needed to get away from the house for awhile. Since his mother died, he hadn't left the house. Tiny went and got him anything he wanted. Family was always coming through looking out for him. Even Sweets stopped by and dropped off a bag. Danny still thought Sweets was behind the shit that happened to him, but he couldn't get any information to pin it on him.

Then there was all that shit Anthony was talking about. Getting out of the game. Getting out was something that Danny didn't know anyone ever actually did. Motherfuckers didn't leave the game; they were taken out of it. Sometimes a motherfucker would go to jail, get out, and pretend to be free for a while, but then the shit would just creep back up on them. The only way out of the game was in a box.

Danny sat up on the bed, lit a Newport, and tried to think of a life outside of the one he was living. He couldn't get away from it if he stayed on Eberhart. Besides, there was the likelihood that it would go with him, or wait a while and creep up on him. He could be at school, hitting the books hard, and some white boy would pass him a pipe, and the shit would be all over him again. There was no real way out. Maybe there was someplace in between, but there was no way all the way out. Anthony was dreaming, but then that is what Anthony always did.

Danny lit another thirty-seven fifty. He inhaled it nice and slow, savoring the sweet taste of the cocaine. He hit it, held it, then blew it out. It was a habit. That is how he had been smoking joints since he was twelve years old.

The cocaine was giving him a head rush, and the weed was keeping it steady. He watched the numbers on the clock change to 6:15 a.m. Danny smoked the cocaine-laden joint until it was nothing but a roach. He lay back on the bed until the rush subsided. He wasn't sleepy. He had weed and rock, but he was out of straightener. The sun was streaking through the basement window, and the birds were outside screaming at the top of their little bird lungs.

Anthony was right. This is not where they were supposed to be now. They were grown. They should have houses in the suburbs, with fine-ass wives at their sides. They should have children who hugged them when they came home from a day at the office. They should be cursing about the traffic on the way to their nine-to-five jobs. They should be getting pissed off when they watched the news and saw that taxes were going up. Instead, they were nowhere near that place, the place where they dreamed they would be when they got to be as old as they were now.

There was a time when Danny wanted to go to college, but that was a long time ago. He joined the Army so he could get the money together to go to school, but shit happened. He couldn't go through no shit like the military to get the money again. The whole idea of college was probably never meant to be for him anyway. A degree wasn't a guarantee that he would get away from where he was anyway. People with degrees gave money to him all the time.

As soon as the rush ended, he stood up and looked out the window. He lit a cigarette and listened to the birds screaming, thinking it odd that there were still birds in this part of town. Life went on, in spite of all the bullshit that tried to stop it. It seemed like God didn't care, or maybe Man didn't matter as much as he thought he did. Birds were still singing.

The munchies descended on Danny, so he decided to go and get something, maybe a cup of coffee. He put on a shirt and went upstairs. He was sure one of those little restaurants on 61st Street would be open this time of the morning. For the first time he could remember, the house was actually quiet.

He thought of his mother coming down the stairs any minute now, then he realized there was no way that could happen. One of her old friends was sleeping it off on the couch. This mourning shit had to hurry up and end. These people were wearing out their welcome. They hardly ever came to see his mother when she was alive. Why were they all coming through now?

Outside it was hotter than Danny thought it would be, or maybe it was because he was high. On 61st Street, he saw there was almost no one on the street. There was a lady waiting for a bus, and an old man walking up the street. It almost made the street seem clean. Across King Drive, a little restaurant was open. Danny walked in and took a seat.

A woman and man were behind the counter. The man rushed to go to the back room. Danny knew the man was leaving because he wanted to get his gun in case Danny stuck the place up. Danny was tired of people being afraid of him unnecessarily. It didn't matter what he told them. They were going to think what they wanted to think.

Danny sat at the counter and ordered a cup of coffee. The lady tried to hide her nervousness as she poured the coffee in a Styrofoam cup. The man stayed in the back, hiding behind a partition. Danny put some cream and sugar in his coffee and stirred it. The lady moved as far from him as she could be while staying in the same room with him.

Danny took the cup and left. He continued to walk west toward the highway. There was a man lying in the alley between Prairie and Indiana. He was probably drunk, or he could have been dead. Danny stopped and looked at him. The man in the alley was not his problem. Danny threw the cup of coffee at the man, deliberately missing him. When the coffee touched him, the man did move a little, then Danny left.

He walked until he got to the overpass on 63rd Street. He stopped on the overpass and watched the people in their cars driving to work, wondering what their lives were like. He knew they would not have to dodge bullets today. They wouldn't have to worry about someone trying to take their business from them at gunpoint. They would go to their jobs, sit in their offices and worry about some shit that was not life threatening. If something got life threatening, they could call security.

Maybe their lives were not as different from his as he would suppose they were. They worried about losing their jobs, their home, and their way of life. How far were they from the slum?

He turned around to watch the people getting off the bus to get on the El. They were on the paper chase too, but they were a lot closer to where he was. They were on their way downtown, trying to keep hold of legitimate lifestyles.

Danny stood on the bridge and lit up a joint, a salute to the working man and woman. There were a lot more working women on the buses, but the cars were filled with white men, and occasionally white women or black men. He flicked the roach onto the highway, hoping it went inside one of the white men's cars and made him smell like reefer when he got to work. Danny smiled. That would be some shit to explain to the boss.

He headed back to Eberhart because there was nowhere else to go. Anthony started circles running in his brain, igniting long-molded dreams that he had forgotten existed. He wanted to have an office; he wanted to be married to Samantha Stevens; he wanted to come home from work every day and kiss his children goodnight. He wanted to worry about getting the big account with hundreds of thousands or perhaps millions of dollars riding on him. He wanted to be called because he was a big gun in the world and they knew he could pull down the account or make the deal, or whatever it was that they did downtown in all those offices, power lunches, and boardrooms.

Danny thought about the place he was on the road to—to jail, to an early grave. He could hope to make a mint before he died, but that wasn't likely. There was no pension, no health care, no real future in selling drugs. But no one ever sold drugs for a future. You became a dealer because of the here and now. You wanted to make the money, get the car, and impress the girls. Then you got caught up in it, and the power became the drug you would geek.

Calling the shots, the shorties looking up to you, and the bitches dripping off of you. When you got money, you got juice. People listen to you; they want to ride with you. Everything is proper when you dealing and the dough is rolling. After a while, you realize you can't trust anybody, and you go crazy not to; or you think you rule the world and trust don't mean nothing to you anyway.

Danny knew the bitter reality of it. Most men that sold drugs didn't get to be the big boys. They rose so far, then the best they could do is to be someone's lackey. All that shit about being big time was in the movies and rap records. True life wasn't going that way. Yeah, everybody getting into the game thought about being the big man, but very few ever were. But then you could always get big locally. That is what Sweets had done.

Danny knew real dealers who made Sweets look like dog shit. They had cars, boats and houses in the suburbs. But Sweets kept where he was, and kept his lackeys low. Now he was tripping because he wanted to control all the rock in the neighborhood. Sweets could have this shit. There was always a way to get paid, and it didn't have to be getting played and shot at and shit like that. If Anthony was gonna make that move for Danny, then Danny was going to get out of the game.

He walked back to his house. The man was still in the alley between Indiana and Prairie. Danny looked at him and knew he could wind up like that. The man had no doubt been a player at one time, a hustler. Like so many people who play the game, you never knew when to call it quits. You start out with nothing, then you get a little money. The next thing you know, you riding high, then your shit starts to fall. You keep playing because you think you can get back every little bit you lose, but you keep losing more. Then one day you wake up in an alley, because you've run out of friends, and you got nothing in your pockets.

Your whole hustle has changed from scheming on a big deal to begging nickels for a hamburger. If you could make it that far in the cycle, you were still a loser. Most people didn't make the cycle; they got put out of the game in a box. The people in the little restaurant were scared of him, but the young black man was the one who should be scared. It was the young black man who was getting killed by young black men. It was just another part of the paper chase.

Danny got home, went into the basement and smoked another joint, this one without the rock in it. Maybe it would help him go to sleep and kill the dreams that were stalking him. He lay across his bed and smoked to the morning television shows. Happy-ass people getting tall dough a long way from where he was, except when they came by to make some more money on the latest shooting in the hood.

The reefer didn't kill the cocaine, so he didn't go to sleep. He watched the television and the clock. Then he heard the kids walking into the kitchen. He heard Regina in the kitchen, then Anthony left for work—maybe it was Anthony, or it could have been Jaleel leaving out.

Someone knocked at the side door. Danny froze. Maybe it was the paranoia that came with the weed, or maybe it was just paranoia. He didn't want to open the side door. It might be another nigga gunning for him. Danny didn't have a gun anymore, and the knock at the door reminded him that he had to get one with a quickness.

"Who is it?" he hollered as he crossed the floor.

"It's me, Tiny."

"You straight?"

"Yeah."

Danny opened the door. Tiny was standing there, out of breath. There was nothing totally unusual about that. He was hauling all that weight around, so he was always out of breath.

"What's up?"

Tiny came through the door and started down the steps.

"Man, Otis is dead."

"What?"

"Otis deadened."

"How you know that?"

"The police came through my spot early this morning. Me and Otis was running last night, so they come looking for me. But he left my spot about ten o'clock and that was the last I saw him.

They found his ass in the playground just like they did Jimmie."

"The playground at the school, or the one in the park?"

"The one in the park."

Danny sat down next to Tiny on the bed. "Damn. That is fucked up. You think Sweets had something to do with it?"

"Ain't no telling. I mean he could have, but then it could have been Otis in the wrong place, wrong time kind of thing."

Danny got up and looked out the window. "If Sweets was in on it, then he gonna probably come after you next. Either that or he gonna come after me again."

Tiny lit a cigarette. "You really think Sweets was in on the bum rush? I mean I ain't heard shit around the way about it. If he was in on it, then he being a lot more quiet about it than usual."

Danny motioned for Tiny to give him a cigarette. "Hey, man, if it gets out that he made a move on Family, then he gonna lose juice. To be honest, I'm still wondering why I'm alive. They should have deadened me. And see, if I go gunning for him, then I could be wrong. Besides that, I ain't got my gat anyway. Do you know how Otis got killed?"

"I think it was a shotgun. The police asked me if I had one, so I guess that was what they used."

Danny sat back down. He imagined Otis like he was in a movie scene, lying on the ground in a pool of blood, his hands over the hole where his stomach should have been, writhing on the ground. He took another drag on the cigarette. "That's some foul shit, but that's the way it plays out in the game. Sometimes you win, sometimes you don't. Sometimes you get deadened trying."

Tiny stomped out his cigarette. "You know that house Sweets wanted us to crew?" he asked. "It's going full tilt now."

"Yeah, Sweets got his dough rolling. It ain't like they gonna run out of geeks anytime soon. Them motherfuckers will line up for that rock-killa at the police station if they sold it there. I think I'm just gonna take this opportunity to get out of the game. I ain't even looking to get even. Sweets made the move and he on top. Good for him."

"Yo, man, you think Tony gonna make a move on him like he said he would yesterday?"

"I don't know. Anthony might be talking out the side of his neck. I don't know what kind of moves he gonna make."

Tiny stood up. "Yo, man, I'ma pull up."

"All right now."

Tiny left out the side door. Danny locked it behind him. He went back into the basement and looked out the window at Tiny walking down the street. Now Otis was dead. Danny knew by all rights he should have been dead too. He sat on his bed thinking that this all used to be fun, but now motherfuckers were dropping right and left.

Danny rolled another joint, but he didn't light it up. He didn't feel like smoking now. He didn't know what to feel. First he gets bum rushed in his own spot, then one of his homeys winds up deadened in the playground. His brother, sister, and Anthony were right. Maybe it was time to let it go. It just didn't feel like time to let go, though.

He thought about the man in the alley. It would never feel like time to let go, and Danny knew that.

Danny hadn't really worked since he got out of the Army six years ago. He was supposed to go to school as soon as he got out. He had saved money for it with the Veteran's Educational Assistance Program since he joined the Army. When he got out, he was ready to go, but his mother needed the money for something or another, and he gave it to her. She said she was going to give it back, but he knew better than to expect it from her.

Danny lay down and watched the wooden beams on the ceiling until his eyes closed and he went somewhere between the high and real sleep. He woke up at 2 o'clock in the afternoon, and heard people walking around upstairs in the house. He rolled another joint, went out to the backyard and lit it up.

Danny smoked half of the joint by the alley, near the fence. After he finished, he went into the kitchen. Regina stood over the stove, frying chicken. She looked at him and rolled her eyes.

"You seen Jaleel?" she asked.

"I been 'sleep all day."

Regina turned her attention to the chicken in the skillet.

"Do you know where he might have went?"

"Do I look like his babysitter? You his mother. You should know where he went, not me. You the one supposed to keep up with his young ass."

Regina looked at Danny. "Don't start no shit, there won't be no shit. If I wanted a lecture I'd go to class."

Danny left the kitchen and went into the dining

room. There were people all around in there and the front room. They all had something to drink; there was even a forty-ounce on top of the television. Danny spoke to the people he knew and kept walking until he was standing on the front porch.

He waved at the people next door as they spoke to him. He looked out to the street. DeShawn and Laneka were playing in the dirt by the curb. The rest of the block seemed rather quiet. There was no hollering and screaming from next door or down the street. He noticed a boy running down the street from the far end of the block. Then he took a seat on the steps.

At the other end of the street there was nothing except the cars running up and down 61st Street. People were standing on the corner as usual. They were there yesterday, and they would be there tomorrow. The boy who had been running up the street crossed the street, ran past the children in the dirt and onto the porch. Laneka and DeShawn watched him run by, then they followed him. He was out of breath. "Danny . . . Jaleel . . . getting . . . beat up . . . in the . . . playground."

Danny ran down the steps. "Which one?" he yelled at the little boy.

"School."

Danny looked at DeShawn. "Go tell your mother to come here and talk to this boy."

DeShawn took off up the steps and Danny started running toward the school. No wonder the boy was out of breath. The school was three blocks away. Danny slowed to a trot and then a walk when he reached the playground. He could see a crowd of boys on the other side of the playground. That must have been where Jaleel was.

The crowd didn't have anyone over the age of thirteen. Danny felt foolish for even coming. He shouted in his most authoritative voice, "What the fuck is going on here?"

Some of the ten or twelve boys turned around to face him. None of them said anything, nor did they make any attempt to move away from the crowd. Shorties didn't show any respect anymore.

"I said what the fuck is going on here?" Danny yelled again.

As Danny approached the crowd, one of the boys shouted back, "This motherfucker owes me money, and I'm trying to get it from him."

The crowd opened up, and Danny could see Jaleel lying on the ground. He seemed to be okay. At least he was still moving, holding his stomach, groaning. Danny walked over to the boy who was shouting. He reached in his pocket, figuring Jaleel owed ten, maybe twenty on the outside.

"How much he owe you?"

"Two hundred dollars," the boy said.

Danny eyed the boy. He stood off from the group, obviously the leader. Danny assumed the leader boy had his other boys beat Jaleel, then he went over and kicked him while he was on the ground. The boy was cool. He was certainly going places in the world, provided he lived long enough to get there.

"How the fuck he owe you two hundred dollars? Nigga, you ain't seen that much money in your life."

"He owe me that much and he know it."

Danny thought about when he was young. If an older came on the set, you were scared. But this boy wasn't trembling in the least. Twelve years old and two hundred dollars to the bad. What kind of shit was Jaleel getting into? When Danny was twelve, he was happy to get a joint or a piece of leg, and here this youngster talking about two hundred dollars without trembling.

Danny helped Jaleel stand up.

"Why this man say you owe him two hundred dollars?"

"He say I stole some rock from him."

"What?" Danny said in disbelief.

"He say I took his stash. We was over there playing basketball and he put his shirt with his stuff in it—"

The tough boy broke in. "And he went in my shirt and took my shit. My homey saw him do it."

Danny looked down at Jaleel. There was blood on his forehead and around his mouth.

"Did you take this boy's shit?"

"Naw, I ain't got nothing from him."

Danny started going through Jaleel's pockets. He felt a few bags of rock in his pockets, but there was no way it was worth two hundred dollars. It was more like thirty dollars. Danny pulled out the bags and looked at them.

"Where the fuck you get these from?"

The tough boy shouted out, "He got 'em from me."

Danny looked at him. "I thought you said it was two hundred dollars worth."

"It is."

Danny looked at the crowd. "Y'all get y'all's asses out of here now."

The tough boy walked up to Danny. "Can I have my rock back?"

"Hell naw."

"I'ma get my shit back, or I'ma get my money."

Danny stepped up on him, then looked down at him. "The only thing you gonna get is your ass kicked if you don't get the fuck out of my face."

The tough boy turned around. "Yeah, you say that shit now."

When the playground was cleared of little boys, Danny and Jaleel started the walk back home. Danny wanted to ask about the cocaine. He wanted to know how Jaleel even came into contact with it. He was sure it wasn't through him. He never got high around the kids. But Danny also knew that drugs were so prevalent that he didn't have to get it from home. "So, what was you gonna do with this rock?"

"I don't know."

"Bullshit. Don't try to play me. I ain't the one. Look, I don't care what you was gonna do. You really don't need to be fucking with this shit."

Jaleel spoke under his breath. "Who are you to be talking?"

"Oh, so that's how you gonna play it? You gonna be one of them punk-ass motherfuckers they be talking about on television. The motherfucker that lives his life monkey see, monkey do. If that's the way you want to be, go the hell on with it. So you want to be like me. Well, motherfucker, take a good look so you can be me right. I'm twenty-seven and I'm still in my mother's crib. Even when I do make money, it don't go to shit, 'cause I ain't legit. No credit, no way to ever get out of this dead-ass neighborhood. All the people that I got to do business with would just as soon shoot me in the back as look at me, and motherfuckers that is straight up out to deaden me. Yeah, go ahead. Be just the fuck like me."

Jaleel looked up at him. "That's because that's you. I ain't you."

"Who the fuck are you, Superman? But hey, it's your choice. You want to get deadened, get deadened. You could just save yourself some time and put a bullet in your skull."

"Who are you to be talking? You be in the box getting paid. Why don't you want me to get paid too?"

"It ain't like that. You too young to be worried about getting paid. Man, you should be playing. You got the rest of your life to worry about getting paid. But then again, if you off into this shit, the rest of your life ain't gonna be that long. You know Otis, don't you?"

"Yeah."

"Did you know he was dead?"

"He ain't dead. I saw him yesterday."

"They found his ass in the playground this morning. He took a shotgun to the gut."

"How you know?"

"What does that matter? I'm just taking it as a sign that it's time for me to get out of the game."

"I thought Otis was your boy."

"He was."

"Ain't you gonna go and deaden whoever killed him?"

"Nope."

"You ain't right. You supposed to look out for your boy."

"I'm gonna look out for my own ass this trip. I ain't buying in to that shit."

"See, that's how you are. I ain't like you."

"Yeah, you a little tough motherfucker. You can take it and dish it out. Just the next time you getting your ass kicked, don't send for me, 'cause you ain't got it like that."

Jaleel looked down at the ground. "Bet."

They turned the corner to Eberhart in tense silence. They could see Regina on the porch looking out for them. Laneka and DeShawn were playing in the front, and one of the guests was standing next to Regina. From where Danny was, Regina looked angrier when she saw her son. It was the same look he had seen on his mother so many times, especially when he was young. He was glad it wasn't his turn to play this game. He planned to simply excuse himself from the whole situation, then go smoke a joint or something. He just wasn't going to hang around for the bullshit that was coming up.

Regina started screaming at her son as soon as he got into range. Danny saw no reason to fan the flames by telling her what really happened with the drugs. He said it was a simple misunderstanding, the kind kids have when they play.

Danny went into the house, leaving Regina screaming at her son on the porch. He walked past the drinking people sitting in the living room and the dining room. He would be glad when the funeral was over with so these people could go back to wherever they were supposed to be. Drinking killed his mother, and these people mourned her by killing themselves the same way. He couldn't talk. He was killing himself, just using different methods.

Danny went into the basement feeling helpless. There was nothing he could do about Jaleel. He was going to be the junior drug dealer because he wanted to. Danny had no idea how to stop him or change his mind. Otis was deadened in the playground, and there was nothing Danny could do about that. He could get on the revenge trip. He knew that was what he was supposed to do. However, that would just start a vicious cycle 'til everybody was dead. He couldn't do nothing about being bum rushed in his house. He didn't know who did it, and even if he did, what could he do about it? Start another kind of killing cycle? The whole world just seemed to be one big killing cycle.

He began rolling the joint, adding some of the rock he took off the little boy. Was there anything that was worth fighting for? Why couldn't a nigga just get high and live his life? Why did he have to go through the dumb shit? Why couldn't he be coming home from work, roll a joint, put a little rock in it and kick back for the evening, and still be legit? All this sneaking around and people getting deadened—the law was fucked up. The messed up thing was that the law was made by people that didn't get high. Maybe they ought to try it before they put it on the wrong side of the law.

He should be able to have his get high, and

credit cards, and a decent job with a bank account, and not a bankroll hidden in the rafters in the basement ceiling. That was the way it was. The shit started at the top of the hill, and Danny was at the bottom of the hill. The law of gravity meant that the shit would get bigger as it rolled downhill. That was just the way it was.

Danny went out in the backyard to smoke the joint. The rock was good. He could see why the little boy wanted it back. It tasted like the shit that was taken from him. It probably was. As he smoked it, he thought about getting revenge. He could go find the little boy and beat the shit out of him until he told Danny where he got the rock from.

Revenge was the law of the street. It was one of many laws on the street. The laws of the street were easy to learn. If you didn't know them, you could make them up as you went along. There was the law of compensation, the law of love, lust, and sex, and there was the law of out-gunning. That was the big one. If you could take it, it was yours. If you gave it up and you could out-gun the perpetrator, you could take it back.

There were supposed to be laws for Family, but when it came down to it, it was just like the rest of the world. If you could get away with it, then you did. If you got caught, then there was a debt to pay. It could be fifty hits to the head, no cover-up, or it could be slugs to the skull. You were supposed to love, honor, and respect Family. You were supposed to die for Family, and as long as you were alive, you were supposed to be ready to kill for Family. Danny knew, no matter where he went in life, Family would have a place in his heart.

Family would look out for him. All his friends

were Family. When they were shorties, they had been Friends. During high school, they switched flags, and all of a sudden they were Family. What mattered was that they were all still friends. What flag they went under, at least in a very basic way, did not matter.

Danny wouldn't admit it, but Family influence had a lot to do with the way he viewed the world. The Family color was green, so he had it everywhere. He even painted the Family insignia on the basement wall in green. Most of his clothes were green, but none were purple. Purple was the color for Friends. He simply said he didn't like it.

When he watched the news and saw what was termed a gangland shooting, he would immediately assume that there were Friends involved. He thought of Family as better people than Friends. Family had more money, more members, and better organization. Family was a better way to be.

The only white people he knew were Family members. They were they only white people he ever came in contact with. He was surprised to see white gang members. He thought all the white people in Chicago were rich and lived in the big houses or fancy apartments on the North Side. There were also Mexican and Puerto Rican Family. Family was just that way. Friends were that way too.

Even if a gang ran under a different name, you could tell if they were Family or Friends. Did they have triangles or squares in their symbol? Were they right-or left-sided? Family was one way, Friends were the other. If there was one thing worse than being either, it was being neither.

Anthony would say that he was neither, but he was Family. They looked out for him while he was in jail. If they didn't, Anthony would have come back a bitch and he knew it. Even if you didn't run with a gang, you needed their protection. Without it, you would get their abuse. You were truly bad if you could grow up and never align.

Some people mellowed out of gangs, some got hardcore, and some were dead before they could make that decision. Danny knew the best way out was to get legit. Everybody respected the man that was legit. There were people who were Family then went away to college, got jobs and moved to the suburbs. They would come around every once in a while, and hardcore Family was always glad to see them. Legit Family didn't have to involve themselves in the criminal activities that went on, but if they needed a favor, Family would look out for them.

In the same respect, they helped other Family get legitimate, or semi-legitimate jobs. Family was all about looking out for each other. If you wanted to make it up in the ranks, you did whatever you had to do to get the juice. With the juice, you could call the shots over other Family.

There were all kinds of ways to get juice. All of them threatened your life or liberty. You might have to gun somebody, or do a little breaking and entering, or you might be on a crew, selling drugs at the dope spot. The catch was that the deeper into it you got, the harder it was to get out alive. It was like a drug too. The more you got, the more you would want.

Danny finished the joint and went back in the

basement. He wondered if he'd gotten in too deep. Maybe they wouldn't miss him at all. There were already thirty people out to take his place in the hierarchy. Family wouldn't be a problem; Sweets might be a problem. He had to be expecting Danny to make a revenge move on him sometime, if he had something to do with the bum rush and Otis' death. Or Sweets could just be biding his time until he could kill Danny.

If Anthony came through like he said he would, then Danny was going to get out of this. Even if Anthony hesitated, he could talk Regina into moving with the money from their mother's insurance policy. But if Anthony came through, it could truly be a move up. Otherwise, it was a move sideways at best. Danny knew he wasn't stupid. He knew there were stupid people out there, and they were making it in a legitimate manner. If they could do it, he could do it too.

Danny listened as someone walked across the kitchen floor with steps that crossed through the kitchen and came to the basement stairs. He hoped that it was Anthony so he could find out more about what he was planning to do. It was Anthony. He came down the steps in a way so familiar to Danny that it could be no one else.

As Anthony's legs appeared, Danny called out to him. "Yo, man, what the fuck is up witcha?"

Anthony took a seat on the bed. He looked at Danny almost like he didn't know who he was.

"You been thinking about our deal?"

"Yeah, I ain't been thinking about shit else."

"Do you know why I'm asking you to do this?"

Anthony spoke again before Danny had a chance to answer. "I'm doing this for my son. You are doing this for my son. That's what it's all about, bottom line. This ain't about you getting rich, that ain't it. If you do get rich, that's a good thing, but the bottom line is my son, Max. You got to look out for him, whether you get rich or not."

Danny nodded. "That's all well and good, but where you gonna be?"

"Don't worry about that. This ain't about me."

"So, you ain't gonna tell me shit about what you gonna do?"

"Nope, you got other shit you got to focus on. I got shit I got to focus on. Besides, you got Regina and her family to worry about. I mean you got to do right by them too. This is about everybody in the family, even Reggie's faggot ass. I don't know just how he'll fit in, but I'm sure he will. I just want to let you know it's gonna be a lot of pressure on you."

Danny smiled. "It can't be more pressure than standing on a corner selling rock."

"Yeah, but you buying into a lifetime with this. You got to change everything, I mean everything. Don't be thinking you got to do it by yourself. That's why you gonna go to school and do well."

"The first thing I want to do is to get out of this house. I'ma try to talk Regina into taking the money that Mom left us and move with that."

"A damn good start. She ain't got to know what's going on, at least not until it's in full swing."

"I ain't saying nothing. Shit, I don't know what's going on."

"You'll know soon enough. I heard they found ol' Otis dead this morning."

"Yeah, I heard that too. Tiny told me."

"Don't worry about Sweets' ass. I got him covered. This is gonna work out. Just do right by my son."

"Tony, I'ma look out. I said I would, and I will. Don't sweat."

"Straight. You got a joint?"

"Yeah, but they all got killa in them."

"It don't matter. I ain't got the time it takes to be an addict, so fuck it."

They smoked the thirty-seven fifty in silence. When Anthony put out the roach, Danny lit a cigarette. Anthony watched him, still silent, unlike Anthony ever was. Then he spoke. "You know you gonna have to quit smoking. You gonna have to quit a lot of shit."

"I'll do what I got to do. It's just a play."

Anthony looked at Danny like he was recognizing him for the first time since he had come into the basement. "Just don't give up. Don't give up on yourself, and whatever you do, don't give up on my son."

"I won't."

Anthony stood up. "Always tell him about me. Let him know what I did for him, and that he may have to do the same thing someday for his children. Don't let him forget what I did."

Danny looked at Anthony. There were tears rolling down his cousin's cheeks. Danny stood up and placed his hand on Anthony's shoulder.

"How could I let him? You the kind of man legends are made of."

Anthony looked down at the floor. "Look, man, I got to go. I got to go and see my son. You know I wouldn't trust nobody but you to do this shit for me. I don't know, man. Maybe shit is clearer now;

maybe it ain't. That don't matter. I'll lay this shit out for you in a few days so you won't be sweating about what you got to do. Just for a little while, you got to trust me. I know what I'm doing. You just got to trust me."

Danny stepped toward him. "I trust you. You the man. You know what's up better than I do. Just watch your back."

"I don't think that matters anymore. You watch your back."

They hugged. For the first time in their lives, they hugged. Then they shook hands. Anthony left. Danny wasn't exactly sure what happened, so he sat down and lit up another joint. He lay on his back smoking, looking at the ceiling, thinking things didn't have to be this way much longer. There was a chance for a change, and Danny was going to take it. He closed his eyes hoping he was up to it.

chapter fourteen

Regina woke up to the same wall she had been looking at since she was twelve. It was blue now. It had been pink or green at different times in her life. The borders were a constant white. This had been her mother's room until her grandmother died, then her mother moved to the room she would die in. Regina would probably do the same.

She turned on her back and looked at the ceiling. She wanted to get up early today. Tomorrow was her mother's funeral and there were still things left undone. People had been coming over in what seemed like an unending stream since her mother died. She hadn't had the time to do anything she needed to get done. She wasn't even sure if the kids had the right clothes to wear. She shouldn't have trusted Jaleel's grandmother to get clothes for them.

She knew she wasn't right to lay any blame on Jaleel's grandmother, since she did what she could. Jaleel's grandmother was old fashioned, so her sense of style was somewhat off course. Even though she helped out with Laneka and DeShawn, Jaleel was the only person she claimed as her grandchild. There were more than enough women in South Side Chicago that could legally dispute that. Not that it mattered much. Jaleel's father was in prison. He'd been busted on a Class X felony drug conviction. He was not going to see the streets for twenty-five years.

Regina thought about sending Jaleel to stay with his grandmother. She was looking for a second chance to raise a son, and Regina was just looking for a chance. Jaleel had been getting a little crazy lately. He had that fight yesterday, and a few weeks ago the police brought him home. Regina knew it would only be a matter of time before they wouldn't bring him home, and he would become just another statistic.

Staying with his grandmother wouldn't necessarily be a better thing for Jaleel to do, and Regina knew that. His grandmother lived in Englewood, which was not a better place to live. It was notorious for the constant body count it had amassed, and the gangs and drugs that pervaded the community. As bad as Englewood may have been, Regina knew she was up against the same things where she lived. Jaleel's grandmother had the money to spend on Jaleel that Regina didn't—money to get gym shoes, jackets and other things that teenagers felt they needed to survive.

Jaleel was a game that Regina felt she was losing. He had already started down a dead end road, and moving would only delay the inevitable. Jaleel was just another problem she faced in her everyday life. She was the female head of a poor household, a subject that was always talked about on the news. As much as they did interviews, reports and whatnot, they seemed to skip over the real reason behind this latest phenomenon. The lack of a father in the black family was all in the choosing.

When Regina had to face up to it, and she did every day, choosing daddies was something that she was not good at doing. But then again, it wasn't like she actually picked them to be fathers. They just happened. Every man she had sex with in her life was not a father to one of her children. It was a roll of the dice kind of thing. When you're young and stupid, you roll the dice often. You roll the dice with your eyes closed to the consequences that are never too far away—consequences like the girl next door, a cousin, or some girl that had to drop out of school.

Having babies, no matter what anyone said, was a mark of womanhood. It was like a rite of passage. It made you so different. Older people treated you different—not always better, but always different. When older girls had babies, you could see there was something special about it. Something that made you want one too.

As special as a baby may have been, it was almost always an unplanned thing. You didn't get pregnant because you planned to; you got pregnant because you didn't plan not to. Regina knew she never planned any of her children. It wasn't that she didn't know how babies were made. She learned all that penis and vagina shit in the fifth grade, but that was all for the birds, or doctors.

The classes never explained about what made you become wet between the legs, or why it would ever happen. The classes never talked about how your nipples could love to be kissed, or the sensation of someone else's tongue in your mouth. The teachers never told you about how you could not have sex just once; how once that hunger was breached it came back time and time again. The classes never talked about the power you would feel to hear a man begging you, or all the things a man would go through to get you, at least for that first time. The classes never told you that even if you started having sex at fifteen, it could be seven years before you started enjoying it. Sex education wasn't shit.

Regina would never admit it, but to her, babies were like a doll or a pet, only ten times better. They were living and they smiled when they saw her. Babies learned to speak and they were fun to dress and shop for. The biggest problem with babies was that they didn't stay babies. Her babies grew into something that Regina could not see coming. From the first time she learned she was pregnant, Regina had maybe seven months to prepare for a baby. She learned to feed and how to burp a baby. She changed diapers so that she would know how to do it when her baby came.

She didn't know that babies were the easy part. They were so cute when they were struggling with their first words, but then they were telling you to leave them alone. She remembered how bad she felt the first time she lost her temper and hit Jaleel. Hitting had worked on her and her brothers, so it was a tool to use. After a while, she hit him and felt not even a tinge of guilt. By the time DeShawn started getting spankings, it was the only way she knew.

Regina had no idea how to deal with her children and leave room for herself. When she was ready to go, she'd just feed them and leave them with her mother. Regina didn't know anything about being a parent, except how to become one. Her medical knowledge went slightly past bandages. She didn't know how to listen to her children. She could hear what they said, but that was as far as that went. What she didn't know, she didn't have time to learn.

It didn't matter now. She was an adult, and she knew everything anyway. Her children believed she knew everything, just like she believed her mother knew everything at one time. They would find out, just like Regina found out her mother didn't know that much and she was faking it. Regina would fake it until her children were out of the house, one way or another.

The one thing she could do, she did well: involving the fathers or some representative of the father to become involved in the child's life. Jaleel's father and his father's mother were involved in Jaleel's life. He had stayed over his grandmother's. Jaleel had gone to the prison to see his father, but not too many times; maybe twice a year since he was five. His grandmother did give money for him, and she bought things for him.

Laneka's father was dead, so his mother was involved with Laneka. Before he was shot to death, he did the least he could to contribute. Regina had to stay on him to get the money she needed for all the baby things. His being dead hardly mattered now. Laneka didn't miss him, and his mother did what she could, which wasn't much.

DeShawn's father was the most involved, but

he was trying to take more than he was allowed. He'd gotten with this woman and she had been putting ideas in his head. DeShawn was the least of a mistake of any of her children, if there could be such a thing. Regina wanted to believe that she and DeShawn's father had the best chance of getting married and living that dream she had as a little girl—that dream that a man would take care of you, that you could work but you wouldn't have to. DeShawn's father represented the best chance at that.

He was student at Chicago State University when they met. He was on his way out of the ghetto. He was going to be a teacher. Now he was a teacher, and he wanted to take DeShawn away from her. He would never come out and say that she was an unfit mother. After all, she wasn't an unfit lay.

He said he wanted to remove the financial burden that DeShawn put on her family. Regina didn't understand why he had to take DeShawn away for that. He could remove the financial burden by simply buying everything that the child needed. He said he wanted to give DeShawn a two-parent home. He wanted to do what was best for DeShawn. That's what he'd say, but that is not how she heard it. There was nothing about her that was good enough for his son. She lived in a bad neighborhood, she never had enough money, she couldn't get him in a better school, and she beat him.

DeShawn's father sounded a lot like a social service agency. He wanted to do everything but the right thing for the sake of the child. What DeShawn's father failed to understand was that if he wanted to help DeShawn, he would have to do it through her. She didn't understand how his father wanted to do all this for DeShawn, but nothing for Regina. How had she become so evil in his eyes over the last few years? He swore she was taking money that he gave her for DeShawn and using it for her other children. He was right; she did do that.

When he looked at her children, all he would see was his son. She saw her family. As far as her children knew, their fathers did very little for them. Their mother did everything. Besides, she knew if she sent Jaleel to live with his grand-mother, the children most certainly would miss each other. They were not to be split up.

Regina could hear the television on in the kids' room. She wouldn't have to hear it when she moved to her mother's room. Jaleel might take her room, or she might give it to Laneka, even though she was a bit young to have her own room. When Reginald went away, Anthony would have his own room, so maybe she might rent her old room out. They could definitely use the money.

It would be nice if they could take Mama's in-surance money and move to a nicer neighborhood, put the kids in a better school. Then she wouldn't have to worry about them dodging bullets, at least not as much. Maybe she could get her G.E.D. and go to school and get some kind of job skills. Mov-ing would have to be something that everybody agreed on, and they probably wouldn't. Regina felt like she was cursed to stay in the same place and die just like her mother died, just like her grand-mother died, and then her daughter could die there too.

They would certainly get some of the things in the house fixed up; fix the kitchen, get a new boiler, some new security doors. Twenty-five thousand dollars would be gone in no time. Whatever they did, Regina was sure that she would be there to see it need to be done again.

Her mother always figured she would win the lottery and get out of the house. Regina always thought some man was going to take her out of this house. Even after she had her children, she felt that way. Now that they were school age, she settled on the fact that if she left, it would be by her own doing, and she wasn't going to leave. There was no real way for her to get herself and her children out of here. She was on welfare and had no real experience doing anything.

She had been a cashier at an Arab liquor store on 79th Street once. That was before Laneka and DeShawn were born. It was then that Regina realized that all men were basically the same; they just wanted to get laid. If it wasn't the A-rabs in the store, it was the niggas out on the bus stop, all of them talking that same shit. Trying to get laid without coming up off any money, the cheap-ass sonofabitches.

Since then, men had come in and out of her life, but somewhere along the line they stopped being part of the solution. Regina knew that she could use pussy to get a man, but keeping him took something else. It seemed like any man she could keep wasn't worth the effort, and any man she wanted, there was no way to get to. The grass was definitely greener on the other side.

She wondered how the people living in Chatham and Beverly got to be where they were. They didn't start out being a cashier in a liquor store or waiting tables in some shitty restaurant. It didn't matter because they were there, she was here, and all the bridges were burned.

She turned over and got out of the bed. She had a slight hangover. Too many people were coming by, and everybody was bringing something. Most of her mother's friends brought something to drink as opposed to something to eat. Lately she had been spending the day with a drink in her hand. Normally Regina would only drink when she went out to a club or something, or if somebody came by with something to drink. She comforted herself with the thought that what she was doing was ordinary. It was just that more people were coming by with something to drink.

Maybe that is how it started with her mother. You get wore down, and more wore down, then you drink your way through one crisis, then another, then every day is just another crisis that you drink your way through.

She went to the bathroom and showered. On the way back to her room, she checked in the kids' room. Laneka and DeShawn were mesmerized by the television. Jaleel was nowhere in sight. Regina hoped that he was downstairs eating, but he was probably already out in the streets somewhere.

Regina got dressed and went into her mother's room. The funeral was tomorrow, then this wouldn't be her mother's room anymore. A long time ago, the door to the room seemed so big. When she was a little girl, it was her grandmother's room. It used to smell like flowers and it was brighter then. When Grandma got sick, it smelled like medicine or antiseptic. When Grandma passed then Dorothy moved in, that seemed like forever ago.

Regina was ten or eleven then. The difference was one that she didn't notice right off. Her grandmother died and boys started coming out of the woodwork for her. By the seventh grade, Regina's breasts made her the envy of every girl in her class. Her mother tried to fight it. That was how it was done back then; you either fought it or ignored it. Her mother didn't realize it, but she was fighting hundreds of boys, and she was fighting by herself. Even more, her mother didn't realize that the battle she was fighting had already been lost to one of the neighbor's sons when Regina was ten.

By the time Regina was fifteen, boys were coming at her from every direction. She continued to blossom in high school, and the word got out that she was sexually active. She wasn't the only one, either. Sex was all the girls talked about on the phone and in the bathrooms at school. Her mother was still fighting it, but now she was fighting Regina too. She was drinking a lot more by then, and she would drunkenly tell Regina about how bad boys were, as if Regina didn't already know. She'd experienced the power of sex when she was ten. She experienced the consequences when she was fifteen.

Her mother almost died when she found out Regina was pregnant. Dorothy cursed and spat like Regina had been convicted of capital murder. By the time Jaleel was born, Dorothy had accepted it and was even in the delivery room with Regina.

The room brought it all back to her—the fights she had in that room, beatings for getting bad grades, beatings for coming home late, getting cursed out for hanging her ass out of some boy's car window. Regina smiled, thinking about all the times her mother had said that to her. Then it occurred to her that she wouldn't hear it anymore, and she wanted to cry.

The phone rang, and Regina answered it on the first ring. Her mother would have accused her of acting desperate for doing that, but it wasn't like that at all. Regina just didn't like the sound of bells—doorbells, school bells, any kind of ringing. That was one of many things her mother didn't understand about her.

More of her mother's friends were coming over today. There were other people coming over too. Reginald's friends from church were always coming by. At least they would bring something to eat. Regina wanted to cook today, whether people brought food or not. It was the most normal thing she could do. Regina had been cooking the family meals since she was twelve. There was no reason to stop now. The kids had cold cereal for breakfast yesterday, so today they could have pancakes or something.

Regina got up and looked in the kids' room again. She went downstairs, and Jaleel wasn't in the house. He was going to be just like his father and wind up in jail next to him. Regina never did find out what really happened in the playground yesterday, but she suspected there was more to it than Danny said there was. While she would rather that Jaleel be in the house, it was summer, and keeping him cooped up in the house seemed neither smart nor fair. Pretty soon Laneka and DeShawn would be like that. Regina wasn't going to act like her mother did and ride her children about their whereabouts. She would be more understanding than that. At least she hoped she would.

Regina knew her children weren't the greatest kids in the world, but they weren't all bad. Sometimes they were just a little hardheaded and they needed to have their attitudes adjusted. All children were like that. Regina knew girls with children so bad you would want to leave them on the highway. Her kids basically got along with each other. Besides, they were all cute. One thing was for sure, Regina didn't make no ugly babies.

Regina thought about making herself a cup of coffee, but she never really liked coffee anyway, except maybe the kind you get in a restaurant. She busied herself making pancakes for everybody in the house. She didn't make any for Reginald because she was sure he wasn't there anyway.

Dorothy used to make pancakes on the Saturdays she didn't have to go to work. The pancake breakfasts stopped after Regina's grandmother died. Dorothy used to say she was a waitress not a cook, which was true, because she couldn't cook as good as Regina. Dorothy used to be cleaner, too, until she started being drunk all the time. Regina kept the kitchen clean, and most of the rest of the house too. But it was never clean enough for her mother to come home from work and say it was a good job. Instead, she would pick until she found something she could bitch about.

Regina called Laneka and DeShawn down to eat, then she actually went into the basement, woke Danny and asked him if he wanted some pancakes. Of course he did. Anthony came down on the smell of bacon alone. They sat and ate at the table. For a moment, Regina actually saw them as a family, like a sitcom on television. She wondered where Jaleel could be this early in the morning while she sat and ate with the rest of her family.

With the dishes washed and put away, she went into the front room to watch the stories. She sat in her mother's chair. She would have sat there even if her mother was alive, because she'd be at work. As soon as she was settled in, the doorbell rang. She thought it was the beginning of the intrusion of visitors, but it was DeShawn's father.

He came in and took a seat on the old sunken couch. He'd brought something that his mother had sent for DeShawn. She hung the clothes in the closet, and put the toy in the closet also. "Why you putting his toy up? I wanted to give it to him myself."

"He'll get it. He just got to wait until Laneka get something too."

"Laneka's not my responsibility."

"She's my responsibility, and so is DeShawn. That's the way I do it. Either they both get toys or neither of them gets toys."

Regina could tell from the look on his face that he didn't understand. There had been times before when things like this happened and he assured her that he didn't hate her other children. He just hated that they were hers. If DeShawn had been her only child, she was sure that they would be married by now. She often wondered how he could profess all that love for her and not love her children. They were as much a part of her as her arms were. He didn't understand she wouldn't be who she was without them.

He saw Laneka and Jaleel as another man's children. They were not another man's, they were hers, first and foremost. DeShawn was not his, DeShawn was hers, and she was going to see to it that he and his new girlfriend understood that. He still lived with his mother and she took care of him like he was a baby. She cooked his dinner and cleaned up after him. If he thought that every woman in the world was going to obey his whims, he'd better just stay at home with his mother. His wife-to-be might take that shit, but Regina could just send the nigga packing. He wanted to tear her family up.

DeShawn came downstairs, having heard his father in the living room. His father gave him a few dollars to go and buy some candy. Regina told him he could go to the store with Laneka, and that he was to share the money with her. DeShawn and Laneka left, happy to get a chance to get some candy. DeShawn's father saw he was fighting a battle he could in no way win, so he followed the children to the store.

Regina cleaned, dusted and vacuumed. Tomorrow and even later today, the house would be full of people, and it should look like it was cleaned some time. Uncle Dave and Aunt Rose were the first staying guests to arrive. Aunt Rose offered to help Regina with the cleaning, and she offered a drink to help Regina make it through the day. The way the day was going, the help was more than welcome.

Regina held off taking too much help. She had to make sure the kids all had clothes and shoes. Fathers and grandmothers were always forgetting shoes. They could remember everything else but the shoes and the underwear. She caught the bus to the shopping mall on 63rd and Halsted. Cheap shit from one of those Korean places would be okay. It didn't have to last forever, just through the next two days.

After the shopping trip, she came home to see Danny actually sitting in the living room talking to people other than Tiny or Anthony. He was actually being cordial to the guests. That was a surprise. Reginald was in the kitchen with all his good-cooking sissy friends. Anthony was nowhere to be found. The children were in their room, locked onto the television set. Jaleel was not in the house at all.

Regina took the first drink someone offered her. There was plenty to eat. Regina knew Dorothy would have been proud. This was definitely better than a lot of people sitting around crying all the time. Regina only had to feign attention by occasionally nodding and saying "Yes." With a look in the right direction, her drink was refreshed or her plate was filled automatically.

Danny got up and headed out the back door. Regina followed him. There was no reason; she just wanted to get out of the house for awhile. He lit up a joint. For a moment she watched him from the porch, then she walked out and joined him by the garage. "So, how you doing?" she asked him.

"I'm straight."

"I mean about you getting hit in the face 'n stuff."

"I'm all right. I'm still alive."

He offered the joint to her. She took it.

"So, you gonna still sell drugs?" she asked.

"I hope I won't have to."

"So do I."

Regina passed the joint back to Danny. He took a long pull.

"You know they found Otis in the playground."

"Dead?"

"Yeah. Shotgun," Danny said, looking at the ground.

She took the joint from Danny. "Well, let's be glad it wasn't you."

She inhaled from the joint, held it for a few seconds and blew the smoke out. "So, what happened at the playground yesterday with Jaleel?"

"It wasn't nothing you need to worry about. Just some shorty shit happening. Shorties will be like that."

"How did Jaleel get beat up?"

"He was winning and some punks jumped in. Same ol' story." Danny frowned. "You know I was thinking that with the money from Ma's insurance, maybe we could move out of this house, maybe sell it or something."

"You want to move?" Regina couldn't believe that this was coming out of Danny's mouth.

"Yeah. Get the hell away from here. Maybe try to find a place in Chatham or over in South Shore or something. Might even move out to the suburbs. What you think about that?"

Regina chuckled. "Hey, I'm down with that. But even if we do move, how long will Mama's money last us? That ain't all we got to do with that money. I mean I had some other plans too. Besides, we still got to get the house fixed up some, then we can at least rent it out and get some money that way.

"If Anthony come through like he say he will,

then we'll be on our way. Let me worry about the details. We gonna get out of here."

"Do you think Reginald will be mad if we take the money and move away from here?"

Danny sucked on what was left of the joint then threw it to the ground. "I don't give a fuck if Reginald gets mad."

They walked to the house in silence. Inside, one of Regina's old boyfriends was sitting on the couch waiting to see her. At first she was glad to see him, then she wondered why he would come by. She knew that men always liked to catch you when they thought that getting laid was easier than other times, when you were weak. She also knew that more often than not, they were right to come around.

They went out on the porch and talked. He put his arm around her. She sort of melted into some comfortable familiarity that he brought with him. She was in his arms, she was drunk, and she had smoked something with Danny. Getting laid was not a bad idea. No, they didn't teach you this in school, but that is where you learned it. She looked up to him, and they kissed, and she was sure that she wanted it to go further, all the way.

Right now she was not particular about who it was with. This boy showed up at the right time. The new boy that she was seeing was not there. He should have been, if for no other reason than he should know how men are. Besides, he was not yet tried and tested. This boy had passed the test of sex some time ago.

Yeah, she wanted to go, but where could they go? Certainly not in her house. Maybe they could go to his apartment, now that he had an apartment. When he was coming around before, he was living with his mother, and they had to get a room at the no-tell motel. His apartment was much better than a room, where she would wait in the car until he came back, then creep through the lobby with a feeling of small shame.

There were hands all over in the car—her hands, his hands. There were kisses at the stoplights. By the time she got to his third floor apartment, she was dripping wet between her legs. The apartment was dark, not that it mattered. She just wanted him, just for a time. He was taking his clothes off, and she could almost hear Anthony ask, "How many of your friends have died from it? They will."

"We need to use some protection," she said.

"We didn't use no protection before."

"It's a new day. Either we use protection or we don't have a reason to use protection."

He produced the protection. He fulfilled her lust, and she his. It had been some time, too long, since Regina had been this way with a man. There was no pretending that things were going anywhere, no vows of love everlasting, and no lies. When it was over, she got up and dressed. When she asked him to take her home, he complained that it was so late that she might as well stay.

Earlier in her life, that kind of shit might have worked, but there were things that she had to do. She told him to take her or to pay the cab fare, so he took her home. She was amazed that men would still try this kind of bullshit at all.

Back at the house, things were pretty much as she left them. The people were still there, Jaleel was still not in the house, Laneka and DeShawn were still glued to the television set. Someone handed her a rum and cola, so she sat and listened to Reginald's friends gossip to each other, about each other. Regina remembered them from church, but they had never been over to the house before. She watched them talking, all animated and feminine. Who did Reginald ever think he was fooling?

Danny, Tiny, and two of Reginald's friends sat at the kitchen table playing bid whist. It was hard to tell that there was going to be a funeral tomorrow, but this is the way her mother would have wanted it, a party that lasted a week.

She asked Reginald if Anthony was home. He was upstairs in his room. Regina went to see him. She was fucked up enough to listen to anything that he had to say. She stood at the door and knocked.

"Come in."

Regina walked through the door and saw Anthony laying across his bed, looking at the ceiling. "Hey, Tony, how you doing? Why you ain't downstairs with the rest of us?"

"I'm straight. Tell me something, Regina. Why is it that when a bitch has my child, she can do any damn thing she wants to with him, but I got to ask if I can take him to the store? That is bullshit."

Regina sat next to Anthony on the bed. "What happened?"

"I went to see my son, and that bitch that call herself his mother took him off somewhere."

"Why she got to be all that?"

"I wish I knew. Man, all them bitches be on T.V.

talking all that shit about niggas ain't shit, then when a nigga try to do right by his children, bitches be blocking. A motherfucker can't win."

"I don't know, Anthony. I mean you don't know what's happening with her. Check it out. DeShawn's daddy wants to try to take him from me. Now he talking all that shit about his son this and his son that. Fuck that motherfucker. He ain't got shit coming."

Anthony smiled. "That's because he a bourgie-ass punk. I told you that when the motherfucker first come creeping around. He'd be standing on the porch trembling 'n shit. I knew he wasn't gonna be right."

Regina took a sip out of her drink. "So, how do you know that Vanessa don't feel that way about you? 'Cause see, I don't look at it like he trying to take his son. I look at it like he trying to break up my family. But you don't know what 's up with Vanessa."

"I know she a pipe-head bitch."

"She fucking with the pipe?"

"Yeah. Not only that, but she fucking with some dope-dealing, punk-ass Friend. I don't want my son in bullshit like that."

"Good luck with that. That's some bad-ass drama there."

Anthony sat up on the bed. "Regina, answer me something."

"What?"

"Would you look out for Max for me?"

"Is that part of the big plan you got for Danny?"

"What did Danny tell you?"

"He ain't said nothing about the plan, except that you had a plan. But you said that the other night at the table or in the yard or somewhere you said it. He did say something earlier about if you look out for him the way you said you was, then we could move."

"That is super straight. He making plans 'n shit. That shit is straight. That makes me feel good. So, you gonna move?"

"If I can, I will. You gonna move with us, ain't you?"

"Not only am I gonna move with you, I'm gonna move for you," Anthony said, smiling

"Anthony don't do nothing stupid. We just lost Mama. Don't go doing nothing stupid."

"Don't worry. This ain't stupid."

Regina took another sip from the glass. "Do you think Jaleel gonna turn out like Danny? You know, running the street all the time, being in a gang and stuff like that?"

"Being where he is, the odds are that he will turn out that way. I don't really know what you can do about it."

"I was thinking of sending him to stay with his grandmother. You think that might help?"

"Hell no. She fucked up once, and there ain't no reason to think that she learned to do things any differently since. She could wind up raising him to be just like his father, to be just where his father is. If you ain't gonna raise him, ain't nobody. You know that he knows that it's a paper chase, and I tried to put it on his mind to chase the paper slow. Fast money is a bad and dangerous thing if you ain't ready for it."

"So, what you think I ought to do?"

"Show him how to live. Stop telling him shit. Do shit for yourself, shit like going to school and getting a decent job. Look for some balance in your life. Make time for your kids and yourself. The best thing you can be for your kids is good to yourself."

"You know, Anthony, they be talking that same shit on television all the time, but shit don't happen like that. Where do you get started on some shit like that? I mean, I be thinking about doing shit like going to school 'n shit, but that ain't no promise there."

Anthony looked in her dazed eyes. "You know you right, but peep this. If you do it, you might get somewhere. If you don't do shit, you definitely going nowhere. It's tripped out, but once you focused, you can see shit clear as hell. That's what you need, Regina. You need to get focused on a goal or something."

"Yeah, that shit looks good on paper."

"Just think about it, Regina. Get focused and kick some ass."

Regina sat there, looking at the floor, then she stood up. "You gonna come downstairs? They playing cards."

"Maybe."

Regina walked out the door. Instead of going to the steps, she went to her mother's room. She came in, turned on the light, and sat on the bed. It was the first time she sat on the bed since she had seen her mother on it. She didn't want the bed. She would buy another one. She laughed, realizing it was the same thing her mother did. As soon as her grandmother was buried, her mother bought a new bed.

Regina looked out the window. It was all stuff that she had seen before—the houses across the street, the cars, the lights from 61st Street. She looked toward the park and watched a group of people coming toward the house. Jaleel was in the group, and Regina watched as he and a girl broke away from the group. The rest of the group, which was nothing more than other teenaged boys and girls, continued walking, but Jaleel and the girl stopped and kissed. A quick flash of memory reminded Regina. This is where it all began.

She watched them. She wanted to say something, but she didn't know what. Jaleel didn't seem old enough to be kissing. He was thirteen; it was summer. Things like that happened. They would keep happening, then one summer romance would turn into a baby one April or May. Yeah, shit like that happened.

She sat back down on the bed, and thought about spending the night in this room just to see what it would feel like. She had lived in this house all of her life, and she had never spent the night in this room. When her mother had gone out of town, she had spent all day in it, but never the night.

Regina took a sip of her drink. There was no way she would spend the night in this room. If it weren't the biggest room in the house, she probably wouldn't move into it at all. She should let Danny have it. After all, he was the oldest. She would take it, though. It was her right. But not tonight. After her mother was buried. Maybe Anthony and Danny were telling the truth. She could move out of the house, and she would never have to sleep in the dead room.

She wondered if her mother ever wanted to get out of the house. She must have wanted things to be better than they were. The house was like a trap that held her mother until she died in it. Now with her mother dead, Regina could finally get out of this hellhole before it killed her and her children too.

A breeze came through the window, parting the curtains, then died down. Regina sent a silent thank you to God for being able to get out of the house, or at least to dream of getting out. She was amazed that as many people in her family were alive at all. There were so many people she knew, who had lost a loved one or two. It wasn't from old age or even bad health, but mostly the violence that just sucked people down the dead hole. She knew it was only a matter of time before death came and took someone young out of the house. If it wasn't Danny, she wouldn't be surprised if it was Jaleel. Regina thanked God again for just the chance to get out. She just hoped it was soon enough to save everybody.

chapter fifteen

Reginald stood at the window looking out over the lake. Dennis sat in a chair across the room. Neither of them spoke, then Reginald began to cry. It was soft murmurs and tears. Dennis started to cross the room and comfort his old friend, but Reginald motioned him away. "I'll be okay. Just give me a moment. "

Reginald walked into his room. His mother's funeral was in a few hours, and there was nothing for him to do. He wanted to be helping, but everything had already been taken care of. He lay across his bed and thought about his mother. He hoped she'd gone to heaven because her life had been rough enough.

There was nothing to do but think about his mother. He didn't feel like getting laid. Maybe later, after all of this was over with. Things like that would take care of themselves. He wondered if he should drive to his mother's house to ride in the limo to the church. He could have Dennis take him. He didn't really want to leave his car there anyway. He looked at the walls in his room, surprised that they had become so familiar to him so quickly.

This room was nothing like the room he grew up in at home. These walls were green with purple trim. The walls at the house were some weak blue with white borders. There was no adventure in them, no life. Those walls had been blue ever since he could remember, something about being a boy's room. He wondered what the room was used for before Danny was born. He couldn't remember ever hearing it called anything other than the boy's room. All at once, the room on Eberhart seemed to be a million years ago and in a far-off place, yet fresh in his memory like something that happened earlier in the day.

He assured himself that moving in with Dennis was a good thing to do. Anything would be better than staying in the house on Eberhart. Here he would not only have the freedom to be and say what he wanted without fear of repercussions. He would also have privacy, a room of his own.

His eyes wandered over to the radio sitting on the floor in the corner of the room. Reginald had picked it up from work yesterday. He hoped that it was close enough to what Tremont wanted for Tremont to be happy. If it wasn't, there was nothing he could do about it for a while. Tremont was going to have to come over here and pick it up.

Dennis came in the room and asked if he wanted a ride. Reginald got up, put on his black, raw silk jacket and headed for the door. They made the ride in relative silence, listening to a tape of a church service.

Reginald could see the two black limousines as

soon as they turned the corner. Inside the house was a small crowd; Uncle Dave, Aunt Rose, and some other close friends. The kids were all dressed and they did look nice. Danny wore a black suit, which Reginald had no idea he owned. Anthony was wearing a shirt, black tie, and pants. Regina was made up, and she actually looked pretty. Reginald could see traces of Dorothy in her face.

One of the drivers got out of the limousine and came to the front door. Regina saw him and started crying. She didn't want to go. She hated funerals, especially this one. Reginald looked down at DeShawn. He was crying too. The other children had blank looks on their faces.

Reginald took Regina's hand. "Nobody wants to go, but we have to."

Regina nodded softly through her tears and allowed herself to be led to the car. She rode with her children, Uncle Dave and Aunt Rose. Danny, Reginald and Anthony rode in the second limo. The ride to the church was in complete silence. They arrived at the church and were ushered inside to the front pew.

Before they sat down, they walked by the casket and viewed the body. Danny was first. He looked in the casket then proceeded to his seat at the far end of the pew. Reginald looked in, straightened something on his mother's dress, then took his seat. Regina was next. She held on to her youngest children's hands. They all looked in together. Jaleel followed them. Anthony was last. He leaned into the casket and whispered, "See you soon."

Reginald didn't like the way his mother's body looked. Dead people never looked right. She hadn't been in an accident or anything, so she should have looked perfect. Her skin was darker, and somehow her hair was wrong. He knew he should have checked with the funeral home before they brought the body here, but he had never done anything like this before, and no one told him how things went. She looked older than she did when she was alive.

Reginald looked at her from his seat. It was easy to say that wasn't his mother, but he knew that was all that was left of her. The choir began singing softly as people filed pass the body. Reginald scanned the choir stand and was glad to see Tremont. After people passed the casket, they would stop and offer their condolences to the family.

Soon the church was filled. There were friends of the family, but mostly there were other church members. The casket was closed and the service began. Reverend Warden and three associate ministers sat in the pulpit. They all appeared to ignore the casket.

One of the associate ministers walked up to the front of the pulpit. He looked down at the family sitting in the front pew, and gave them a sympathetic smile. Then he looked out over the people in the sanctuary. He gave a weak welcome then opened his Bible.

He thumbed through the pages until he found the one he was looking for. He began reading form the fifth chapter of John, the twentieth verse. "For the Father loves the Son and shows Him all things . . ." He finished with verse 29. ". . . those who committed evil deeds to a resurrection of judgment."

He closed his Bible and looked at the family again. "May Dorothy be risen to life eternal."

He returned to his seat, then another associate minister approached the pulpit. He closed his eyes and bowed his head. "Heavenly Father, we are gathered here today, in the midst of all our grief and sorrow, to say thank you. We thank You that we knew Dorothy, and that we were blessed to have her as part of our lives. We thank You for allowing us to be a part of her life too, Father. Lord, we know that no ones lives in these bodies forever, yet we are never ready to accept the passing of a loved one. Dorothy's passing caught us all by surprise. In her passing, we see that life cannot be depended upon. What we call life here in this world is temporary at best, and we never know how close we are to being called home. Lord, You have, however, given us something that we can depend on. We will have it today and forever. That is Your love, God. We thank You for that love. We also want You to know that as long as You love us, we can only remain thankful. We are thankful that Dorothy Evans rests in Your arms today and forever more. We hope that the memories that we have of Dorothy serve as an inspiration to those that knew her, but didn't know You. Because You, Father, are the only thing on which we can depend for eternity. In Jesus' name we pray. Amen."

The minister returned to his seat. Edward struck a chord on the piano and the choir stood. It seemed for a moment he didn't know what he was going to play, then he started a slow, mournful gospel song. Reginald knew the song. It was one he and Edward had co-written because of the many funerals of friends they went to. It was called "The Other Side." The refrain ran through Reginald's mind. "There's a love we know but we don't understand, a love we can call our own, a love from the other side."

Reginald watched Tremont singing. Tremont looked at him once, but when he saw Reginald looking, he quickly looked away. Reginald continued to stare at him as long as the song lasted. When the song ended, Aunt Rose went up and thanked people in the sanctuary for the cards and letters they received. Before she left, she announced that the choir would sing another selection.

Pastor Warden got up and approached the pulpit. "I know this may seem out of order somewhat. Mrs. Evans sure liked to hear her son sing, so I'm gonna ask Reginald to come up here and sing a selection in memory of his mother.

Reginald got up and walked over to the piano where he told Edward to play "Beams of Heaven". Reginald went to the microphone in the choir stand. He looked out over the audience. The church was full from front to back. His mother couldn't have known all these people. He lifted his head toward the ceiling. He didn't like to look at people when he sang. At least he didn't like to start out looking at them, particularly now. He didn't want to see the casket that held his mother's body, not now. He focused on a point near the ceiling on the back wall, took a deep breath then he shook it off. He grabbed the mike with both hands and took another breath then realized that Edward was playing the introduction for a second time. There were calls from the congregation for him to take his time. He took another deep breath and began to sing

The singing helped him, or maybe it was the song. He just knew that while he sang, he felt better. He sang knowing he didn't have all the answers or all the questions. He felt removed, like he could touch God from where he was. Perhaps he could stay there as long as he continued to sing. Then, just like a bubble bursting, it was all over. He was still singing, but through the music he could hear crying, and God was gone. He had to stop singing. There were tears streaming down his face. He finished the second verse and turned around. The choir picked up where he left off as he headed toward his seat.

Before he could reach his seat, he started singing again. He looked from the casket to where his family was sitting, Regina had fainted. Anthony and Danny were both crying. Reginald looked over the congregation. Almost everyone in the church was crying. He held one note as long as he could, then he passed out.

He came to in the pastor's office. Someone was holding smelling salts under his nose. Reginald immediately wanted to go back out front, but an usher blocked his way. "I'm all right," he said as he brushed past the usher, and returned to his seat on the front pew.

Someone else was praying in the pulpit. Regina was okay, and everything seemed to be under control. The person praying took his seat and Reverend Warden rose from his chair and approached the pulpit. He looked down on the people in the congregation. He faced the family and nodded his head to acknowledge them.

"It is a shame that we are gathered here for an occasion such as this one. The shame of it is that we would not have all come here to celebrate her birthday, we would not have come here just to tell Dorothy we loved her, but now we are all here to say good-bye. Not that we can tell Dorothy good-bye, because we can't. We can only say good-bye to the hopes and dreams we had that involved Dorothy. We are here saying good-bye with flowers she cannot smell, with words she cannot hear, with cards that she cannot read.

"Too often in our lives it is the passing of a loved one that shows us how much we loved that person. That is a shame. As we move on in our lives, we can only take our memories like small bags of treasures into tomorrow with us."

To some she was a mother, to some a friend, to some a sister. To all of us she was a measure of love. While we hold her in our memories, I want us to consider the love we have for each other. There is a love that God would have us share with each other, brother to brother, sister to sister, each to everyone and everyone to each, from those people we don't know to those we know intimately. After all, this is how God would have us to behave."

Reginald listened to the pastor, saying "Amen" at the appropriate times with the rest of the congregation. However, his attention was more centered on Tremont in the choir stand. By concentrating on Tremont, he didn't have to look at the casket in front of him containing his mother. Tremont was a pleasant alternative to a casket and the preacher.

Pastor Warden finished his preaching, then during the invitation, twelve people joined the church. The eulogy was read the casket was reopened, and the choir sang again as people filed out of the sanctuary.

Instead of going straight to their cars, some people stopped and talked to the family in front of the church. The limousines were there, but only the children were in them. Reginald was talking to the pastor, Edward and Mark when Tremont came up to him. Edward excused all of them while Tremont and Reginald talked.

Again Tremont expressed his condolences and Reginald graciously accepted them. Reginald asked Tremont if he were in a hurry to get home, and if he would join him over at Dennis' apartment after the repast at his mother's house. Tremont accepted the offer. He would ride to the repast with Dennis, and they would meet there.

Reginald and the rest of his family got into their respective limousines and went home. They were met there by people already waiting on them with drink in hand. Everybody came in and started drinking.

They sat around and reminisced. Reginald was on his third glass of wine, and Tremont had drunk a beer and moved on to cola with a little rum in it. Regina sent her children off to bed. Danny and his friends went into the basement and smoked joints. Anthony just up and left, then Reginald decided it was time to go. He, Tremont and Dennis said their good-byes to the people remaining, then left. Tremont sat in the back seat of the car with his second rum and cola. Reginald brought the wine he had been drinking.

They rode in each other's silence and listened to the gospel music on the radio. When they got to the apartment, Dennis excused himself, saying he had to get up and go to work in the morning. Reginald and Tremont sat in the front room. Tremont commented on the view, but other than that, nothing was said for a while.

"You want to listen to some music?" Reginald asked. "Dennis got that stereo over there, but I ain't sure how it works. But if you can figure it out, then turn it on. By the way, I got you a stereo from work. They had an employee sale. I saw it there and thought about you. It's in the room. If you want, you can go in there and get it now."

Tremont walked over to the glass cabinet that held Dennis' rack system. "I'll get it later."

He knelt down and eyed the system for a minute, then pushed a button and there was sound coming from the speakers. He turned it down then changed the station from the gospel music to a contemporary urban format. The radio station was playing what they referred to as "music for lovers only."

Tremont returned to his chair and sat sipping from his drink and looking out the window at the lake. Reginald sipped his wine and watched Tremont. The glow from the streetlight spread softly across the ceiling, and the only other light was from the stereo.

Tremont broke the silence. "So, how you feeling now?" he asked Reginald.

"I'm okay."

"You know you really sang this evening. I mean that was probably the best I've ever heard you sing in my life. "

"Thank you. "

In the soft light in the room, Reginald could see

that Tremont was almost finished with his drink. "Do you want something else to drink? There is some more wine in the refrigerator."

Reginald got up and found the wine and a glass, and handed it to Tremont with the hope that he would be drunk enough to spend the night. Reginald didn't feel like driving him home. Tremont settled back in his chair and looked out the window at the moon hanging in the sky over the lake.

"Nice view, isn't it?" Reginald asked.

"Yeah, it's pretty good. I guess it looks better in the daytime."

"Not really. I mean it doesn't look worse, it just looks different. The moonlight on the lake is like a dream, and sunlight on the lake is blinding at times."

Tremont took another sip from his glass. "Yeah, I've seen it. Not from up here or anything. You know, like driving down Lake Shore Drive."

The music took over the room. Reginald watched Tremont. He wanted to go across the room and kiss him. He wondered what Tremont was thinking about or if he was thinking at all.

Tremont looked at his watch and sat straight up. "I better get going. It's after twelve."

Tremont stood up, and Reginald watched as his legs wobbled under him while he tried to walk to the door. "Why don't you call your grandmother and tell her you spending the night here? I'll take you home in the morning. I mean if that's all right with you."

Tremont asked for the phone and Reginald left the room while he called his grandmother. When Reginald came back in the room, Tremont was no longer on the phone.

"She said it was okay to stay. But where am I supposed to sleep?"

"You can sleep with me in my room. I know that the couch is too uncomfortable to sleep on. I mean as long as you don't mind sleeping with me."

Reginald could see the hesitancy in Tremont's face. "Well, I ain't slept with nobody since I was little."

"I won't mind. You go on in there and make yourself comfortable. I want to spend a little time . . . you know, off to myself. You go on in there and go to sleep. I'm going to have to get up extra early in order to get home and get to my house for the burial."

Tremont acquiesced. Reginald pointed out the bedroom and the bathroom to him. Tremont went to the room, and Reginald returned to his chair in the front. He listened as Tremont went from the bedroom to the bathroom. He listened as Tremont used the bathroom then went back to the bedroom. The bedroom light went off. Reginald continued to sit in the front.

He imagined that Tremont was sleeping in the nude, that Tremont wanted him as much as he wanted Tremont. Maybe Tremont simply didn't know how to express this desire, because it was so new to him. Reginald would be more than happy to show him a few ways to express himself.

Reginald listened past the music to Tremont rustling the sheets in the bed each time he turned over. He looked at his watch. He would go in the room in another half an hour.

Fifteen long minutes later, Reginald left for the room. When he entered the bedroom, he looked to make sure Tremont was sleep. He silently crossed the room and hung up his clothes, tossing his underwear into the hamper in the closet. When he sat on the bed, he could feel Tremont's body heat through the sheets.

Reginald lay down, then quickly got under the sheets and felt Tremont's underwear. He tugged at the band. Tremont shifted his weight. Reginald knew that he would be waking soon, so he moved even more quickly. He pushed Tremont's leg out of his way and began kissing him on his inner thigh. The response was just what Reginald wanted and expected. Reginald moved Tremont's underwear out of the way and placed his erect penis in his mouth.

Tremont woke up moments before he experienced an orgasm in Reginald's mouth. He realized what was happening and tried to push Reginald's head off of him. Reginald would not relent. When it was over, Reginald came out from between Tremont's legs. He looked at Tremont and smiled. Tremont looked confused.

"What were you doing to me?"

Reginald continued to smile. "Did you like it? I think you did. It was just a little fun. I didn't hurt you, did I?"

"No, but—"

"But nothing. Don't worry about it. You didn't get hurt and I didn't get hurt. It was all right."

Before Tremont could respond, Reginald kissed him full on the mouth. Tremont tried to pull away, but Reginald held him. After the kiss, Reginald nuzzled Tremont's neck.

"Tremont," he began breathlessly, "I think you are you beautiful. This was the only way I knew to show you how I felt about you. I know you might not have thought you were ready for this, but I thought you were."

Tremont was still tense. "But I didn't know you were like this."

"Yes, you did. You knew it the same way I knew it about you. It was not as though we actually had to tell each other with words. There were other things going on between us. The way we were so comfortable with each other, the way we became friends so fast—all of that told us."

"But it wasn't supposed to be like this. We were just supposed to be friends."

"We are still friends. This will just make us closer. This is just another aspect of our relationship. This is just something special between us."

"But it was supposed to be like Paul and Timothy or something like that."

"It still can be like that, like that and better. This is something special between us. We don't have to let anyone else know unless we both agree to tell. Is that okay with you?"

Tremont hesitated. "I guess so."

Reginald reached down between Tremont's legs and began stroking his genitals again. Tremont responded with an erection, and Reginald performed oral sex on him again. When it was over, Reginald took Tremont's hand and placed it on his own penis. Tremont tried to pull it away, but Reginald held it there. He used Tremont's hand to masturbate until he reached his orgasm, then he let him go. Tremont lay down and faced away from Reginald, who cuddled with him, kissing his back and licking his ear.

Reginald whispered to him, "I could hold you

like this forever." Tremont didn't say anything, so Reginald continued. "You are so special to me. I just wanted you to know how much you meant to me. I didn't want it to happen like this, but I guess the stress from my mother dying was just too much. I just wanted to be close to someone. I chose you. I'm sorry if you weren't ready for all of this, but I just had to. I wanted you so much. I just couldn't hold it in anymore."

Tremont didn't say anything. Reginald lay there listening to him breathe. He felt guilty about what he had done, but he would not relent now. He held Tremont tighter. He wanted him to know what it was like to be held. Reginald went to sleep holding Tremont. In the morning, Reginald performed oral sex on him again. Tremont was a little more cooperative, or at least Reginald thought he was. When they were ready to go, Reginald reminded him to get the radio. Tremont picked it up. Reginald kissed him again.

Reginald had Dennis drop him off then take Tremont home. When Reginald got out of the car, he gave Tremont's hand a squeeze. He felt Tremont squeeze back. At least he thought he did.

chapter sixteen

How do you start the last day of your life? That depends. If someone has chosen this day to kill you then you begin the day in fear. If you have chosen that day to die, then you are in total control. Anthony decided that a joint and a good breakfast would be the perfect start. Aunt Dorothy's burial was to be today. It would have to happen without him. He would be going to the burial ground on his own time, soon enough.

For the first time since he'd come from jail, he shaved. His face looked younger without that scraggly beard, his jail hair. He was glad to have it off. After washing, he walked downstairs to eat breakfast. He would need to get some vitamins and minerals. This was going to be a tough day.

He sat at the table as the rest of the family got ready to attend the burial. Reginald was not there, but then he never really was there anyway. He was always someplace else. He was at choir rehearsal or he was doing something else at the church of the eternally fucked up souls.

Danny came up the stairs, already dressed. "Yo, Family, ain't you going to the burial with the rest of us?"

"I'm sorry, man. You know I loved Dorothy like she was my own mother. Shit, she was the only mother I ever really knew, but I got other shit I got to do today."

"Like what?"

"My mission."

"Can't it wait?"

"Nope. As a matter of fact, I'm using the burial as my alibi. There are people that will expect me to be there, so I have to use that to my advantage. Aunt Dorothy would understand, and if she don't, we can talk about it soon enough."

"So, you really gonna do this shit."

"Hey, look. Bottom line, you the one that's got shit to do. Don't be faking me out 'n shit. See, I've got to totally trust you. If you fuck up, there won't be nothing I can do about it."

"Well, if you take care of Sweets, then I'll come through."

"Sweets is like the least of what I got to do. He ain't gonna be a problem at all. So, when you hear that he's deadened, you in. Bet?"

"Bet."

They shook hands. Danny left the table and went upstairs. Soon after, the children came down, Jaleel and DeShawn both in suits, Laneka in a black dress with a white lace collar. Anthony couldn't remember seeing them all so dressed up at once. It would be a nice way to remember them. They sat at the table eating cold cereal. Regina came down and reminded them not to spill anything on themselves. She looked at Anthony and saw that he wasn't dressed. She asked him if he was going to the burial. He said no.

"Why not?"

"You'll know soon enough."

"You fucked up, Anthony. My mother raised you, and you can't even go to her burial. You are so fucked up. Fuck it. I ain't got time for this. I just ain't got the time." Regina rolled her eyes, turned around, and went back upstairs.

The kids just looked at him and ate their cereal in silence. Jaleel finished first, and left as soon as his bowl emptied. Laneka and DeShawn both saved their milk so they could have seconds of their no-name fruit ring cereal. Anthony watched the two of them. They seemed like they had never been apart. It was hard to imagine there was a time when there was a Laneka and no DeShawn. Now they were natural allies.

Danny, Reginald and Anthony had been like that once. Their grandmother called them the Three Musketeers. They always thought she was saying "Mousketeers." By the time they knew what the difference was, they were no longer that way. They grew older and grew apart, not what they imagined life to be.

Anthony figured it was because they no longer had common enemies like they used to. Laneka and DeShawn still had the common enemy of boredom and the common ally of imagination. But he, Danny and Reginald had lost it. Today he would renew the fight. He would revive a commonality about their enemies. He could not kill it on his own. Danny would have to come through, and even Reginald's faggot ass would have to cooperate to some degree, and they would all be the better for it.

There was a time when the three of them would have secrets that no one else would know. This should have been one of those times, but since Reginald got the Holy Ghost he wasn't one of them. Reginald was totally out of the loop on this. He hadn't heard a word about it. There was no reason for him to know. If he did know, he would start spewing all that Christian shit. Danny could tell him later.

What Danny knew was only the outcome. He had no idea what was about to happen. Danny was looking at it like it was some kind of dare that Anthony could back out of. Danny probably thought that Anthony was just faking, full of shit. Nobody had faith in this act. Anthony still wasn't sure what the act was. It wasn't solid in his own mind.

Watching the kids eat, Anthony realized even more how important this shit was. If he could pull it off, the whole family could get out. This was the pulling together that bullshit-ass black leaders were always talking about. He wondered what they would be saying tomorrow. They wouldn't see it as people coming together to get shit done, but bottom line, that is what it was—people acting together to save the children. Anthony smiled. He was going to save the children. Not all of them, just the ones he cared about.

The kids took their last slurp of cereal and left the table. Jaleel came back into the house, Anthony stopped him before he went through the kitchen.

"Yo, man, what the fuck is up with you? Danny told me you got into some shit over some drugs 'n shit. What is up with that?"

Jaleel gave Anthony a hard-as-I-am look and said, "I hope you ain't about to give me that drug lecture, 'cause I already heard it."

"Nope, I'm about to give you the are-you-fucking-crazy lecture. That's the one I used to get all the time, and it's the only one I really remember."

Jaleel shifted his weight from one foot to the other. "I don't need no kind of lecture."

"Oh well, Homes Malone. Just what do you need? Or do you got it all right now?"

"I just need people to quit trying to tell me what to do."

Anthony leaned toward him. "How the fuck you gonna make it in jail? 'Cause you gonna go. Yeah, one of them motherfuckers will grab your little ass and make you into a bitch. How you gonna handle that? Or maybe you could wind up just like Otis and James, deadened in the playground."

"Nothing'll happen. I'll just be dead."

"Oh, so your life ain't shit."

"That ain't what I said."

"Then what the fuck are you saying, you little punk ass motherfucker?"

"Why I got to be all that?"

" 'Cause that's what you are, a little punk-ass, runny nose, smelly-ass, teenage motherfucker. Don't know a goddamn thing, but your ass can rule the world. I ought to kick your motherfucking ass just to show you what you don't know."

"I know I'm getting my money on."

"Motherfucker, you don't know a damn thing about money. That little bullshit you call money is just what the man wants your ass to die for, one or two thousand dollars. See, that's some dumb-ass nigga shit going on there. Man, why don't you learn to think of money by the billions? Fuck a few grand. See, when your ass don't be paying attention in school, you think a grand is some dough, but if you went to college, you would find out it ain't shit."

"You ain't go to college."

"Yeah, 'cause I fucked up. So, you want to fuck up like me?"

"No."

"Man, look. It's easy to be another stupid nigga on the planet Earth. Be somebody it ain't easy to be. Be a true bad-ass. Check this out. You think them basketball players in the NBA got the dough rolling, right?"

"Yeah, they do."

"Think about the motherfucker that pay they asses. They got dough rolling, totally righteous, totally legit. That is a hard motherfucker to be. That's why it ain't that many of them, but you got a bigger dick than all them motherfuckers, so kick they ass. See what I'm saying 'n shit?"

"Yeah, sort of."

"Hey, Jaleel, bottom line, just make me one promise."

"What?"

"If you get outta this hood, you don't come back. Don't be a punk and let real life beat you. "

"Yeah, I guess so," Jaleel said slowly.

"Bet?"

"Bet."

They shook hands and Anthony left the table. Jaleel didn't know what to do. Another reason Danny had to come through. Anthony found some paper and a pen, and wrote down the things he specifically wanted Danny to do. He put the letter in an envelope, stamped it, but didn't seal it.

He looked out the front window to see the funeral cars pull up. He watched as all the family he knew, except for Reginald, got into the funeral cars. They sat there waiting for Reginald to come from wherever he was. Sure enough, a car pulled up and Reginald got out, leaving two other sissies in the car.

Anthony knew it was wrong to assume they were sissies, but they were with Reginald, and that seemed reason enough to assume that. You lay down with faggots, you get up a faggot, end of story. Reginald was never going to get his shit together, not as long as he was in church. At least as long as he was in that church.

Anthony remembered when they all went to church. He and Danny went to get the girls. There was a lot to do in church besides getting saved. During service, he and Danny would sneak into the basement and meet some girls in a classroom or a closet, and they would actually give up the leg, right there in the church. And the church wondered why so many girls turned up pregnant. Anthony felt there were only three kinds of men in church. Pimps and faggots made up about 90 percent of the men in church. The rest were there really searching for God, or on their way to becoming pimps and faggots.

He remembered when Reginald began searching for God. He was really serious about the shit.

He was a little preacher. Danny went off to the Army, Anthony went to jail, and Reginald was still going to church. Goals had changed.

Anthony watched the cars pulling off from the curb. He felt a tinge of regret that he couldn't be with them, but he had shit to accomplish. The house was totally silent except for Anthony's breathing. He turned on a radio just to hear some noise.

He walked over to the old bureau and opened the bottom drawer, he felt around under some clothes and pulled out the revolver he'd gotten from the police two weeks ago. This was certainly going to come in handy today. He changed clothes twice before he felt comfortable with the gun in his pants. He rolled a couple of joints and took some eye drops with him.

He left the house about 9:30. The money would be leaving the store about 10 o'clock. He had more than enough time. He walked slowly, lighting up a joint. The joint didn't really change things.

He thought about going to see his son, but there wasn't enough time. He would have to remember him as he saw him last, sleeping. He wondered if he would ever be able to see him again, or if this was it for eternity. Could he rest in his grave knowing that Max would be taken care of?

He felt the letter in his back pocket. It gave him a small comfort. Maybe even with the letter, Danny was still going to fuck it up. Maybe he ought to just change his mind, turn around and go back home, chicken out. No one had ever been arrested for thinking about committing a crime. Maybe there was another way to accomplish all this shit.

He watched a police cruiser slow down at the

end of the block. No way was he gonna let motherfuckers like that win. Anthony knew this was his chance to beat the motherfuckers. They were going to beat on him until he died anyway. This was it. The ultimate expression of love, life, hate, and death. He was going to win, or at least he was going to go down fighting.

He got to the store, sweating. It was hot, but it wasn't that hot. He went around to the back of the store. The big white Cadillac was there, and a gray Mercedes next to it. The old man's son was picking up the money. Anthony looked at his watch then waited across the alley. These were creatures of habit. The man would be leaving at 10:00, not a moment before.

Anthony was perfecting the crime in his mind when the back door opened. Anthony came out of the shadows from across the alley, still wondering whether or not this man should die for their money. Life would decide for him. Anthony knew there would be no one watching. After being in the community for so many years, there was a tendency to get lax.

The man was unlocking the car door when Anthony crept up on him, raised the butt of the gun, and brought it down as hard as he could on the back of his head. Unlike the movies, the man didn't crumple. He started to turn around. Anthony smacked him in the face with the gun. He didn't want the man to see him. He hit him on the head again, and the man went to his knees. There was blood coming out of the gash on the back of his head. When he hit the ground, Anthony kicked him, partially to get him away from the car, mostly just to kick the shit out of him.

Anthony snatched the bag away from him and checked to make sure the money was in it. Jackpot, goddamn it! Anthony pulled the keys out of the door and kicked the man again. He dragged him across the lot into a gangway where he would not easily be spotted by a passerby. Once there, he kicked him a few more times and hit him with the gun again.

He got in the car, drove a few blocks away and looked at the money again. They had pre-counted and stacked it into thousand-dollar bundles. There were twenty-eight. The dope-selling motherfuckers was making money. He pulled off, smiling. Now on to the next phase of the plan.

He drove to the clinic on 61st and Woodlawn, and parked the car across from the clinic. He checked the glove compartment. There was a 9mm, fully loaded with two clips to spare. The white boy wasn't all stupid, but he wasn't ready either. Anthony smiled again. Finally, he understood why the niggas in jail were always bragging about this shit. It was fun, in a little boy kind of way.

He wiped his fingerprints and dumped the car, leaving the keys in the ignition. It wouldn't be sitting there long. This shit was working. He stuffed the guns into his pants and headed home. He tried not to look suspicious as he walked with his hand under his shirt to keep the guns from falling down his pants.

When he got to the house, he smoked another joint. That whole episode didn't take an hour out of the day. Shit was rolling now. The joint worked this time. He was calmer and focused. Straight.

There were little drops of blood on his clothes,

so he decided to change. This time he added a jacket to help hide the guns better. He also got a duffel bag to put his money in. He unwrapped a thousand dollars and put it in his pocket.

Time to take care of part two. He waved to the people next door as he left.

He walked toward the spot on 61st Street where Sweets liked to be seen. He was there, just like it was planned. Anthony called him away from the crowd.

"Yo, man, I need you to look out for me."

Sweets shook Anthony's extended hand, giving the sign of Family recognition. "What up?"

"I need you to run me over to the West Side."

"Naw, Family, you don't need me to do that."

"Aw, Family. Man, now come on. I know you know about that shit that happened to Danny the other day."

"Yeah, I heard his mother died."

"Not that. I'm talking about when he got bum rushed 'n shit."

"Yeah, I heard about that too."

"Well, I told him that I could get some work for him. He knew I wasn't going to the funeral 'n shit, so I made a few calls. You know, Family that looked out while I was in California. Well, anyway, one of my brothers gonna hook me up, 'cept Danny's dumb ass took the fucking car keys."

Anthony reached into his pocket and pulled out the thousand dollars. "He loaded me up to get the work 'n shit. The spot where he usually get his shit is asking eight hundred, but I know I can get it for six, and I can keep the difference. Hey, you do this for me and I'll look out. Shit will be straight."

Anthony spotted the crooked smile on Sweets' face and he knew he had him. He was in there. Sweets was geeking not for the money, but for the connection.

"Yeah, man. You my man. I'll look out." Sweets shooed his faithful away from the car. He got in and unlocked the door for Anthony.

Anthony got in. "Super straight. Good looking out. I was scared for a minute I was gonna have to catch the bus 'n shit."

"Where on the West Side you got to go?"

"Over by Chicago and Cicero. I'll let you know exactly where when we get close by."

"Bet."

Sweets got on the highway and headed north. Anthony wondered how he was going to get Sweets. Should he do him in the car, or get him out? There was no question as to whether Sweets would live or die. The question remained how. Once they were on the West Side, Anthony randomly gave Sweets directions, trying to figure out what to do. Finally, Sweets turned the corner onto a street full of abandoned buildings. Anthony told him to go around the back and park in the alley.

Sweets parked in the alley. Anthony reached under his shirt and pulled out the 9mm he'd gotten out of the glove compartment.

"Yo, Family, get out."

Sweets looked at the gun. "Man, what the fuck you trying to do? "

Anthony reached over, turned the car off and pulled the keys out of the ignition. "Get the fuck out the car."

"Man, I ain't never think you try to pull no shit

like this. Why you want to stick me up? I ain't do shit to your cousin."

Anthony kicked him toward the door. "Man, get the fuck out of the car."

Sweets opened the driver's side door. Anthony grabbed a handful of his shirt. "Move slow."

Anthony scooted across the seat as Sweets got out of the car. "Man, why you doing this shit? You know you ain't gonna get away with this shit. All my boys saw us leaving together and they gonna be on your ass."

Anthony got out of the car, still holding Sweets' shirt. He motioned for Sweets to go in the backyard of one of the abandoned buildings. Sweets started into the yard. "You crazy-ass motherfucker, I'ma fuck your dumb ass up. I'ma fuck your monkey ass up. Man, quit playing, motherfucker. "

When they walked through the gate, Sweets tried to run. Anthony shot him in the back. Sweets stumbled to the ground. Anthony walked up to him and kicked him. "Time to go to hell, you punk motherfucker."

Anthony fired two shots then kicked Sweets. One more shot, then he bent over and checked Sweets' pockets. He removed two wads of money then turned around and walked back to the car. In the car, Anthony checked under the seat. There was a loaded tech nine, the kind of gun the police were always displaying on the television news.

Finding the gun was like a message from God that he was doing the right thing. He drove 'til he got to the highway, and headed back downtown. Other than occasional glances in the rearview mirror, Anthony was calm, ready for the next part of the mission.

He arrived downtown and decided that he would buy some new clothes. He parked the car on a lot, giving the attendant a twenty-dollar tip. He put the money from Sweets and the guns in the bag in the trunk. This was better than "so far so good." It kept getting better as it went along.

He walked from the parking lot to one of the most expensive clothing stores he knew of. As he walked, he noticed all the people sitting outside and eating. There were very few black men in suits. That is where he should have been, a black man in a suit working in an office downtown, plotting corporate takeovers, marketing campaigns and shit like that.

Instead, he looked like one of the brothers out there waiting on the bus stop, trying to get to that second shift. He was going to strike a blow for them, although they wouldn't see it that way. They would see another nigga making it hard for people in power to trust them. Fuck the people in power. They weren't coming up off shit. Fuck them.

It was that "problem with authority" thing all over again, all those trips to the principal's office in school. The teachers couldn't take the challenge of someone who wasn't buying all that dumb shit wholesale. Problems with authority led to a worthless life. Anthony didn't like it, but it was a bottom line kind of thing. It was the same thing in church and all those civil rights groups. It was the same thing with the Muslims too. They didn't like to think they were like that, but they were. Whether it was a cause or an effect really didn't matter. The result was that Anthony wouldn't follow anybody.

This, the land of individual rights, liberties, and personal freedoms, couldn't stand a motherfucker that was different. Being a black man was as different as one could get. Everybody was constantly faking out everybody else. The rich get richer, and the poor get to watch. America always had been the land of the big lie, the big lie made up of millions of little lies.

It started with a lie, the Columbus scam, then the Pilgrims, then the whole independence scam. The history books were there to make shit shine, and draw you into the scam. The truth was found in the business pages of the daily newspaper. Next week there would be a story about him in the business pages. The business pages, where you go down in history.

Anthony watched the white men walking around in suits like they had important shit to be about. He wondered if they could take an ass kicking from the police like he had done so many times. He wondered how they lived in their suburban huts, on their tree lined, clean streets. They didn't have to worry about a motherfucker gunning somebody and shooting them by accident. They could buy their drugs once a month, and not every time they got five dollars. How did it feel to have your bills paid and your money flowing, knowing it was only going to get better?

Yeah, every now and then there would be some shit where they would lose a job or a company would close, but they weren't into beating each other over the head, not yet. Tonight there would be a bunch of them wondering how close they came to dying that day. They would whisper to their wives and children, "I was down there when it happened. It could have been me." Where Anthony grew up, they never said shit like that. They all knew how close they were.

Anthony got to the store and bought a suit, some socks and shoes, and a shirt and tie. He watched the clerk nervously package the clothes. He was all but trembling when Anthony handed him the money.

"Fuck you, you pussy-ass motherfucker. I ought to fuck you up. Gimme my shit."

Anthony snatched the change from the man. When he walked out of the store, he was smiling. That shit was still fun. He walked to a fast food restaurant and changed clothes in the bathroom. He looked at himself in the mirror. There was something missing. He decided that he needed a briefcase and a pair of glasses. He went to another store to buy those things, and again he leered at the clerk, making her extremely nervous. He was glad to know he could do it in a suit too.

Anthony walked back to the car, all the while admiring himself in the windows as he passed by. This was the way he should have been. He should have gotten the breaks to dress up and go to work. It was well past the time for blame, but as he walked, he wondered if he had been a conformist in school, if he had been a follower, could he be living that dream now. The fact was that he was neither, and he was where he was, and he was going to do what he was going to do. He had the pioneer spirit and was ready to take what he wanted for his family.

He reached the car, took the money out of the bag and put it in the briefcase. He left the guns in the trunk. It was about noon when he hit the first bank. He went inside and bought three thousand dollars worth of series EE savings bonds. He put them in his son's name, with Danny as the benefactor if anything should happen to him. This time he was calm and businesslike. The clerk hardly paid him any attention. This is what it was like in the land of the liars. Anthony was faking his ass off. He was clipping the ends off of his normally drawling words to sound more professional.

He repeated that same action at nine other banks. It was so cool, he thought. He felt like he could do this the rest of his life. He could see himself living in a suit like the one Sweets had just paid for. He went to one more bank and purchased a safe deposit box. He only put Danny's name on the access list. He put the remaining money and the bonds in the safety deposit box and left the bank smiling at about 4 o'clock in the afternoon.

The streets were a lot more crowded now. He walked as fast as anyone else was walking. He went back to the car and put the .38 and the tech nine in the briefcase. He put the 9mm in his belt and closed the jacket over it. He mailed the letter containing the key then took off toward Woolworth's.

Anthony saw a pay phone and decided that he wanted to hear his son's voice. He called, and Vanessa answered the phone.

"Let me speak to Maxwell."

"Don't start tripping," she snarled into the phone.

"Just put him on the phone, will you?"

He could hear her put the phone on the table.

"Hello?" He sounded so sweet and pure. He would do well to live his life like that.

"Hey, my man, my main man. How you doing?"

"Fine."

"You know who this is?"

"My daddy."

"You know I love you, don't you?"

"Yeah."

"You love me too?"

"Yeah."

"Okay, I just wanted to be sure."

"Okay."

"All right. Bye now."

"Bye-bye."

Anthony hung up the phone. Now there was nothing to it but to do it. State Street was crowded now. The buses were running back to back. Anthony knew some people were going to be extremely mad because he was going to fuck up the bus traffic, which of course was going to fuck up regular traffic. Oh well. They would live through it—at least most of them would.

He stood outside the store, surveying it. He had been in there many times, but he didn't know where the offices were. They were probably on the second floor.

He went in. The store was pretty crowded. He went upstairs and asked a cashier where the management offices were. She pointed him to the back of the store.

Anthony went to the back and knocked on the door. A small white man opened the door.

"Yes, may I help you?"

Anthony could tell by the tone of his voice that the man was telling him he was in the wrong place. He reached into his jacket and pulled out the 9mm. "Open the door, you punk sonofabitch."

The man did as he was told, backing into a desk as he tried to get out of the way. Anthony stepped inside. It was an office much like Anthony imagined it was. There were some black people in there.

"Okay, all the black people are free to go."

The black people left the room in a hurry. For once, being black paid off in a big way. They didn't appear as grateful as Anthony would have liked them to be, but they were scared.

As soon as they were gone, Anthony shouted, "For the first time in your life, and probably the last, you are about to be affected by racism. I have killed my quota of black people today, and now I must kill my quota of whites."

He fired the gun while they were still hearing him, shooting the man who opened the door. Then he shot a lady sitting at a desk. He fired on the man again. Then he shot a man crouched behind his desk. He shot him twice in the head. He shot another woman, then another. He heard the first woman moaning, so he shot her again. Another man tried to rush him.

"Take that, hero." Anthony shot him twice. Then he walked to the back of the office, where he found two more people. He opened the briefcase and took out the tech nine, firing two short bursts. He reloaded the 9mm and fired a single shot at them.

He took the .38 out of the case and jammed it into his belt then snatched the other clip and put it in his pocket. He headed out to the door. He heard moaning again. Didn't these people watch television? Didn't they know to make it through a massacre you play dead? He shot the woman who was moaning. She stopped.

He walked out of the office, fully expecting to see the security guards coming at him. There was one coming up the steps. "Yo, motherfucker, you ready to die for eight bucks an hour?"

The guard ran down the steps, then another came out of the aisle and ran down the steps too. Anthony heard a scream from the front of the store. The cashier was still there.

"Come on out. I ain't gonna shoot you. I ain't killing nothing but white people and police."

The lady came out. Anthony smiled at her. "You know what you can do for me? When the people from the news ask you what happened and why I let you go, tell them this was a dream deferred. So much for that raisin in the sun shit."

The lady started walking toward the stairs. Anthony thought about using her as a hostage, but there was no point to it. The police would simply have killed both of them. He looked out the front window. There were people still running out of the store, the police were blocking off the street, and the news crews were pulling up to the scene.

He pointed the tech nine out the window and fired a burst toward the police. He got one. They all scattered, except the one lying in the street, holding his throat. A cop tried to help his comrade, but Anthony fired again, holding the other officers behind the cars.

Anthony turned around and ran downstairs. The store looked empty. He knew they were going to be coming for him, but there was no way he was going to die in this store. He fired a burst at the plate glass window in the front of the store. He could see a news truck from where he was. He emptied a clip from the 9mm on it, injuring a reporter. He reloaded the 9mm and fired a burst from the tech nine.

He emptied the last clip from the 9mm on police cars. He was surprised they weren't shooting back yet, probably scared they might hurt some civilians or something. He wasn't a civilian anymore; he was a target. He could see the SWAT van on the set. They had a bead on him and he knew it. He threw the 9mm out of the broken window. With the .38 in his left hand and the tech nine in his right, he ran through the broken window. He fired a few bursts from the tech, hoping to get a good look at a police officer to get with the .38.

There was one pulling up. He had a suit on. Anthony fired twice. The driver's side window broke, and the suit slumped forward. Then everybody was shooting at him. He kept spraying until the tech was clicking. The tech flew out of his hand. He dropped to the ground, did a roll just like in the movies, then came to a half stand. He could feel his body jerking from the bullets hitting him. These were some no-shooting motherfuckers. One more. He just wanted one more. He fired, hoping he could hit someone.

When the police stopped shooting at him, he lay crumpled on the ground. The gray suit he'd bought was now red, front and back. They ran up on him, weapons drawn, ready to shoot him some more. Two bullets had ripped his head apart. There was no use in trying to feel for a pulse.

"Eleven people, including the alleged gunman and two police officers were killed in downtown Chicago today. The gunman, tentatively identified as Anthony Evans from Chicago's South Side, was killed by police in a shootout in front of the Woolworth's where he allegedly killed eight employees of the store. Our reporter, Janice Wilforth, is on the scene. Janice, can you tell us more about what happened on downtown State Street today?"

"Yes, Ted. I'm speaking with an employee who was in the store at the time of the shooting. Ms. Scott, can you tell us what happened? "

"Well, I was at my register, and he asked me where the office was. I told him it was at the back of the store. He went back there and then not too much later, I heard gunfire. It really caught me by surprise, so I did what I always do when I hear gunfire. I dropped to the floor. I didn't even think to run or nothing. Then he came out of the office and heard me scream. I don't know why I screamed. You ain't supposed to scream. But he said to tell the news people this was about a dream de . . . de . . . something."

"Deferred?"

"Yeah, a dream deferred. Then he said something about a raisin in the sun. Oh, he said it wasn't no raisin in the sun. Then he told me to go and to remember what he said."

"Why do you think he let you go?"

"I know why he let me go."

"Why?"

"He let me go because I was black. He said he wasn't killing nothing but white people and police officers. "

"Do you believe that the killings were racially motivated?"

"That's what he said."

"Well, Ted, it appears that the killings were racially motivated. This is Janice Wilforth reporting for Channel Ten Action News team. Back to you, Ted."

"This is Ted Janiewski of Channel Ten Action News team. We'll be right back with more on this breaking story after these messages."

Regina looked at the television, her jaw slack. Reginald's head dropped. Danny stared at the television and the words came slowly. "What the fuck?"

chapter seventeen

This shit was unreal, totally and without a doubt unreal; but then it was real, cold steel real. Anthony was dead, with his mug shot all over the television. He was dead in the street at a place called spot, as in "that was the spot where they killed him, that crazy nigga." He was crazy, killing white people like he did. Danny knew Anthony thought it all out, but there was no way Anthony could have known what was going to happen afterwards.

The press was swarming around the block like crazed wasps. They interviewed everybody on the block. They were interviewing people that Anthony didn't even know, and everybody was talking like they had really been with him.

The press had everything on him. That he had been to jail several times, that he had a son, what school he went to, every damn thing. They probably knew the last time he pissed.

Danny looked out the front window at them. They were talking to the cameras, about five different reporters. They all faced in different directions so that no one would appear on someone else's report. Danny watched them. He wanted to shoot one of them to really give them some news. Yeah, fuck one of them up, and let them feed on that for a while.

The news people talked to the community leaders, who understood his anger, but couldn't condone his violence. It was the same shit they said about the riots in Los Angeles. What the fuck did they understand about shit, especially this shit? Anthony, in all his genius, hadn't told nobody about how to get through this shit. People always saying shit, and they was going to keep saying it. The rest of their lives, the people in the hood would identify them as Anthony's folks.

But they would survive this shit, and better yet, there was some money to be made from it. Danny figured that soon enough the people from television would want to make a movie, or better yet, the big screen people from Hollywood would be on the set. There was already those bullshit news shows calling, and they were giving up the dough to get Anthony's story from the people closest to him. Danny wanted to fire up a thirty-seven fifty, but he couldn't leave the house to get any, and he'd smoked all his up. He was supposed to be giving the shit up, but these were hard times, and he didn't like being stuck in the house. He knew if he could make it through a rough time without getting high, he could do without it all together.

Regina looked out the window in her mother's bedroom. She watched the boys from across the street making faces behind the reporters so they could see themselves on television later. Eberhart never had this much drama before. The police had been on the block a thousand times, and the news people had even come around once or twice, but it had never been like this. Regina could turn on the television and see the front of her house, but she wouldn't turn it on. Why had Anthony gone and done some shit like this? What the fuck was he thinking? Pretty soon the kids would be going back to school. They would have to hear this shit from their friends. Jaleel was getting cagey, and the kids wanted to go out, but there was no way to get them out without getting on the news. Those people were actually out there overnight. Tonight she was going to find a way to get the kids over to somebody's grandmother's house.

Regina picked up a glass and took a sip of water. She didn't want to drink anymore, especially after that binge she had just recovered from. If she didn't watch it, she would wind up like her mother, cold and dead before she was old. She turned away from the window and saw the last bottle of vodka on the shelf in the closet. What the hell. She could drink her way through this. At least a little buzz wasn't going to hurt anything.

Outside the house, Reginald walked up the stairs. He had to park almost a block away, and as soon as they saw him, the press rushed him. They stuck microphones in his face and began screaming questions at him. He thought about telling them the truth, telling them that Anthony was playing them for suckers from the grave. Instead, he faced the cameras and lights.

"There was no way we could know what Anthony was going to do. Our hearts go out to the families that lost loved ones in the shooting. We know how they feel; we lost a loved one too."

Then the throng of reporters parted and Tiny made his way through the crowd. He pushed some more reporters out of his way, and got Reginald up the steps and to the front door. Reporters were still screaming questions, but Tiny stood between them and Reginald as he unlocked the door. When the door opened, the reporters made a surge for the house. Tiny blocked them all. Once Reginald was inside, Tiny backed his way into the house. Reginald thanked Tiny, but Tiny brushed it off, saying he always wanted to do that.

Regina came down stairs with a glass of vodka in her hand. Reginald looked at her and frowned. She frowned back.

Danny looked at Reginald. "Don't start no shit. We got enough shit to deal with as is."

"I wasn't going to say anything."

Danny sat on the couch. "I'm going to go and get the body when they release it. I'm going to have him cremated."

"Is that what he told you he wanted? Was that part of his big plan?" Regina asked, being snide.

"Regina, you can keep that shit to yourself. I don't need it, not in the least."

"Well, look who's a big man now."

Reginald said, "Man, look. Both of you all can keep that shit. I mean goddamn, now is the time for us to be coming together and shit, and you all want to be fucking up. Fuck both of you."

"I was just wondering what brought this big change on. When Mama died, you didn't know how to do shit, and now you calling the shots."

"There ain't been no change," Danny said, looking down at the floor in front of him

Tiny broke in. "Later for all that. What are you all gonna do about all them reporters you got all over the block?"

"We ain't got to do nothing about them. Shit, there ain't nothing we can do about them. What, we gonna call the police on them or something like that? Shit, I'm trying to find a way to get some money from them while they here."

"Danny, is money all you ever think about?" Reginald asked.

"Hey, it's a paper chase. Bottom line, we can't get Anthony back, and we can't undo what he did. Hey, the best thing we can do is to get better because of it, and getting paid is getting better."

"But there is a lot more than money going on in this," Reginald responded.

"See, Reginald, that's what you don't know. This is all about money."

"How so?"

"All that shit Anthony did was about getting dough, and I don't think he would be mad if we make some more money. Hey, we can get out of this neighborhood. Shit, we can get out of the city. Hey, all the money we can get is going to help."

"So, why did he do it for money?"

"He wanted me to take care of his son. Actually, he wanted me to take care of the family. He had some insurance and shit, and I'm supposed to use that money to go to school 'n shit. He left some money specifically for his son, so that he wouldn't grow up and be a dumb-ass pipe head or nothing like that."

"So, why did he have to kill those white people downtown?" Tiny asked.

"Well, think about it. He couldn't straight up commit suicide or the insurance policies wouldn't pay off, so he just pulled it off the way he did."

Tiny sat down on the sunken couch. "He was a thinking-ass crazy motherfucker. I just thought he snapped on them people downtown, but homey had a plan. My mellow."

"Tiny, do me a favor and don't tell nobody about this shit until we outta here. Straight?"

"Bet."

Reginald sat down. "So, what are we going to do now?"

"What do you mean we? I thought you was going to move out."

"I am going to move, but then so are you, and I am a member of the family still, so I think I ought to be helping to make decisions with you." Reginald faced Danny. "So, you going to school?"

"Yeah, that's the plan."

"What school you going to?"

"I don't know. Probably Chicago State or something like that. But all that can wait. We got to get the hell out of here. That's the first matter we got to deal with."

Regina took a sip out of the glass. "I'll be glad when we get the fuck out of here."

"Where y'all gonna go?" Tiny asked, knowing he was going to lose his best friend.

Danny answered him. "I don't know. Maybe to South Shore, or maybe even the suburbs, or maybe out to Chatham.

Reginald asked, "What are you going to do about Maxwell?"

"I don't know. I'm on my way to see his mother, then I'll see what's up with that."

Tiny spoke, "What are you gonna tell the news people on your way to the car?"

"I'm gonna tell them to get fucked."

Reginald put him in check. "Don't get out of hand. We best keep the media on our side if we want to pull this off right, so don't go out there and be the ugly nigga on television."

Regina chimed in. "You know they want to get the ugliest, dumbest, most stupid-ass nigga on the planet to represent all the black people, so be straight when you perpetrate. Besides, someone looking at the news might have to give you a job someday."

Danny walked out the front door. Someone was interviewing one of them old bitches from down the street. As soon as they saw him, they rushed the front porch.

"Can you tell us about your cousin? Why did he do that? How do you feel about what he did?"

The questions were coming too fast, and he couldn't see anything for the lights shining in his eyes. For a moment, he thought about putting the mack to one of the black women reporters that were out there. Maybe another time.

"I can't say why he did what he did. He just snapped. I don't know why he killed those people at the store, but my mother used to work there, and they laid her off. Then, that night, she had a heart attack and died. Maybe he was on some kind of revenge thing or something. I can't say. He never talked to us about what he was feeling or doing. He just did stuff and we might find out about it later. But that was the first time that

I've ever known him to hurt anyone. That's all I can say right now."

The questions started up again, but he just walked through the crowd of reporters like he was a rich white motherfucker with nothing to fear. He got in his car and drove off, almost hitting a reporter and a cameraman on the way out.

Danny drove straight down King Drive. The rest of the world was still normal. There were still baseball games in the park, the basketball courts were still crowded, and there were still people getting high in the stands. Everything was going on like nothing happened. To them it was just some shit on the news.

Farther down King Drive, life went on the same. Just a crazy ass nigga with a gun on the news. Down here with the manicured lawns and the shaped bushes, Anthony was just another reason for gun control. Back on Sixtieth, he was a hero. All those people making guesses about why he did it, there was no way they could have guessed right. Hey, a crazy nigga don't make no moves for the future.

Sweets was out of the picture, and the liquor store had been robbed. Danny knew that Anthony had done all of that. He did what he said he was going to do. He looked out in a big way. Now the pressure was on Danny to do the same. Danny was looking at changing his life. When he talked to Anthony about it, it seemed so far away that he wouldn't have to worry about it. It was on his ass now, on his ass like a lead weight.

Danny wasn't ready to make those moves, but hey, he gave his word, like telling Family that you would keep their grave clean. Bottom line, word was word, and he knew he was going to have to do it. Fuck the dumb shit. He was going to have to do it.

This shit about getting Anthony's son was a real mystery. How the hell was he supposed to get that done? He was just going to have to play it as it lay, and hope the shit came out right. Anthony had thought of a lot of shit, but he left no instructions. This was just something else that Danny was going to have to pull off, besides going to school and living straight.

Danny pulled up in front of Maxwell's house. He was playing in the front, looking like he could have been anybody's child, not the child of a man who killed ten white people in a downtown store yesterday. Danny had seen him enough times, when he brought Anthony over, to know what he looked like. He had even looked in on Maxwell for Anthony when he was in jail. But that was all he knew about Maxwell, just what he looked like.

Danny got out of the car and went up on the front porch. All the while, Maxwell was watching him the way that children watch strangers. Danny didn't know how to feel for him. Should he feel sorry for him because he just lost his father, or should he feel happy for him because he was banked to the rim? Even more, how was he supposed to relate to him? He wasn't his daddy. We wasn't anybody's daddy, but he was going to be responsible for Maxwell from now on. This was truly tripping.

The door opened and Vanessa asked, "Yeah, what you want?"

"We have to talk."

"Talk about your crazy-ass cousin going out

there killing all those people like he did? Talk about him getting killed in the middle of State Street? Or you want to talk about him leaving his son without a father? Just what do you want to talk about?"

"Can I come in?"

"Yeah, come on. You ain't gonna shoot me, are you?"

"Don't be tripping."

He walked in and sat on the couch. She closed the door and sat in the chair opposite her.

"So, what you want to talk about?"

"You know what Anthony did?"

"Yeah. Who don't? I mean it ain't been nothing else on the news."

"Well, he didn't exactly leave his son alone."

"How you mean?"

"Well, he wanted me to look out for him."

"Oh, so you gonna take care of him. Well, who gonna take care of me? Not that Anthony was taking care of me."

"You grown. You can take care of yourself."

"So, how you supposed to be taking care of him?"

"He left money for me to take care of him with."

"Ain't that some shit. He didn't just leave the money with me. What did he think, I was gonna blow it or some shit? He could have just gave me the money, and I could take care of my own child. Fuck him!" She turned away from Danny and looked at the floor.

"Look it ain't got to be all that. I'm just letting you know that, hey, if you need something, then I'll look out. Don't be serving me drama."

"You got some rock?" She looked up at Danny.

"No, I don't fuck around."

"You a goddamn lie. Your ass is selling the shit. I know that."

"Look, part of the deal with Anthony was that I would give up the shit and get into a real life. You know, go to college and get a downtown job. So, I don't fuck around, all right?"

"Yeah, right. Where you gonna go to school?"

"I ain't made no decisions about that yet. Besides, all you got to know is that I'm gonna be there for Maxwell."

"Yeah, you can be there for him, but who gonna to be there for me?"

"I ain't got shit to do with that. Anthony said you was spending too much time with the wrong people and your future was looking bleak. He just wanted to make sure his son didn't wind up forgetting him, and he wanted to see that he got a better life, or at least a good shot at it."

"Yeah, but what about my chance for a better life? I don't want to wind up in a hell hole. I mean I want to get both of us out of this shit. Anthony is dead. I got to look out for me and mine."

"Look, I don't know how this shit is gonna turn out. We got some more talking to do, try to iron this shit out. There may be a way we can both work this shit out to our benefit. For now, though, I'm going to pull up before you start tripping on me 'n shit. Besides, I got some other shit I got to do. When you feel like you ready to talk, then give me a call. And if Maxwell needs anything, you can call sooner."

Danny headed toward the door. Vanessa sat in the chair, shaking her head. When she got up to let him out, she asked if he had any money on him. He gave her twenty dollars. Outside, he spoke to Maxwell then got in his car and drove off.

He stopped at a funeral home on Cottage Grove to find out what to do about Anthony. He stood in the funeral home, realizing that he would be attending another funeral so soon. The funeral was a temporary thing. There was a lot of life behind funerals, and somehow that did not seem right that people would have to continue to live beyond burying people they were supposed to have loved. Love for the living is what drove people on, not love for the dead. Bury the fucking dead, spill for them and move the hell on.

He would have to move, and move his family too. Now was a good time to fire up a thirty-seven fifty. He wondered if the pressure was getting to him, or he was starting to geek. This was fucked up. There were still reporters in front of the house. They were interviewing the neighbors again. Some of them were talking to their cameras. There were no parking places, so he parked a block over.When he turned the corner on Eberhart, they rushed him again.

"Get the fuck out of my face. I don't feel like talking to you motherfuckers."

They continued to press him with questions. He reached out and grabbed a fist full of one of them and pulled him face to face. Danny cocked his arm. The man, who had reported in the gulf war, was visibly shaken.

"Is there something about 'fuck off' that you don't understand?"

The man shook his head, and Danny let him

go. The crowd of reporters backed off and cleared a path for Danny to get to the door. He opened the door and was surprised to find the house dark. He could hear someone moving around upstairs. The kids, at least two of them, were watching the little color television he'd just gotten for his mother. He started to tell them something about making sure the television was put up or something, then he remembered that his mother was dead and it wouldn't matter.

Regina was in his mother's room, laying across the bed. She was on her back, listening to the radio.

"Where Reginald?" Danny asked.

"I don't know. He said he would be back, so I guess he will."

"What's the matter with you?"

"Nothing. I was laying here thinking."

"Thinking about what?"

"Thinking that we ain't never gonna get outta here. We gonna be in this house forever."

She was frowning, almost on the edge of tears. Danny could feel it. But now was not the time to collapse. This was not the pressure, not the real pressure anyway.

"We gonna get out. We got dough, and we got it legit. We gonna get out of this motherfucker."

"Yeah, we got money, but we ain't got no credit history or nothing, and anyplace decent they check your credit history. You ain't got one. Shit, you ain't even got a job yet. Shit, by the time all that shit is in place, ain't no telling who else is gonna be dead."

"So, that's where Reggie can help us out. He got his papers straight already. We'll be outta this motherfucker before school starts. Don't be giving up all early 'n shit. Goddamn, you already being negative. Besides, I've learned ain't nothing you can't get with money. It's just a matter of finding the right price."

Regina sat up and looked out the window. There were still a few trucks and reporters out there. She took a sip out of the glass on the nightstand. "Where are we gonna go?"

"Someplace better than here."

"You think that's going to make a difference in the way things turn out?"

"The question you should be asking is are you gonna make a difference. Are you ready to make this move?" Danny sat on the bed next to her

She looked at him with her eyes glazed. "What you all hype about? You sound like Anthony with that shit."

"Before Anthony died, we talked about this shit. I mean he brought up some stuff in me that I hadn't even remembered. I mean now I got the chance, a straight-ass chance. Take a look around. You see all them motherfuckers out there? They stuck here. I mean if they won the lotto, they would still be here mentally 'n shit. But this is about making a mental move along with a physical move. Hey, all we got is a chance, and we gotta get prepared to take it, and to take it well."

"A chance don't amount to shit. Hell like you say, they got a chance to win the lotto. All you got to do is buy the damn ticket."

"But it just ain't about chances. Odds come into play. The thing is to put the odds in your favor. That's what all this shit is about. Check this. You don't want your kids growing up in this shit, do you?"

Regina shook her head. "I didn't want me growing up in this shit."

"Well then, let's get the fuck out of here and commence to perpetrating like the rest of these motherfuckers, like them motherfuckers out there on the lawn 'n shit."

"What are we gonna do with the house?"

"Fuck, we can sell it or rent it. Shit, we could burn the motherfucker down. So long as we get out of it, I don't give a shit."

They heard the front door open downstairs, and then Reginald walking around in the dark.

"We up here!" Danny shouted.

They waited in silence as Reginald walked up the stairs.

Reginald entered the room. "What y'all doing?"

Danny watched Reginald standing in the door. "I was telling her that we gonna get out of this house with a quickness, and how you gonna help us."

"And what am I supposed to be doing?"

Regina told him," You got to help us to get a place to stay. We ain't got no credit, and we can't get a lease with no credit."

Reginald looked at the floor. "I don't know about all that."

Danny stood up, walked over to the door and closed it. Reginald followed him with his eyes.

Danny turned and faced him. The anger in voice was clear. "Yo, man, you said you was gonna look out. This ain't no time to be punking out 'n shit. Man, Anthony died so we can make this move.

I'll take your monkey ass out with a quickness you don't cooperate. I swear, man, I'll fuck you up."

Reginald never looked away from him. "You ain't got to go through all that. I'll do what I got to do."

"Thank you." Danny walked past him out the door. Reginald listened to him going through the house. "What the hell is wrong with him?"

Regina took another sip out of the glass. "He all hype about this shit. I just ain't a true believer. Next thing you know, he gonna start going to church."

Reginald smiled. "I don't think so. But tell me something. You think he actually gonna pull this off?"

Regina shook her head. "I don't know. Like I said, he all hyped about it. He feel like it's his big chance. I hope he make it. That's all I got to say about it. I hope he make it."

Reginald looked at her sitting on the bed, just like her mother would have.

"What are you going to do?"

"Well, as long as I can, I'm going to perpetrate. I might go to school or something. What are you gonna do?" Regina took another sip from the glass

"I'm going to move in with a friend of mine. Maybe I can get you all in that same building with us. Anyway, I got this new guy that I'm seeing, so I'm going to see how that goes."

"Is that the guy you moving in with?"

"No." Reginald looked away from her.

"How do you think you got to be that way?"

"Born like that, I guess. I still like women, and

one day I may find one and settle down with her." Reginald knew that was a lie, but he liked the way it sounded.

"You ain't gonna fake on us, are you? I mean we gonna need you, and I want to get the kids out of this shit-ass neighborhood, get them into some good school. I guess that Danny got it right. This is our chance, our one chance, and I don't want to blow it. The trip part is that it's gonna take all of us to pull it off, but I still don't know what my part is."

"You got to do what Ma did. You know, hold us together. She did it for as long as she could. You got to keep things in check and stay on Danny's ass. Besides, you the only one of us that can cook."

Danny was in his room, lying in the bed, looking at the wall. He wondered if he was up to all this shit he was putting on himself. How would he do in school? It had been a long time, maybe too long. His eyes wandered over the gang symbol painted on the wall, then to the faded red stairs.

How was he going to be a role model for anybody, especially a little boy? That shit Anthony said came to mind. Was this how it was going to be? Was Anthony going to be haunting him from the grave? How was Maxwell's mother going to act? Had he ordered too much shit to eat? He sat up, walked over to the dresser, and turned on the television. At least the news wasn't on yet, so he wouldn't have to watch all the shit about Anthony. Anthony was going to be haunting him the rest of his life.

Whatever gave Anthony the idea that he was

the one to do this shit? It didn't matter now. Anthony had saved his life. Danny pushed around a few things on the dresser, looking for nothing in particular, just to see if there was something there. In the midst of the mess on his dresser, he found a joint. Danny looked at the joint. He held it in his fingers, wondering if it was a thirty-seven fifty.

He put it to his lips, then he took it down. He knew that tomorrow was forever the day to begin a change, because tomorrow was forever tomorrow. He opened a drawer and put the joint in it. Maybe someone else would die and place another world on his shoulders. Maybe he could use a joint in the next couple of days, but after the last couple of days, he knew he didn't need one now.

Danny closed the drawer, walked over to the bed and sat down. He turned on the radio then turned off the light. He took off his clothes and threw them on a chair at the end of the bed, then lay down in the dark, listening to old songs on the radio. They were songs that took his mind back to his childhood, his grandmother on the porch as he ran up and down the block. He lay on the bed, matching the old songs to times in his life. He remembered dancing for his mother's smile, taping freshly colored drawings on the old refrigerator door. He felt tears welling up in his eyes and did not even try to hold them back. It was here that tomorrow would begin, for real.